THE SOLDIERS' HOMECOMING

Brett, Logan and Sam were best friends and three of the finest soldiers in the Australian SAS K9 division. But one day Sam was killed, tearing their friendship group apart and leaving Brett and Logan with memories that would haunt them for ever.

Now, back in Australia, Brett and Logan are adjusting to life outside the army.

But they haven't counted on two gorgeous, intriguing, captivating women who swan into their lives and present them with challenges they've never faced before!

Available in March

THE RETURNING HERO

and

HER SOLDIER PROTECTOR

Available in April

HER SOLDIER PROTECTOR

BY
SORAYA LANE

Published in Great Britain 2014
by Mills & Boon, an imprint of Harlequin (UK) Limited,
Eton House, 18-24 Paradise Road, Richmond, Surrey, TW9 1SR

© 2014 Soraya Lane

ISBN: 978 0 263 91273 9

23-0414

Harlequin (UK) Limited's policy is to use papers that are natural, renewable and recyclable products and made from wood grown in sustainable forests. The logging and manufacturing processes conform to the legal environmental regulations of the country of origin.

Printed and bound in Spain
by Blackprint CPI, Barcelona

Writing for Mills & Boon is truly a dream come true for **Soraya Lane.** An avid book-reader and writer since her childhood, Soraya describes becoming a published author as 'the best job in the world', and hopes to be writing heart-warming, emotional romances for many years to come.

Soraya lives with her own real-life hero on a small farm in New Zealand, surrounded by animals and with an office overlooking a field where their horses graze.

For more information about Soraya and her upcoming releases visit her at her website, www.sorayalane.com, her blog, www.sorayalane.blogspot.com, or follow her at www.facebook.com/SorayaLaneAuthor.

As a little girl I begged frequently for a dog of my own. Thankfully I only had to wait until my seventh birthday before I was gifted an eight-week-old Australian Silky Terrier named Chloe. So this book is dedicated to my amazing parents for giving this dog-loving girl her dream come true!

CHAPTER ONE

LOGAN MURDOCH SURVEYED the waiting crowd. After years spent serving overseas, usually in the desert and lugging an eighty-pound pack on his back, he had no intention of complaining even if he had to wait another hour for his superstar client to arrive.

"Stand by for arrival in five minutes."

He touched his earpiece as the other security expert's voice came on the line.

"Cleared for arrival in five minutes," he responded.

Logan moved down the line, checking that all the waiting fans were securely behind the low, temporary fencing. A couple of policemen were on guard, keeping an eye on the large crowd, and he had a security team ready to help if he needed them. He reached down to give his dog a pat, before moving out with one minute to go to wait for the car. Logan had already led his dog around and inside the entire perimeter to check for explosives, and now their primary objective was to get the client safely from the car into the building.

"I have a visual on the car. Stand by for immediate

arrival," he said, before talking to his dog. "Stay at heel," he commanded.

His dog knew him better than any human possibly could, and the verbal command was just procedure. One look and Ranger would know what he was thinking.

The car pulled up to the curb—jet-black with dark tinted windows—and Logan stepped forward to open the back door. He'd researched his client, knew all there was to know about her in the public domain, but nothing had prepared him for seeing her in the flesh. For the slim, tanned legs that slipped from the car, the beautiful face turned up toward him or the star power she exuded from her small frame. She was gorgeous.

"Ms. Evans," he said, holding out his hand to assist her. "Please follow me immediately through the front door. Will you be signing autographs today?"

Her eyes—big blue eyes that were as wide as saucers—met his, and she shook her head. Logan might never have met her before, but something told him she was terrified.

"Yes!" someone from inside the car barked. "Candace, you're signing autographs. Go."

Logan tightened his hold on her hand as she stepped out, and suddenly they were surrounded by flashes that seemed like bulbs exploding in front of them.

"Easy," he told Ranger, his grip on the dog's leash firm. "Let's go."

He released her only when she loosened her hold, then he walked with his palm flat against her back, his dog on his other side. If she wanted to stop to talk to fans, then that was her decision, but anything that alerted him to a potential problem? Then he'd be the one calling the shots, never mind what her manager or whoever he was wanted her to do.

"Don't leave me," she whispered just loud enough for him to hear, a tremble in her voice.

"I'm right here until you tell me to go," Logan replied, moving his body closer to hers, realizing his instincts had been right. "I've swept every inch of this place, and my dog never makes mistakes."

Logan watched her nod, before bravely squaring her shoulders and raising her hand in a wave to her fans. The flashes from the paparazzi were still in full swing, and now everyone in the crowd seemed to be screaming out to the woman they'd queued hours to meet. He'd been doubtful that she needed such high-level security, but the worry in her voice told him that maybe it had been justified.

"Candace, over here!" one girl was yelling. "Please, Candace, I love you!"

Logan steered her forward, stopping only when she did. He noticed the slight shake of her hand as she signed multiple autographs, before angling her body toward the building. He took his cue.

"Autographs are over," he announced, at the same time as the crowd started yelling again.

They walked straight toward the door, stopping for a few more fans just before they disappeared inside.

Logan touched his earpiece. "We're in the building. Secure the exits."

As the doors shut behind them, Candace collapsed against the wall, her face drained of color.

"Ms. Evans?" he asked, at her side in a heartbeat.

"I'm fine. It's just overwhelming," she muttered, resting her head back against the wall. "I didn't think I was going to be able to make the walk from the car."

Logan dropped Ranger's leash and told him to stay, before crossing the room to fill two glasses of water.

"He won't hurt me, will he?"

Logan glanced back and saw that his dog was sitting to attention, ears pricked, eyes trained on her. Ranger was looking at her as though curiosity was about to get the better of him.

"Lie down," he commanded, smiling as Ranger did as he was told. "He's a big softie and he knows his manners. The worst he'd do is lick you if I let him, and he sure seems to like the look of you."

Her smile wasn't convincing, but she did seem to relax. He passed her a glass of water, trying not to look too intently at her bright blue eyes, or the long blond curls that were falling over her breasts. In real life she was beyond stunning—much shorter than he'd have guessed, and tiny, like a doll.

"Tell me why you're so scared," he asked. "I'm guessing it's more than just the bombings that have happened around the world lately to cause a seasoned superstar like you to panic."

Candace nodded, sipping her water before passing it back to him.

"I've received threats," she told him. "The first few to my house, then a package sent to my last tour bus and another to my manager. I was fine to start with, but it's starting to get to me."

Crap. He'd guessed there was more to this story, but the fact that he was head of security and hadn't been correctly briefed was a major breach of trust from everyone involved.

Logan kept his face neutral, not wanting her to see him as anything other than trustworthy and dependable. It wasn't her fault that not all the information had been passed along—he would save his anger for someone who deserved to be blasted. *Like maybe his boss or her manager.*

"I've worked with Ranger for five tours in warzones, so there is no chance an Improvised Explosive Device is coming anywhere near you without him detecting it," Logan told her. "The only thing you have to do is make sure your people keep me fully briefed at all times. No secrets, no lies."

The smile she gave him was shy, but it lit up her face, made her eyes swim to life. "Will you stay with me until I go on? I have an interview to do soon, but I'll be in my dressing room until the show."

"Yes, ma'am." There was no way he was going to walk away when he'd finally seen her smile like that.

"I don't even know your name," she said, pushing off from the wall she'd been resting against as her entourage came down the stairs at the end of the hall, having been escorted into the building through a separate door.

"Logan," he said. "And this here is Ranger."

"Call me Candace," she told him, her eyes never leaving his as they spoke. "If you're in charge of keeping me safe, you can at least call me by my first name."

Logan smiled at Candace and picked up Ranger's

leash, before following a few steps behind her. He might have moaned about being asked to work security by the Australian Army, but this job was turning out to be a whole lot more interesting than he'd expected. She was here to perform to a sold-out crowd and help promote Australia to the rest of the world at the same time, and being her private security detail might just prove to be the most enjoyable work he'd done in his career with the SAS.

Personally enjoyable, anyway. Not to mention it was a job that wasn't going to haunt him in the middle of the night like his last few assignments.

For the first time in weeks, Candace was relaxed. The tightness in her shoulders had almost disappeared, and she wasn't on edge, looking sideways to make sure no one was following her who shouldn't be. Ever since the letters had started to arrive, she'd hardly slept and almost cancelled the last leg of her world tour, but she hated letting anyone down.

And then Logan had escorted her past the waiting crowd and into the building, and the fear and terror had slowly seeped from her body.

She'd had plenty of bodyguards over the years, usually hulking guys who could deal with any physical threat. But with the latest spate of bombings around the world and the situation with the letters, she didn't just want men capable of brute strength around her. She'd asked for the best, and it looked like she'd received him.

"We'll take it from here."

She glanced across at her manager, Billy. He always

had her best intentions at heart, or at least she hoped he did, but right now she wasn't interested in doing what she was told.

"I've actually decided I want Logan to stay with me," she said.

Eyebrows were raised in her direction, and she almost laughed at the stern expression Logan was giving them in response. She doubted that he was easily intimidated, or that anyone here would have the nerve to cross him, especially not with his fierce-looking dog at his side.

"This way," Candace said, nodding toward the room with her name on it.

He followed, dog at his side, each of his footsteps covering more ground than two of hers. It was oddly comforting having his heavy boots thumping out of rhythm with the click of her heels.

"So are you in private security now?" she asked, wondering how someone who'd served in warzones was even assigned to work with her.

He chuckled. "Would you believe me if I told you I'm still SAS, but that the Australian government was so determined to have you here to promote their new tourism campaign they decided to send me here to head the security team?"

She shook her head, pushing open her door. Logan walked past her, his dog doing what appeared to be a quick check of the room.

"You're not kidding, are you?"

"Nope. But I can't say that I mind. After years on

patrol in the middle of nowhere, it's a nice change of pace before I retire."

She sat down on the sofa and gestured for him to do the same, unsure of whether she believed him or not. "What do you feel like? Sushi? Something more substantial?"

He raised an eyebrow. "You're ordering lunch for both us?"

"Ah, yes," she said, not sure why he found that so unusual. "Unless you do something different at this time of the day in Australia?"

He shook his head, a wry grin on his face. "If you're buying lunch, then I definitely have no complaints about this gig."

"I have a bit of a ritual that I always eat Japanese food before a show. I'm thinking sashimi and miso soup, but maybe you'd like something more."

"Candace, I'm used to eating dehydrated army food when I'm working, so if you feel like sushi, I say sure."

"That settles it then. I'll order." She stood up to use the phone, ordering way more food than they'd ever consume.

Candace turned back around, eyes locking on Logan's as he met her gaze. It wasn't something she was used to—a man not intimated by meeting her, not fazed by the circus they'd confronted when he'd escorted her from her car. *She* knew that she was no one special, but men usually reacted badly to her fame or her money, and the way Logan was behaving was the complete opposite. He was just staring back at her like she was… ordinary. Although she guessed a lot of it, dealing with the crowds and stress earlier, was more to do with his training than anything else.

"Can I ask you something?"

He shrugged. "Shoot."

"You're the first guy in years who's treated me like a regular woman and not a celebrity. Is it your training or just how you are?"

He leaned back, crossing his legs at the ankle and stretching out his big body. Logan was tall and fit, the T-shirt he wore snug to his athletic frame, pants stretching over his thigh muscles. She'd sure hit the jackpot where he was concerned.

"*Aren't* you a regular woman?"

She felt a blush crawl up her neck and heat her cheeks. It had been a *long* time since a man had drawn that kind of reaction from her, but he'd said it like it was the most logical answer in the world. Which she kind of guessed it was.

"Of course I am," she said, refusing to be embarrassed. "It's just that men usually avoid me, look at me like I'm some freak show because they've seen me on television or in magazines, or otherwise they're all over me. Even most of my bodyguards have never gotten used to dealing with the whole fan and paparazzi thing."

"Sounds like you haven't spent much time with real men," he said with a chuckle. "Or maybe it's just that Australian men aren't so easily intimidated. A pretty lady is a pretty lady, no matter who she is, and at the end of the day, I'd rather a camera in my face than a semi-automatic."

He thought she was pretty? "Well, maybe I should

spend more time *down under*. Is that what you call it here?"

"Yeah, that's what we call it."

Candace could tell he was trying not to laugh.

"So, are you going to hang around for the concert?"

"Is that an invite?"

"There's a VIP pass with your name on it if you want to stay. And I can't say I'd mind you hanging around, knowing that you're keeping an eye on things that could go boom."

"Sure thing. Can't say I've ever been given the VIP status before, so it'll be a nice change."

Candace cleared her throat. "Ah, do you have a partner or anyone I should add to the list, too?"

"Yeah, but he's probably not that interested in a show."

"Oh." He was gay? She sure hadn't seen that one coming, and it wasn't exactly easy to hide her disappointment. "If you're sure, then."

Logan met her gaze, his eyes dancing with what appeared to be…humor? "You've already met him, actually."

She swallowed, trying to figure out why he looked like he was about to burst into laughter again. "I have?"

"Yep. He's pretty big, beautiful brown eyes…and he's staring at you right now."

It took her half a second before she locked eyes with the dog staring at her, his black tail thumping against the ground as she showed him a hint of attention, like he'd figured the joke out before she had.

"That wasn't funny," she said, shaking her head and refusing to smile.

"Sorry, couldn't help myself."

"So, just the one pass, then?" she asked.

"Just the one," he confirmed, standing up when a knock at the door echoed throughout the room.

Candace watched as Logan accepted the food and kicked the door shut behind him. He wasn't hard to watch, the kind of guy she'd always notice no matter where she met him—tall, built and with close-cropped dark hair that matched his eyes. But he was strictly off-limits, eye candy only, because she was staying true to her promise not to get involved with anyone at the moment.

He paused, stood there looking down at her before crossing the room again.

"Candace, I won't be offended if you say no, but are you busy after your show?"

Why did he want to know, and why did he suddenly look so...staunch? "Why's that?"

Logan cleared his throat "I thought you might like a night out in Sydney, you know, to just have fun once you're done with work." He laughed. "I've been working around the clock for months, and I have a feeling you don't take much time off, either."

Candace stared at him, taken aback. He'd just managed to surprise her twice in less than a few minutes. "It's not that I don't want to, but it's just not that easy for me to hang out in public." Was he asking her on a date or did he think taking her out was part of his job description?

He put the containers down on the low table between the two sofas and sat down, leaning forward, eyes on hers. "You're in Australia, not America, and the places I'll take you, if it's just the two of us, no one will even realize who you are." Logan held his hands up. "But I have thick skin, so you can just turn me down and I'll forget I ever asked."

She took the plastic tops off the containers and reached for a pair of chopsticks, before looking up and seeing the serious expression on Logan's face. He was serious. And she had no idea what to say to him.

"You promise I'd be safe? That it would just be the two of us?"

"I promise," he said. "You'll just be a girl in the crowd instead of a superstar."

A shiver cascaded down her spine, spreading warmth into her belly. *Now that was something she liked the sound of.* "I'll think about it, but it does sound nice." It sounded way better than nice, but she didn't want to lead him on, not until she'd had time to think about it.

"Well, you just let me know when you're good and ready," he said. "Now it's time for you to tell me exactly what I'm about to bite into here, because I haven't ever seen anything that looks like this before."

Candace didn't usually even talk much before a show, tried to rest her voice, yet here she was chatting with a cute guy and thinking about going out with him. Maybe Australia was exactly the place she was supposed to be right now, to take her mind off everything that had been troubling her since…way too long.

* * *

Logan fought not to grimace as he held the chopsticks—
awkwardly. He wasn't opposed to trying new things,
but the food sitting in front of him looked downright
scary. Not to mention the fact that he was more comfortable using a good old knife and fork.

"When you said Japanese, I was kind of thinking
about the over-processed chicken sushi that I find at
the mall."

Candace gave him her wide smile again, the one
that was making him wish he'd met her under different
circumstances. Although, someone like her wouldn't
exactly have crossed paths with him if he hadn't been
assigned to mind her. She was an international superstar
and he was…a soldier turned bodyguard for a couple
of days. Which was why he'd taken his chance to ask
her out while he could. That would teach his friends for
pestering him about being single too long and not enjoying enough human company—he'd stepped completely
outside of his comfort level with Candace.

"So, I probably should have explained to you that
sashimi is raw fish, huh?"

Logan raised his eyebrows and wrangled with the
chopsticks some more, trying to mimic her actions. Except she was already dunking her first piece in the soy
sauce and popping the entire thing in her mouth, which
meant she was way ahead of him.

"Here goes," he muttered, leaning over the table so
he didn't spill any, his other hand ready to catch anything that fell.

"What do you think?" she asked.

He swallowed. "I can't say I've ever wanted to eat raw fish before, but I guess it's not half bad."

"I do have one kind with a cooked prawn on top. Here," Candace said, opening another box and then pushing it his way. "Try this."

Logan shook his head. "I can't go eating your favorite foods hours before your big concert. I'm the help, not a guest."

She rolled her eyes. "If we eat all this I can order more, so just take whatever you like, okay?"

Logan stared at her, wondering if he was about to see her diva side firsthand. He had a feeling someone that beautiful and talented was bound to be difficult. "You're sure?"

"Look, most celebrities have a rider about exactly what they do and don't want backstage or in their dressing room. Me? I just ask to have someone ready to run out and grab me great Japanese food and bottled water, and I request good lighting for my hair and makeup team." She smiled, shrugging at the same time. "I like the fact that everyone thinks I'm easy to deal with, so trust me when I say we can order more. These people are used to divas requesting a certain number of candles with a particular scent, flowers, bowls filled with expensive chocolates and imported candy. You get my drift?"

Logan got the picture. "Okay, pass me the prawn one, then."

"That's more like it."

Candace pushed the container closer to him, as well as a cup with a lid on it.

"What's this?"

"Miso soup. You'll love it."

Logan took off the lid, staring into the brownish liquid. "You sure this stuff won't kill me?"

"Positive. Now stir it with your chopsticks and take a sip. The green stuff is just seaweed, and there might be a few pieces of tofu floating around, too."

"Tofu?" he asked, pausing before the cup touched his lips. "You're killing me. I don't even think Ranger would eat tofu."

As if he understood exactly what they were saying, Ranger let out a low whine that made Candace laugh.

"Tofu," Logan muttered, taking a sip.

It wasn't half as bad as he was expecting, so he had some more, careful to avoid anything solid that was floating around in the soup. He was probably the only person in the building who hadn't tried this type of food before, but he was a soldier and a rancher—he was more used to simple steaks, vegetables and fries than the latest cuisines. Not to mention he was having to act like a regular guy instead of one who usually couldn't go a day without exercising like a crazy thing—sprinting as hard as he could to outrun his demons.

"So, what do you think?" Candace asked, pulling her long hair from her face and throwing it back over her shoulders.

"I think," he said, clearing his throat and putting down his chopsticks, "that it's time I went and did another perimeter check."

He was starting to become way too comfortable sitting around with Candace, eating fancy food like he did it every day.

Smoke billowed around him, obscuring almost everything. He walked slowly, not able to see even one of his feet, but he never let go of Ranger's leash. And then he stumbled, looked down and realized he'd just walked over another human being, facedown in the sand.

Logan cleared his throat, pushing away the memories that always hit him when he was least expecting them. If he wasn't on duty, he would have changed his shoes and hit the gym. But today that wasn't an option, and neither was giving in to his memories.

CHAPTER TWO

CANDACE TOOK A deep breath, mentally preparing for the concert. She'd been given her sixty-minute countdown already, which meant it was time to start running through her exercises, have a little something to drink, stretching out so she was all limbered up and dressing in her first costume.

But preparing for the performance wasn't taking up all her energy like it should have been. Instead she was thinking about a certain man who'd as good as knocked the wind from her earlier in the afternoon.

She'd been single for so long, not to mention the fact that she hadn't met a man who'd even remotely interested her for close to a year. Maybe that was why Logan had surprised her so much. Because even if she stayed true to her promise to remain single, she could still appreciate a good-looking man. And Logan was a fine-looking addition to the male species.

Candace cleared her throat and was about to start rehearsing when there was a knock at the door. She didn't call out because she was saving her voice, but she did cross the room to see who it was.

"Hey."

The man she'd been trying her best not to think about was standing in the hallway.

"How did you get past my security detail?" she asked in a low voice.

Logan grinned. "It just so happens I know the boss."

She laughed and pulled open the door so he could come in. She was about to ask him in when he held his hand up and shook his head.

"I'm not going to disturb you, I just wanted to check that you felt safe," he told her. "I personally handpicked the men working tonight, so you've got nothing to worry about, and I'm going off duty now for a quick break."

Candace thought for a second before saying what was on her mind. "What do you think about escorting me to stage and watching from the wings?"

"Like my own private concert?" he asked, raising an eyebrow.

She grinned. The idea of having Logan close by in case something *did* happen would be reassuring.

"What if I made you a trade?" she asked.

He cocked his head, clearly listening.

"I'll say yes to the night out you suggested, tonight, if you look after me for the duration of my performance."

Logan didn't even blink he answered her so fast. "You're on."

Candace met Logan's gaze, determined to keep her head held high. He was a handsome man who happened to be protecting her, and one she'd agreed to go on a date of sorts with. It didn't mean she had to go all bashful and forget the confident woman she usually was.

"Well, that's settled then," she said. "I'm going to keep running through my routine, so if you could come back in about forty-five minutes?"

Logan nodded. "Yes, ma'am."

Candace forced herself to stop staring at the tall, heavily muscled hunk standing outside her door and shut it instead, slowly slithering to the floor once she did so, cool timber against her back. She was behaving like a silly girl, flirting with a man who probably had no interest in her other than to parade her around a few hotspots on his arm. How many times before had she had someone say to her that they wanted to take her on a quiet date, only to find the paparazzi tipped off the moment they arrived at a restaurant or club? Or a man pretending he wasn't interested in her fame, only to find out he was a wannabe film star or singer with a CD he wanted to slip her during drinks or over an entrée. *That* was why she'd sworn off men for the time being.

Deep down, she wanted to believe that Logan was different, but until he'd proven that he wasn't the type of guy she was used to, she needed to tread lightly. No falling for her bodyguard, no touching her bodyguard and definitely no letting herself think, at any stage, that he could be anything more than fun.

She'd tried serious, and it hadn't worked. She'd even tried marriage, too, and that hadn't worked out well at all. When it came to men, she'd realized that maybe she just wasn't good at picking them, and it was probably something she'd inherited from her mom. Her mom might have been an incredible businesswoman, but she'd also had to raise Candace singlehandedly because of her poor decisions when it came to the male species.

Candace sighed, reached out for her first outfit, ran her hands down the silk, shut her eyes and imagined herself on stage, wearing it. Listening to the crowd. Holding the microphone as the band started to play. Hair and makeup would be back any minute, and so would her stylist.

She could do this. She'd performed a hundred times before, and Logan had promised her that the venue was safe and secure. She needed to forget the stupid threats and just do what she did best. Because no matter what happened to her, no one could ever take away her love of singing. Performing was the love of her life and it always would be.

This was her time to shine.

"You a fan of country music?"

Logan glanced at the woman standing beside him, her headset pulled back so she could talk to him. She was holding a tablet, and until now she'd had her eyes glued to it and had been speaking intently into her headset.

"I can't say I've ever really listened to it before," he admitted. Truth be told, he'd never listened to it because he'd never really liked it before, but watching this particular performance was fast converting him to the genre.

"She's pretty incredible to watch," the woman said, pulling on her headset again. "I get to see a lot of performers, but she's hands down the most talented and nicest we've hosted yet."

Logan smiled in reply and turned his attention back to Candace. As the song finished she wowed the crowd with her mesmerizing, soft laugh, before turning around and waving toward the band so they could have their own round of applause. He was pleased that she'd asked him to watch, but he'd actually been employed to stay until the end of her concert anyway. He just hadn't told her that.

"Thank you for having me here tonight!" she told her fans. "Australia is one of the most beautiful countries I've ever visited, and I wish I had more time to spend here."

The applause was deafening, but Logan could no more take his eyes off her and walk away than he could stop breathing. If there was such a thing as star power, she had it—on stage she wasn't the sweet, soft-spoken woman he'd spent time with earlier in the day. Up there, her presence was almost overpowering, and the screaming fans only seemed to make her light up more in front of them, her confidence soaring as they encouraged her.

As she burst into another song, Logan leaned against the wall where he was standing. The past year had been nothing short of hard, unbearable, and being here tonight, watching Candace, was the kind of night he'd needed, even if it was technically work.

When Sam had died...*hell.* He didn't want to go back there. Losing one of his closest friends so soon after his parents' accident, then coming so close to losing another under different circumstances, not to mention deciding to retire—he'd only just pulled through. But the rush he'd felt when Candace had said yes to a night out with him had given him a much needed boost. He was ready to add some nice memories to his thought bank, and Candace was exactly the kind of memory he'd prefer to dwell upon.

He looked up as the next song came to an end, and the next thing he knew Candace was running toward him.

"What did you think?" she asked, eyes flashing as she glanced at him, a big smile on her face as she ran in her heels. "The crowd is crazy here!"

She kept moving, not pausing, so Logan spun and jogged to keep up with her, even as she was surrounded by a group of people who started to tug at her clothes and talk a million miles an hour.

"You were great out there," he managed when the crowd paused for a nanosecond.

"You really think so?"

There was an innocence in her gaze that made Logan smile, because this was the woman he'd glimpsed earlier. The one who was so used to being told by others what they thought she wanted to hear, that she no longer knew who to believe, who to trust. She wanted to know whether she could believe him—it was so obvious it was written all over her face, and he had no more intention of lying to her than anyone else.

"I know so," he told her honestly.

The words were barely out of his mouth before she disappeared into her dressing room, and Logan turned his back when he realized the door wasn't going to be closed. It seemed like only minutes later that she was running back out again, heading toward the stage, and instead of trying to keep up with her this time he just walked behind. She was still being plucked and prodded, her outfit pulled into shape and her hair fiddled with just before she was due back on stage. The woman with the tablet from earlier was flapping her arms at a group of dancers, before starting a countdown and sending them on as the music started again.

Just before she disappeared, Candace turned and locked her gaze on his, smiling for barely a second before throwing one hand in the air and returning to the stage.

There was no doubting she was a brilliant performer, but she was also like a little girl desperately in need of someone to look after her and trust in. To tell her the truth when she needed it, but also to shield her from harm.

"I'm not that person," Logan muttered to himself, even as his instinct to protect reared within him before he could stamp it out.

He'd protected and looked after people all his life, and still he'd lost those he loved. Some of the people he cared most about in the world, and some strangers whose faces he'd never forget until the day he died, too. Looking after Candace while she was on stage and during her press conference tomorrow was his job, and one he intended on doing well, and tonight was about having fun with a beautiful woman. There was no need to overthink the situation or turn it into something it wasn't.

He wasn't going to be the one to rescue her, because

he was still waiting to be rescued himself. Tonight was going to be great, but after that he'd never see her again, which meant she wasn't his to worry about. Or protect.

Candace took one last bow after her second encore song before walking from the stage. It had been the kind of night she loved, the type that made her remember how lucky she was to perform for a career, even though her nerves had jangled whenever she'd let her mind stray to the hate mail she'd been receiving. There were always those times when she wondered if that person was in the crowd, watching her, but with Logan standing in the wings and the security amped up for the evening, she'd tried to make herself just relax. And for the most part it had worked.

Her heart was still pounding, adrenaline making her feel a million dollars, as she disappeared into the darkness of the wings, her eyes taking a moment to adjust from the bright lights she'd been performing under.

"I think you've made me like country music," a deep male voice said.

She recognized Logan's Australian twang the moment she heard it, and her heart started to race a little more.

"I'd say I don't believe you, but I kind of want to," she said with a laugh.

"I'm actually thinking of joining your insane fans and lining up for a CD and T-shirt. It seems to be the thing to do."

She laughed, brushing her hand against his as she passed and then snatching it back like she'd connected with a flame. It had been a long time since she'd just touched someone impulsively like that, and it wasn't something she wanted to make a habit of. Especially not with a man, even if she was enjoying his company.

"You can have a free T-shirt, I'll even autograph it for you," she teased.

"So what time do you want to head out?" he asked, following her.

Candace took a slow breath, still energized from her ninety minutes on stage. She always felt amazing at the end of a performance, exhaustion never setting in for hours after she finished.

"We'll need to wait until the crowds die down. I don't mind signing a couple of autographs, but I'm not going to ruin my buzz by being mobbed. Not tonight."

Logan shook his head. "I think we're best to leave immediately, before anyone expects you to depart. My truck's parked around the back and we should be able to get in before anyone realizes it's you, so long as we move quickly."

Candace wasn't convinced, but then she also usually timed these kind of things all wrong anyway and ended up in the middle of a hundred fans, trying to reach her getaway car. Or else her manager set things up to happen like that for maximum publicity when she gave him explicit instructions to the contrary.

"I don't believe you, but I'm prepared to give you the benefit of the doubt," she said.

"Good. I'll go check the exit now and be back in ten minutes," he told her. "Shall we meet in your dressing room?"

Candace nodded. "Let's do it."

The idea of a night out was exciting—she'd become used to feeling fantastic, on a high from singing, then going straight back to a hotel room, alone. Most of the time she ended up ordering room service, watching an old movie and going to bed, before receiving her wake-up call and taking a car to the airport early the next morning. Before she'd become recognizable, she'd always had a fun night out after any gig, which was why tonight was like a blast from the past for her. Add the tourism campaign she was the face of, and she didn't have a hope of Australians not realizing who she was.

It was yet to be seen whether she could even manage to leave the building without being recognized or followed, so she could easily end up holed up in her hotel room just when she least expected it.

Candace closed her dressing room door the moment she stepped inside and slipped the feathery minidress off, letting it pool to the floor. She rummaged around in her case for the casual clothes she'd packed, in case she needed them, pulling out a pair of dark blue skinny jeans and wriggling her way into them. She didn't have anything other than a T-shirt to wear, so she flicked through the tops hanging on her racks, wishing they weren't all so costume looking, until she spotted a sequined black tank. Candace pulled it over her head, grabbed a studded leather biker jacket, and slipped into a pair of dangerously high heels she'd worn on stage earlier in the evening.

Glancing at the clock on the wall, she stopped, took a deep breath, then sat down at her dressing table. Her makeup was excessive—thick false eyelashes and spar-kly eyeshadow—but she didn't have time to change it. Besides, Logan had seen her looking like this all evening. She did run her fingers through her hair to flatten it down a bit, teasing the hairspray from her curls so it felt like real hair again, so it was touchable.

There was a knock at the door. Candace jumped, glaring at her reflection at the same time. It was just Logan, and it wasn't like she hadn't known he was coming, but her nerves had been permanently on edge for weeks now. Maybe she could talk to him about it and see what he thought the best way to react to the threats was.

"Just a minute!" she called out.

Candace jumped up to grab her purse, checked her credit card, phone and hotel swipe card were all inside and swung open the door.

"Wow."

Logan's approving smile and the way he looked her up and down made her laugh. He seemed to say what he was thinking, and she liked the fact he was a straight shooter with her.

"Are we cleared to leave?" she asked, trying to ignore what he'd just said even though she couldn't stop smiling.

"I told your manager and the rest of the team that you're feeling ill, and you wanted me to escort you straight to the hotel. I said we'll be exiting from the side entrance, and I have a feeling there'll be a lot of fans waiting there, if you catch my drift."

"So we can't go?" she asked, hearing the disappointment in her own voice.

Logan gave her a wry smile, a dimple flashing against his cheek at the same time. "We're going out the very back. My vehicle's parked down the alleyway, so no one will see us."

"So you lied to everyone?" she asked.

"I expanded the truth," he said, winking as he gestured for her to follow him. "I have a feeling your manager is more interested in getting publicity than a quiet getaway for you, and given that I'm your head of security, all I care about is your safety. You say no fans or paparazzi? That's what I give you."

Candace shook her head. "I think I underestimated you," she said with a chuckle.

"I also told them that you'd be exiting in fifteen minutes, so if we're going to do this, I think we should hurry, just in case someone comes looking for you before we go."

He waited for her to nod, then clasped her hand firmly, walking fast in the opposite direction to which they'd arrived earlier in the day. Candace had to almost run to keep up with his long, loping stride, but she didn't care. Logan was going to get her out of here without being mobbed, without even having to come face-to-face with her manager, and she might actually have a drink at a bar before anyone figured out who she was. Adrenaline was starting to fill her with hope.

Her phone started to beep in her purse, and she managed to open it without slowing down. She glanced at the screen.

"It's Billy, my manager," she told Logan when he looked down.

"Text him from the car when we're driving away," he said. "You can tell him we've gone once we've hit the main road, but not before."

Candace slipped the phone back into her purse and hurried along with Logan, trying to concentrate on not falling off her stiletto heels. A few little white lies weren't going to hurt anyone, especially not her manager, who didn't seem to care that she'd spent the past few weeks frightened out of her own skin about the thought of being in public.

"So did you believe me when I said I'd get you out of there?"

Logan glanced over at Candace and saw that she was staring out the window, watching the world as it blurred past.

"No," she replied, sighing and turning in her seat to face him. "If I'm completely honest I didn't even want to let myself hope that I'd get out of there that easily."

"So I don't need to ask you if you're still keen for a few drinks and something to eat?"

Candace laughed and it made him smile. "I'll stay out until someone starts flashing camera bulbs in my face."

"You're on. The places I'm taking you no one will ever find us."

She was looking out the window again, and he took his foot off the gas a little so they weren't going so fast. For someone who hadn't found it easy being back or dealing with people, he was finding it weirdly easy to talk to Candace. She should be the one person he had nothing in common with, but for some reason he was drawn to the fact that she was an outcast just like he was, albeit a different one. It settled him somehow.

"That kind of makes you sound like a serial killer," she finally responded, like she was just thinking out aloud. "Which makes me wonder how I ended up letting you whisk me away from everyone who's supposed to be looking after me and keeping me safe."

"I'm the one who kept you safe today, so you don't have a lot to worry about," Logan told her, taking his eyes off the road for a second to make sure she was listening to him, looking at him. "If I'm perfectly honest, you have a manager who makes sure you get mobbed when he knows you hate it, and the rest of your entourage probably have way less interest in making sure you're kept out of harm's way than I do."

She shut her eyes and put her head against the rest. "I know you're right about my manager. Deep down, I think I've known it for a while. I just didn't want to acknowledge it."

He didn't answer. He knew he was right, but he didn't need to make her feel worse than she probably already did.

"Until you said that, I guess I've been trying to bury my head in the sand and pretend like everything's fine."

Logan fought the battle to bite his tongue and lost. "The guy's seriously bad news. How long have you put up with him for? I know you have more experience with the whole celebrity thing than I ever will, but that's a layperson's take on him."

Candace sighed. "He's been with me for years, and

he used to be a lot better than he is now, that's for sure," she muttered. "Things have kind of been going downhill for a while now."

"How about we stop talking about work and just have a nice night?" Logan suggested, wishing he'd just kept his mouth shut instead of insulting her people. For once in his life he wasn't screwing up—usually something he only managed to achieve in his work life—and he needed to just enjoy the company of a beautiful woman.

"You betcha," Candace agreed. "Hey, where's your dog tonight?"

Logan grimaced. "I left him at home. He was pretty pissed."

"You know, for a dog he's kind of nice."

"You're a cat person, aren't you?"

She laughed, like she was embarrassed. "Sure am. I was attacked by a German Shepherd when I was a little girl. In fact, I still have the scars to prove it. I've just never really warmed to dogs since. Stupid, I know, but just the way I am."

"Understandable." Personally, he wasn't fussed on cats, but he wasn't going to tell her that. "I've had dogs all my life, but then I've never had one be anything other than loyal to me."

"Back home I have a pair of Birman cats called Indie and Lexie, and if I'm completely honest they've probably done me more damage with their claws than your dog has probably ever done to you with his teeth."

They both laughed. Logan changed the subject for a second, wanting to point out to Candace where they were going.

"See just over there? That's Cockle Bay and it's where I'm taking you for dinner."

"I thought we were just going for drinks?" she asked, her nose almost pressed to the window, looking where he'd pointed.

It was the reason Logan had brought her here, because he knew how amazing the harbor was to visitors. Him? He'd grown up with it and was used to it, but every time he'd returned from a tour it had always put a smile on his face, told him he was home.

"If you're not hungry, we can always skip dinner."

"Don't be silly. After all that energy I used on stage, I'm famished," she admitted. "And dinner sounds great."

Logan parked his four-by-four and jumped out, grabbing his jacket and pulling it on. He walked around the vehicle and opened the passenger door, waiting for Candace to step out.

"Thank you," she said. "You know, it's kind of strange for me getting out on this side of the road."

Logan waited for her to grab her purse, before shutting the door and leading the way, walking slowly so she didn't have to hurry beside him.

"Your shoes are insanely high."

"I know, but aren't they fab? They were a gift from my favorite designer."

He raised his eyebrows. "You're talking to a soldier, sorry. But they do look cool, I guess, for a pair of shoes, that is."

Candace laughed. "I definitely need to spend more

time with real people. Of course you couldn't care less about my shoes!"

He shrugged and pointed ahead. "We're going to a place called Jimmy's and they have the best seafood in Sydney. Plus they're right on the water."

Candace started walking even slower, a smile spreading over her face that he couldn't miss as they passed a couple who didn't even look at them.

"You have no idea what it feels like to just walk along the street and not be noticed. I've missed this for so long now."

Logan looked up, taking comfort in the bright stars twinkling in the dark sky—the same stars he'd looked at every night when he was on tour even though he'd been on the other side of the world. When he was at home in the Outback, they always seemed brighter, but they were still just as pretty to look at in the city.

"When I was on my first couple of tours, white soldiers were pretty easy to notice. I remember the first time we went through a village, and the women were screaming out to us, begging us to help them. I couldn't understand what they were saying, but the pleading, desperate looks they were giving us told me that I was their last chance. That that's how they thought of us." Logan took a deep breath, wondering why he was even telling Candace all this. He hardly ever spoke about his tours, except with Brett, but for some reason he just needed her to know. "These little children were hanging on to us, grabbing us as we walked through on patrol, and we gave them all the food we had. It wasn't until the next day that we found out all the men had been killed by local insurgents, and the women were left to fend on their own, terrified that they'd be next, and with no way to provide for their children."

Candace had almost stopped walking now, her eyes like saucers, filled with tears as she stared at him. Her hands were clenched into fists at her sides.

"What happened to them?"

Logan shook his head. "I don't know. But I can tell you how awful it was to be recognized, as someone who those people thought could save them, when in reality all I could offer was some dried snacks and a candy bar. And it happened to us over and over again."

"So, what you're saying is that I need to stop caring about being recognized for who I am?" she asked, her voice soft.

"No, what I'm saying is that sometimes being recognized for the right reasons is okay. The people who want to see you just want a smile and an autograph, and they're things you can give them. It's when you're powerless that being recognized is something to be scared of."

Candace shook her head, a sad look on her face. "I sound like a selfish, self-centered idiot for even saying all that, when you compare it to what you went through. But I guess it's just that I struggle with the whole fame thing. I'm a singer and I love what I do. It's just the publicity that I find really difficult." She sighed. "Unfortunately one doesn't come without the other in this industry."

"No, Candace, that's not what I meant," he said as they started to walk again. "I guess I just want you to know that I probably understand some of what you go through on a daily basis, even though our worlds are light-years apart."

They walked in silence for a minute, almost at the restaurant. She knew what he meant, but she still felt stupid for moaning aloud about being recognized. She was lucky and she knew it, but lately being surrounded by fans had turned from flattering to downright scary.

"Have you ever tried Morton Bay bugs?" Logan asked, changing the subject.

Candace gave him a look like she was trying to figure out if he was joking. "I have no idea what you're even talking about, but they sound revolting."

He laughed. "Definitely not revolting, I promise you. They're kind of like lobster, but different. Better."

"You're serious, aren't you?" she groaned as he opened the door. "You're actually going to make me eat something called a *bug as punishment for the sashimi*."

"It's a stupid name for what they are, but yeah, you're definitely going to be eating them." Logan chuckled as they stood and waited to be greeted. "Grilled with garlic butter, fresh bread on the side and…"

"Logan?"

He spun around, taking his eyes off Candace and her cute smile. "Hey, Jimmy."

His old friend raised his eyebrows, looking from him to Candace, before his eyes widened. Logan gave him a look that he hoped he understood, not wanting their night ruined before it even started.

"The kitchen's closing soon, but I can squeeze you two in if you order quick," Jimmy said, grabbing two menus. "How you been, anyway? I haven't seen you in ages."

Logan motioned for Candace to follow, touching his hand to her lower back and guiding her forward.

"I've been okay, can't complain. Especially since I'm back for good now."

Jimmy walked them through the restaurant and waved toward an alfresco table, complete with low candles on the table and a view out over the water. Even though it was dark, the water was twinkling under the lights from all the restaurants and the luxury yachts moored nearby. The night air was warm, slightly muggy still after the hot day.

"Do you even need these?" Jimmy asked with a grin, gesturing at the menus.

Logan grinned straight back at him, pulling out a seat for Candace. Jimmy obviously knew exactly who she was—maybe he was just too starstruck to remember his manners, or his job.

"Let's start with two buckets of prawns and sourdough bread, then Morton Bay bugs for two, and maybe a Caesar salad."

Jimmy was nodding, but he was also spending most of his time glancing at Candace, who was looking out at the water, her body turned away from them.

Logan leaned in closer to his childhood friend, giving him a playful whack across the back of the head.

"Don't you breathe a word of this to anyone until we're gone. No tipping the media off, no telling your girlfriend."

Jimmy made a face like his head hurt, but he was

still grinning. "Can I at least get an autograph before you leave?"

"Keep everyone else away from us and I'll make sure you get one. Deal?"

Jimmy's smile grew wider. "And a big tip, too, right?"

"You do know I have a dog that could eat you in a few mouthfuls, don't you?" Logan said in a low voice, smiling as Candace turned to face them.

Jimmy just laughed. "I'll get your order in and bring you some drinks. Champagne?"

Logan sat down and glanced at Candace. "Bubbly or beer?"

She made a thoughtful face before one side of her mouth tilted up into a smile. "Let's have a beer. Why not?"

Logan didn't let the surprise show on his face, even though he'd never have picked her choosing beer over champagne in a million years. "You heard the lady. Two beers, bottles not glasses."

Jimmy shook his head and walked off, leaving Logan to burst out laughing. Candace seemed to be finding the entire thing as hilarious as he was.

"He knew who I was the moment we walked in, didn't he?" she asked in a soft voice, like she wasn't in the least bit surprised.

Logan wasn't going to lie to her. "Yeah, he did. But there's no way he's going to make a fuss or say anything, okay?"

She nodded. "So you don't think it'll be in the papers that I was spotted out with a mystery man, knocking back beers? Knowing the paps, they'll probably say I was out of control and ready for rehab."

"You missed the part about us digging into two massive buckets filled with prawns, that we'll be eating with our fingers like barbarians instead of fine dining."

Candace dipped her head when she laughed, looking up at him like she wasn't entirely sure whether he was ever being serious or always joking. "And here I was thinking you'd brought me to a classy restaurant."

"Believe me, nothing in the world is better than fresh seafood eaten with your fingers, washed down by an ice-cold beer. We don't need five forks and silver service to eat incredible food."

"Well, I'll have to reserve judgment until I've experienced it, but I'm guessing you're probably right."

He leaned back in his chair. "See the beautiful super yachts out there?"

She nodded, following his gaze.

"When you come here earlier in the evening, there are waiters running back and forth from the restaurant to the boats, carrying silver trays of seafood and champagne. It's crazy, but a lot of fun to watch."

"I was right going with my gut feeling on promoting Australia to the world," she said with a laugh. "Next time I'm ready for a vacation, I'm heading straight back here."

CHAPTER THREE

CANDACE LOOKED BACK out at the water to avoid looking at the man seated across from her. There was something exciting about being out somewhere different, on the other side of the world, and with someone she hardly knew. And for the first time in forever, she actually felt like herself, like the old her, the one she'd started to slowly lose a few years earlier. When her marriage had started to crumble, so had her self-confidence, and then when her mom had died…she pushed the dark thoughts away and focused on Logan.

"Is this somewhere you come often?"

Logan leaned forward, both hands on his beer bottle. She took a sip of hers while she waited for his response.

"I've been coming here for years. Every time I came home from deployment, this was the first place I headed to for a meal," he told her. "There were three of us with a standing date."

"As in three soldiers?" she asked, curious.

Logan twirled his beer bottle between his hands. "Yeah."

Candace could sense there was something else going

on, something unsaid, but she didn't know him well enough to pry. She knew what it was like to want to keep some things private.

"It must have been a relief coming here for the amazing food after what you had to eat over there," she said, wanting to give him an out if he needed it.

Logan looked up and met her gaze. "It was. There's only so much dried jerky and dehydrated food a guy can eat, right?"

She laughed, but it died in her throat as their waiter approached the table with an enormous amount of food.

"No way."

Logan grinned and leaned back as two large silver buckets filled with prawns were placed in front of them. She'd never seen so much seafood in her life.

"You're telling me that this is just for starters?" she asked, groaning.

The waiter returned with two dishes of some kind of sauce and freshly quartered lemons, as well as a bowl of warm water, which she guessed was for them to dip their fingers in to after eating.

"In Australia, we have a saying that you can't eat enough seafood," Logan told her.

"You do?" Candace watched as he picked up one of the prawns and pulled the head off, before peeling the shell.

"No, I just made that up to make you think this was a good idea." He gave her a wink that made her heart thud to her toes. "If you don't want to get your hands dirty I can peel yours?" he offered.

"I appreciate the gesture but I think it's about time

I got my hands dirty." She was sick of people running around and doing everything for her, and tonight was about her just being her. "You show me what to do and I'll do it."

"You just have to grab your beer bottle between your palms so it doesn't get all greasy. Like this," Logan explained, demonstrating with a quick swig of his beer before dipping his prawn into the sauce.

Candace just shook her head, finding it hard to believe that she'd been performing live in front of twenty thousand people only an hour earlier, and was now sitting at a restaurant, tucking into a meal with the man who'd been assigned her personal head of security. Add to that the fact she hadn't been asked for even one autograph…it was insane. She shouldn't have trusted him so easily, but she hadn't been so relaxed in a long time. Maybe she'd wake up and realize it had all just been a dream, but if it had been, at least it had been a nice one.

She peeled her first prawn and dipped it in the sauce.

"Good?" he asked.

"Amazing," she murmured, hand over her mouth as she spoke. "You were right."

They sat in silence for a while, both eating their prawns and sipping beer. Something told her that Logan wasn't usually a big talker—that he was comfortable not saying anything at all, and she liked it. Where she'd grown up, the men had a motto of speaking only when they'd had something worthy of being said, but her adult life had been filled with men who couldn't say *enough* to make themselves sound important.

"So have you always lived in the city?" she asked.

Logan looked up, finishing his mouthful and dipping his fingers in the lemon water to clean them. She watched as he dried his hands on the napkin.

"I actually grew up in the Outback," he told her, finishing his beer before leaning back in his chair. "I'm based here a lot of the time, but when I'm not working I head straight back there just to be away from the city and out in the open air."

So, that's why she felt so comfortable around him. It had been a while since she'd hung out with a country boy.

"Your family all ranch out there?"

He grinned. "We call it farming here, but yeah, it's my family property."

Candace paused, slowly peeling a prawn. "So your dad runs the place or a brother?"

Logan took a deep breath, she could see the rise and fall of his chest, before he waved to a waiter and gestured for another beer. He glanced at her, but Candace shook her head—hers was still half-full.

He cleared his throat. "My parents both died a few years ago, and my sister lives on a farm with her husband," Logan explained. "The property has been in our family for generations, so I'd rather die than sell the place, but I've had to have a manager employed while I've been serving so the place can continue to run smoothly."

Candace sighed. "I shouldn't have been so nosey, Logan. I'm sorry."

"It's fine. Sometimes it's just hard to say out loud,

because admitting it makes it real, as stupid as that sounds."

She knew exactly how that felt. "My mom died a couple of years ago, and if I'm honest, that's why I've put up with my management team for longer than I should have. She was the one who dealt with all that stuff so I could just focus on singing, and I'm still pretty lost without her. She was the business brains and I was the creative one, and it had always been just the two of us. We made a good team."

Logan took the beer that arrived at their table, his eyes leaving hers to look out at the water. She did the same, because it seemed wrong to keep watching him when he was obviously troubled about what they were talking about. He was silent.

"I didn't mean to just unleash all that on you," she apologized. "I don't usually spill my thoughts so easily, but…"

"It's nice to tell someone who actually gets it, right?" he finished, gaze meeting hers again.

"Yeah," she murmured, "something like that."

"Losing a parent is tough, and it doesn't get easier, so don't believe anyone if they try to tell you otherwise," he told her. "But you do learn to live with it."

Their table was cleared then and within minutes two large white plates were placed in front of them.

"So these are the bugs, huh?"

Logan nodded, but he was more reserved now than he'd been before—his enthusiasm dulled.

"You just scoop the white meat out of the shell," he told her. "It's incredible."

Candace spread her napkin over her lap, smoothing out the wrinkles, before picking up her fork and following Logan's lead. He was right—again—the food was great.

"Thanks for a lovely evening," she told him when she'd finished her mouthful. "It was completely unexpected and I appreciate the gesture."

He gave her a weird look. "Sounds like you're ready to leave."

"No, I'm just grateful that I've actually enjoyed a night in someone else's company. You've given me some perspective at a time when I needed it."

Logan went back to getting every last piece of meat from the shellfish, and she forced herself to stop watching him and just eat, too. There was something so refreshingly real about him.

"Another beer?"

She looked at her bottle and was about to say no, before she changed her mind. "You know what? Yeah. I'd love another. Why not?"

"So, I told you where I grew up. How about you?"

"I grew up on a ranch, too. My parents split when I was a baby, so we moved to my grandparents' ranch. I used to ride my horse and sing into a hairbrush, pretending it was my microphone. I spent every day outside, even if it was raining, just making up songs and enjoying the fresh air." She smiled just thinking about it. "It was the best childhood I could imagine, and my grandfather made up for my not having a dad. He was great."

He chuckled. "Ever wish you could go back in time?"

"I don't know about back in time, but I'd love to go

back to living on a ranch. I have a place in Montana, but it's not somewhere I get to very often these days, so it's not really where I call home."

"Why don't you just make time?"

Logan's question was serious, his voice deep.

"That's a very good question."

"Candace, when do you fly out?" Logan asked.

She pushed her plate away and reached for her beer. "Day after tomorrow."

Logan pulled a bread roll apart and took a bite, looking back out at the water again. There was a lot going on his mind, she was sure of it, but it was like he chose his words carefully, thought everything through before he said it. Their Caesar salad arrived while they were mid conversation, but there was no way she was going to able to eat even a mouthful of it.

"Why?"

"I was just thinking that spending some more time in Australia would do you the world of good."

"Meaning that I need to unwind?"

His eyes were still on the water, looking into the distance. "Meaning that if you want to remember what it's like to just be a human being in the world, here's probably the place to do it. The Outback heals the soul, or at least that's what I've always believed."

"Is that what the Outback did for you?" she asked, studying his side profile, the angle of his jaw and the fullness of his lips.

She glanced away when he turned, catching her staring.

"Yeah, it did," he said. "The Outback saved me when

nothing else could, and every time I go back there it reminds me what life is truly about. I guess it's my place in the world."

Candace didn't know why, or how, but when she saw the hurt in his gaze, the honesty of what he was saying, tears sprang into her eyes. This man who'd been so kind to her, so polite and respectful, had a power of hurt inside of him, and even glimpsing it made her sad. Whatever he'd been through was more than just losing his parents—he'd seen pain, grief, like she'd probably never know. What he'd experienced as a soldier must have given him memories that he'd never be able to shed.

"Excuse me, I'm just going to find the ladies' room," Candace said, grabbing her purse, before crossing the restaurant.

A waiter pointed her in the right direction and she disappeared into the first restroom, locking the door behind her. Candace stared at her reflection in the mirror, studying her face, seeing the makeup, the woman she was on stage, and not the girl she felt like inside.

The past few months, she'd been miserable except for the few times she'd been on stage or in the studio. So unhappy that she'd clung to what felt safe, what she thought was right, but one evening in the company of someone like Logan and she was starting to question everything. Today had been full of adrenaline and anticipation, she'd been excited when she'd said yes to going out with Logan, and now she was starting to spiral down, like a party girl coming off a high.

Logan was kind and handsome, and in all honesty she was probably drawn to him because he was capable of protecting her. But in less than two days she'd be flying away from Australia and never coming back, which was why she should never have agreed to tonight. Men were supposed to be off her radar, and after everything she'd been through, that's where she wanted them to stay. So getting her hopes up about an Australian soldier who'd probably never even think about her again, who probably just wanted what every other guy wanted from her, was beyond stupid.

Candace reapplied her lip gloss and gave herself a long, hard stare in the mirror. The best thing she could do was call it a night, not get involved in any way with Logan. For her sake and for his. She'd been stupid to agree to it in the first place.

Logan stood when Candace reappeared. He knew he was frowning, but the look on her face wasn't helping him to stop.

"You okay?" he asked.

"I'm fine," she replied, but he could tell from the smile she fixed that it was a face she'd perfected to hide how she really felt. He'd spent most of his working life studying people and situations, and he doubted he was wrong.

"Are you ready to head somewhere else for a drink, or…" He paused, watching the way her gaze darted away, the change in her eyes. "You're ready to go back to your hotel, aren't you?"

Candace nodded. "I think maybe we should call it a night."

Logan hesitated before reaching for her hand, not sure what he'd done to upset her.

"Candace, if there's something I've done…" he started.

"No, it's absolutely nothing you've done," she whispered, but as she spoke tears glinted in her eyes.

"It's been a long time since I've made a girl cry," he said, doing the only thing he could think of and pulling her toward him for a hug. "Whatever it is, I'm sorry."

She hardly moved, but her hand did reach up and grasp his shirt as he put his arms around her, held her so she could compose herself.

"I don't know why you're being so kind to me," she murmured, just loud enough for him to hear.

Logan sighed, inhaling the fresh scent of her hair, the aroma of her perfume. It had been a while since he'd been with a woman, and being this close to Candace was something he was already starting to crave.

"You sure you don't want another drink? Something else to eat?"

She ran her hand down his arm as she stepped back, eyes fixed on his. Logan was watching her, waiting for her to reply, when a flash went off, followed by what seemed like a hundred more. Logan leaped in front of Candace, instinct warning him to protect her no matter what, anger burning inside him as he realized the threat was only a photographer who'd managed to find them.

"Crap," he muttered, taking her hand firmly in his.

"It's okay, it's just one pap," she said.

He didn't care if it was one or twenty, he was still pissed at the intrusion. The photographer was escorted from the restaurant within minutes, but Logan knew it had been enough to rattle Candace. He had his own personal reasons to hate the media, and he wasn't going to let them ruin Candace's evening, not when she'd been so excited about an anonymous night out.

"Word will be out soon, so I'll take you straight to the hotel," he told her, before remembering what he'd promised Jimmy. "Before we go, I did promise our waiter an autograph in exchange for his discretion. If he was the one who tipped that guy off, I'll kill him, but I think I made it clear enough already what the consequences would be, so I doubt it would have been him."

Candace's smile diffused his anger as easily as someone blowing out a candle.

"Logan, we've sat here alone without anyone bothering us for the best part of a couple of hours. I don't care about one photographer finding us, but you're right about word not taking long to spread."

"So you're not angry?" He was confused—and he was seriously pissed.

Candace plucked a pen from her purse and signed an unused white napkin on their table.

"This is for your friend," she told him. "Do you want me to settle the bill and give it to him?"

Logan was reaching for the napkin when he froze. Had he just heard that right?

"You're not paying the bill."

"Of course I am," she said. "I wouldn't have it any other way."

"I asked you out for dinner, and I don't care how PC

the world is supposed to be, but you taking care of the bill is ridiculous."

"Logan—" she started, but he cut her off.

"Do you really want to insult me?" he asked.

"I'm just used to…"

"Jerks, if they let you pay. I don't care who you are. The only thing I care about is that you're a woman and I'm a man, and that means I take care of our bill tonight."

He watched as she shut her mouth and shrugged, clearly giving in. "Well, all right then. Thank you for a lovely meal, Mr. Neanderthal."

Logan burst out laughing as they walked to the front of the restaurant. "I know I'm old-fashioned, but seriously. Just because you're famous doesn't mean you shouldn't be treated like a lady."

He paid and passed his friend the napkin as they said goodbye, before walking out the front door.

"And just because you're a soldier doesn't mean you have to…"

Her words faded as someone yelled her name, and Logan sprung straight into work mode, putting his arm around her shoulders and hurrying her forward. There were a couple of guys trying to get close with their cameras, but he ignored them and just focused on propelling Candace away.

"We'll be fine once we get to the car," he told her, his palm firm on her shoulder.

"They'll follow us straight to my hotel."

"You want to go somewhere no one can bother you?" he asked.

"Please."

"Then I'll give them the slip and we can head straight to my place. No one will ever find you there."

Logan didn't know why he said it, why he'd even thought to take her back to his house, but he had and now there was no going back. The last time he'd let a woman into his home had been…Logan swallowed and moved faster, listening to Candace's heels as they beat a rhythm against the sidewalk. When he'd admitted to his friends that it had been a long time since he'd let a woman into his life, he hadn't been exaggerating.

He'd enjoyed tonight because he hadn't let himself dwell on the past, and if he wanted to survive having Candace at his place, then that's what he'd have to keep doing. There was no point thinking about the woman who'd hurt him, or anything else about what had happened in the past few years.

For months, he'd been telling himself that it was time to move on with his life, to put his past behind him, but some things were easy to think and a whole lot harder to put into practice. Especially when the darkness of his memories crept into his brain just when he was least expecting them.

CHAPTER FOUR

CANDACE COULD FEEL her heart racing—it was like her pulse was thumping in her head it sounded so loud. Fleeing the paparazzi and heading for Logan's place had seemed like the safe option when he'd suggested it, but now she was starting to panic. It was one thing to have dinner with the man in a public place, but going back to his house? Not something she'd ever usually do, especially with someone she'd just met, without anyone else knowing where she was.

They pulled up in front of a row of two-story houses. There wasn't a garage, so Logan parked on the street, and she waited for him to come around to open her door. It gave her time to calm her breathing and think about how to handle the situation.

"We managed to lose all of them, and I doubt they'll come looking for you in the suburbs."

She stepped out of the vehicle and shut the door behind her, before following Logan to the front door of his house. Nerves made her stomach flutter, but she ignored them. It was time she started trusting her own instincts.

"I should probably call my manager, just to let him

know where I am." Candace didn't like the fact that no one in the world knew where to find her if they needed her. Although come to think of it, she did have a tracking device on her phone, so her manager could locate her if he made an effort.

"Candace, you can do whatever you like, but if it were me? I'd be telling him you were safe and that you'd see him tomorrow. Unless you're okay with that same shark frenzy we just escaped from turning up outside here with telescopic lenses."

She grimaced. "You really don't like him, do you?"

"If I'm completely honest with you, I have my suspicions that the hate mail and threats you've been receiving aren't real. I don't want to point fingers, but there's only one person I can see who could be responsible, if my theory is correct."

Candace was sick to her stomach hearing his words, but she also realized that Logan could be right. She'd never have thought it before, *had never thought it,* but she also wasn't prepared to defend Billy without looking into it further. Without her mom to guide her, she knew she could have overlooked *something,* but if Logan's hunch was correct…She swallowed but refused to push the thoughts away like she usually would. She had only herself to rely on now, and that meant investigating the situation thoroughly if she needed to.

"Say you're right," she said. "What do you think I should do about it?"

"Ask him outright. I bet you'll figure it out the moment you catch him off guard and see the look on his face. Just trust your instincts, because they don't often let you down when you listen to them."

It was a serious accusation to make, but she would do exactly what Logan had suggested. What did she have to lose if she was wrong?

Logan flicked the lights on as he walked inside and she jumped back as his dog came bounding toward them.

"Hey, boy, settle down," he instructed, bending to give his dog some attention. "You remember Candace?"

She stayed in place, back to the front door, not certain about the excited canine. He was sitting to attention, perfectly obedient, but she still wasn't ready to trust him quite yet.

"Look, I just know Billy's type, and I'm a pretty good judge of people," Logan said, which made her flip her attention back to him and away from the dog. "I've spent enough time with dogs to know that they sense things in people, and I've started to understand the signs."

"So you think I should get a dog and let him choose my crew?" she joked.

Logan smiled, but his expression was still serious. "No, I think you need to listen to your gut and trust your own instincts. If it's not him, you'll know."

Well, that was exactly what she'd done by coming here, trusting her gut, and she was already doubting herself.

"This is a nice place you've got," she said, changing the subject.

Tomorrow she'd figure out how to deal with her manager. Tonight, she just wanted to forget all the stuff that had been troubling her for so long. If she was going to start trusting her instincts, then she was going to start with how she felt about Logan.

Candace looked around, liking the white hall and the open-plan living space she could see into. Logan motioned for his dog to move away, and they all walked through the house.

"Have you lived here for long?" she asked.

Logan crossed the room to the fridge and she sat at one of the high-backed chairs at the counter that split the living room from the kitchen.

"I purchased this place soon after my parents died, but I'm not sure if I'll keep it."

He held up a beer and a bottle of water, and she pointed to the water.

"Are you planning on going back to your ranch?"

Logan shrugged. "I want to spend a lot of time there, but I haven't really decided what to do with myself. Once this job is finished, I should officially be discharged for retirement from the army, and so will Ranger."

She smiled when he passed her the water and she opened it, taking a sip. "I'm guessing you get to keep him?"

"Yeah. That grey muzzle of his means he's done his time. He's worked as hard as any human soldier since he was a couple years old, but the stress and discipline eventually gets to them, just like it does us. I paid to get him home, and my parents actually started a foundation to make sure working military dogs receive the retirement they deserve."

"I love feel-good stories like that. Working for charity means a lot to me."

They were silent a while, Logan standing with his beer in hand, looking at his dog, and Candace looking around at his home. She knew that soldiers didn't earn a heap of money, and his house was furnished beautifully in a masculine kind of way, which was making her realize that his family must have been relatively well off. It shouldn't have mattered, but it made her curious about who he was and why he'd spent so many years in the army if he hadn't had to, financially.

"Logan, why did you take me out for dinner tonight?" she asked, unable to keep the question to herself.

His dark eyes locked on hers, sending goose pimples across her skin, making every part of her body tense.

"There was something about you that reminded me of myself," he said, his voice an octave lower than it had been before. "I liked you, and I guess I also wanted to show you that you could just spend a night out in Sydney like a regular woman. But it kind of backfired in the end, because we never even made it to a bar."

Candace swallowed, not sure where her confidence was coming from but suddenly needing to know more, wanting to know what Logan thought of her. She knew it was needy, that she should have just shut up, but the way he was looking at her, the way she was reacting to him, was more than just platonic.

"So this wasn't technically a date?" she asked, dropping her gaze and fiddling with the label on her water bottle.

"Do you want this to be a date?" he asked straight back.

Candace didn't look up, not straightaway, but she heard Logan move, his boots echoing out against the timber floor until he was standing beside her. He reached for her bottle and pulled it away, sliding it across the counter just out of her reach. Then he took her hand, his palm closing over it, waiting for her to respond.

She forced herself to raise her chin, to meet his stare.

"Candace?"

"I don't know," she whispered, her voice cracking. "I honestly don't know."

"Do you want this?" he asked, bending slightly, his mouth stopping barely inches from hers.

Candace didn't say anything, *couldn't say anything,* because as badly as she knew she should say no, she wanted it. Her body was humming like an electric current was running through it, all her senses firing to life, desperate to connect with Logan.

He paused for what felt like an eternity, before cupping her cheek and touching his lips so gently to hers that she almost didn't feel it. His lips hovered, pressed lightly, before his entire mouth moved against hers. She matched his pace, loving the feel of his warm, soft lips, the touch of his palm against her skin.

Candace sighed as he pulled back, like he was giving her the chance to change her mind, and she reached for his shirt, pulling him back toward her. His mouth was firm to hers again, tongue softly teasing hers, desire making her stomach flip with excitement as Logan's hands skimmed her waist before settling on her hips. His fingers were still then, the only part of his body moving was his lips, and Candace wanted more. She was hungry for him, craving the kind of contact she'd avoided for so long.

Candace ran her hands down Logan's chest until she reached the hem of his T-shirt, slowly touching beneath it, connecting first with the waistband of his jeans and then with bare skin. She let her fingertips explore his rock-hard abs, the warmth of his skin and the hardness of his muscles, making her moan into his mouth.

She had half expected him to pull back, to tell her no, but there was nothing about Logan's body language that was saying *no*. His hands matched hers, disappearing under her top and touching *her* bare skin, the slightly rough edge of his fingertips making the sensation even more erotic.

"Logan," she moaned, knowing she should stop but giving it only a fleeting thought.

His mouth became more insistent, crushing her lips before he started kissing down her neck, to her collarbone, his tongue tracing across the tops of her breasts.

Candace fisted her hand in his short hair, fingernails scraping his scalp.

"You want me to stop?" he mumbled, lifting his head to look into her eyes.

She shook her head. "No."

Logan didn't need any further encouragement. His mouth met hers in a wet, erotic kiss, before he scooped her up into his arms as if she were weightless, carrying her through the kitchen, marching down the hall. Candace sighed against his mouth, her lips moving in a lazy movement in time with his, their kiss less intense now but still making her belly flutter with anticipation.

It had been so long since she'd kissed a man, since she'd been intimate, and instead of being scared of it like she'd thought she would be, she could feel only a burning sense of desire. That even though she'd never had a one-night stand in her life, been with a man she wasn't in a committed relationship with, there wasn't a bone in her body that didn't want this right now. She was always the good girl, the one who stayed out of the media and never made a wrong step, but she was on the other side of the world with a man who'd shown more interest in keeping her away from the limelight than trying to be in it himself. So if she was going to do something reckless, then why not with Logan?

She'd tried marriage, tried settling down, and it had been disastrous. But this? This felt right in every way possible.

"Candace, we don't have to do this," he mumbled, walking with her in his arms until he could set her on the bed.

"I want this," she whispered as he covered her body with his, her legs looping around his waist so he couldn't get away, locking him in place.

"I'm not going to ask you again, but I will stop if you ask me to," he told her, propping himself up on his elbows and looking down at her, his hazel-brown eyes like pools of the darkest chocolate in the half-light. "You just say the word, and I'll stop, okay?"

Candace nodded, suddenly feeling vulnerable with this gorgeous, big man lying on top of her, yet being so careful with her at the same time. The last man she'd been with had never put her first, had hurt her with his mind and with his fists, which made her even more attracted to Logan. The fact that he was so strong yet so gentle told her that she'd been right to trust herself, at least in spending one night with him. In letting him be the first man to get close to her since her divorce.

"Thank you, Logan," she whispered.

His eyebrows shot up. "For what?"

"For just letting me be me tonight."

He dropped a slow, careful kiss to her forehead. It shouldn't have, but it felt more intimate than all the touches, all the kisses, they'd already shared.

"I haven't been me in a long time, Candace, so this is a first for me, too."

She had the feeling like they were two lost souls who'd found one another, two people who'd crossed paths for a reason, if only for one night. Logan had shared some of what he'd been through with her, and she'd hinted at her past, too—just enough so they both understood that they were the way they were for a reason.

Logan stared at her, his gaze unwavering, until she arched her body, stretching up to catch his mouth, to start the dance that they'd started in the kitchen. His gaze went from thoughtful to something that scared and excited her in equal parts, his mouth insistent, his hands even more so as he pushed up her top, sliding it up high so he could touch her stomach and then her breasts, his fingers teasing her nipples through the lace bra she was wearing.

Candace was just as desperate for him, wanting his bare skin against hers, needing to feel his naked body pressed to her own. She wanted Logan to make love to her, and she wanted it now.

Logan was trying hard to hold back, to let Candace set the pace and not push her, but after months serving overseas and hardly even *seeing* a woman, having Candace beneath him was sending him stir-crazy. She had a body like he'd never touched before—her waist was tiny, her limbs long and slender, and her breasts… He stifled a groan. They were full and luscious, and he wanted them free from the scrap of lace she had them covered with.

When she arched her body into him this time, her chest pressed to his, he took his chance to reach behind her and unhook her bra. He wanted to touch her, taste her, feel every part of her. And his impatience was starting to get the better of him. It wasn't often he could block everything out—his past, the memories—but with Candace, right now he couldn't think of anything else.

"Candace, you're so beautiful."

Her shy smile spurred him on even more because it was so unexpected.

"You're sure you want this?" He had to ask, needed

to make sure she'd thought this through. "I don't want you to regret anything in the morning."

Candace reached for him, cupped her hands around the back of his head and pulled him lower, her lips warm and pillowy as they traced his mouth.

"No regrets, Logan," she murmured. "I want you to make love to me."

Logan groaned as one of her hands left his neck, her fingernails trailing lightly down his skin, pushing at his jeans like she was as impatient as he was.

This time, he wasn't holding back, wouldn't push her away or ask her if she was sure. He'd given her a chance to say no, and she'd made it perfectly clear what she wanted. Now, he was going to give her exactly what she'd asked for.

Logan stroked Candace's long hair, gently fingering the curls that were splayed across his chest. They'd been lying in silence for a while, just lying in the dark. It wasn't a silence he wanted to break, either—she seemed as comfortable as he was with saying nothing at all, bodies pressed together, his fingers caressing either her hair or her skin.

He shut his eyes, starting to drift into sleep.

The sound of a plane's engine, the dark silence as it stalled and started to spiral, falling toward the earth.

Logan blinked and went back to stroking Candace's hair, touching a strand of it to his face as he focused on her again and stamped the dark thoughts away. He was not going to ruin this perfect moment with lurching back into the past.

"Logan, can I ask you something?" Candace's words were soft and husky.

He stopped twirling her hair and brushed his knuckles softly across her cheek as he propped on one elbow to look at her. She was lying on her back, and now he was on his side, facing her. Staring into her eyes seemed to help him to forget everything else.

"You seem to find it easy to talk about some of the things you've been through, and I guess I…" Her voice trailed off. "I guess it's just unexpected from someone who's been through what you've been through."

Logan wanted to look away but he didn't. "What I've told you is a very small part of what I've been through, Candace. There are some things I'll take to my grave that I should probably talk about but never will, and other things that I *can* talk about for reasons I don't understand." What he didn't tell her was that his head so was full of his memories that he wouldn't even know where to start.

She reached for his hand and linked her fingers with his. "So why did you tell me what you did, about being on patrol, being recognized, all those stories?"

He dropped his gaze to their hands, craving the contact, the touch of her skin to his. "There's something about you that reminds me of, well, me," Logan tried to explain. "I've been through a lot, and I saw something in you that made me want to talk to you. I don't know why. I've never wanted to before, but…"

She turned and snuggled into him. "You don't have to explain. I shouldn't have asked."

Logan dropped a kiss to her forehead, moving to her lips when she tilted her face up to him.

"That's the crazy thing. I'm usually so protective over my past, yet with you I wanted to talk." It was strange, because she also helped him to forget.

She laughed, just a soft, husky giggle. "Yeah, that's probably because you know enough about me to hold me for ransom over your secrets."

Logan raised his eyebrows. "Meaning I could sell all our sex secrets and whispered conversations to the media?"

"Exactly," Candace confirmed.

Logan just smiled and pulled her into him, lying back on the bed and shutting his eyes. He didn't need to say anything in response, because if she didn't trust him, it wasn't something she'd joke about. And there was no way he'd ever spill the beans on anything about Candace, or any other woman he'd ever been with, for that matter.

The last woman he'd shared his own bed and memories with, so many years ago, had hurt him beyond belief. She'd betrayed him when he'd trusted her, made him wary of any other woman and what she could do to him if he let her close. But Candace, she was different, because she felt she had too much to lose to betray him, or his confidence.

It might only be one night, he might never see her again, but it had been worth it. Because Candace had shown him that he wasn't the only damaged person in the world, and it had done him good to see the world through someone else's eyes for once. Or maybe it was because he knew it was only one night that he'd allowed anything to happen at all.

Candace lay awake, her head on Logan's shoulder, hand resting on his chest. She was listening to his breathing, feeling the gentle rise and fall of his chest, as she thought about what she'd just done. She had no regrets and doubted she would, but there were so many things running through her mind that she knew she'd never be able to fall asleep, even if she was exhausted.

Logan had shown her what it was like to just be a woman attracted to a man. She had no intention of making one-night stands a habit, and it wasn't like she'd ever had one before, but tonight had been…just what she'd needed. Her body was relaxed and satisfied, but her mind was working in overdrive, thinking about all the things she needed to do to get her life and her career back on track. And what he'd said about her manager—she didn't want it to be true, but Logan's words had made her wonder. Deep down, she wasn't even that surprised, in fact, if it was true she'd almost be relieved that there wasn't some psycho out there wanting to kill her! Ever since her mom had passed away, she'd ignored the fact that she no longer had someone she could trust in her life, to make all the big decisions for her.

But she was also thinking about the fact that she needed a getaway plan—she'd probably never see Logan again, and she didn't want things to be awkward between them when he woke up. Better to have a beautiful memory of what had happened than an awkward parting, or at least that's what she was thinking as she lay beside him.

"No!"

Candace jumped, pushing away from Logan as his body convulsed. She pulled the sheets up to cover her naked body, eyes trained on the man she'd just been cuddled up to. She'd been lying in the almost dark for so long that her eyes were fully adjusted, and she could see the sweat that had broken out across Logan's forehead, his hands clenched at his sides like he was about to start a fight. What the hell was happening?

"No!"

His voice was loud this time, the order clear, and Candace had shivers working like propellers down her spine, the familiar taste of fear like bile in her mouth. She knew it was a dream, probably a night terror that had something to do with what he'd been through, but she was still scared. Because she'd seen a violent man up close and personal, and it had terrified her.

What if he hurt her? Candace jumped clear off the bed. A whining noise made her spin, her heart still racing, but she realized it was only Ranger, and he had absolutely zero interest in her. He had run to Logan, was sitting beside the bed, head cocked to the side, emitting a low whine. Maybe he was used to his master's behavior? Or maybe he was just as scared by what was happening as she was.

Candace knew it was stupid, but she also knew what it was like to be on the receiving end of a man's fist, of being hurt by someone she'd never expected to hurt her, so she wasn't going to stay too close to Logan. And she definitely wasn't going to risk waking him. She'd seen enough television shows about soldiers with post-traumatic stress to know she could end up with his hands wrapped around her throat if he mistakenly thought she was the enemy.

"I'm sorry, Logan," she whispered, dressing in the dark as he continued to toss and turn, the sheets starting to tangle around him. She should have tried to help him, but she didn't, *couldn't*.

Candace found her shoes, slipped them on, then disappeared out into the living area. She pulled her phone from her purse, saw she'd missed a heap of calls while it had been on silent, but ignored them all and went online instead. She searched for the name of a taxi company, found out Logan's address, called to order a cab, and sat down on the sofa while she waited.

Running out on Logan wasn't something she'd wanted to do. It wasn't something she'd ever done before to any man, but she'd set the wheels in motion now and there was no turning back. What they'd shared had been incredible, a night she'd never forget for as long as she lived, but they'd made each other no promises, and now it was time to head back to the real world.

Even if right now that world held little appeal.

CHAPTER FIVE

LOGAN STRETCHED AND threw one hand over his eyes to block out the sun. He went to pull the pillow over his head instead before he realized what had woken him.

Bloody phone.

He reached for it, sitting up as he also realized that he was alone in his bed when he should have had a gorgeous blonde tucked up beside him. Where on earth had she gone so early in the morning?

"Hello," he muttered, shutting his eyes again as he hit the pillow.

"Tell me the media have gone crazy and lost their minds?"

Logan groaned as he recognized his best friend, Brett's, voice, before sitting back up again and pulling his jeans on so he could see if Candace was still in the house. He tripped over his dog, who was looking at him like he was the crazy one. He did that a lot lately, especially in the morning, and he had no idea why.

"Logan?"

"Sorry. What have you seen?" He checked the kitchen and living area, before ducking into the bathroom. All empty. *Crap!* How had he managed to sleep through her leaving?

"Oh, you know, just you leaving Nick's Seafood restaurant with Candace-*freaking*-Evans, and then her spotted arriving back at her hotel at about three this morning looking mighty disheveled."

Double crap. Logan swallowed the expletives that he would like to have yelled out. At least it was Brett telling him rather than some stranger confronting him.

"Are you sure she was seen at the hotel?"

His friend laughed. "You mean you lost her? Hey, Jamie, he didn't even know where she was, so they must have gotten the whole one-night stand thing wrong."

Logan grimaced as he listened to Brett call out to his wife. If it was all over the news, then there was little chance of anyone else believing that nothing had happened, and the last thing he wanted was the whole world to know what Candace had been doing the night before. He couldn't care less what anyone said about him, but he knew that she wasn't exactly the kind of woman used to making headlines for being scandalous.

A noise made him look up and Ranger let out a loud bark.

"Look, I spent the day with her yesterday…"

"And the night?" Brett was laughing, like he found the entire thing beyond hysterical.

"Oh, man!" Logan ducked out of sight when he saw that the front of his house was surrounded by a bunch of guys with cameras. The last thing he needed was to be photographed bare-chested in jeans he hadn't even buttoned up properly.

"What?"

"There's bloody paparazzi outside my house. How did they find my place?" Not to mention *why* they'd want a photo of him when they knew Candace wasn't even with him.

"From the fierce looks you gave them last night it's a wonder they wanted to go near you again."

Logan went around the house pulling all the blinds and drapes down so no one could see in.

"Look, she's a sweet girl and we had a nice night together. *End of story.* Now I have to go and make sure she's okay, because she obviously slipped out on me in the night."

Brett laughed again. "Guess that serves Jamie right for telling you it was time to meet a woman. We just didn't expect you to set your sights quite so high."

Logan was usually ready to spar with Brett whenever he became annoying, but today he wasn't going to take the bait. He could deal with his friend later.

"I have to go. I'll call you later."

"I'll email those pics through to you," Brett said. "You know, in case you want to check yourself out."

"Later."

Logan hung up and opened his fridge, pulling out a carton of juice. He managed to take a few sips before curiosity got the better of him, and he grabbed his phone again and checked his emails. Sure enough, Brett had already hit Send, because there was a link waiting for him to click on.

Naughty night out in Australia for America's sweetheart. Candace Evans waves goodbye to good girl reputation with mystery man.

Logan took a deep breath, refusing to let his anger get to him. He clicked through the shots and saw them leaving the restaurant together, a zoomed-in photo of them holding hands, one of them driving away in his car, then hours later Candace running into the hotel, her hair all messed up and one hand held across her face.

It wasn't like they'd actually caught them doing anything, but they'd built a story around nothing and put up a few photos together to try to prove a point. The worst thing was that she'd run from him, and he had no idea why she'd just disappear like that after they'd spent the night together. Had someone sent her the photos and spooked her?

Whatever had happened, he was going to make sure that she was left alone at the press conference this afternoon. Sure, the media might go crazy when they realized he was her bodyguard, but then again they might think they'd made a huge mistake and he'd just been minding her.

Either way, he was heading to the hotel now to see if she was okay.

His phone bleeped again, this time with a text. He flicked through to his messages, anger rising again when he read the words.

Looks like you had an interesting evening. Heads up that the press junket has been cancelled, so you're officially off duty on this one.

Great. Even his boss knew what he'd been up to, or allegedly up to, the night before. And Candace had obviously gone into hiding if she was giving up her afternoon appointment. Still, he was going to see her. If she was still in the country, he'd track her down. What Candace didn't know about him was that he wasn't exactly a one-night stand kind of guy, either, and he wanted her to know that he'd be there for her if she needed him, until her flight out.

Candace had made him see that he needed to move on with parts of his life that he'd ignored for so long, and for that alone he needed to thank her. Usually when he freaked out over anything, he went for a run or hit the gym. In fact, he usually did it every morning because his dreams freaked him out night after night, but today was different. Today he actually had to confront the problem head-on instead of try to outrun it.

Candace stared at her laptop screen. She was a sucker for punishment, and she still couldn't help clicking through and looking at each photo one more time. She'd looked before her shower, and now she was sitting on her bed, hair wrapped in a towel, torturing herself again.

She felt like a fool.

Being with Logan wasn't something she regretted, even if she did regret the paparazzi getting snaps of her and making it clear to the world what she'd been up to. It was the fact that it had taken Logan's comments for her to realize how bad her manager was—she'd hidden behind the fact that her mom wasn't around any longer, instead of dealing with something she knew was detrimental to her career. But those days were gone. The first thing she'd done in the taxi was text her manager and tell him she was okay, that she would be arriving back at the hotel within twenty minutes, and then when she'd arrived to quietly slip into her room, the place had been buzzing with photographers. There was only one explanation for it, and she was going to be giving him his marching orders and sending him packing before the end of the day, after she asked him whether he was responsible for the letters she'd been receiving.

Then she was going to figure out how to apologize to Logan for running out on him in the middle of the night, before figuring out what to do for the next few days. It was time for her to take a break, figure some things out, and find a beach to relax on where she wouldn't be disturbed. She didn't have any more concerts scheduled on this tour, and she'd been too busy for too long without taking time out for herself, punishing herself with work to avoid dealing with everything that had happened.

Her hotel phone rang but she ignored it, uninterested in whoever it was. She'd made it clear she didn't want to be disturbed, and she meant it.

Candace padded barefoot back into the bathroom and let her hair down, running her fingers through it and then working some product into the roots. She would do her hair and makeup, then deliver the verdicts that she'd decided upon.

It was time for her to take control of her own life, her own destiny, and that started today.

CHAPTER SIX

"LOGAN, IT'S CANDACE."

He stopped dead, flicking his phone off speaker and pressing it to his ear instead.

"Candace? I thought you were long gone."

There was silence for a moment, and Logan had to check that they hadn't lost the connection. The last thing he'd expected was for Candace to call.

"I was wondering if you had time to meet up," she asked, her voice low.

"Business or pleasure?" Logan cringed the second the words left his mouth. *Pleasure* hadn't exactly been the best phrase, given what had happened between them.

"Coffee," she said. "I'm at a different hotel, just down the road from where I was before."

"I can't believe you're still in Australia." *Unbelievable.* Almost two days later and he'd been sure he'd never hear from her again, especially when she'd never answered her door when he'd known she was in her room that next morning.

"You're still here, in Sydney, right? I mean, I thought you might have already left for the Outback."

"I leave tomorrow," he told her. "I'll head to you now, if that's okay with you?"

"Sure. Meet me in an hour at my hotel. I'll be in the café, and I'm wearing a short brown wig."

Logan said goodbye, zipped his phone into his pocket and tapped his thigh as a signal to Ranger. It would take him at least fifteen minutes to run home if he sprinted, but given that he was about to cut his workout short, he wasn't complaining. Ranger bounded along beside him and Logan tried not to overthink the phone call he'd just received.

He wasn't going to even bring up what had happened between them unless she did, and he was most definitely not going to offer to help her or take her out again. She had a bunch of professionals at the ready if she needed them, and he was done with the army and with working any kind of security, at least for now. From next week onward, he was just Logan Murdoch, civilian. He was going to spend time on the land, forget about the future for a while, and figure stuff out.

Or at least that was the plan.

He blanked everything out of his mind, focusing only on the soles of his shoes as they thumped down on the pavement. Logan concentrated on each inhale and exhale of breath, the pull and release of his muscles, his dog matching his pace as he ran directly at heel.

Exercise was how he kept in control, how he stayed focused, and it was the only constant he'd had in his life for a very long time. Candace might have rattled him, but he was going to stay in control and not let anyone distract him. And that included her.

Candace's legs were so fidgety she was fighting the urge to get up and start to pace. But then that would have only drawn attention to herself, and the whole point of sitting quietly and wearing her brunette disguise was so no one even thought to glance twice at her.

She still didn't know exactly what she was going to say to Logan, but starting off by thanking him for being so honest with her about her management team, and then apologizing for disappearing on him, was probably a good starting point. The guy had been nothing but nice to her, and he deserved an explanation about what had happened between them, and for how right he'd been about Billy. He'd set her on the right path and he deserved to know.

"Candace?"

She turned when a deep, low voice said her name. Heat flooded her body when she saw Logan, standing with his hands jammed into his jean pockets. There had never been any doubting that he was incredibly sexy, but seeing him in the flesh again brought back a certain amount of memories that she'd been trying to repress. Namely his mouth, his rock-hard abs, his…

Candace jumped up and kissed Logan on the cheek, stamping out those thoughts. "Hey."

"Wow, you look…" He hesitated. "Different."

"I don't know if I'm fooling the hotel staff, but so far no one has bothered me," she admitted. "It won't last long, but I'm planning on checking out first thing tomorrow."

Logan went to sit down, then stopped. "You want a coffee?"

Candace glanced at her empty cup. "Another chai latte would be great."

She watched as he crossed the room to order, rather than waiting for someone to come and serve them, before sitting down across from her. It was all old-fashioned decadence here, and big, strong Logan looked the completed opposite of the hushed-toned men in suits walking past. He looked relaxed in his jeans and shirt like only a confident, strong man could, and she liked that he had such a strong identity of who he was—or at least that's the impression he gave.

"Logan, I want to apologize for just leaving in the middle of the night. It wasn't something I've ever done before, and you deserved better."

She struggled to read his expression, but he didn't look angry.

"I'm not going to lie. I was looking forward to waking up to you beside me," he said, staring into her eyes and not giving her one chance to look away. "But I get it. You saw the photos and you freaked."

Candace took a slow, deep breath. So he thought she'd seen the pics on her phone and run. That she could live with. If he'd thought she was stone cold and happy to just bed him and then leave? Not something she'd have been able to swallow very easily.

"I'm just sorry that I dragged you into all this. You were just trying to be nice to me and…"

"Stop," he said, reaching for her hand then hesitating, like he'd acted before realizing what he was doing. "We had a great evening together and it didn't end quite as planned. We're both grownups and we never made any promises to one another. Right?"

So in other words he didn't care? Candace pushed aside the feelings of hurt, the emotion clogging her throat. This was why she wasn't a one-night stand regular, because she couldn't handle the blunt truth of a man being honest with her.

"Logan, I wanted to thank you for being honest with me," she started, reminding herself of the real reason she'd wanted to see him. "You were more honest with me than anyone has been in a long while, even though you hardly even knew me."

He raised an eyebrow. "This sounds serious."

She nodded, waiting for their coffees to be placed in front of them before continuing. "I fired my manager and pretty much everyone else I've been working with, and I'm going to take some time off before rehiring anyone. Just be me for a while."

He sat back, gaze fixed on her. "What changed? Why now, after all this time?"

Candace tried to relax, but with Logan staring at her she was finding it hard enough just to focus on breathing and saying what she'd rehearsed in her mind.

"I've used losing my mom as an excuse for too long now, and it wasn't until you read the situation for what it was that I realized I'd been putting things off for too long. I'm sick and tired of letting people make decisions for me, and you were right about everything. I've been

spooked about those letters for so long that it was starting to consume me, and it was my manager all along."
She blew out a deep breath. "All I've ever wanted to do,
all my life, is just sing. But now that Mom's not here to
cover my back for me, I need to step up and take more
control of everything, rather than just burying my head
in the sand."

He reached for his coffee cup and took a sip of the
steaming black liquid. "For the record, I'm not one of
those people who'd ever use you, and I will never talk
to anyone about what happened between us. Or about
the whole manager situation for that matter."

Candace couldn't help it—suddenly her eyes filled
with tears and she was reaching for a napkin to blot
them away.

"Candace?"

Logan was suddenly at her side, moving to the chair
next to hers, his arm around her.

"Candace, please don't cry."

She shook her head and blinked the tears away, refusing to turn into an emotional mess.

"I'm sorry, it's just I'm not used to…" Her voice
trailed off. "*You*. The way you are with me."

Logan kept his arm around her, and when she turned
to him she could see confusion in his expression.

"I'm not sure what you mean?"

Candace looked up at the bright lights above, wishing she knew how to tell him what she meant.

"I'm not used to a straight talker, and I'm sure as
heck not used to being with someone who doesn't have
an ulterior motive. Who won't sell me out to the press."

She shrugged. "I'm just so tired of watching my back and not knowing who to trust, especially after what I've been through the past few weeks. I've been scared for so long, looking over my shoulder all the time, and it was just a ploy to create more press about me. Press that I didn't even want."

They were silent, just sitting there, Logan not saying anything in response for what felt like an eternity.

"Candace, I'm heading out with a couple of friends tonight. Why don't you join us?"

She knew she must have looked wide-eyed, but she could hardly believe what she was hearing.

"You mean to say you'd actually go out in public with me again? After what happened last time?"

Now it was Logan shrugging. "Look, it's no big deal. You can even wear your wig if you like. We'll just be heading to a bar for a few drinks, nothing too exciting, and I doubt we'll even be noticed if we're careful."

Logan dropped his arm and moved back around to his seat, his coffee cup in his hand again.

"You're sure your friends won't mind?"

"Brett has been my best mate for years, and I've known his wife almost as long. We're just hanging out for some drinks before I leave tomorrow. Catching up for a few hours."

Candace stared into her latte, wishing she'd been brave enough to just say yes from the start.

"If you're sure…"

Logan had no idea where that had come from. Why had he even asked her? The plan had been to see her, listen to what she had to say, then walk away. What happened to her not being his problem? To her not being part of his life? To not letting anyone too close?

"I'm sure," he heard himself say. "It'll be fun."

The words were just falling out of his mouth now like he had absolutely zero control over the link between his brain and his vocal cords, and that definitely wasn't something he was used to. He usually found it harder to talk than not.

"If anyone recognizes me or it becomes awkward, I'll just leave."

"Candace, it'll be fine. Want to meet me there or should I swing past and collect you?"

"If you wouldn't mind coming to get me?"

Her voice was low, a shyness there that made his protective instincts flare up, and told him exactly why he'd asked her. He liked her, sure, was beyond attracted to her, but he was also able to sense the vulnerability that for some reason she wasn't great at hiding around him. Anyone who saw her on stage or in public would think she was full of confidence, but he'd already seen firsthand that there was a lot more to Candace than met the eye.

"I'll pick you up at eight," he said.

Logan rose, unable to take his eyes off her. Even with a pair of crazy-high heels on she was still short beside him, and part of him just wanted to tell her to grab her things and come with him now so he could look after her. But he didn't. Because he had things to arrange for the morning, paperwork to deal with, and because he *did not* want to get involved.

Spending the night with a woman he'd never expected to see again had been one thing, but he knew he wasn't ready for anything else. There wasn't enough room in his mind or his heart to worry about another human being, to give what someone like Candace deserved. And besides, it wasn't like she'd indicated that she wanted anything else, either.

They could have another fun night together, and then they'd say goodbye for real.

"Thanks, Logan," Candace said, suddenly reaching out for him, her palm soft against his forearm as she stopped him from walking away. "After everything, just, thanks."

She didn't let go of him straightaway, and they stared at one another, not moving. Logan clenched his jaw as memories of their night together came flooding back to him—her hands on his skin, her body against his as he'd traced every part of her with his mouth and fingers. This girl.... God! She was under his skin and no matter what he tried to tell himself, being this close to her made it impossible not to want her.

"I'll see you tonight," he said, clearing his throat when he heard how husky his voice sounded.

"See you tonight," she repeated, slowly releasing him and taking a step back.

Logan gave her one last look, hesitated one second too long. Before he could even think through what he was doing, he'd closed the distance between them again, wrapping his arm around her so he could put his hand flat to the small of her back, lips closing over hers. It was a hungry kiss that he hadn't even known he'd been waiting to plant on her mouth, and she didn't disappoint. Candace kissed him back like she was as hungry for contact as he was, before raising her hand and placing it on his chest to push him back slightly.

"The purpose of the wig was to *not* draw attention to myself," she whispered, eyes dancing as she stared up at him.

Logan chuckled, shaking his head. What had Candace done to him? So much for being the guy Brett called Mr. No Emotion. He'd gone years without having any issues of self-control around the opposite sex, and now he was behaving like a deprived addict.

"I'll try to be on my best behavior tonight," Logan muttered.

Candace stroked his face, gently, like she was touching something fragile. She didn't, *couldn't,* know it, but that was exactly what he was. No one else saw it—everyone treated him based on his physical appearance and based on the rank he held—when inside he knew he was as vulnerable, if not more so, than anyone else. He just hoped she couldn't see too much of who he was, because he was certain the darkness of his thoughts, his memories, would send her running.

"I'll see you at eight," he said.

Logan backed away and turned, walking in a straight line toward the lobby and the front doors. This time he made it to his car, unlocking the vehicle and jumping behind the wheel. Ranger nudged him, dancing from paw to paw in excitement at not being left alone for too long.

"Don't ask," Logan muttered, giving the dog's head a scratch.

What he should have been concerned about was how much he was starting to treat Ranger like a pet instead of an elite military dog, and how easily they'd fallen into bad habits since they'd been home. Instead he was thinking about a blonde who'd looked just as sexy as a brunette, and who was starting to drive him crazy.

He picked up his phone and dialed Brett, hitting speaker and putting his phone on his lap.

"All set for tonight?" Brett said as he answered.

Logan fought the urge to thump his head on the steering wheel. Instead he yanked on his seat belt and started driving, needing to be distracted.

"There's been a slight change of plan," he told Brett.

"Don't even think about it. Jamie will kill you if you cancel."

"I'm not cancelling. I'm, ah, bringing someone."

Logan waited for the laughter, but all he heard was silence.

"Anyone I know?"

"Look, I need you guys to just not make a fuss. Just treat her like any other girl I might have met and brought along for a drink."

"Except you've never brought a girl along before," Brett said with a laugh. "In fact, I don't know when I last heard the words Logan and date uttered in the same sentence."

"I'm warning you..." Logan told him, knowing he could trust his best mate but going all stupid and protective over Candace anyway.

"No need. It'll be fun. Want to just meet us there?"

"Yeah, I'll see you there."

Logan hung up and let his head fall back against the rest. Asking Candace out had been crazy, but the fact he was heading out with Brett and Jamie would mean there was no pressure, that everything would be fine. So long as he didn't end up taking her back to his place again, it would just be a night out with friends.

Ranger whined and Logan took his eyes off the road for a split second to glare at him.

"I know, I know, but it's only one night."

His dog ignored him and stared out the window, and Logan tried to think about going back home to the Outback instead of what the night was going to be like. Because he couldn't convince his dog, and he couldn't convince himself that seeing Candace for a few hours over a drink was ever going to be enough. Or that he'd be able to hold back and not end up trying to make something happen between them again.

Weakness wasn't something he'd ever struggled with before. He'd had to fight a lot of other emotions, deal with loss and a lot of crap over the years, but no one could ever have accused him of being weak. Until a gorgeous, sexy country singer had walked into his life and turned everything he'd ever known, ever felt, up on its head.

Next thing he knew he'd be playing her music and singing along to her songs like a lovesick puppy.

Candace had a pile of rejected clothes strewn across the bed. After trying almost everything on, she'd settled on a pair of skinny jeans, a T-shirt with sequined sleeves and a pair of super-high stilettos. Logan was insanely tall and while she liked the fact that his size made her feel protected, she didn't like only reaching his shoulder if her shoes weren't high enough.

She fluffed her hair, tousling her curls, and applied one final brush of lip gloss. Candace was about to reach for her purse when her phone beeped. She grabbed it and scrolled through her emails, smiling when she read the first new message.

Candace Evans spotted getting cozy with mystery man in L.A.? Source sees her being rushed through customs and into the arms of another stranger.

She blew out a sigh of relief and flicked her phone to silent before jamming it into her purse. Her tip-off had worked, which meant no one would be expecting her to still be in Australia, and definitely not at a local bar hanging out with some regular people. She just had to hope that enough gossip sites passed around the message.

Candace left the light on in her room and turned the message on the door to Do Not Disturb, then headed for the elevator. Her heart was pounding, nerves making her hands damp. The anticipation of seeing Logan again was putting her more on edge than she ever was just before a concert. It was crazy, and she hadn't been like this around a guy for a very long time, but something about the sexy soldier-turned-bodyguard had her stomach doing cartwheels.

She'd promised herself that she wouldn't ever fall for a man again, that she was better off being single, but while that might have been easy before, it didn't seem quite so straightforward now. Because Logan had shown her that not all men were jerks, and no matter how hard she wanted to resist him, her willpower had failed her from the moment she'd agreed to go out with him the first time.

The elevator dinged and Candace took a deep breath and walked out. She hadn't bothered to put her wig on, but she did keep her head down as she walked toward the lobby doors. She doubted anyone would bother staring at her too hard, and all the excitement over her concert had well and truly died down.

"Candace."

She glanced up just as she almost walked straight into Logan, his deep voice stopping her. He was standing with his arms folded, waiting like he'd kill anyone with his bare hands if they so much as came near her.

"Hey," she said, wishing the sight of him had settled instead of unnerved her.

"I was half expecting a brunette tonight," he joked, turning so he could put his arm around her and walk them both out of the hotel. "It's kind of like the whole Miley Cyrus versus Hannah Montana thing."

His joke blew all the nerves from her body, somehow made her relax.

"How on earth do you know *anything* about Hannah Montana?" she asked, laughing as he opened the door to his vehicle.

Logan leaned in toward her, one arm braced on the

door. "Ten-year-old niece. I was trying to be a good uncle."

Candace laughed to herself as he shut the door. *This* was why she liked Logan so much—being in his company was…refreshing. It made her feel like she was a world away from everything, and right now that was the best feeling she could imagine.

"So tell me about your friends," she said, angling her body so she could stare at Logan. "Do they know you're bringing someone along with you?"

He glanced at her before starting the engine, and she was just watching as his mouth opened to reply when—

"Argh!" Candace squealed and almost hit her head on the ceiling.

"Ranger!" Logan barked, pushing his dog back and reaching for her, his hand covering her thigh. "I'm sorry. I was just about to warn you and then…"

"Your dog stuck his tongue in my ear. Actually in my ear," Candace complained, wiping at her face and glaring at the dog in the backseat. But her anger quickly turned to laughter when she saw the confused look on Ranger's face.

"It's fast becoming one of his party tricks," Logan confessed. "We both apologize, don't we, Ranger?"

Candace reached back and gave the dog a stroke on the head, finding it hard to believe that the dog had actually molested her, not to mention the fact that she was voluntarily touching him.

"It's okay. I guess that was just him saying hi," she said, not wanting to get the dog into trouble now that she was actually starting to like him. "Next time I suggest warning your passenger, though."

Logan stroked his hand across her thigh before putting it back on the wheel, and she wished she had the nerve to just grab it and put it back in place.

"He was all upset seeing my bags packed, so I told him he could tag along for the ride."

Candace leaned back in her seat, keeping an eye on the dog in case he decided to get frisky again.

"Anyway, you were asking about Brett and Jamie?"

"Yeah. Tell me about them."

Logan made a noise in his throat that made her think he didn't really want to discuss them, but then he took one hand off the wheel and seemed to relax.

"Brett is one of my oldest friends. We met our first day of training, and we both ended up going through to the SAS and then the doggies division."

"Has he retired now, too?"

Logan nodded. "Yeah, he was injured pretty bad on his last tour."

She watched as Logan's jaw tightened, a visible tick alerting her to the fact that this might not be something he was comfortable discussing with her.

"Is he, ah, one of the guys you mentioned the other night? One of the two that you used to meet up with at the restaurant?" Candace hoped she hadn't pushed him too far by asking.

Logan didn't say anything straight away, but he did put his fallen hand back on the wheel, the whites of his knuckles showing how hard his grip was. She wished she knew what was going through his mind, wondered if it was the same memories that he fought in the night.

"There were three of us. Brett, Sam and me. They were on tour together about a year ago, working a routine patrol, when an IED bomb went off and killed Sam."

Logan paused and Candace just stayed still, silent.

"Brett lost his dog in the blast, too, and he's so lucky to be alive himself."

She had no idea what to say. "Logan, I'm sorry."

He shrugged, but she knew he wasn't finding it easy to talk about, that it wasn't something he'd ever be able to truly shrug off, no matter how convincing he might look.

"When Brett came home, things kind of became difficult between us when he, well, he kind of fell in love with Sam's wife. His widow, I mean. It's all a bit of a complicated story, but at the end of the day it was the best thing for both of them."

Jeez. When Logan had said he'd been through a lot these past few years, he actually had.

"You must have found that pretty hard to deal with?" Candace said. "Understandably so, I mean."

"I was a jerk when I should have listened to them, but Jamie can tell you more about all that if she wants to. All I care about is that they're both happy now." He glanced across at her. "I'm not usually the guy who overreacts, except when it comes to the people I care about."

Candace shifted in her seat as Logan focused on the road again.

"And you," he added, his voice low.

She stopped moving, wondering if she'd heard him right. "Me?" Candace forced herself to ask.

Logan pulled over, parking the car, but she couldn't take her eyes off of him. What did he mean by that?

Once the vehicle was stationary, he turned his body to face hers, reaching for her hand. She let him take it, their fingers linking.

"There's something about you that I can't stay away from, no matter how much I tell myself I should."

Candace was like a spider caught in a web—Logan's gaze was impossible to escape from, and she didn't want to. It was like he was saying the words that were in her head, telling her what she was thinking.

"Meaning you wish you hadn't asked me out tonight?"

"Meaning," he said, cupping her face in his other hand, "that it probably would have been best for both of us if I hadn't, not that I didn't want to."

She knew exactly what he meant, because she'd been telling herself the same thing, knowing that it would have been best to move on and not think about Logan, let alone see him again. But like a bee was lured to nectar time and time again, so it seemed was she to him.

"You're leaving in the morning, right?" she whispered.

Logan nodded, just the barest movement of his head. "Yes."

"Then it's just one more night. We'll both be heading our separate ways tomorrow."

He leaned toward her, placing a feather-light kiss to

her lips. Logan didn't say anything, and he didn't need to. Whatever it was they had between them, whatever was pulling them together, wasn't something either of them seemed to understand. But by tomorrow, neither of them would have a choice.

"Let's go meet your friends," Candace said as he dropped his hand from her face.

Logan smiled and jumped out of the car, and Candace quickly touched up her lip gloss in the mirror.

CHAPTER SEVEN

LOGAN TOOK CANDACE'S hand as they walked toward the entrance of the bar. He hoped no one made a fuss and recognized her, especially not after last time. All he wanted was a quiet evening with friends, a couple of beers and to make the most of his only night left with Candace. So much for telling himself that he was going to play the part of the perfect gentleman tonight. After what she'd said in the car, his mind was all over the "just one more night" line she'd given him.

"They're just over there," he said into her ear, pointing toward where Brett and Jamie were standing near the bar.

Candace squeezed his hand and they headed straight over. He could see the grin on Jamie's face even from across the room once she spotted them, and he knew it wasn't just because it was Candace he'd brought with him. She'd been trying to set him up with someone, *anyone,* for longer than he liked to admit, and even though he'd repeatedly turned her down she'd been pretty insistent that it was time he met someone. Pity he'd have to let her down gently that this wasn't a relationship that was going anywhere.

"Hey!" Jamie said, kissing his cheek and holding her hand out to Candace. "Great to meet you."

Candace smiled and shook hands with both Jamie and Brett, and Logan gave them both a hug.

"What do you want to drink?" Logan asked Candace.

Candace raised her eyebrows and looked at Jamie. "What are you having?"

"A mocktail because I'm driving. But whatever you do, don't let either of these boys talk you into a Long Island Iced Tea."

They all burst out laughing, except for Candace, who just looked confused.

"Come sit down and I'll tell you all about it," Jamie said with a grin, looping her arm through Candace's. "Logan, ask the bartender to make her something delicious. He's good like that."

Logan reached out and touched the small of Candace's back just before she walked away, receiving a sweet smile in response when she glanced over her shoulder. He stared at her as she moved, watched the gentle sway of her body, the long curly hair that hung like a wave down her back and that he was desperate to fist his hands in.

"Hey," Brett said, nudging him in the ribs. "You going to get these drinks or do I have to?"

Logan snapped out of it and stared at Brett.

"I'm losing it," he admitted. "I'm losing the plot and there's nothing I can do about it."

Brett sighed and leaned across the bar to order the

drinks, clearly deciding he was useless for the time being. "Next round's on you," he muttered.

"Brett, I'm serious. She's done something to me and I can't snap out of it."

"So you like her. What's the big deal?"

Logan put one elbow on the bar to prop himself up. "The fact that she's way out of my league, not to mention she leaves tomorrow." He ran a hand through his short hair. "And you know me, I'm just not interested in being with anyone after, well, everything."

Brett chuckled and passed him a beer. "You can pretend all you like, but you're interested in being with her. Otherwise you wouldn't be telling me all this. Besides, you can't dwell on the past forever, no matter how bad it is. At some point you're going to have to move on."

Logan raised the beer bottle and drained almost half of it. "She's under my skin. I want her but I don't, and…"

He had no idea what he was trying to say, because he didn't even know what he wanted. It was impossible to even think straight with her around. Deep down, he doubted he could give enough of himself to any woman, certainly not Candace, but he knew he was starting to think about her as more than a one-night thing. He'd be lying if he told himself he didn't want more. A lot more.

"Logan, she's a beautiful girl, and you've had fun with her. You telling me you want more than that, or are you just pissed that you can't have her in your bed for a few more nights?"

"Don't talk about her like that. It has *nothing* to

do with me just wanting her in bed." Logan knew he sounded angry, and he was.

"Whoa," Brett said, putting his beer down and holding up both hands. "I was just trying to make a point. You don't have to bite my head off."

"Well, don't," Logan grumbled, even though he knew it was him who'd been in the wrong.

"You remember when I was first with Jamie, and I tried to tell you how I felt about her?"

"Was that before or after I gave you the black eye?"

Brett punched him in the arm, but he was still grinning. "The point is, I felt differently about Jamie than I'd ever felt about another woman. I could have lost you as a friend just for telling you, for trying to explain, but she was worth it. *She's still worth it.*" He shrugged. "Your past is never going to go away, so you're just going to have to deal with it."

Logan watched as Brett glanced across to where the girls were seated, and he angled his body so he could see them, too. They were sitting together, heads bent as they discussed something that made them both burst out laughing. Jamie was one of his closest friends, and he'd been right to think that she'd be perfect for Candace to spend time with. And everything Brett was saying was right, even if it was blunt.

"Don't be so much of a hard head that you lose someone you feel that way about, that's all I'm saying," Brett said, picking up his beer bottle and another mocktail for Jamie. "Jamie was worth fighting for, and that would have been the truth no matter how high the stakes. You just have to decide if Candace is worth the fight, whatever that fight turns out to be."

Logan collected his drinks and walked beside his friend, knowing he was right. He often kept everything bottled up inside and refused to talk, but telling Brett what he was thinking had been the right thing to do.

"It's about time I told you I'm sorry for being a jerk when you tried to talk to me about Jamie," he admitted. "I should never have been so harsh on you, and every time I see the two of you together I know what an idiot I was. I hope you know that."

Brett just shrugged. "You were looking out for her, I get it. And you've said sorry enough times for me to believe you, so how about we just move on, huh?"

"Yeah, but until now, maybe I didn't know how you really felt. I meant it when I apologized back then, but all of a sudden I actually get it," Logan mumbled, eyes locked on Candace as he headed toward her. "As much as I want to forget about her, to ignore the way I feel…"

"You just can't," Brett finished for him. "Trust me, I get it."

"So what do I do?" he asked just before they reached the table. "What am I supposed to do?"

"Stop overthinking it," Brett said in a low voice. "If it feels right, just go with it. For once in your life switch that part of your brain off and just enjoy the moment."

"Hey," Candace said with a smile as Logan sat down beside her on the leather seat.

The table was tucked away, a low-hanging light casting warm shadows around them in contrast to the darkness of the bar.

"Try this and see what you think," Logan told her, sliding the drink across to her.

Candace grinned and leaned forward, at the same time resting her hand on his thigh. Logan stiffened, couldn't help how rigid his body went, like it was on high alert, but if she noticed she never said anything. What Brett had said had been right, trouble was that the last time he'd just lived in the moment, he'd had his heart ripped out and stomped all over. Add to that his fear of losing anyone he actually cared about again, and he was one screwed up individual, he knew.

"So what were you two busy talking about?" Brett asked, kissing Jamie when she turned to face him.

"Oh, you know, just telling Candace some stories about you two," Jamie responded. "It's always fun having someone new to share info with."

"I was telling Jamie about my fear of dogs, and how Ranger decided to make love to my ear with his tongue on the way here."

Logan just shook his head when the other two burst into laughter. He'd hoped they'd just be themselves around Candace, and they were, which was making the whole situation seem…like some sort of double date. They weren't treating her any differently than they would any other girl.

He cleared his throat. "I'm heading back home first thing tomorrow, Jamie, did Brett tell you?"

"Don't tell me you want me to babysit Ranger?" Jamie asked. "Or is that something Candace wants to do now that he's shown his love for her?"

Both Candace and Jamie giggled, and Logan exchanged looks with Brett. His friend was giving him a look he'd only seen when they'd been serving, a look that told him he had to do what he had to do. Before, it had been about war, about making decisions that could affect his entire team, and now it was about putting his own heart on the line and putting himself at risk. Which wasn't something he was comfortable with at all. Now, the decision he made was only going to affect his own life, which was why the whole thing was scaring him.

"What are your plans, Candace? You heading back to the States?" Brett asked, giving Logan a moment to gather his thoughts.

Candace was toying with her straw. She took a delicate sip before answering. "You know, I don't have any definite plans as yet, but I'm planning on staying in Australia for a few more days, maybe longer."

Logan almost choked on his beer. "You are?" He turned so he was staring straight at her.

She glanced across at him, her eyes not settling on his. "Yeah. You kind of convinced me that I needed a break."

"When you said you were going to take some time off, I didn't realize you meant *here*. I figured you were going back to your ranch in Montana."

Suddenly it was like there was just the two of them in the room, that Brett and Jamie weren't even part of the conversation. How had she not mentioned this earlier? Why hadn't he asked her?

"You're going tomorrow, and I didn't want you to feel like…" Her voice trailed off, her sentence unfinished.

"I could have changed my plans," he muttered. If

he'd known there was the chance of spending more time with her, of this being more than a one-night thing… he would have what? He still didn't know how he felt about Candace, what he thought, what he was capable of offering.

"Candace, you should see Logan's property while you're here," Brett said, interrupting them just as Logan was about to tear his hair out. "I know you've probably travelled to a lot of beautiful places, but there's nothing quite like the Outback."

An awkward silence fell over the table. Even the ever bubbly Jamie was quiet, which made the whole situation feel more pressure cooked than it was.

"I'd love to see it one day. I'm sure it's pretty special," Candace said, but she kept her head down, eyes on her cocktail.

"Brett, why don't we go get another round of drinks?" Jamie suggested, standing and tugging on Brett's hand.

"But we haven't even…" He stopped talking and just stood up when Jamie gave him a fierce look that Logan caught from the corner of his eye.

Logan let them leave before turning to Candace. His mind was jumbled, his thoughts all over the place, but he kept thinking about what Brett had said and he realized he didn't want to regret anything when it came to the woman seated beside him. It was time to man up and he knew it.

"You should have told me you were staying in Australia," Logan said, going to reach for her hand then hesitating, before forcing himself to get out of his comfort zone and just do it. "I just presumed you were heading back straightaway."

Candace's hand was warm in his, but her eyes were staring at their connection, not back into his. She was deep in thought and he wanted to know what was going through her head, what she wanted from him.

"Candace?" he asked, wishing he hadn't sounded so angry.

"I didn't want to tell you because I don't even know what this is between us," she said, finally looking up at him. "I couldn't exactly ask you not to go back home, to stay for another few days just to keep me company."

Logan's heart physically felt like it was going to stop. The pain he felt at seeing her eyes swim with tears was too much for him to handle, because it was him hurting her and that wasn't something he'd ever intended on doing.

"I have no idea what this is, either, Candace." It was the truth and he didn't know what else to say.

"A couple of years ago, I made a decision that I was better off alone than with a man in my life," she told him, still letting him hold her hand. "And then I met you, and I forgot all about the promise I'd made myself. I want you to know that I've never had a one-night stand in my life until you, Logan, and I'm fairly certain it's not something I'll ever do again."

Logan stared back at Candace, wondering what on earth she saw in him to make her want to spend any time with him at all. Why she trusted him, why they both seemed able to confide in one another.

"I don't have a lot to offer, Candace, not emotionally. But I'm not ready to say goodbye to you yet."

She leaned into him, her cheek to his chest. Logan circled his arms around her body, held her to him and shut his eyes, wanting to remember what it was like to have the tiny blonde against him. To be with a woman who made him feel things he'd never expected to feel again in his lifetime, to simply have Candace tucked against him. For as long as he lived, he'd never forget her warmth, the vulnerability he'd glimpsed—it was a comfort like he'd never experienced before.

"Come with me tomorrow," he said, his voice low.

Candace went so still he couldn't even feel her breathing.

"You mean that?" she asked, keeping her face to his chest.

Logan blew out a breath, not sure how he'd just ended up inviting a woman he barely knew back to his family home. But he had, and deep down he knew he wanted it more than anything. This time, he wasn't going to let his fears make decisions for him.

"Yeah, I mean it."

Candace eventually sat upright, one of her hands touching his face as she stared into his eyes.

"Screw doing what I think I should," she said, the corners of her mouth tipping up into a smile. "I think it's about time I just do what feels right."

He couldn't have said it better himself. Logan kissed her, forcing himself to keep his mouth soft to hers when all he wanted was to lose control. He usually hated any kind of public affection, but he wasn't exactly behaving like himself around Candace and there was no way he was going to *not* kiss her with her looking up at him like that.

"We leave you guys for, like, ten minutes, and already you're making out like a pair of lovesick teenagers."

Logan didn't pull away from Candace immediately, but when he did he glared at Brett. Trust his friend to push him in one direction then tease him about it as soon as Logan followed his instructions. But without Brett's chat, maybe he would have kept his mouth shut instead of taking a leap of faith.

"I think that round was supposed to be mine," Logan muttered, wrapping an arm around Candace and letting her snuggle under his shoulder.

"Yup. You owe me thirty bucks."

The drive back wasn't long, and in a way Candace wished it had been. The moment they'd buckled up, Logan had reached for her hand and held it, and they'd been like that the entire way back to her hotel. Even though they hadn't said a word, they hadn't needed to, and Candace had no idea what she would have said to him, anyway. They'd kind of said it all at the bar and the silence between them was comfortable.

"Here we are," Logan announced when he pulled up outside.

Candace reluctantly let go of his hand, wishing she'd just suggested they go home to his place.

"Do you want to come up?" she asked.

Logan stared straight ahead for a second, like he

wasn't sure what to say, or was having some sort of battle over what he wanted to say and what he thought he should say.

"I can't leave Ranger the whole night in here, but I'll come up for a little bit," he said.

Candace fought the heat starting to spread into her cheeks, finding it hard to believe that she'd been the one to ask a man up to her hotel room. Spending time with Logan was sure making her do a lot of things for the first time.

She jumped out and they both walked into the lobby, side by side but not quite touching. They headed straight for the elevator, and Candace toyed with the idea of putting her arm around Logan before deciding to just stand still and stop fidgeting.

"So this might sound like a weird question, but how exactly do we get to the Outback?" she asked, hoping that didn't make her sound like a dumb blonde. She had no idea whether it was two hours away or ten, and if she had to prepare for an insanely long drive or not.

"Not silly at all," he said, touching his fingers to hers when the doors opened. "I probably should have explained when I asked you."

"Don't tell me we have to go by bus or something?" She didn't want to sound like a princess, but...

"We fly," he said, stepping back so she could select her floor. "The catch is that I'm the pilot."

Candace spun around, her jaw almost hitting the floor. "No way." Logan sure had a way of surprising her when she least expected it.

He grimaced. "Yes way, but if it makes you feel any

better I've had my private pilot license since I was nine-teen, so it's not like I'm trying to clock up flying hours just for experience these days."

She couldn't believe what she was hearing. "And the plane's yours?" she asked.

"It's not that unusual for a large Outback station to have a plane," he told her, clearly trying to be modest. "We have a couple of small helicopters based on-site for mustering, but I keep the plane here a lot of the time so I can go back and forth."

Okay, she thought. Maybe the reason he wasn't eas-ily intimidated by her was because he had a lot more family wealth than he'd ever let on before. Either way it didn't bother her, but it did make her even more in-trigued about the man she'd just agreed to go on a mini-vacation with. There was so much about Logan that was still a mystery to her.

"If you're comfortable taking me, I'm comfortable flying with you," Candace told him.

They exited the elevator when they reached her floor, stepping out side by side.

"Just in case you're getting any grand ideas, it's just a nice reliable four-seater, nothing over-the-top, so don't expect reclining chairs or champagne."

She smiled. "I don't care what the plane looks like, just so long as it gets us to where we need to go and safely."

A look crossed his face, either sadness or anger, she just couldn't quite put her finger on it, but something changed in him at that exact moment.

"We'll get there," he said in a quiet voice that she hadn't heard before. "Don't you worry about that."

Candace wasn't sure what she'd said, but something had rattled him, she could sense it. She wasn't going to pry, though—if he wanted to talk about something that was troubling him, then he could bring it up when he was good and ready. She hated being pushed when something was on her mind.

"So will I have Ranger strapped in beside me?" Candace asked as she swiped her room key. "Or will I be relegated to the back so he can have your wingman seat?"

Logan chuckled. "He's a seasoned flier after all the miles he clocked up in the army, so you don't have to worry about him turning into a quivering mess and wanting to sit on your knee. He knows his place in the back with his harness on."

They walked into the room and Candace dropped her key and purse onto the side table before flopping down onto the bed.

"Talk about a cheap date. Two cocktails and I'm buzzing."

Logan sat beside her, his thigh grazing hers. "So what did you think of my friends? They weren't too full-on?"

Candace lay back on the bed, kicking off her stilettos. "You're kidding me? They were fantastic. Jamie was hilarious, just the kind of company I've been missing. I really liked her."

"Yeah, she's a great girl." Logan was silent for a while, obviously thinking something over, when he suddenly turned to her. "Candace, I want you to know that I've never taken anyone I've been involved with to my family home before."

Candace went still, staring at the ceiling fan before pulling herself up and sitting back against the pillows. "You haven't?"

He shook his head. "I was dating someone a while back, someone I thought I was going to marry, but my parents died before I had the chance to take her there. I haven't been seriously involved with anyone since."

"I'm sorry," Candace said, wishing she could think of something more helpful to say and coming up with nothing.

"When they died, we'd already gotten engaged, and I was so angry that she hadn't met them, that we hadn't spent time together as a family. It seemed so stupid that I'd never made the time to take her home when it should have been a priority."

"So what happened?" Candace asked, her voice deliberately low.

Logan kicked off his boots and moved up the bed, lying beside her, his head almost touching hers. She waited, hardly breathing she was trying to stay so quiet.

"I've experienced a lot of loss, it's just part and parcel of what I've always done for a job, but losing my parents?"

Candace moved her hand so it was touching Logan's, her fingers linking with his, letting him know she was there for him.

"I still don't know how I managed to pull through.

And then the fiancée I thought was in love with me turned out to be a gold digger."

Now that was something she understood all too well, and why she rarely trusted her instincts when it came to men anymore.

"I don't know what to say, but I can say that I've been in that same position with a couple of men before. Nothing hurts more than that kind of betrayal."

Logan squeezed her fingers. "To be honest, that's why I'm telling you," he said. "Charlotte made a few comments that made me suspicious, that made my friends question her real motives, and so I told her that my parents had been in debt and there wasn't any inheritance left over once the debtors had been paid."

Candace sighed. "Don't tell me. She left straight-away?"

"Yep, she was gone from my life faster than I could blink. Her stuff was moved out of our city house within the week," Logan said, moving so he could put his arm around her. "So I lost my parents and my fiancée within a few weeks of each other."

Candace turned, too, so she could snuggle back into Logan. She'd been thinking about getting him into bed ever since he'd kissed her in the bar, but now that they were here, all she wanted was to lie in his arms. The fact that he trusted her enough to confide in her meant more to her than anything, especially when on so many levels she understood what he'd been through.

"Better to have her walk out before you were married, or after you'd had children. I know it's kind of a cliché to say that, but it's true."

Logan's hand tucked under her breast, keeping her close, the warmth from his body making her want to shut her eyes and just enjoy someone holding her, making her feel wanted.

"Logan, I don't know a lot about Australia, but I'm guessing your ranch is kind of, well, impressive," Candace said. "You're obviously in a—" she struggled to find the right word "—*comfortable* position."

Logan's breath was hot against her ear when he chuckled. "You want to know my net worth before you agree to spending more time with me? Is that what you're saying?"

Now it was Candace laughing. "I couldn't care less how much money you have, but from the story you've just told me I have a feeling you're a more eligible bachelor than you've let on."

"If I'm honest with you, we have one of the biggest privately owned Outback stations in New South Wales, and my sister and I inherited everything jointly," he told her. "It's something I'm proud of, but at the same time I'd rather slip under the radar without anyone taking any notice of me, if you know what I mean."

"And yet you've dedicated the last, what, ten years to the army?"

"Something like that," he said, his mouth against her hair. "I just wanted to prove myself, make my own mark on the world before I took over the day-to-day running of the station. It made my dad proud, and I'd always planned on working side by side with him once I'd finished with the SAS."

Candace kept her eyes shut, loving the feel of Logan

stroking her hair, running his fingers gently through her curls before starting at her scalp again.

"What Charlotte did to me, it screwed me up where women are concerned. I'm not the guy who'll ever settle down, because I couldn't ever trust anyone that much again."

That made her eyes pop open. It wasn't that she had any illusions about Logan wanting to marry her, but the fact that such a nice, genuine man was too afraid of being hurt to love again? It made her sad. She often had similar thoughts, but to actually believe that falling in love would never happen? That wasn't something she believed, no matter how disillusioned she felt sometimes.

"Logan, you deserve to have children one day, to carry on your family's legacy and be happy."

When he spoke, his voice was gruff. "My parents set the best example for what a marriage is, and they were the best parents a kid could ever wish for. If I can't be the same husband, and dad that my own father was to me and my sister, then I don't have any interest in trying."

She understood, but it didn't mean she agreed with him. To her he just sounded like a wounded person not wanting to admit that one day he'd be whole again.

"Can you stay a little while?" Candace asked as Logan's touch lulled her into a happy, almost asleep state.

He didn't say anything, but he didn't stop touching her, either. She should have turned to him, should have kissed him and enjoyed having a man like Logan in her bed, but she also didn't want to give up the feeling of simply having his arms around her. It had been a long time since she'd trusted someone as much as she trusted this man, and it was something she wanted to selfishly indulge in a little while longer.

"We leave at nine tomorrow morning," Logan murmured in her ear. "I'll be gone when you wake up, but I can either come back and collect you, or you can make your own way to the airport."

Candace was barely conscious she was so relaxed. "There," she murmured. "I'll meet you there."

She tried to stay awake, but as she was slipping into sleep she decided not to fight it. For all she knew, it might be the only time she was cuddled to sleep for a long time.

Candace woke with such a fright it was like a bolt of lightning had struck her. It took a moment, a split second as she struggled to remember where she was and figure out what on earth was happening, but when she did the panic was like a noose around her neck.

"Logan!" she gasped, trying to push herself up.

He was calling out, tossing and turning, the pain and desperation in his voice almost unbearable.

"Logan!" she called out, scrambling from the bed and landing on her feet.

One second Logan was thrashing, the next he was sitting up, looking disorientated, his hands above his head.

"Candace?" Logan's voice was rough, croaky.

She didn't say anything for a moment, just tried to catch her breath.

"Candace?" His voice was more panicked this time.

"Here," she said, leaning forward. "Logan, I'm right here."

He reached to flick the bedside lamp, illuminating the room so she could see him properly and him her.

"What happened?" he asked.

Candace took a big, shaky breath, before sitting on the edge of the bed.

"You were having one of your night terrors and I woke you."

Logan's expression changed, his face falling. "I'm sorry. I don't know what happened."

She reached for him, clasping his hand. "I think you might have these more than you realize," Candace told him, trying to be as gentle with her words and her touch as she could. "Logan, you, well, the other night when I left, it wasn't because I knew about the photos."

He pushed his legs off the bed, head falling into his hands as he sat there. Candace wanted to comfort him, but she also knew that talking about this probably wasn't something he was comfortable with. Wasn't something that would come easily to him.

"I've done this before with you?" he asked when he finally raised his head.

"The other night I woke to you thrashing around and I know I should have done something, but instead I just left," she told him. "I thought maybe it was a one-off thing, and I also didn't think I was going to see you again."

Logan stood, his body dominating the room with his size. "I don't know what to say. I shouldn't have fallen asleep, and I just, I mean…" His voice trailed off, like he was in pain. "I didn't realize that I ever lashed out when I was dreaming. If I'd known I would never have put you in danger like that."

"It's not your fault, Logan. And I'm here for you," she said, even if she *was* scared of it happening again. "I can help."

"Candace," he started, walking around the bed and dropping to his knees as she sat on the bed, reaching for her hands before gently touching her face and then dropping his head into her lap. "I'm sorry."

Tears flooded Candace's eyes, spilled over even as she tried her hardest to push them away. This man— this strong, big man—was literally on his knees before her, and it almost broke her heart.

"It's okay, Logan. Everything's going to be okay."

When he raised his head, she could see that his own cheeks were tearstained. He slowly rose to his feet, and she could hardly breathe, couldn't take her eyes from his face.

"I have to go," he said.

She shook her head but he just nodded, walking backward.

"You can stay," she whispered.

"No, Candace, I need to go. To think. I'm sorry."

Candace watched him leave then lay back on the bed and pulled the covers up, dragging them over her head and hiding away from the world. A part of her wanted to run after him, to grab him and tell him that he couldn't go, but she also knew that he wasn't the kind of man to be forced into anything. If he needed time, he needed time. End of story. He was a complicated guy and she understood that more than he probably realized.

If you love someone, you always need to be strong enough to let them fly.

It was a saying her mom had strongly believed in, and when she shut her eyes, she could hear her saying it, whispering it to her one night when she was a little girl. Then, it had been about her beloved dog, loving him enough to say goodbye the next day at the vet clinic. Now, it was about a man. The only difference was that this time, she wasn't ready to admit how she felt. Not yet.

Logan slammed his fist into his steering wheel so hard that the horn beeped loudly into the otherwise silent night.

All this time thinking no one knew about how much he struggled, about the memories that terrorized him, and there he'd gone and lost it in front of Candace. The fact that she'd seen him…it hurt. Because he'd always been so good at making people see what he wanted them to see, without admitting how hard it had been, coming back from war and losing his parents. Even Brett didn't know the full extent of what he went through every single day—the memories he lived with.

He reached for his dog and stamped out the thoughts that were trying to take over his mind once again, wishing there was something he could do to make them stop. When he was with Candace, his mind actually felt calm, which was why he'd never thought about how he might react in his sleep when he was beside her.

But he'd blown it now. There was no chance she'd turn up in the morning. He'd sealed his own fate there, so now he just had to live with the fact that his past was part of his future, whether he liked it or not. He'd tried to run away from it, and he'd found someone who made him forget, and it still hadn't worked.

Logan started the engine and pulled away, from the hotel and from Candace.

CHAPTER EIGHT

LOGAN TAPPED HIS thigh to tell Ranger to walk at heel, his bag slung over his back, heading for the plane. He'd hardly had any sleep last night, had lain awake thinking about Candace, about his night terrors…*everything*. But he still wanted to head home, and he wasn't so weary that he couldn't make the relatively short flight. Every time he got into the pilot's seat he remembered things he didn't want to recall, but each time he was also pleased that he hadn't given into his fears and stayed grounded. And if he was ever going to get himself together, he needed to keep facing his fears head-on.

He stopped and looked at the plane, prepped and ready for him to fly out in, and his hand fell to Ranger's head.

"Time to head home, buddy," he muttered.

"Logan!"

Logan stopped moving. He'd just presumed Candace wouldn't show, that whatever they had was over after what had happened, but…

"Logan!"

He spun around, not wanting to believe it was her until he could actually see her.

"Candace?" He murmured her name, eyes locking on her as she ran in his direction, her blond curls loose and flying out around her.

She had someone struggling to keep up with her, beside her, and Logan was pretty certain that it was probably a poor security guard who she'd managed to slip past.

"Sorry, Mr. Murdoch. She just…"

"It's fine," he said, once they'd reached him. "It's fine. Sorry for the inconvenience."

"You said nine," Candace panted, out of breath. "It's only one minute past and you'd already given up on me? Surely you know me better than that."

Logan shook his head, speechless. "I didn't expect…"

"You didn't expect me to turn up, did you?" she asked, finishing his sentence. "You thought a little scary dream was going to send me running for the hills?"

He shook his head. "I guess not."

"When we first met, you brazenly asked me out, and I did the one thing in the world I would never usually do," she said. "And that was say yes to you."

Logan stared at her, unable to take his gaze off her bright blue eyes—eyes that had only the night before been filled with tears and were now full of light.

"You pushed me out of my comfort zone, and if you hadn't done that, who knows how long I would have kept on going, stuck in the rut I was in."

"I still don't understand why you're here," Logan

said. Candace could be anywhere in the world right now, and she was waiting to board his plane with him?

"I'm here because the time I've spent with you has been amazing, and because I want to see exactly what this property of yours is like."

He relaxed as she reached for his hand, felt as if all the stress, all the fury that had been building since he'd left her, had just fallen away.

"I'm still invited back to your ranch, aren't I?" Candace asked in a quiet voice.

Logan bent down to kiss Candace's cheek, wishing he could come up with something better to say than simply *yes*.

"I was a jerk last night, Candace, and if I could take it all back, I would."

"You're human, and the thing is that humans make mistakes. Let's just move on from all that, okay?"

Logan nodded, drawing her in close so he could hold her in his arms, feel her soft, warm body against his. It was all he'd thought about as he'd lay alone in his bed, wishing she was still pressed back into him, letting him spoon her.

"Thank you," he whispered.

"There's just one thing," Candace said, hand to his chest as she leaned back and looked up at him.

Logan raised his eyebrows. "What's that?"

"I left a heap of luggage inside the terminal there. Would you be a darling and go grab it all for me?"

Logan burst out laughing and pulled her tight against him for another hug. Talk about surprising a guy in more ways than one.

"I'll get you and Ranger on the plane first, then I'll go back in," he muttered. "But you do realize that there's only so much weight a light aircraft can carry, right?"

She glanced over at his shoulder bag, forlorn on the tarmac, and he followed her gaze.

"Lucky you travel so light then, huh?"

Logan gave her a play punch on the arm and indicated for Ranger to walk with them, wanting her safely seated before he left her.

"I hope you're not this bossy once we get there."

Candace took his hand, her palm swallowed up by his when he closed his over hers. Next time he had the chance to open up to her, he was going to have to man up and deal with it instead of walking away. Because Candace deserved more, and if he was honest with himself, so did he. The fact that she'd turned up was a miracle, and it wasn't one that he was going to take lightly.

Candace took a deep breath as they started their descent. It had only taken a short time, and part of her wished they could have stayed up in the air longer. The view had been incredible the entire way, the day clear and fine, and flying across the Outback had been incredible. When she'd watched the movie *Australia* she'd thought the scenery had been manipulated to make it look so incredible, but she'd even seen kangaroos as they'd flown lower across the Murdoch property, hopping around freely in a way she wouldn't have been able to even imagine had she not seen it with her own eyes.

"You don't really eat kangaroos here, do you?" Candace asked, staring out the window, unable to look away.

"I don't personally, but yeah, a lot of restaurants here serve the meat now."

An involuntary shudder slid down her spine. "That's gross. I can't believe anyone would want to kill such a beautiful animal."

"It's even worse when you find a kangaroo shot by a hunter, or hit by a car, and there's a little joey alive in her pouch."

That made Candace snatch her eyes away from the view. "No."

Logan nodded, but his gaze and concentration never strayed from what he was doing. "Sad but true. When I was a kid I rescued one and she was like a pet for years. We pulled her out of her dead mother's pouch and she ended up being like one of our dogs."

Candace looked back out the window as they fast approached the ground. Logan sure had a way of surprising her.

"This should be nice and smooth, just a little bump when we first touch down," he told her.

Candace glanced over her shoulder at Ranger, sitting alert, his body braced by a harness that was keeping him secure and in place.

"Your dog is incredible. I can't believe he's so well behaved," she said, holding on as they landed and eventually came to a stop.

She watched as Logan flicked switches, looking completely at ease with what he was doing.

"The dogs that make it through SAS training have to be super canines," he said, stretching his arms out above his head. "Ranger had to be completely fearless, whether we were on patrol or being helicoptered into a situation. Sometimes he would be harnessed to my back if we weren't able to land, and we'd parachute to the ground together."

"No way!" It didn't even sound possible that a dog could do that kind of stuff.

"Yes," Logan said with a laugh. "I know it's crazy, but the dogs are probably worth more to the army than we humans are, because at the end of the day there are plenty of guys out there capable of doing our job, with the right training, but not many dogs who could make the cut."

Logan went back to unclip Ranger, and then he was opening his door and disappearing. The next thing, her door opened and he helped her down to the ground.

"You know, I'm almost starting to like dogs because of him," Candace said, stretching and looking around. Her eyes landed on two horses in a nearby field, their ears pricked, bodies dead still as they watched the plane and what was happening. "But I love horses *way* more."

Logan reappeared with some of her luggage, and nodded toward the house. It was a decent walk away, and she felt almost bad for having so much stuff.

"I'll take this lot and the butler can come get the rest."

"You have a butler?" she asked, rushing to catch up to him.

The look Logan gave her made them both laugh.

"Okay, I really fell for that one. But surely you have a trailer or something?"

He bumped his body against hers. "Don't sweat it. I'll come back with the quad bike later."

Ranger ran off ahead and Candace was almost as eager, desperate to see the house that was obviously so special to Logan. She knew it was a big deal him asking her here in the first place, and if she was honest with herself, *not* turning up had never really been an option. Logan had probably been beyond embarrassed about what had happened the night before, and she didn't want him to think he had to deal with his troubles alone.

"So who lives here when you're not around?" she asked.

"We have a manager in a separate house, and his wife keeps the place tidy for me, stocks the fridge when she knows I'm coming back, that sort of thing."

They crossed over toward the house and Candace couldn't help but smile. "It's beautiful."

He was silent for a moment as they walked up to it. "Yeah, it is."

She imagined it still looked the same as it had when his parents had been in residence. It was built from timber with a wide veranda that stretched around the entire house, the almost white paintwork in immaculate condition. As they stepped up toward the front door, Candace touched the handrail and let her hand stay on it until they reached the veranda.

"I can't believe how beautiful this house is. I never realized it would be like this."

Logan moved past her and opened the door.

"You don't keep it locked?" she asked as she followed him inside.

"This is the Outback, not the city. We're miles from our closest neighbor and there's not really any risk of a break-in."

When he put it like that she guessed it made sense—it just wasn't something she was used to.

"So what's the plan for today?" Candace asked. "Horseback riding, a picnic, a swim in some amazing water hole?"

Logan chuckled and set her bags down in the hall. "I actually want to show you something. I was thinking we'd take a horseback ride there, if you're keen."

Was she keen? "I've been dying to get back in the saddle for months. Just give me a quiet horse, though, because it's been a while."

"That I can do," he said. "Now follow me while I give you a quick tour of the place."

Candace grinned and followed him, happy to look through the house. Taking the high road, and a risk, had been worth it, because she felt like the girl she'd left behind before her first album had launched, and she'd been missing that girl a lot lately. She just wanted to have fun, enjoy her life. It wasn't that she wanted to walk away from her career, because she could never stop singing, but creating a sense of balance was something she was determined to achieve.

"These are your parents?" she asked as they passed the hallstand.

Logan stopped, the smile that had been on his face dying. He touched the edge of one of the frames. "Yeah, that's them."

"Well, they look lovely," she said, touching his arm. "It's such a shame I couldn't have met them."

"My mom would have been in a huge flap if I'd brought you here when she was still alive. She'd have been baking up a storm and sending Dad to work in the garden, ordering him around like the queen was about to visit."

Candace liked the mental picture, had a feeling that she'd have probably loved his parents, too. Because that sounded a lot like her grandparents and her mom—just nice people who genuinely cared about their kids.

"So which room am I staying in?" she asked as Logan started to move again.

"That depends if you want to sleep in my bedroom or a guest room," he said, giving her a cheeky wink over his shoulder.

"Let's just see what happens today, shall we? I don't want you getting too cocky, soldier."

She was also a little scared of him having another one of his episodes, but she wasn't going to admit it, not to Logan. *And not one hundred percent to herself, either.*

"So what is it you want to show me?" Candace asked, loving the feel of the sun beating down on her shoulders and the gentle sway of the horse beneath her.

"We're almost there," he replied.

She admired Logan's strong silhouette as he rode slightly ahead of her, his big chestnut gelding tall and well muscled, just like his rider. Where she came from, men were always in the saddle, and it always made her laugh when city folk talked about horseback riding like it was a girls-only sport. Nothing made her admire a man more than one who could ride well and knew how to treat animals.

"Logan, I've been wanting to say that if you'd like to talk about what happened last night, I'm all ears," she said, wanting to get it off her chest to clear the air now rather than have it come up later.

"Can we just wait a minute?" he asked, his face not giving any hint of what he was thinking or feeling. "It'll all kind of make sense soon."

Candace didn't push the point, just accepted it and enjoyed the different scenery as they rode. Everything was so different to what she was used to, but the cattle grazing as they passed had the strange effect of making her feel like she was closer to home than she had been in a long while, even though she was on the other side of the world.

"It's in here," Logan said, heading toward a large shed.

She followed him and dismounted when he did, leading her horse closer and dropping her reins like he did. It wasn't something she was used to doing, but the horses seemed to understand exactly what was required of them.

"They won't move," Logan told her. "Come with me."

He bent down to put a key into the padlock that was securing the door, and she bit her tongue instead of asking why he locked this door in the middle of nowhere yet didn't bother with the house. She could see how tense his body was, that what she was about to see was something that meant a lot to him.

"Logan, what's in here?" she asked, curious and worried at the same time.

He yanked the door open and secured it back so that light flooded the big barn. Candace took a step inside, then another when Logan walked ahead of her. She watched as he dropped to his haunches, before looking back at all the metal and parts in front of her. It took her a second to figure it all out, but then she realized what she was looking at, what the wreckage had once been.

"This was a plane?"

She was staring at the back of Logan's head, waiting for him to explain.

"All my life, flying has been like second nature to me," Logan said, not moving. "I was up in a plane with my dad as soon as I was old enough to tag along, and I got my pilot's license as soon as I was old enough."

Candace swallowed, trying not to hold her breath as she listened to Logan. The way he was talking, the fact that they were standing in front of a wreckage, told her that this story wasn't going to end well. That what he was about to tell her was going to be hard to hear and even harder for him to say.

"Logan, what is this I'm looking at?" she asked.

"My parents died when the plane they were in crashed. My father had clocked up more hours flying than anyone I've ever met before, but the thing he loved killed him and my mom."

"Oh, Logan." Candace blinked away the tears in her

eyes and moved to stand behind him. "I don't know what to say."

"I'd just arrived back into the country when it happened, and even though they were supposed to notify next of kin first, the media got wind of who it was and I saw it on the news before my sister had a chance to phone me."

Now Candace *was* holding her breath.

"I dealt with the accident the only way I knew how, and that started with me insisting that I identify the bodies."

She listened as he sucked back a big breath before continuing on.

"They were badly burned, so..."

Candace put her arms around his waist and pressed herself to his back, just wanting to touch him, to hold him and let him know that she got how hard it was for him to talk, to share what he'd been through. That she was there for him.

"You had all the parts salvaged, didn't you?" she murmured against him.

"My training just kind of kicked in and I insisted on a second, independent investigation once the police one ended inconclusively. I just couldn't understand how a man like my father could be killed doing something he was capable of doing with his eyes shut. Nothing about it seemed right to me."

"Did they find anything?"

"Yeah, but it still doesn't stop me questioning everything, scouring through the report and then coming in here to go over every piece of the plane myself whenever I come home."

She released him enough that she could stand beside him, her arms still around his waist, head tucked against him.

"Yeah, but we can only deal with things the best way we know how."

"When I dream, the terrors I have at night, it's their bodies I see," he told her.

She moved around his body and watched as he shut his eyes, wished she could take away even a little of the pain he was feeling.

"I see them flying, then crashing, watch as they burn alive, and there's nothing I can do to help them. Then suddenly they disappear, and it's my friend Sam I see, being blown to pieces in front of me, his body burning and then somehow ending up alongside my folks, so they're all dead together."

"Have you talked to anyone about this before?" she asked. "Someone who could help you deal with what you're going through?"

Logan shook his head and gazed down at her. "You're the only person I've let close, the only person who's outright asked me about my dreams, and the only person I've ever opened up to about it." He paused. "But I don't want to talk about it anymore, Candace. I want to leave this in the past."

Logan hoped he'd done the right thing, but after so long carrying his pain on his own, it was almost a relief to finally get it off his chest. To show someone the barn he'd kept locked for so long, to talk about his memories. Because he couldn't hide his night terrors from Candace, not after she'd witnessed it firsthand, and he couldn't pretend like they didn't happen any longer, either.

"I don't know what to say, Logan, but I'm pleased you told me."

"It's been a long time since I've felt at peace with the world, but when I'm with you, I don't know. I just feel different."

"Me, too," she said, standing on tiptoe and kissing him. "This isn't something you need to deal with alone, and if you want to talk about your parents all night or not at all, it's fine by me."

Logan had a better idea. It was time he closed this chapter of his life, shut the doors to the wreckage and walked away from trying to find answers that didn't even seem to exist.

"You know, every time I fly my plane, I think about my dad up there in the sky, and I hope he didn't even know what happened when they crashed," Logan admitted, walking hand in hand with Candace from the barn and only dropping the contact to shut the door. "I get a bout of nerves every time I start the engine, but then that passes and I can hear his voice in my head, talking me through every step of the process."

Once he'd locked the door, he turned to find Candace standing as still as a statue, just staring at him.

"You okay?" he asked, forgetting his memories and suddenly worried about her instead.

"I'm fine. Better than fine."

"You know, when I'm with you, everything else just seems to fade away."

"Yeah, for me, too," she whispered in reply, tilting her head back so Logan had to kiss her, so that he couldn't think about anything else. "Everything else just seems to disappear."

"I can't make you any promises, Candace," he whispered, looking down at her. "I would never hurt you, and there is nothing more I want from you than just you, but I'm not…"

"Shhh," she murmured. "Just stop talking and let's forget. Everything."

Logan fell to his knees so he was directly in front of Candace, pulling her down then pushing her back gently until she yielded. He had one hand at her back to guide her down, cushioning her fall as she lay on the grass, rising so he was propped above her.

That was something he could do, something he *wanted* to do. He only hoped that she didn't expect more from him than he could give.

CHAPTER NINE

CANDACE STRETCHED AND pulled herself closer to Logan. She couldn't get enough of him—not his body, not his hands on her, not the feel of being cocooned against him. And now here they were, with hardly any clothes on, lying out under the hot Australian sun.

"We really need to cover up, otherwise we're going to fry like crisps," Logan said, but without making any attempt to move.

"But it feels so good," she murmured, shutting her eyes and basking in the warmth. "Just a bit longer."

"Candace, I don't want to ruin the moment, but I have this feeling that we're setting ourselves up for a fall."

She sighed, putting one hand flat to his chest and using it to prop herself up.

"Can't we just enjoy ourselves and pretend like everything's, I don't know, all going to work out."

Logan smiled up at her, and she leaned down to kiss him, loving the soft fullness of his mouth against hers.

"We can pretend so long as we both know that this is just a short-term thing."

"I know," she said, even though she was still trying to convince herself that she would see Logan again, that somehow they might be able to make something work. "I guess it's just nice to believe that things happen for a reason sometimes, that everything will work out for the best, in the end."

"This did happen for a reason," he told her, stroking a hand up and down her back. "You changed things that had been bothering you for a long time, and I finally showed someone what I've had hidden here. Opened up about what I've been going through."

A low bark made Candace jump. She looked over her shoulder and saw Ranger standing there, a stick dropped at his paws, and a curious look on his face.

"Is it weird that I feel funny about your dog staring at me when I'm practically naked?"

Logan sat up, reaching over for the stick and throwing it. "Yeah, that's definitely weird."

Candace play punched his arm but he just grabbed hold of her, a devilish look on his face.

"This is really bad timing, especially given the whole pretending we're in a bubble conversation we just had, but I had a message early this morning from my old commanding officer, and I have to fly out in a couple of days and head to base. After that, I'll receive my official discharge papers."

Candace shouldn't have expected more, had told herself time and again that this was just a temporary thing, something fun, with Logan. But knowing they only had a couple of days together still hurt.

"I guess I need to book my flight back to the U.S. then," she said, trying to keep her voice upbeat.

"Candace, if there was any way I could just hide out here for the next week, even the next month with you, I would," Logan told her, brushing her hair from her face. "If you want to stay here on your own for a little bit, I'll come straight back once I'm done with work. If you need a vacation where no one will find you, this place is perfect and you'll always be welcome here."

"I can't do that," she murmured, wishing as she said it that she'd just kept her mouth shut and nodded. "The longer I put off seeing my attorney back home and figuring out my management, the worse it'll all be. I've been too good at avoiding things for way too long and I need to head back and deal with it, no matter how good an extended vacation here sounds."

She leaned into Logan's touch, like a cat desperate to be petted.

"If we'd only met in another lifetime, or maybe in a few years..." Logan said.

Didn't she know it?

"You know, we're not so different, you and I," she said.

Logan laughed. "Yeah, except for the fact that I'm a soldier and you're famous."

She touched his cheek with her fingertips. "You might be a soldier, but you're also a ranch owner, and a kind, decent man. There's a lot about your family and your wealth that I think you've kept from me. And besides, I'm just a singer who got lucky. At heart I'm still just a country girl with a big voice, and in my mind that's who I'll always be."

Candace touched her forehead to his, eyes shut because she couldn't bear to look into his eyes.

"But we still come from different worlds. I love the Outback and I've waited my whole life to come back here, and you have a life in America," he told her in a quiet voice. "Even if we weren't so different, we still couldn't ever make this work. Believe me, I've thought it through. Too many times to count."

Hope ignited within her, a gentle tickle that turned into a full-on flip inside her stomach. *He'd actually thought about it?* Even if it was a lost cause, she still liked the fact that he cared enough to think about them being together. She knew it was impossible, that they lived on opposite sides of the world and couldn't possibly make anything long-term work between them, but it wasn't like she hadn't spent time wondering.

"So I guess we just enjoy the next two days and then part ways," she said, needing to say it out aloud to truly get her head around it.

Logan squeezed her hand. "For the record, I've been more content being with you than I've been, well, in forever."

Candace refused to become emotional, because they were both adults making an adult decision. She'd been with men who couldn't tell the truth, and she knew exactly what it was like to be lied to, so the fact that Logan was being honest and open with her wasn't something to mourn. He'd set the bar high for any other men she might meet in the future, and for that she needed to be thankful.

"Can I ask you one question before we stop talking about how little time we have together?"

Logan nodded. "Shoot."

Candace took a shallow breath and blew it straight back out again. "If we did live in the same country, if things were different, would you want to be with me? As in, in a relationship?"

She couldn't believe she'd even asked him that, but she had and she didn't regret it. She needed to know.

"Hell, yes," he whispered straight into her ear. "I can tell you, hand on my heart, that you're the only woman I've ever wanted to open up to. You're special, Candace, and don't let anyone ever make you think differently."

It was all she needed to hear. All the pain of past relationships, of men treating her like a free ticket to a life they wanted, it all just washed away. Because Logan was different, and she needed to make the most of every second in his company.

"Have I mentioned that my all-time favorite movie is *The Bodyguard?*"

Logan smiled as she looped her arms around his neck. "Any scenes you want to reenact?" he asked.

"Oh, there're plenty," she told him, pushing him down so she could straddle him. "In fact, we could role-play *those* scenes all day."

"I wasn't ever very good at drama at school, but I'm a pretty fast learner these days."

She laughed. "Then get ready to play my fantasy role."

And then all at once Logan had her arms pinned at her sides, mouth hot and wet against her skin. Maybe they could role-play later, because this wasn't something she had any intention of putting an end to.

Logan hadn't been so happy in years. Having Candace at home with him, on the property that was more special to him than any other place in the world, had been the best thing he'd ever done. It might only be temporary, but it had at least showed him that maybe he wasn't as screwed up as he'd thought. Damaged, sure, but maybe not beyond repair as he'd thought, *believed,* for so long.

"So what do you say to a walk down memory lane with me?" Logan asked as they rode back to the house, side by side.

Candace gave him a lazy look, like she was ready to fall asleep. Or maybe she was just feeling as relaxed and chilled out as he was.

"What do you have in mind?"

He chuckled to himself as he thought about what they could do, where he could take her. It had been a while since he'd just enjoyed the land he'd grown up on, reminded himself of why he liked the Outback so much. Wherever he'd been in the world, no matter how much pain he'd been in or how bad he'd struggled, this was the place he visualized.

"When we were kids, my sister and I used to ride bareback to a deep water hole, tether the horses and swim. Then we'd eat the lunch Mom had packed us and chill out in the shade for a while."

"Sounds like fun," she said, "although maybe we should stay out of the sun for the rest of the day and do it tomorrow."

"Deal," he agreed. He was more than ready to put his feet up and just chill for the rest of the afternoon and evening. "We can have a barbecue tonight and sit out on the veranda for a while. Listen to the wildlife."

Candace rode a little closer to him. "Speaking of wildlife, there aren't any crocodiles in that water hole, are there?"

He laughed. "We're in New South Wales, sweetheart. It's way too cold down here for crocs."

"Well good," she said. "The last thing I need to worry about is my leg being bitten off."

Logan chuckled and nudged his horse on when she tried to slow down and nibble some long grass. Candace had asked him before whether he'd want to be with her, whether they could have made things work if she lived in Australia or he in America, and he'd told her the truth. Maybe he wouldn't have been so open if there actually *had* been a chance of things working between them, but there wasn't, and he hadn't seen the point in not being honest with her.

Candace had been the breath of fresh air he'd been waiting for, and thinking of never seeing her again wasn't something he wanted to dwell on. All he cared about right now was making sure they made the most of the less than forty-eight hours they had together.

Because after that, she'd just be a memory that kept him going when things got tough.

The water was colder than she'd expected, but the feeling of swinging off an old tire that was attached to a tree overhanging the water hole was worth the initial shock factor.

"Ready to go again?"

Logan's enthusiasm was rubbing off on her, the smile on his face impossible to ignore.

"You're loving this whole feeling of being a kid again, aren't you?" she teased.

He responded by pulling her back farther than he had before, letting go so she flew out over the water. Candace screamed as she let go and landed with a plop, going completely under before emerging. She moved out of the way so Logan could do the same, launching like a missile into the deepest spot, his enthusiasm contagious.

"I can't believe how much fun this is," he said. "It's been years since I've even been down here."

She giggled. "My fans would be horrified that I'm such a kid at heart, but yeah, it's pretty cool."

Logan swam to her, blinking away the water that had caught on his lashes, his short hair looking even darker as it slicked back off his head.

"Would they be horrified about this?" he asked, clasping the back of her head and dragging her body hard to his.

Candace wrapped her legs around him, and her arms, making him tread water to keep them both afloat. "Oh, I think they'd definitely be horrified. Mortified, in fact."

"What about by this?" he asked, flicking the clasp on her bra so that the garment fell forward.

She slid her arms from the straps and watched the bra float away, wrapping her arms around Logan's chest so her bare breasts were against his skin.

"This swimming idea of yours was a pretty good one," she murmured as she kissed him again, nipping his bottom lip when he tried to slide the rest of her underwear off.

She refused to think about leaving, about the short time she had left with Logan, because she hadn't been this happy in years, and there was nothing she could do to stop the clock. All she could do was enjoy being in the arms of a man who was so different to any man she'd ever met before. These memories would last her a lifetime, of that she was certain.

"What say we paddle to shallower water, soldier?" she asked.

Logan tucked her under his arm like he was a lifesaver and headed for shore. "Done."

CHAPTER TEN

"THIS IS A pretty extravagant barbecue," Candace said, smiling up at Logan as he finished ferrying food over to the table.

"I only have one chance to impress you with my grilling, so I wasn't going to take any chances," he told her with a wink.

She laughed as she looked at her plate. "I probably should have made us a salad. You know, so that there was *something* green on our plates."

"What, you don't like my carnivore special?"

Candace looked at the array of meat on her plate and couldn't wipe the grin from her face. He'd done his best to impress her, but she was guessing that aside from grilling meat, he really didn't have any other culinary skills. She slipped Ranger a piece of steak under the table, no longer scared of the big dog's constant presence.

"It's really beautiful here, Logan. I never knew what an amazing country Australia was."

He leaned back in his chair, looking up at the sky. It was almost dark, but Candace could still see his face perfectly. They'd lit candles and placed them on the table, but it wasn't quite dark enough for them to need the extra light.

"It's paradise," he admitted. "Even when I stay here for weeks without leaving, I never stop appreciating how beautiful it is."

Candace wished she could have stayed longer, that she'd just taken Logan up on his offer to stay here while he was away, but she also knew that doing that would be putting off the inevitable.

She looked up at the sky, at the inky blackness peppered with white, and then turned her focus back to Logan.

"What do you say we finish dinner then turn in for an early night?" she asked.

"I think," he said, reaching for her hand across the table, "that you might just be a mind reader."

Candace was finding it hard to fall asleep. She'd snuggled up to Logan after they'd made love, and he'd promptly fallen into a deep slumber, but she couldn't stop thinking about leaving. About the fact that their holiday romance was almost over. Or that at any moment he could have one of his nightmares and end up thrashing around beside her.

She knew that he'd snuck out of bed the night before, because she'd woken to find him gone. He'd slept in another room, and then come back to their shared bed early in the morning. But tonight he'd fallen asleep without probably even meaning to.

Candace tried to shut off the overthinking part of

her brain and closed her eyes, listening to Logan's steady heartbeat beneath her, enjoying the warmth of his body. But just as soon as she'd relaxed, as if on cue, his heart started to race so loud that she could hear it. Before she had time to move, he was yelling out, his arm thrashing, smashing into her face as she tried to roll out of his way.

"No!"

"Logan, wake up!" she screamed, landing on the floor and yanking a blanket with her to cover her naked body.

Ranger was at her side, confused, and she held on to him as Logan leaped up, looking like a wild man in the moonlight spilling in through the windows.

"Candace? Where, what…"

Then he saw her and his shoulders dropped. He looked horrified at what he'd done.

"Sweetheart, I'm sorry," he murmured, walking around the bed and reaching a hand out to her. "I'm so, so sorry."

"Logan, you can say sorry all you like, but you need to do something about this," she murmured, knowing she couldn't just pretend like he was okay, act like everything would be fine just because he'd managed to talk to her about his nightmares. "You need help."

"It won't happen again, I can sleep in a different room, I…" He ran a hand through his hair before walking a step backward and sitting on the bed.

Candace stood up, her body shaking as she lifted a hand to her face, touching gently across her cheek.

"Logan, you hit me," she whispered, her voice cracking with emotion.

He stared at her, raised his hand then let it fall to the bed beside him. "Candace, I…" Logan took a deep breath. "Did I hurt you?"

"Logan, you need to talk to someone. If not me, then a professional, but you can't torture yourself in your dreams like that every night. It has nothing to do with you almost hurting me, and everything to do with you hurting yourself by not getting help. This isn't just going to go away."

"I don't have a problem and I don't want to talk about it. I can deal with this on my own," he growled out. "And for the record, what happened just now has everything to do with me almost hurting you. I don't care about me, but I *sure as hell do* care about what I could have done to you."

Candace closed her eyes for a beat. "Yeah, I think you do have a problem, Logan. One that could be fixed if you weren't so scared about facing your past."

He stood up, hands clenched at his sides. "This was a mistake. We don't even know each other and now you're trying to tell me…you know what, I think we're done here, Candace. I am who I am, and I can't change that."

Candace was done with being patient, because Logan was being a bullheaded macho male now, and she wasn't going to let him get away with it. She didn't care if she'd had a fantastic time with him—they also had to deal with reality. Maybe she'd been right to doubt her ability to make a judgment call when it came to men.

"I think you're right," she said, jutting her chin up and wishing she was taller. "Whatever this was, it's over."

Logan stood and stared at her, like he was going to reach for her, going to say something that would turn the entire situation around. She waited, never even blinking as she watched him for fear of crying, but in the end, he turned and walked out of the room.

"I think we should leave tomorrow," she said, willing her voice not to crack.

"Yeah, first thing in the morning."

She watched Logan go and didn't falter until he shut the door behind him. Then she collapsed onto the bed, face buried in the pillow and sobbed like she'd never cried before in her lifetime.

After so long protecting her heart, not letting anyone get too close to her, Logan had snuck past her defenses and managed to hurt her when she'd least expected it. When she'd thought there was nothing he could do to wound her. She should never have let herself be put in this situation, should have protected her heart instead of being vulnerable to Logan. Letting him get closer to her had been a stupid thing to do, and she should have known better.

Either way, there was nothing she could do to stop the pain shooting through her body like a drug being pumped through her veins. Whatever she'd had with Logan, it was over, and no matter what she tried to tell herself, dealing with never seeing him again was...

She swallowed the emotion that choked in her throat,

refusing to let it sink its claws in to take hold. But the pain was too much, the ache in her heart...

Unbearable.

Logan slammed his palm down onto the kitchen counter and hung his head. He was a total idiot. A bloody fool. And because he was incapable of dealing with his problems, he'd just walked away from the one woman he could have just been himself around. Who didn't care who he was, what his family name was, or what he'd been through. The one person who had simply been trying to help him.

Candace had given him a chance to open up and be himself, to acknowledge the nightmares that woke him almost every night, that haunted him, and instead he'd walked out on her and as good as told her it was over. All because she'd been brave enough to confront him, to try to get him to admit that he needed help.

Logan slumped forward, exhausted and unsure what he was supposed to do next. He should have turned around and walked straight back into his bedroom, begged for her forgiveness and just admitted he needed professional help, but his pride or some other stupid emotion was stopping him. He'd never acknowledged what he went through every night to anyone other than Candace, and talking to anyone else, dealing with it properly, wasn't something he was ready for.

He'd told Candace so much, had admitted so much to her that he'd hardly ever spoken to anyone else about, and yet when it came to admitting his shortfalls, acknowledging his true weakness...

Logan sat back, took a deep breath and straightened his body. The best thing for both of them was for this to end now, to stop things before they went any further when they both knew there was no future for them as a couple anyway. The whole idea of bringing her here with him had been stupid. Ridiculous even.

If that was true, though, then why did ending things with Candace seem like the stupidest thing he'd ever done in his life?

CHAPTER ELEVEN

"So I GUESS this is it, then?"

They'd both been silent on the journey back to Sydney, and now they were standing outside the plane, Candace's luggage sitting on the tarmac. Logan had Ranger on his leash, at his side, and he'd asked someone to come and get all of Candace's things. Which gave them about another five minutes together.

"I'm sorry things had to end this way," Candace said, not taking her sunglasses off.

Logan didn't hesitate—he stepped forward, took her handbag and put it down, before wrapping her in a tight hug. He shut his eyes as she tucked into him, snuggled to his chest, her arms holding him just as tight around his waist. She probably hated him for what had happened, but he wasn't going to let her get on that plane without at least trying to show her what she'd come to mean to him.

"I'll never forget you, Logan. No matter what," she whispered, just loud enough for him to hear.

Logan kissed the top of her head, before putting his hands on her arms to hold her back. Her eyes were swimming with tears when he pushed her sunglasses to the top of her head, and if he wasn't fighting it so hard, his would be, too. All the times he managed to stamp out his emotions on tour, and here he was about to cry. Because this was about more than saying goodbye; this was about him being forced to deal with his past, with his terrors.

"One day, when you're old and gray, surrounded by ten grandchildren, you can smile and think about the naughty Australian vacation you had when you were a young woman," he told her, staring into her blue eyes. "Just promise me that you'll always remember me with a smile, because that's how I'll remember you, even if things didn't work out as, well, you know."

Candace shook her head, like she was trying to shake away her emotion.

Logan bent down to kiss her cheek, tasting the saltiness of her tears as she let him touch her skin.

"Goodbye," she said when she broke away.

Her bags were being loaded onto a cart behind them, and he knew it was time for her to go. They should never have even crossed paths in the first place, which meant they'd always been on borrowed time, and after the way things had gone last night, he was lucky she was even talking to him right now.

Logan watched as she gave Ranger a hug before straightening.

"You, my boy, are very special, you know that? I think I might just like dogs now that I've met you."

"Goodbye," Logan said as she walked away.

Logan waved then thrust his hands into his jeans'

pockets, eyes never leaving her as she turned and walked away. Candace was gone, and it was time for him to get on a plane himself and close the final chapter of his life as a SAS soldier. And maybe, just maybe, he'd think about what she'd said to him.

It was goodbye to the job he'd loved, and the woman he could so easily have fallen in love with, all in one day. Time to move on. Pity it wasn't as easy as it sounded. All he could do now was take his life one day at a time, and figure out what his future held. Because right now he was more confused than he'd ever been, and he also knew he'd been a jerk for not sucking up his pride and admitting his shortfalls to her. Because Candace had been there for him like no other woman probably ever would be.

Candace boarded the plane and smiled at the flight attendant who took her bag and put it in the overhead cabin. She took her seat, pleased she'd purchased both the first class seats that were side by side. The last thing she wanted was someone trying to make small talk with her, and she sure didn't want anyone to see her crying.

But there was something different about Logan, and she knew it. There was nothing she could think about him that would change her mind, and there was nothing she could do to pull herself from the mood she was in. After what had happened during the night, and then actually walking away from him…it was all too much. He'd behaved badly and she didn't regret what she'd said, but it still hurt.

"Would you like a drink before takeoff?"

Candace refused to take her grumpiness out on anyone else, so she forced a smile and nodded. She may as well drink something that would take the edge off her pain, or at the very least knock her out for part of the long trip home.

"Champagne," she said after a moment's hesitation. "Please."

Maybe she needed to celebrate the few days she'd just had, minus their argument. She needed to toast it and then forget it, because in the end Logan wasn't a man she could never have been with. Not when he refused to do something about a problem that was so serious, and not when they lived on opposite sides of the world.

"Here we go, ma'am. A glass of champagne for you."

Candace took the glass, shut her eyes and took a sip. It was heavenly. She had fourteen hours before she touched down at LAX, and a few more glasses were probably exactly what the doctor would order. She could pass out and sleep until the plane landed.

No more tears, no more feeling sorry for herself. She was a woman in charge of her own life now, she'd met a man who'd changed the way she thought about *everything,* and she was going home to start over. When she thought about Logan, she needed to learn how to smile instead of frown, and make the memories of her time with him last forever. She needed to simply remember the *good* times she'd had with him and forget the rest.

Today was the first day of the rest of her life. And if there was one thing Logan had taught her, it was that she had to trust her own instincts and learn to put herself first.

CHAPTER TWELVE

LOGAN STOOD OUTSIDE the plane and stretched. He was
exhausted. Not the kind of bone-tired exhaustion that
he'd experienced on tour, but he was still ready to col-
lapse into bed and not stir until late the next morning.
The smart thing to do would have been to stay in the
city for the night, but he'd already let his apartment and
his only option would have been to crash at Jamie and
Brett's. He doubted any respectable hotel would have
let him arrive with Ranger, even if he explained how
highly trained he was, and he didn't want Jamie's pity.
The way she'd look at him would only remind him of
what he'd lost since last time he'd seen her.

"I'm getting old," he muttered to his dog, bending
to give him a scratch on the head. "We were definitely
ready to retire."

Ranger looked up at him, waiting for a signal that
it was okay to run off, and Logan waved him on. He
threw his pack over his back and headed for the house.
*So much for planning to be gone only a few days, a week
at the most.* He'd ended up being talked into spending
time with some of the newer recruits in the K9 division,

which he was pretty sure was his superior's way of trying to push him into a teaching position. It wasn't that he hadn't enjoyed it—he had, and Ranger had, too—but after so long thinking about coming back home, he was more than ready to make it happen. Not to mention the fact that he wasn't ready to make any long-term commitments just yet.

Logan stopped when he noticed a light on in the house. *Weird.* He hadn't phoned ahead and told the manager he'd be back a day early, which meant they wouldn't have bothered to go and turn lights on, and... *crap.* There was smoke coming from the chimney. Either his manager had decided to take some serious liberties and move into the main house, or there was a squatter or someone in there. His sister was away at a conference, and she was the only other person who had a key, and the right, to enter their house.

He broke into a jog, whistling out to Ranger to come back. His dog was trained to sniff out bombs, but he was also a lethal weapon when it came to providing protection when he had to be. Logan knew he was better with the dog at his side than a weapon, especially if there was an intruder.

He moved quietly up the steps, breathing slowly and filling his lungs as he trod, before trying the door handle. It was unlocked. Logan pushed it open, glanced at his dog and tapped his thigh so he stayed right at his side, and closed it behind them. He listened and heard only the low hum of the television, so he walked silently down the hall, pausing to listen before turning into the kitchen. There was a cup on the counter that he hadn't left there, and a couple of shopping bags sitting on the floor.

Someone had definitely been making themselves at home in his absence, and he wanted to know right now what on earth was going on.

Logan could see the television from where he was standing, saw the closing credits of a movie, but he couldn't hear anything else. He stepped carefully, not wanting to make any of the wooden floorboards creak, hardly breathing as he saw a foot sticking out. That someone was lying on his sofa.

"What the hell…" Logan's voice died in his throat as he leaped around the corner of the sofa.

No. He must be dreaming. Seeing things.

He bent to silence Ranger, still staring at the woman lying, asleep, her lips slightly parted, long blond hair messy and covering the cushions beneath her head and shoulders.

Candace. The woman he'd done nothing but think about these past two weeks was actually in his home, lying on his sofa. Logan had been so close to trying to track her down, but he hadn't even asked for her phone number before they'd parted ways, which he'd been telling himself had been smart, not having any of her contact details.

But now she was here? He couldn't believe it. *He didn't believe it.*

Logan bent to retrieve the television remote, hitting the off button, and disappearing to find a blanket. In his room the bed was slightly crinkled, and when he went to yank the comforter off, a hissing noise startled him. Then Ranger's low growl put him on high alert.

"Leave it," he ordered, wondering what kind of animal had gotten into his room.

A head popped out from between the pillows, followed by a yawn and a stretch. Candace was in his house, and she'd brought her cats with her? Logan pulled the comforter off despite the kitty's protests and put a hand on Ranger's head to settle him. The poor dog looked like his eyes were going to pop out of his head and he didn't blame him. Heck, *his eyes* had just about popped out of his head when he'd seen Candace.

"Easy, boy. It's just a cat. You're still the boss."

Logan returned to the living room, put a few more logs on the fire and stood above Candace, still wondering if he was imagining the whole thing. He was insanely tired, so it wouldn't be impossible for him to be dreaming, but…He reached down to stroke her hair from her face, smiling when she stirred slightly. There was no imagining that. Candace was on his sofa, asleep, and he wasn't going to waste any more time in joining her.

He sat on the edge of the sofa, gently scooped her and moved her across a little, then lay beside her, covering them both with the comforter and wrapping one arm around Candace. The feel of her body, the smell of her perfume, the softness of her hair against his face— they were things he'd tried to commit to memory and been so worried he'd forget.

Logan wanted to lie awake, or even better wake Candace up so he could find out what on earth she was doing back in Australia, but the desire to sleep was too strong to ignore. He relaxed his body into hers and shut his eyes, letting slumber find him. Tomorrow he could ask her all about it. Tonight, he was just going to enjoy having her beside him and falling into the sleep he'd been craving for hours. And after all the therapy he'd gone through, the therapy he'd finally admitted to needing, he was at least confident that he wouldn't hurt her.

Candace had the strangest feeling that she couldn't breathe. In her dream, there was something stuck on her chest, pressing her down, but when she opened her eyes the panicked feeling almost immediately washed away. *Logan.* Light was filtering into the room, so she knew it was early, which meant he must have arrived in the night and found her asleep.

She wriggled to move his arm down, the weight of it across her chest too heavy, and then turned on her side to stare at him. She had no idea what he was going to say or how he was going to react, and the idea of telling him what she'd done absolutely terrified her, but she was going to do it. *Fear was no longer going to stop her from doing what her heart told her was right.*

Candace touched one hand to Logan's cheek, trailing her fingers across his skin. He hadn't shaved for at least a day, so the stubble was rough against her fingertips. It took every inch of her willpower not to trace the outline of his lips, parted and full in slumber. But what was even more amazing was that they'd both slept—he hadn't woken like he had every other time she'd spent the night with him.

"Now that you've woken me, you'd better kiss me," Logan mumbled, eyes still shut.

She smiled, not surprised he'd tricked her and been awake, but she also did as she was told. Candace wriggled closer to him, their bodies intertwined, slowly touching her lips to his in a kiss so sweet it made her sigh. Logan's mouth moved slowly, lazily, against hers, like he was still half asleep, and it suited her fine to start things out slow, to just enjoy being this close to the man she'd thought of constantly since the day she'd left him.

"Now that's what I call a nice way to wake up," he mumbled.

Candace kissed him again, not so gently this time, one hand snaking around his neck and running through his hair as she pulled herself closer to him.

"Mmm, this morning just keeps getting better and better."

She pulled away only to look at him, to see if he'd opened his eyes, and he had.

"Hey," she said, staring into his hazel brown gaze.

"Hey," he said straight back, stretching his legs out and then slinging one over hers.

"Were you surprised to find me here?"

Logan chuckled. "Surprised would be putting it mildly."

She had no idea what he was thinking, but he hadn't exactly been opposed to her kisses, and he *had* cuddled up to her on the sofa while she was sleeping, which told her that he obviously wasn't unhappy to find her.

"I guess I should have called ahead first, huh?"

He raised an eyebrow. "It would have stopped me

from almost having a heart attack and thinking squatters were in my house."

"Sorry," she said, starting to wonder whether she had been crazy to just move in while he was away, without asking him.

"Then again, being exhausted and actually sleeping through an entire night with you by my side was worth the near-death experience."

Candace sat up, wanting to tread lightly with what she was about to say. "Logan, I can't believe you slept the whole night without…"

"Freaking out and having my terrors," he finished for her. "Yeah, it looks like I did."

She lay back down again, this time covering his chest, her cheek flat to his body.

"I can't believe it."

"Well, believe it," he said, rubbing her back. "You've changed me, Candace, in more ways than I'd like to admit. Because I finally got the help I needed."

She listened to him take a deep breath, his expression serious. "The way I reacted the other night when you confronted me," he started.

"Was a knee-jerk reaction to being pushed too hard," she interrupted, the kindness in his eyes making her want to just hold him and never let go. "I should have known that it wasn't something you could be pushed into dealing with."

"But pushing was exactly what I needed," he told her, stroking her cheek. "I was being pigheaded, and I owe you an apology."

"Can I tell you something?" she asked.

"Of course."

"I want to explain why I was so scared of you the other night," she started.

Logan frowned. "Because I understandably scared the crap out of you?"

She gave him a half smile, nestling in closer to him. "No, because the last man I was with, the one I thought was different than the rest because he wasn't interested in my fame or my money, he…"

Logan touched her hair, left his hand there and waited for her to continue.

"He was my husband, Logan, and he hit me, and when I went to leave, to call for help, he grabbed me so tight around the throat that I thought he was going to strangle me."

It was as if all the blood had drained from Logan's face when she glanced up at him.

"So when I struck out at you…"

Candace grabbed his hand and touched his fingers to her cheek. "You didn't even make a bruise here, Logan, but yeah, when I woke up to you going crazy it really scared me. Kind of brought a heap of memories back that I've been trying to forget. It was just all too much, one nightmare too many."

"No wonder we get on so well," he said, refusing to react to what she'd told him, to get angry when there was nothing he could do about what had happened to her. "We're both kind of screwed up about the past, huh?"

"I guess you could say that," she muttered, closing her eyes as he leaned down to kiss her. "I've met a lot of men that seemed so right at the start, but with every relationship that's failed, it's just made it so hard for me to trust in anyone. Because it's not just men who've used me, or tried to, it's been so-called friends, too."

"So you being here?" he asked.

Candace shut her eyes, knowing she needed to tell him what her being here actually meant. That she hadn't just flown in for a few days, that this was a whole lot more permanent than that. *If he'd have her.* That all she'd done since she'd left was think of all the reasons why she shouldn't have lost her temper with Logan, why she needed to take a leaf out of her own book and open up to him, to talk to someone about her past and why it haunted her so badly.

"Logan, I kind of took a risk just turning up like this, but something you said to me, something we talked about, just kept running through my mind after I'd left."

He was watching her intently, waiting for her to continue.

"I'm not just here for another vacation," she admitted.

"I kind of guessed that when I found one of your cats on my bed," Logan told her, his grin telling her that he knew exactly what was going on.

"When you said that if we lived in the same country, if we'd met at a different time or place, that things could have worked out between us…" She paused. "Did you mean it?"

He sighed and stroked her hair. "Of course I meant it."

"So, does the fact that I kind of just moved to Australia mean…" Candace stopped talking, knowing he knew exactly what she was trying to say to him.

Logan sat up, back against the armrest of the sofa. "You mean to say that while I was away working, you flew halfway across the world with your cats in tow to move into my house and surprise me?" He paused. "And forgive me?"

Candace's face flushed, the heat rising up her neck and into her cheeks. "When you put it like that you make me sound like a crazy person."

"You," he said, pulling her against him so she was firm to his chest, "are not a crazy person."

"So you do want me here?" she mumbled.

"Yes, I want you here," Logan said, squeezing her and dropping a kiss into her hair. "You and your crazy cats will always have a home here, Candace. Always."

From the moment she'd walked through the door with all her things, Candace had started to worry. What had seemed like such a great idea back in L.A. had seemed stupid and childish once she'd arrived, but having Logan by her side, seeing the look on his face when he'd woken with her in his arms, had made everything okay. It was the first time she'd ever taken a risk, except for the time her mom had forced a record label executive to listen to her songs, and both times they'd changed her life for the better.

"So now that you're here, are you going to be my barefoot housewife, cooking me three meals a day and tending to my every need?" Logan joked.

Candace laughed. "You wish, soldier. You wish."

Ranger came over and poked his head between them,

looking for some affection, and Candace stopped touching Logan and ran her hand across the dog's fur instead. She couldn't believe that after a lifetime of being scared of large dogs, she'd warmed to Logan's big canine so quickly.

"Poor boy was traumatized by your cats last night," Logan told her.

"Sorry, Ranger," she cooed. "Those mean old cats might try to take over, but you stand firm, okay?"

They sat in silence for a long while, Candace stroking Ranger's head and Logan running his fingers gently through her curls.

"I don't want to ruin the moment, but have you really thought about what it'll be like living here, when you're so used to such a, well, a glamorous lifestyle?" Logan asked. "And just because I've started to get help doesn't mean we aren't going to hit a few road bumps along the way." He paused. "I did dream last night, Candace, but it wasn't as bad and I was able to deal with it. To pull myself out of it somehow and use you to push the memories away and fall back asleep."

Candace's heart started to beat faster.

"So have you really thought this through?" he asked again.

Yes, it was *all* she'd thought about when she was trying to figure out whether moving was a good idea or not, but at the end of the day, she knew that having a partner in life was way more important than anything else. Her success as a recording artist wasn't going to keep her warm in bed at night, or give her someone to confide in and travel with, to start a family with. And the fact that Logan had actually done something about his terrors? That just made her decision seem all the more *right*.

"Logan, I've been performing for eight years now, and even though I love it, I don't think it's enough anymore."

"And you're sure this is what you want, though?" he asked. "Don't get me wrong, I want you here, but I don't want you to look back in a few months, or even a few years, and wish you'd thought it through more."

"I want you," she said, taking her hand off Ranger and pressing it to his cheek, looking up into his eyes. "It might mean a change of pace, but I'm okay with that. I'm *ready* for that. Because I honestly believe that this is where I'm supposed to be."

Logan's eyes crinkled ever so slightly at the corners, his smile making her entire body tingle.

"Why do I feel like you have this all planned out?" he asked.

She laughed. "Well, it just so happens that I've had a lot of time to think this through."

Logan groaned but she kissed him to stop it. He ran his fingers down her back and hoisted her up on top of him, letting her sit on top but taking charge of her mouth.

"Don't you want me to tell you all my great ideas?" she asked, pulling back.

Logan leaned up, cupping the back of her head and forcing her back down, kissing her again.

"No," he mumbled when she fought against him again, laughing. "Just let me enjoy being with you for a while before you map my whole life out for me. Unless, of course, you've written a song about me?"

"Yeah. I called it 'Bodyguard'," she joked.

"Oh, really?"

"Logan!" she protested when he tried to flip her beneath him.

He stopped, rolling to his side and dragging her with him. "Fine, go on then. I can see we're not going to have any fun until you tell me all your plans."

Candace laughed, but he was right—she did have everything all planned out, because planning had been the only way she'd been able to convince herself to take a risk, follow her instincts, and move halfway across the world.

"I figured we could keep a place in town, so we're only a short flight away from the city when we want to head in, but we'd obviously spend most of our downtime here."

"When you say downtime?" he asked.

"I have a tour next year that I can't cancel, so I was thinking that you could be my bodyguard," she said. "You *and* Ranger."

"Oh, you were, were you?" Logan muttered.

"It'll be busy at times, and I'll have to go back to L.A. to record another album at some stage, because I've already signed for one more, but after that we can decide on what works for us both, together. What do you think?"

Logan was trying hard not to laugh. As Candace talked excitedly, she reminded him of a little bright-colored parrot chirping a million miles an hour. It was impossible not to smile just watching her talk so animatedly, but his gaze was constantly drawn to her mouth, those pillowy lips of hers his weakness.

"Logan?"

He switched his gaze back to her eyes. "What was the question?" Logan had no idea what she'd even been talking about at the end there, but whatever she'd said he was inclined to just agree.

"I said does all that sound okay with you? I don't want to sound like I'm trying to organize your life, but it's going to take a bit of juggling at the start."

Logan smiled at the worried expression on her face, trying to reassure her. "Sweetheart, so long as I have you by my side and I get to spend a decent chunk of the year here at home, I'm happy. Everything else we can figure out as we go."

He'd never been more pleased to have his life organized for him, especially now that he was confident he could deal with his past, that he'd received the help he needed. And help was only a phone call away now, so he didn't have to burden Candace with everything when he needed to talk through his night terrors some more.

"You're sure?" she asked, bottom lip caught between her teeth.

"I spent the past couple of weeks in a foul mood even though I promised you I'd think about you and smile," he told her honestly. "I couldn't believe that I'd finally met someone I could actually be with, who I wanted to be with, and I only got such a short time with her. Or that I'd acted like such a jerk when I should have been taking care of her."

Candace seemed to melt into him, her entire body relaxing at hearing his words.

"Really?"

"Really." Logan pushed her up a little and hooked a finger under her chin, tilting her face up so he could look into her eyes. "You're the best thing that has ever happened to me, Candace, and I will do whatever it takes to make this work."

"Me, too," she sighed.

Logan was about to kiss her, but he hovered for a moment. "You do realize that Ranger has to come everywhere with us, though, right? I promised him a retirement by my side, and after what he did for me on the tours we went on, I can't go back on my word."

"Okay, so you *and* your goofy dog."

Logan broke their kiss as soon as he'd started it. "Who you calling goofy? Ranger has…"

"I know how awesome your dog is," Candace said with a laugh. "So just shut up and kiss me, would you?"

Logan didn't need to be asked twice. He kissed Candace slowly, groaning when she raked her fingernails through his hair, forcing himself to take things slowly. Because there was no rush now—they had all day together, and the day after that. *The month after that.*

He might have lost a lot, seen things that he'd never forget and that would haunt him for the rest of his life, but now he had Candace. And for all the darkness of his past, he now had her like a shiny bright light beaming into his future. There was no way he was ever going to let her walk away again, not if he could help it.

"I love you," he whispered as she pulled back, looking up at him.

Candace had tears swimming in her eyes, but her smile told him they were happy tears.

"I love, too, Logan," she whispered back.

Logan shook his head as he pulled her in for another kiss. How he'd managed to end up with Candace Evans in his life, in his heart, he'd never know. But he sure wasn't complaining.

EPILOGUE

"Have I thanked you for being my bridesmaid?"

Jamie laughed, and Candace watched as she filled two spiraled glasses high with champagne.

"If you tell me one more time…"

"Sorry," Candace apologized, taking her glass and taking a nervous sip. "I just still can't believe that it's just the four of us here, that I'm about to get married."

"Stop," Jamie ordered, her hand closing over Candace's forearm. Her grip was light, but her intention was clear. "I don't want to see that panicked look in your eyes again, because I have no desire to chase you down the street if you go all runaway bride on me."

Candace took a deep breath, staring at her slightly shaking hand. "I just find it hard to believe that after so long, after everything, I'm standing here."

"Well, believe it," Jamie said, holding her glass high so they could touch them together. "I never believed that I would ever be with anyone ever again after my first husband died, but sometimes we just have to accept that things happen for a reason. Those men out there waiting for us?"

Candace nudged aside the blinds, searching for Logan. She saw his big silhouette almost immediately, sitting on the beach in just a pair of shorts. His skin was golden, his dark hair damp, off his face like he'd just run his fingers through it. She hoped he wasn't having any last minutes nerves, wasn't trying to devise a plan with Brett to make a run for it.

She pushed those thoughts away. It had been a year since she'd moved to Australia, and not once had Logan given her the impression that he was unhappy. It had been the best twelve months of her life.

"We're pretty lucky, huh?"

Candace blinked away the tears that had filled her eyes, wishing she didn't keep getting so emotional. Everything seemed to set her off these days—just the thought of standing in front of Logan and saying "I do" was enough to make her want to burst out crying.

"I was so lost when I met Logan, and he just took me under his wing like I was a broken bird in need of tender loving care. He healed me, Jamie," Candace said, tears now falling slowly down her cheeks. "I never thought anyone ever could, but he did it like it was the easiest thing in the world."

Jamie plucked a tissue and crossed the room to gently wipe her cheeks. "You know you saved Logan, too, don't you?"

Candace took the tissue and dabbed closer to her eyes and then her nose. "Logan was fine just the way he was. I was the fragile one."

She knew more than anyone else ever would that Logan had been suffering, that he'd been in so much pain from his past, but she also knew how strong he was. There wasn't a doubt in her mind that he'd have found a way to pull through and find happiness.

"No." Jamie shook her head, taking her own look out the window. "Logan has always been so good at hiding how he feels, making us all think he's okay, but the truth is that he's been hurting and alone for a long time. He didn't cope well when Brett and I told him we were together, and I'm not sure he's ever gotten over Sam's death, or what happened to his parents. Add his last tour to the Middle East into the mix?" Jamie sighed, before turning back around and reaching for her champagne flute. "We were worried about him. Until he met you."

Candace blinked away the last of her tears and sipped her drink to take her mind off everything. Deep down she knew that Jamie was right, but she was just so grateful for what Logan had done for her that it was hard to believe she could have done the same for him.

"I think we need to get dressed," she announced, putting her glass down and walking over to the wardrobe.

She opened the door and couldn't help the smile that spread across her face when she saw her dress. It was white, covered in the tiniest white jewels that caught the light like diamonds. Candace had already placed the same jewels in her hair, just a handful of them so they looked like raindrops against her blond curls, which were loose and tumbling around her shoulders.

"I still can't believe that you didn't even bring a makeup artist here," Jamie said with a laugh. "You're used to a whole entourage, and instead you've just got me."

"Well, believe it," Candace said, untying her robe and letting it fall to the floor so she was just standing in her underwear, before stepping into her dress. "The best thing we ever did was decide to come here, just the four of us. Although I'm sure we'll find out that there was a rogue long lens taking snaps of us when we get back."

"I don't care who takes a photo of me, I'm just in shock still that we're here," Jamie replied, zipping up the dress without having to be asked. "I still can't believe we have a butler just for our villa."

"It's Hayman Island, baby," Candace said with a drawl, imitating Logan when they'd first arrived. "Get used to living in the lap of luxury."

"And I will never stop thanking you for as long as I live. Seriously, I know you're used to the rich and famous lifestyle, but for us regular people, this is beyond incredible. It's the vacation of a lifetime for me."

Candace wriggled, getting her dress right, before spinning to look in the full-length mirror.

"Don't mention it. You deserved an amazing vacation, and for the record, I will never get used to coming to places like this. I still have to pinch myself." She sighed. "Besides, what fun would Logan and I have without you two? I foresee plenty of trips in the near future."

"Yes to that!"

Jamie took off her robe and slipped her dress on, and

Candace turned her back slightly to give her privacy until she felt her friend's hand on her arm.

"I think I also owe you thanks for letting me wear something beautiful. Last time I was bridesmaid I think the bride intentionally wanted to make us look terrible in case we stole the show!"

"Well, you do look beautiful," Candace told her, touching up her lip gloss before picking up the single, long-stemmed white tulip that had been resting on the bed.

They linked arms, took one final sip of champagne each, and stared at one another.

"Do you think they'll even be off the beach yet?"

Jamie laughed. "Sweetheart, those boys have spent all their adult lives in the military. There's not even a chance they'll be late to this."

Candace knew it was silly, and they only had to walk out the door and down the beach a little, but part of her was worried that Logan wasn't going to be there, that she'd just dreamed the past few months and reality was going to come crashing down.

"There he is."

Jamie's whispered words made Candace stop walking, clutching her friend's hand tight. She was right; he was there. Standing on the beach, barefoot, linen pants rolled up, wearing a half-buttoned loose white shirt and a smile that made her want to run into his arms.

"Oh, my gosh," she muttered, but the words just came out as one garbled sentence.

"Take a deep breath and just start walking."

Candace did as she was told, eyes locked on Logan's as they walked, even from this distance. She was aware that Brett was standing close to him, that there was a celebrant there, too, but all she could really see was the man she was about to marry. Tears welled in her eyes again, but she forced them back, wanting to bask in the happiness of being on an almost secluded beach, with the three people who'd grown to mean so much to her in only a year.

"I hope he knows how much I love him," she whispered to Jamie, still fighting the urge to run to him in case it *was* all a dream that she was about to wake up from.

"He does," she whispered back, "but tell him again anyway."

Logan took his eyes off Candace for a split second to glance at Brett.

"Do you think she's going to regret this? I mean, look at her."

"Sorry, mate. I only have eyes for the woman walking beside her," Brett said with a laugh. "But yeah, she probably will. I mean, you're just some commoner, right?"

Logan knew he should have waited, that he was supposed to stand with Brett until the girls reached them, but seeing Candace walk toward him was too much. He wanted her by his side, in his arms, and he wanted her now.

Thank God he was her bodyguard and had an excuse to be at her side all the time, because even seeing her walk alone made his protective instincts go into overdrive. He was so used to taking care of her when she was working that he couldn't stand to see her walking on her own.

"Where are you going?" Brett muttered as he left him.

Logan didn't bother answering, he just stared at Candace as he closed the distance between them, only stopping when he had his arms around her and his lips pressed to hers. Today was about telling the world she was his, that he was ready to be with her forever, and he was more than ready to stake his claim.

"Logan!" she exclaimed when he broke their kiss.

"What? I was impatient waiting down there."

He gave her a wink and took her hand, laughing at the eye roll Jamie gave him. Not that she could get away with teasing him after the way she behaved with Brett.

"You look absolutely beautiful, Candace," he told her, raising their hands to drop a kiss to hers. "And you, too, Jamie."

Jamie made a noise in her throat and joined Brett, and Logan kept hold of Candace's hand until they joined them. When they did, he took her other hand in his, so they were facing one another.

"Have I told you how much I love you?" Candace whispered, standing on tiptoe as she spoke into his ear.

"You can tell me those words as often as you like, because I will never tire of hearing them."

"Well, I do, and I'm so glad we decided to come here."

A noise made them both look up, and Logan gave the celebrant an apologetic smile.

"Can we just skip to the part where we say I do and I get to kiss the bride?" Logan joked. "No need to waste your time doing the entire ceremony."

Everyone laughed along with him, and he dipped his head for a sneaky kiss before their informal ceremony started. For a man who thought he'd never find happiness, would always be alone, life hadn't turned out half-bad. *In the end.*

"That," Logan said, kissing her mouth, "was," another kiss, "perfect."

Candace laughed, stretching out on the sun lounger before Logan held down her arms and lay down on top of her.

"Are you referring to our wedding or the amazing food?"

"Neither. I was talking about you and me being naked in the shower."

"Logan!"

"Honey, there's a reason we checked into a private villa. No one's going to tell me off for talking dirty with my wife, especially not at the per night price we're paying."

Candace swatted at him halfheartedly, at the same time as she stretched her neck out so he could kiss her. She groaned as his tongue darted out to trail across her skin, making every part of her tingle and think about exactly what they'd been doing in the shower only a short time ago.

"What you're doing to me right now definitely needs to stay private," she said with a laugh.

His hand skimmed her body, caressing her hip and running down her thigh.

"Logan!"

He raised his head, locking eyes with her. The stare he was giving her sent a shiver down her spine, a lick of pleasure that made her push Logan back up a little so she could run her hands down his bare chest. The physical reaction she had to her husband made it hard to concentrate on anything else when he was this close, and this bare, to her. But she wanted to tell him something that she'd been waiting all afternoon to share with him.

"Logan, there's something I want to give you."

He dropped a kiss to her lips before pushing up and moving back to lie on the lounger beside hers. The sun had almost completely faded now, but lying outside their villa was just as magical in the half-light as it was during the middle of the day.

"You do remember that we agreed on no gifts, right? This vacation is more than enough, for both of us."

Candace reached beneath the lounger, her hand connecting with a small box. She pulled it out and sat up.

"I promise that it cost less than twenty dollars, so you can't complain."

Logan's eyebrows pulled together, like he was trying to figure out what she could possibly have in the box. Her heart was racing, beating a million times a minute, her eyes never leaving Logan's. She still couldn't believe what she was about to tell him.

"Well, I would have guessed a snorkel or something

for our Great Barrier dive tomorrow, but that small? Hmm."

Candace passed the little box to him, wondering if she'd gone a little overboard by putting a bow around it. Maybe she should have just told him.

"Just promise me that you won't freak out," she mumbled.

Logan squeezed her hand, looking worried, as he reached for it. She looked at how tiny the little box was in his hand as he undid the bow and slipped the lid off.

"What...?"

She held her breath, barely able to even keep her eyes open as his face froze, recognition dawning.

"Is this what I think it is?" he asked.

Candace moved to sit beside her husband as he took the white plastic stick from the box as carefully as he would hold a broken bird, his eyes never leaving it. The pink word *pregnant* was bold, not something he could miss, although she got why he might not believe it straightaway.

"Logan?" she whispered.

He finally turned, the stick still in his hand. "We're having a baby?"

Logan's voice was deep, the emotion in his voice impossible to miss as he stared at her.

"It's very early still, but yeah," she replied. "We're having a baby."

He carefully put the test back in the box and put the lid back on, before slowly turning around and holding his arms out, pulling her against him.

"We're having a baby," he whispered, his lips against

the top of her head, kissing into her hair. "We're actually going to have a baby."

"Is that okay?" she whispered back, crushed against him.

"Hell, yes, that's okay!" he exclaimed, hands on her upper arms as he pushed her back, held her at arms' length. "Honey, aside from marrying you, this is the best thing that's ever happened to me. Honestly."

"Promise?" she asked, tearing up at listening to him say the words she'd been hoping to hear.

"I promise," he said straight back, lying down and pulling her on top of him so her body covered his. "Hand on my heart, I promise."

"At least we know why I've been so darn emotional," she joked.

"Come here, Mama," he said, yanking a strand of hair to make her lean down more.

"Logan!"

"Just shut up and kiss me," he demanded. "I only have, what, eight months of you to myself? That means I'm going to be making the most of every moment before I have to share you."

Candace crushed her mouth to Logan's, kissing him like she'd been deprived of his mouth for an eternity.

"So, you'd like more of that?" she asked, loving his hot breath against her skin, before touching her lips to his again and teasing him with her tongue.

"Yes," he murmured, "God, yes."

"Well, then, Mr. Murdoch, let's not waste a minute."

Candace shut her eyes, focused only on the feel of Logan's mouth pressed to hers, his hands as they roamed up under her dress, caressing her bare skin. They were alone on one of the most beautiful islands in the world, she was with the man of her dreams and very soon they'd have a family of their own.

Life couldn't get any better than this, and if it could, she didn't care. For her, this was perfection.

* * * * *

He'd promised himself to stay away from her, but the trail of her haunting fragrance drove him to follow her out the front door to the truck.

"What are you doing?" She sounded panicked.

Jarod ground his teeth. "Isn't it obvious? We have unfinished business, Sadie. While we're alone, now is as good a time as any to talk." He stretched his arm along the back of the seat, fighting the urge to plunge his hand into her silky hair as he'd done so many times in the past. "To pretend we don't have a history serves no purpose. What I'm interested to know is how you can dismiss it so easily."

"I've dismissed nothing!" Her voice was shaky. "But sometimes it's better to leave certain things alone. In our case it's one stone that shouldn't be turned."

"I disagree."

IN A COWBOY'S ARMS

BY
REBECCA WINTERS

MILLS & BOON

Published in Great Britain 2014
by Mills & Boon, an imprint of Harlequin (UK) Limited,
Eton House, 18-24 Paradise Road, Richmond, Surrey, TW9 1SR

© 2014 Rebecca Winters

ISBN: 978 0 263 91273 9

23-0414

Harlequin (UK) Limited's policy is to use papers that are natural, renewable and recyclable products and made from wood grown in sustainable forests. The logging and manufacturing processes conform to the legal environmental regulations of the country of origin.

Printed and bound in Spain
by Blackprint CPI, Barcelona

Rebecca Winters, whose family of four children has now swelled to include five beautiful grandchildren, lives in Salt Lake City, Utah, in the land of the Rocky Mountains. With canyons and high-alpine meadows full of wildflowers, she never runs out of places to explore. They, plus her favorite vacation spots in Europe, often end up as backgrounds for her romance novels, because writing is her passion, along with her family and church.

Rebecca loves to hear from readers. If you wish to e-mail her, please visit her website, www.cleanromances.com.

To Dr Shane Doyle of the Crow Nation in Montana
for his assistance with some aspects
of the culture you can't find in a book.

Chapter One

"Zane? I'm glad you called me back!"

Zane Lawson was the brother-in-law of Sadie Corkin's late mother, Eileen, and uncle of Sadie's half brother. The recently retired navy SEAL had just gone through a painful divorce, yet Sadie could always count on him.

"You sound upset," Zane said. "What's wrong?"

She picked up the Vienna sausage two-year-old Ryan had thrown to the floor and put it in the sink. Her half brother, who had clear blue eyes like his mother, thought he was a big boy and didn't like sitting in the high chair, but today she hadn't given him a choice.

"I got a call from the ranch a little while ago. My father died at the hospital in White Lodge earlier this morning."

Quiet followed for a moment while he digested the news. "His liver?"

"Yes."

"I thought he had years left."

"I did, too. But Millie said the way he drank, it was a miracle that diseased organ of his held up this long." Daniel Corkin's alcohol addiction had caught up with him at a young age, but the impact of the news was still catching up to Sadie. It had been eight years since she'd last seen him. She felt numb inside.

"With news like this, you shouldn't be alone. I'll drive right over."

"What would I do without you?"

"That goes both ways. Have you made any plans yet?"

She'd already talked to Mac and Millie Henson, the foreman and housekeeper on the Montana ranch who'd virtually raised Sadie after her parents' bitter divorce.

"We've decided to hold the graveside service at the Corkin family plot on Saturday. That's as far as I've gotten." She had a lot of decisions to make in the next five days. "I'll have to fly there on Friday."

"Rest assured I'll go to Montana with you so I can help take care of Ryan. See you in a couple of minutes."

"Thank you. Just let yourself in," she said before hanging up. No two-year-old could have a more devoted uncle than Zane.

Ryan had never got to meet his father, Tim Lawson. Tim had owned the software store where Sadie had been hired after she'd moved to San Francisco to be with her mother, Eileen, eight years ago.

Sometimes her mom dropped by the store to go to lunch with her and that's how Eileen had met Tim. It must have been fate because the two had fallen in love and married soon after. But Tim had died in a car accident while Sadie's mother was still expecting their baby. Tragically, Eileen had passed away during the delivery from cardiac arrest brought on by arrhythmia. Age and stress had been a factor.

Sadie suffered from the same condition as her mother. In fact, just before she'd left the ranch, she'd been advised to give up barrel racing and had been put on medication. If she ever married, getting pregnant would be a huge consideration no matter the efficacy of today's drugs.

Sadie had continued to work in sales for Tim's store even after new management had taken over. Since Eileen's death, however, and taking on full-time duties as a mother to Ryan, she worked for the store from home.

Tim's younger brother, Zane, had been a tower of strength, and the two of them had bonded in their grief over Tim and Eileen's deaths.

Zane knew the whole painful history of the Corkin family, starting with Sadie's great-grandfather Peter Corkin from Farfields, England. Due to depressed times in his own country, he'd traveled to Montana in 1920 to raise Herefords on a ranch he'd named after the town he'd left behind. When he'd discovered that Rufus Bannock, a Scot on the neighboring ranch who ran Angus cattle, had found oil, the Corkins' own lust for oil kicked into gear, but nothing had turned up so far.

Sadie's father, Daniel Corkin, had been convinced there was oil to be found somewhere on his eighty-five-acre ranch. His raging obsession and jealousy of the Bannock luck, coupled with his drinking and suspicions about his wife's infidelity, which were to-

tally unfounded, had driven Eileen away. When she'd
filed for divorce, he said he'd give her one, but she
would have to leave eight-year-old Sadie with him.

Terrified that if she stayed in the marriage he'd
kill her as he'd sworn to do, Eileen had given up custody of their daughter, forcing Millie Henson, the
Corkin housekeeper, to raise Sadie along with her
own child, Liz.

Zane also knew Mac and Millie Henson were
saints as far as Sadie was concerned, and she felt
she could never repay their goodness and devotion.

It was their love that had sheltered her and seen
her through those unhappy childhood years with an
angry, inebriated father who'd lost the ability to love.
The Hensons had done everything possible to provide
a loving family atmosphere, but Sadie had suffered
from acute loneliness.

Once, when she was fifteen, there'd been a mother-
daughter event at the school. Never really understanding how her mother could have abandoned her,
Sadie had been in too much pain to tell Millie about
the school function and had taken off on her horse,
Candy, not caring where she was going.

Eventually stopping somewhere on the range,
Sadie, thinking she was alone, had slumped forward
in the saddle, heaving great, uncontrollable sobs.
With only her horse to hear, she'd given way to her
grief, wondering if she might die of it.…

"WHAT'S SO TERRIBLE on a day like this?"

Sadie knew that deep voice. *Jarod Bannock*.

She lifted her head and stared through tear-drenched eyes at the striking, dark-haired eighteen-year-old. She knew two things about Jarod Bannock. One, his mother had been an Apsáalooke Indian. Two, every girl in the county knocked themselves out for his attention. If any of them had succeeded, she didn't know about it—although he was a neighbor, her family never spoke of him. Her father, whose hatred knew no bounds, held an irrational predjudice against Jarod because of his heritage.

"I miss my mother."

Jarod smiled at her, compassion in his eyes. "When I miss mine, I ride out here, too. This is where the First Maker hovers as he watches his creation. He says, 'If you need to contact me, you will find me along the backbone of the earth where I travel as I guard my possessions.' He knows your sadness, Sadie, and has provided you a horse to be your comfort."

His words sent shivers up her spine. She felt a compelling spirituality in them, different from anything she'd experienced at church with Millie.

"Do you want to see some special horses?" he asked her. "They're hard to find unless you know where to look for them."

"You mean, the feral horses Mac sometimes talks about?"

"Yes. I'll take you to them."

Having lost both parents himself, Jarod understood what was going on inside her better than anyone else. Wordlessly he led her up the canyon, through the twists and turns of rock formations she'd never seen before.

They rode for a good five minutes before he reined to a stop and put a finger to his lips. She pulled back on Candy's reins and waited until she heard the pounding of hooves. Soon a band of six horses streaked through the gulch behind a large, grayish tan stallion with black legs and mane. The power of the animals mesmerized her.

"You see that grullo in the lead? The one with the grayish hairs on his body?"

"Yes," she whispered breathlessly.

"That's his harem."

"What's a harem?"

"The mares he mates with and controls. Keep watching and you'll see some bachelor stallions following them."

Sure enough a band of eight horses came flying through after the first group. "Why aren't they all together?"

"They want control of Chief's herd so they can mate with his mares, but he's not going to give it to them."

She darted him a puzzled glance. "How do you know his name is Chief?"

"It came to me in a dream."

Sadie wasn't sure if Jarod was teasing her. "No it didn't." She started laughing.

The corner of his mouth twitched. It changed his whole countenance, captivating her. "He has a majestic bearing," he continued, "like Plenty Coups."

From her Montana history class she knew Chief Plenty Coups was the last great chief of the Crow Nation. "Where do these horses come from?"

"They've lived here for centuries. One day Chief will be mine."

"Is that all right? I mean, isn't it against the law to catch one of them?"

A fierce expression crossed his face. "I don't take what doesn't belong to me. Because he's young, I'll give him another two years to get to know me. He saw me today, and he's seen me before. He'll see me again and again and start to trust me. One day he'll come to me of his own free will and eat oats out of my hand. When he has chosen me for himself, then it will be all right."

Sadie didn't doubt he could make it happen. Jarod had invisible power. A short time ago she'd thought she was going to die of sorrow, but that terrible pain had been lifted because of him.

THAT WAS THE transcendent moment when Sadie's worship of Jarod Bannock began in earnest and she'd fallen deeply in love.

For the next three years Sadie had spent every moment she could steal out riding where she might run into him. Each meeting became more important to both of them. Once he'd started kissing her, they lived to be together and talked about marriage. Two days before her eighteenth birthday she rode to their favorite spot in a meadow filled with spring flowers—purple lupine and yellow bells. Her heart exploded with excitement the second she galloped over the rise near Crooked Canyon and saw him.

His black hair gleamed in the last rays of the sun. Astride his wild stallion Chief, he was more magnificent than nature itself. The stamp of his Caucasian father and Apsáalooke mother had created a face and body as unique as the two mountain blocks that formed the Pryor Mountains on both sides of the Montana-Wyoming border. Through erosion those mountains had risen from the prairie floor to eight thousand feet, creating a sanctuary for rare flora and fauna; a private refuge for her and Jarod.

She'd become aware of him as a child. As she'd grown older, she'd see him riding in the mountains. He'd always taken the time to talk to her, often going out of his way to answer her questions about his heritage.

His mother's family, the Big Lodge clan, had been part of the Mountain Crow division and raised horses. They were known as *Children of the Large-Beaked Bird.* Sadie never tired of his stories.

He told her about archaeological evidence of his ancestors in the area that dated back more than 10,000 years. The Crow Nation considered the "Arrow Shot Into Rock" Pryor Mountain to be sacred. Jarod had explained that all the mountain ranges in the territory of the Crow were sacred. He'd taught her so many things....

She looked around the meadow now. Two days before her birthday their talk had turned into a physical expression of mutual love. They'd become lovers for the first time under the dark canopy of the sky.

To be that close to another human, the person she adored more than life, filled her with an indescribable joy that was painful in its intensity. They'd become a part of each other, mind, heart and body.

She never wanted to leave him, but he'd forced her to go home, promising to meet again the next night so they could slip away to get married. He intended to be with her forever.

He pulled her against his hard body one more time, covering her face and hair in frenzied kisses. She was so hungry for him she caught his face in her hands and found his mouth.

After a few minutes he grasped her arms and held her from him. "You have to go home now."

"Not yet—" She fought to move closer to him, but he was too powerful for her. "My father will think I'm still at Liz's house studying for finals."

He shook his head. "We can't take any more chances, Sadie. You know as well as I do that with his violent temper your father will shoot me on sight if he finds out where you've been tonight. You need to go home now. Tomorrow night we'll leave for the reservation and be married. From then on you'll be known as Mrs. Jarod Bannock."

"Don't send me away," she begged. "I can't stand to be apart from you."

"Only one more night separates us, Sadie. Meet me here tomorrow at the same time. Bring your driver's license and your birth certificate. We'll ride over to the firebreak road where I'll have the truck and trailer parked. Then we'll leave for White Lodge.

"The next morning you'll be eighteen. We'll stop to get our marriage license. There'll be no waiting period. All you have to do is sign a waiver that you accept full responsibility for any consequences that might arise from failure to obtain a blood test for rubella immunity before marriage. That's it. After that we'll drive to the reservation."

She'd gone to the reservation with him several times over the years and once with his sister, Avery. Everyone in his Crow family had made her feel welcome.

"Remember—you'll be eighteen. I've made all the preparations for our wedding with my uncle Charlo. As one of the tribal elders, he'll marry us. There'll be at least a hundred of the tribe gathered."

"So many!"

"Yes. Our marriage is a celebration of life. You'll be eighteen and your father will have no rights over you by then."

She stared into his piercing black eyes. "What about your grandparents?" Sadie had loved Ralph and Addie Bannock the moment she'd met them. "How do you think they really feel about us getting married?"

"You have to ask? They're crazy about you. I've already told them our wedding plans. They're helping me any way they can. Earlier today my grandmother told me she can't wait for us to be living under the same roof with them until we can build our own place. Don't forget they loved your mother and like to think of you as the daughter they were never able to have. Surely you know that."

The words warmed her heart. "I love them, too." Sadie shivered with nervous excitement. "You really haven't changed your mind? You want to marry me? The daughter of the man who has hated your family forever?"

"Your father has something wrong in his head, but it has nothing to do with you." His dark brows furrowed, giving him a fierce look. "I made you an oath." He kissed her throat. "I've chosen you for my wife. How could you possibly doubt I want to marry you after what we've shared?"

"I don't doubt it," she said, her voice trembling. "You know I've loved you forever. Having you as my husband is all I've ever dreamed about. Oh, Jarod, I love you so much. I can't wait—"

He caressed her hair, which cascaded to her waist, and then his hands fell away. "Tomorrow night we'll be together forever. But you've got to go while I still have the strength to let you go."

"Why don't we just leave for the reservation now?"

"You know why. You're still seventeen and the risk of getting caught is too great." Jarod reached into his pocket and pulled out a beaded bracelet, which he fastened around her wrist. "This was made by my mother's family. After the ceremony you'll be given the earrings and belt that go with it."

"It's so beautiful!" The intricate geometric designs stood out in blues and pinks.

"Not as beautiful as you are," he said, his voice deep and velvety soft. "Now you have to go." He walked her to her horse. Once she'd mounted, he climbed on his stallion and rode with her to the top of the hill. They leaned toward each other for one last hungry kiss. "Tomorrow night, Sadie."

"Tomorrow night," she whispered against his lips.

Tomorrow night. Tomorrow night. Tomorrow night. Her heart pounded the message all the way home.

REMEMBERING THAT NIGHT now, Sadie felt the tears roll down her face. Their love affair had turned into a disaster, permanently setting daughter and father against each other. She was forced to leave for California and never saw Jarod again. And the Hensons had been left to deal with their drunken boss until the bitter end. Guilt had swamped Sadie, but she'd had no choice except to leave the ranch to prevent her father from carrying out his threat to kill Jarod.

While her mind made a mental list of what to do first before she and Zane left for Montana, she hung up the phone and took a clean cloth to wash Ryan's face and hands. "Come on, sweetheart." She kissed his light brown hair. "Lunch is over. Time for a nap."

While she changed his diaper, she looked out the upstairs window of the house she'd lived in with her mother and Tim on Potrero Hill. The view of San Francisco Bay was spectacular from here.

But much as she loved this city where her mother had been born and raised—where she'd met Daniel when he'd come here on business—Sadie was a Montana girl through and through. With her father's death, her exile was over. *She could go home.*

She longed to be back riding a horse through the pockets of white sweet clover that perfumed the land in the spring. Though she'd made friends in San Francisco and had dated quite a bit, she yearned for her beloved ranch and her oldest friends.

As for Jarod Bannock, eight years of living away from him had given her perspective.

He was a man now, destined to be the head of the Bannock empire one day. According to Liz he had a new love interest. Obviously he hadn't pined for Sadie all these years. And she wasn't a lovesick teenager who'd thought her broken heart would never heal after her father's treachery against Jarod. He'd been the one behind the truck accident that had put Jarod in the hospital. But that was ancient history now. She was a twenty-six-year-old woman who couldn't wait to take her half brother back to Farfields Ranch where they belonged.

Ryan might end up being her only child, which made him doubly precious to her. One day Ryan Corkin Lawson would grow up and become head of the ranch and make it a success. In time he'd learn how to do every chore and manage the accounts. She'd teach him how to tend the calves that needed to be culled from the herd.

That had been Sadie's favorite job as a young girl. The sickly ones were brought to the corral at the side of the ranch house. Sadie had named them after the native flora: yellow bell, pussytoes, snowberry, pearly. Ryan would love it!

Before she left his room, she hugged and kissed the precious little boy. While she waited for Zane, she went into the den and phoned the Methodist Church in White Lodge, where she and her mother had once attended services.

In a few minutes she got hold of Minister Lyman, a man she didn't know. Together they worked out the particulars about the service and burial. The minister would coordinate with the Bitterroot Mortuary, where the hospital would transport her father's body.

To the minister's credit he said nothing negative about her father. He only expressed his condolences and agreed to take care of the service. After thanking him, she rang off and sat at the computer to start writing the obituary. She could do everything online. Within a couple of hours the announcement would come out in the *Billings Gazette* and *Carbon County News*. How should she word it?

> *On May 6, Daniel Burns Corkin of Farfields Ranch, Montana, passed away from natural causes at the age of fifty-three after being the cruelest man alive.*

Too many words? On second thought why not make it simpler and put what the munchkins sang when Dorothy arrived in Oz.

> *"Ding Dong! The Wicked Witch is dead!"*

"HEY, BOSS."

"Glad you came in the truck, Ben. I need you to get this new calf to one of the hutches before a predator comes after it. She has a broken foot from being stepped on." There was no need to phone Liz Henson, White Lodge's new vet. Jarod's sister, Avery, could splint it. "Would you help me put her in the back?"

"Sure." Together they lifted the calf, careful not to do any more damage, but the mother bellowed in protest.

"I know how you feel," Jarod said over his shoulder. "Your baby will be back soon."

Ben chuckled. "You think she understands you?"

"I guess we'll find out the answer to that imponderable in the great hereafter." Jarod closed the tailgate and then shoved his cowboy hat to the back of his head, shifting his gaze to the new foreman of the Hitting Rocks Ranch. The affable manager showed a real liking for his sister, but so far that interest hadn't been reciprocated. Ben needed to meet someone else. "You were going to tell me something?"

"Avery sent me to find you. I guess your phone's turned off."

"The battery needs recharging. What's up?"

"She wanted you to know Daniel Corkin died at White Lodge Hospital early this morning of acute liver failure."

What?

Jarod staggered in place.

Sadie's monster father had really given up the ghost?

"The Hensons were with him. They got word to Liz and she phoned Avery."

The news he hadn't expected to come for another decade or more sent a great rushing wind through his ears, carrying painful whispers from the past that he'd tried to block out all these years. They came at him from every direction, dredging up bittersweet memories so clear they could have happened yesterday.

But Jarod managed to control his emotions in front of Ben. "Appreciate you telling me." After a pause he said, "If Avery can't tend to the calf, I'll call Liz. You go on. I'll follow on my horse Blackberry."

Ben nodded and took off.

Long after the truck disappeared, Jarod stood in the pasture to gentle the calf's mother, adrenaline gushing through his veins. Sadie would show up long enough to bury her father. Then what?

He threw his head back, taking in the cotton-ball clouds drifting across an early May sky. With Sadie's mother buried in California, it no doubt meant the end of Farfields. Sadie hadn't stepped on Montana soil in eight years. The note he'd received in the hospital after his truck accident when she'd left the ranch had been simple enough.

Jarod,
You begged me to consider carefully the decision to marry you. I have thought about it and realize it just won't work. I'm going to live with my mother in California, but I want you to know I'll always treasure our time together.
Sadie.

For eight years Jarod had done his damnedest to avoid any news of her and for the most part had succeeded. *Until now...*

By the time he rode into the barn, twilight was turning into night. He levered himself off Blackberry and led him into the stall.

"You're kind of late, aren't you?"

Jarod couldn't remember when there wasn't a baiting tone in Ned's voice. Out of the corner of his eye he saw the youngest of his four cousins walking toward him. Ned's three siblings were good friends with Jarod.

He scrutinized Ned, who was a year younger than him. Even that slight age difference upset Ned, but the rancor he felt for Jarod ran much deeper for other reasons. They were both Bannocks and lived in separate houses on the Hitting Rocks Ranch, but the fact that Jarod's mother had been a full Crow Indian was an embarrassment to the bigoted Ned. He liked to pretend Jarod wasn't part of the Bannock family and took great pleasure in treating him like a second-class citizen.

Ned was also still single and had always had a thing for Sadie Corkin, feelings that were never reciprocated. "It took me longer than usual to check out the new calves. How about you? Were you able to get the old bale truck fixed today or do we need to buy a new one?"

"If it comes to that, I'll talk it over with my dad."

Grant Bannock, Jarod's uncle, was a good man. But he had his hands full with Ned, who'd been spoiled most of his life and did his share of drinking. Jarod often had to keep a close eye on him to make certain he got his chores done. Not even Tyson Bannock, Ned's grandfather and Ralph's brother, could control him at times.

Ned had always dreamed of marrying Sadie Corkin and one day being in charge of both ranches. But that dream was in no one's interest but his own. Ralph Bannock, Jarod's grandfather, was the head of the ranch and his closeness to Jarod was like pouring salt on Ned's open wound.

Jarod patted the horse's rump before turning to his cousin. "Was there something else you wanted?"

Ned had looped his thumbs in the pockets of his jeans and stared at Jarod, who at six foot three topped him by two inches. Jarod saw a wild glitter in those hazel eyes that felt like hatred, confirming his suspicions that this encounter had to do with the news Ben had brought him earlier. Now that Sadie would be coming back for the burial, Ned wanted Jarod out of the picture.

"I thought you should know old man Corkin kicked the bucket early this morning."

Jarod didn't bother telling his cousin he was way ahead of him.

"If I were you," Ned warned, "I wouldn't get any ideas about showing my face at the funeral since he hated your guts." Jarod noted the heightened venom in his voice.

There'd been a lot of hate inside Daniel that had nothing to do with Jarod. In that regard Sadie's father and Ned had a lot in common, but no good would come of pointing that out to his cousin.

Jarod's uncle Charlo would describe Ned as an "empty war bonnet." The thought brought a faint smile to his lips. "Thanks for the advice."

Ned smirked. "No problem. Because of you there's been enough tension between the Corkins and the Bannocks. Or maybe you're itching to start another War of the Roses and manipulate your grandfather into buying Farfields for you. To my recollection that battle lasted a hundred years."

"I believe that was the Hundred Years War." Ned's ridiculous plan to acquire Sadie and the Corkin ranch in the hope oil could be found there was pitiable. "The War of the Roses lasted thirty years and the Scots only triumphed for ten of them. If my grandmother were still alive, we could check the facts with her."

Addie Bannock loved her history, and Jarod loved

hearing what she could tell him about that part of his ancestry.

Even in the semidarkness of the barn, he detected a ruddy color creeping into Ned's cheeks. For once his cousin didn't seem to have a rebuttal.

"Do you know what's important, Ned? Daniel's death puts an end to any talk of war between the two families, for which we can all be grateful. I have a feeling this news will bring new life to both our grandfathers. Those two brothers are sick to death of it. Frankly, so am I. Good night."

As he walked out of the barn, Ned's last salvo caught up to him.

"If you think this is over, then you're as *loco* as Charlo." It sounded like a threat.

Jarod kept walking. Daniel Corkin's death had shaken everyone, including his troubled cousin Ned.

Chapter Two

"…And so into Your hands, O merciful God, we commend Your servant Daniel Burns Corkin. Acknowledge, we humbly beseech You, a sheep of Your own fold, a lamb of Your own flock, a sinner of Your own redeeming. Receive Daniel into the arms of Your mercy, into the blessed rest of everlasting peace, and into the glorious company of those who have gone before. Amen."

After the collective "amens," Minister Lyman looked at Sadie before eying the assembled crowd. She hadn't noticed the people who'd attended. In fact, she hadn't talked to anyone yet.

"While they finish the work here, Daniel's daughter, Sadie Corkin, and the Hensons, who've worked for Daniel all these years and are like a second family to Sadie, invite all of you back to the ranch house for refreshments."

The house, with the extraordinary backdrop of the Pryor Mountains, was only a two-minute walk from the family plot with its smattering of pine trees. Sadie had already ordered a headstone, but it wouldn't be ready for a few weeks.

She felt an arm slip around her shoulders. "Let me take Ryan for you so you can have some time alone."

When she looked up she saw Liz Henson, her dearest, oldest friend. They'd been like sisters growing up. Even while Liz attended vet school at Colorado State, they'd stayed in close touch. "Are you sure?"

"Of course I am." Liz kissed Ryan's cheek. "Since you flew in yesterday, we've been getting to know each other, haven't we?" She plucked him out of Sadie's arms. "Come with me, little baby brother, and I'll get you something to eat."

At first he protested, but eventually his voice grew faint. Liz had a loving way about her. Sadie knew he was in the best of hands.

Zane walked up to her. She saw the compassion in his blue eyes. "It was a lovely service. Your father is being laid to rest with all the dignity he would have wanted."

"He wanted Mother with him, but I'm glad she's buried with Tim. He brought her the joy she deserved in this life."

"You brought her joy the day you were born, and she'd be so proud you're raising Ryan. I plan to help you any way I can. I hope you know that."

"You're a wonderful man, Zane. Ryan is so lucky to have you in his life."

"He's a little Tim."

"I know. Those dimples get to me every time," she told him, smiling.

"Yup. Don't forget he's my life now, too!"

"As if I could forget."

Zane, she knew, had reached an emotional cross-

roads in his life and was still struggling to find himself.
There'd been so many losses in his life, her heart went
out to him. Thank heaven they had Ryan to cling to.

The afternoon sun caused Zane to squint. "Everyone's gone inside the house. I'm going to help Liz. If
you need us, you know where to find us."

She nodded. The mortuary staff was waiting for
her to leave so they could lower the casket and finish
their part of the work, but she couldn't seem to get up
from the chair they'd brought for her. Since the phone
call from Millie five days ago, her life had been a blur.
She barely remembered the flight from San Francisco
to Billings, let alone the drive in the rental car with
Zane and Ryan to the ranch. Someone could use her
for a pin cushion and she wouldn't feel a thing.

Sadie counted a dozen large sprays of flowers
around the grave site. Such kindness for a man who'd
made few friends humbled her. The huge arrangement
with the gorgeous purple-and-white flowers kept at-
tracting her attention. For as long as she could remember that color combination had been her favorite.

Needing to know who'd sent the floral offering,
she stood and walked around to gather the cards.
She recognized every name. So many people who'd
touched their lives and had loved her mother were still
here offering to help in any way they could. When
she pulled out the insert from the purple-and-white
flowers, her breath caught.

Sadie,
Your mother and father's greatest blessing. Let
this be a time for all hearts to heal.

*Love, Ralph Bannock and all the Bannocks—
including the good, the bad and the ugly. Hope
you haven't forgotten I'm the ugly one.*

She could hear Ralph saying it. He could be a great
tease and she'd forgotten nothing.

A laugh escaped her lips as she put the cards in
the pocket of her suit jacket. How she'd loved and
missed him and Addie! Sadie had sent purple-and-
white flowers when Addie had passed away, and
today he'd reciprocated. She would have come for
his wife's funeral if there'd been any way possible,
but fear of what her father would do to Jarod if she
came back had prevented her from showing up.

There could have been so much loving and happiness in her family, but her father's demons had put
them through years of grief that affected the whole
community. Suddenly she was sobbing through the
laughter.

Needing to hide, Sadie hurried over to the grand-
daddy pine where she used to build nests of pine nee-
dles beneath its branches for the birds. She leaned
against the base of the trunk while she wept buckets.
How was she going to get through today, let alone
tomorrow?

Her father's flawed view of life, his cruelty, had
occupied so much of her thinking, she didn't know
how to fill that negative space now that he was gone.
She felt flung into a void, unable to get her bear-
ings. And then she heard a male voice behind her. A
voice like dark velvet. Only one man in this world
sounded like that.

"Long ago my uncle Charlo gave me good advice. Walk forward, and when the mountain appears as the obstacle, turn each stone one by one. Don't try to move the mountain. Instead, turn each stone that makes up the mountain."

Jarod...

She hadn't heard that voice since her teens, but she'd recognize it if it had been a hundred years ago. His sister, Avery, had once told Sadie he was known in the tribe as "Sits in the Center" because he was part white and straddled two worlds of knowledge.

Since he'd just picked up on Sadie's tortured thoughts, she couldn't deny he had uncanny abilities. But too many years had passed and they were no longer the same people. The agony of loss she'd once felt had been replaced by a dull pain that had never quite gone away. Wiping the moisture off her cheeks with the backs of her hands, she turned to face him.

He was a twenty-nine-year-old man now, tall and muscled, physical traits he'd inherited from his handsome father, Colin Bannock. But the short hair she remembered was now a shiny mane of midnight-black, caught at the nape with a thong. His complexion was bronzed by the sun and she picked out a scar near the edge of his right eyebrow she hadn't seen before. No doubt he'd received that in the truck accident that left him unconscious.

He wore a dark dress suit with a white shirt, like the other men, but there was something magnificent about his bearing. The powerful combination of his Crow and Bannock heritage meant no man was Jarod's equal in looks or stature.

She sensed a new confidence in him that had come

with maturity. The coal-black of his piercing eyes beneath arched brows the same color sent unexpected chills down Sadie's spine.

The whole beautiful look of him caused her to quiver. Once she'd lain in his arms and they'd made glorious love. Did he ever think about that night and their plans to marry the day she turned eighteen?

After she'd fled to California, she'd prayed he would ignore the words in her note and call Millie. Once he'd left the hospital and got her number in California from the housekeeper, she'd expected his call so she could explain about the traumatic episode at the ranch with her father.

But Jarod hadn't called Millie, and there had been no word from him at all. Learning that he was out of the hospital and on his feet again, she'd prayed she would hear from him. But after a month of waiting, she'd decided he really was relieved they hadn't gotten married, so she hadn't tried to reach him.

That's when she'd given him another name: *Born of Flint*. The Crow nation referred to the Pryor Mountains as the Hitting Rock Mountains because of the abundance of flint found there, which they chipped into sharp, bladelike arrowheads. Jarod's silence had been like one of those blades, piercing her heart with deadly accuracy.

"It's good to see you again, Sadie, even if it's under such painful circumstances," he said. "Ned warned me not to show up, but my grandfather's been ill and asked me to represent him."

And if he hadn't asked you, Jarod, would you still have come?

"He's too tired to go out. Do you mind?"

Did she mind that Jarod's unexpected appearance had just turned her life upside down for the second time?

"Of course not. Liz told me Ralph has suffered re-curring bouts of pneumonia. I love him. Always have. Please tell him the flowers he sent are breathtaking." She plucked a white-and-purple flower from the ar-rangement and handed them to him. "These are from me. Tell him I'll come to see him Tuesday evening. By then I'll be more settled."

He grasped the stems. "If I tell him that, then you have to promise you won't disappoint him. He couldn't take it."

She sucked in her breath. *You mean the way you disappointed me after you said you would always love me? Not one word or phone call from you in eight years about my note? Surely you knew there had to be a life and death reason behind it.*

"Sadie?"

Another voice and just in time.

She tore her gaze away from Jarod. Zane was walking toward her, holding a fussy Ryan. "Here she is, sport." The moment he put the little boy in her arms, Ryan calmed down. This child was the sunshine in her life.

Zane smiled at them. "He was good for a while, but with all those unfamiliar faces, he missed you."

Sadie clung to her baby brother, needing a buffer against Jarod, who stood there looking too splendid for words. She finally averted her eyes and kissed Ryan. "I missed you, too." She cleared her throat, realizing she'd forgotten her manners. "Zane Lawson, have you met Jarod Bannock, our neighbor to the east?"

He nodded. "Liz introduced us."

At a loss for words in the brief silence that followed, Sadie shifted Ryan to her other arm. "I'm sorry I left you so long, sweetheart. Come on. There are a lot of people I need to thank for coming."

She glanced one last time at Jarod over Ryan's head. "It's been good to see you, too, Jarod," she lied. Her pain was too great to be near him any longer. "Thanks for the wise counsel from your uncle Charlo. In truth I *have* come back to a mountain. Getting through the rest of this day will be like turning over that first stone."

As Jarod grimaced, Sadie hugged her brother harder. "Please give Uncle Charlo my regards the next time you see him. I always was a little in awe of him."

AFTER EIGHT YEARS Jarod finally had his answer. She'd meant every word in the note she'd sent him. *Not one phone call or letter from her in all that time.* It appeared the sacred vow he'd made to her hadn't touched her soul.

Gutted by feelings he'd never experienced before, he watched the three of them walk back to the house. They looked good together, at ease with each other. Comfortable. Just how comfortable he couldn't tell yet. Was there something in the genes that attracted the Corkin women to the Lawson brothers?

But the girl he remembered with the long silky blond hair hanging almost to her waist was gone.

Except for her eyes—Montana blue like the sky—
everything else had changed. Her mouth looked
fuller. She'd grown another inch.

Blue jeans and a Western shirt on a coltish figure had been replaced with a sophisticated black suit
that outlined the voluptuous curves of her body. The
gold tips of her hair, styled into a windblown look,
brushed the collar of a lavender blouse. And high
heels, not cowboy boots, called his attention to her
long, beautiful legs.

There was an earthy element about her not ap-
parent eight years ago. He hadn't been able to identify it until she'd caught the towheaded boy in her
arms. Then everything clicked into place. She'd become a mother as surely as if she'd given birth. He'd
seen the same thing happen in the Crow clan—they
watched out for the adopted ones. The experience
defined Sadie in a new way. It explained the hungry
look in the uncle's eyes.

Jarod was flooded by jealousy, an emotion so for-
eign he could scarcely comprehend it, and the flowers meant for his grandfather dropped to the ground.
Not wanting to be seen, he stole around the side of the
ranch house and had almost reached his truck when
Connor caught up to him.

"Jarod? Wait a minute! Where's the fire?"

His head whipped around and he met his younger
brother's brown eyes. Connor had been through a
painful divorce several years ago, but his many steer
wrestling competitions when he wasn't working on
the ranch with Jarod had kept him from sinking into
a permanent depression. This past week he'd been

away at a rodeo in Texas, but after learning about Daniel, he'd come home for the funeral.

"Avery and I looked for you before the service."

"My flight from Dallas was late. I just got here. Come inside with me."

That would be impossible. "I can't, but Avery will be glad to see you got here."

Connor cocked his dark blond head in concern. "Are you all right?"

Jarod's lungs constricted. "Why wouldn't I be?"

"I don't know. You seem…different."

Yes, he was different. The passionate, stars-in-her-eyes woman who'd made him feel immortal had disappeared forever.

"I promised grandfather I wouldn't be long. He wants to hear about the funeral and know who attended. He has great affection for Sadie."

His brother nodded in understanding. "Don't we all."

"How's the best bulldogger in the state after your last event?" The question was automatic, though Jarod's mind was somewhere else, lost in those pain-filled blue eyes that had looked right through him.

"I'm not complaining, but I'll tell you about it later. Listen—as long as you're going back to the house, tell grandfather I'll be home as soon as I've talked to Sadie. How is she? It's been years since I last saw her."

A lifetime, you mean.

"She's busy taking care of her brother, Ryan." That shouldn't have made Jarod feel as if he'd been spirited to a different universe.

Connor shook his head. "It's incredible what happened to that family. Maybe now that Daniel's gone she'll have some peace. Avery told me on the phone she doesn't have a clue what Sadie's going to do now."

"I would imagine she'll go back to San Francisco with Ryan and his uncle."

Connor looked stunned. "Do you think the two of them are…?" He didn't finish what he was going to say.

"I don't know."

"He's old enough to be her father!"

"He certainly doesn't look it, but age doesn't always matter." The way her eyes had softened when she'd looked at Zane Lawson had sent a thunderbolt through Jarod. "Why don't you go inside and make your own judgment. I've got to leave. Grandfather's waiting."

"Okay. See you back at the house."

But once Jarod had driven home, he went straight to his room and changed into jeans and a shirt. Before he talked to his grandfather, who was still asleep according to his caregiver, Martha, Jarod needed to expend a lot of energy.

He'd made tentative plans to have dinner in town with Leslie Weston after the funeral. She was the woman he'd been dating lately, but he couldn't be with her right now, not after seeing Sadie again. He would have to reschedule with her. For the moment the only way to deal with his turmoil was to ride into the mountains. He'd take his new stallion up Lost Canyon. Volan needed the exercise.

Though he started out in that direction, midway

there he found himself changing course. After eight years of avoiding the meadow, he galloped toward it as if he were on automatic pilot. When he reached their favorite spot, he dismounted and slumped into the bed of wildflowers. Their intoxicating scent was full of her.

Jarod remembered that last night with her as if it was yesterday. After their time together, he'd followed her to make sure she reached the Corkin ranch safely. He'd felt great pride that she rode like the wind. She and Liz Henson had provided stiff competition for the other barrel racers around the county, until Sadie suddenly quit. When Jarod had asked her about it, she'd said it had taken too much time away from being with him.

When he could no longer see her blond hair whipping around her, he'd set off the long way home, circling her property to avoid being seen. But before he'd reached the barn he'd had the impression he was being followed.

IN A LIGHTNING move he turned Chief around and bolted toward the clump of pines where he'd detected human motion. As he moved closer he heard a curse before his stalker rode away, but Jarod had the momentum. He knew in his gut it was Ned. In half a minute he'd cut him off, forcing him to stop.

He looked at his cousin. "Where are you going in such an all-fired hurry this time of night?"

"None of your damn business."

"It's a good thing I knew it was you or I might have pulled you off Jasper to find out who's been keeping tabs on me. I would think you'd have better things to do with your time."

"You've been with Sadie." Ned's accusation was riddled with fury.

It was possible Ned had seen him and Sadie together tonight, but he decided to call his bluff, anyway. "If you know that for a fact, then why isn't my grandfather out here looking for me right now, waiting to read me the riot act? Wait, I've got an idea. Why don't you ride over to the Corkin ranch and ask Sadie to go for a midnight ride with you?"

When Ned said nothing, Jarod continued his taunting.

"Oh, I forgot. Her father forbid any Bannock to come near her years ago. Have you forgotten he vowed to fill us full of buckshot if he ever caught one of us on his property? Of course, if you can figure out a way to get past Daniel, you can see what kind of reception you'll receive from her."

"Damn you to hell," Ned snarled as Jarod headed for the barn in the distance.

Grandfather would be furious with him for baiting Ned. It was a mistake he shouldn't have made this close to leaving with Sadie, but his cousin had chosen the wrong moment to confront Jarod, who was too full of adrenaline not to react.

For two cents he'd felt like knocking him cold. Ned had been asking for it for years, always sneaking around to catch him with Sadie. No doubt he planned to tell Daniel in the hope Sadie's father would finish Jarod off. For his grandparents' sake, Jarod had never stepped on Corkin property and he'd held back his anger at Ned. But Ned's obsession with Sadie seemed to be getting out of control.

Worse, Jarod couldn't get that night years ago out of his mind.

Once he'd removed Chief's saddle and had brushed him down, he entered the ranch house and found his grandparents in the den. That was the place where they always talked business at the end of the day. It was time to put his plans into action.

Addie hugged him. "I'm glad you're home. You missed dinner. Are you all right?"

"Yes. Everything is set for our marriage. Thank you for standing behind me in this."

"If your father were still alive, he'd understand and approve. We know it's the Crow way to marry young. You're a lot like your dad and have always known what you wanted."

"I'm thankful for your understanding and help, but right now my biggest concern is Ned. He must have been following me tonight. In order for him not to find out what's going on, I'm setting up a smoke screen. I'll pretend Chief is favoring his hind leg.

"After chores tomorrow I'll put Chief in the trailer and drive him to the clinic in White Lodge. If Ned finds out I paid a visit to Sam Rafferty for an X-ray, it should throw him off the scent long enough for us to be married."

"That's as good an idea as any," his grandfather said. "We decided not to tell Connor and Avery your plans. It's crucial they know nothing so that Ned doesn't pick up on any change in their behavior.

He's a talker when he drinks and it could get back to Daniel."

Jarod nodded. "Where are they?"

Addie smiled. "Connor's in town with friends and Avery is spending the night with Cassie while they study for their finals. They'll be graduating from high school in two weeks."

"Sadie will be getting her diploma right along with them, but by then she'll be my wife. Here's what I'm going to do. After I leave the vet clinic, I'll drive up to the mountains where Sadie and I will meet. From there we'll go to the reservation to be married and spend a couple of days with Uncle Charlo and his family. We'll be home Sunday night in time for her to be back in school."

His grandfather got up from the chair and hugged him. "When you two arrive, we'll all celebrate."

Jarod's heart was full of love for his grandparents, who'd always supported him.

"Tell me what you need me to do before I leave tomorrow afternoon and I'll get it done."

"Why don't we go over the quarterly accounts after breakfast?" Ralph suggested.

"Sounds good."

He hugged his grandmother hard, then left the den and headed down the hall to the kitchen. After filling up on a couple of ham sandwiches and a quart of milk, he took the stairs two at a time to his bedroom at the top.

His watch said twenty after ten. At this time tomorrow night he'd be with Sadie on reservation property. He knew a private spot where they wouldn't be disturbed. They'd stay there until it was time to drive to White Lodge for their marriage license.

You're going to be a married man, Bannock.

If he had one regret it was that his siblings wouldn't be there. But when he brought Sadie home as his wife, they'd understand the measures he'd had to take to protect Sadie from her out-of-control father.

"So, Dr. Rafferty, you don't think there's a need to take an X-ray?" Jarod asked, walking Chief out of the trailer to the paddock behind the clinic with the vet.

"Not that I can see," Sam Rafferty told him.

"His limp does seem to be a lot better. Last night I was really worried about him."

"Horses aren't that different from people. Sometimes we wake up in the morning and everything hurts like hell. But the next day, we feel better."

"Well, I'll take your word for it nothing serious is wrong."

Sam nodded. "Give him a day of rest and see how he does."

"Will do. How much do I owe you?"

"Forget it. I didn't do anything."

"You can't make a living that way." Jarod put a hundred dollar bill in the vet's lab coat pocket. "Thanks, Doc."

"My pleasure." They shook hands before he led Chief back into the trailer and shut the door.

Jarod started the truck and drove his rig away from the clinic. Out of the corner of his eye he saw Ned's Jeep down the street across from the supermarket.

That was no coincidence—Ned must still be tailing him.

Twenty after five. The sun would set at nine. Jarod would have driven to the mountains immediately, but he couldn't do that with Ned watching him. It would only take a half hour to reach Sadie. He had three hours to kill. Might as well drive Ned crazy.

After making a U turn, he parked near the supermarket and went in to buy a meal at the deli. Then he took it out to the truck and sat there to eat while he listened to music. Ned had finally disappeared, but Jarod knew he was somewhere nearby watching, hoping to see Sadie show up and join Jarod. The fool could wait till doomsday but he'd never find her here.

The sun sank lower until it dropped below the horizon. It was time to make his move. His heart thudding in anticipation of making love to Sadie for the rest of their lives, Jarod started the truck and turned onto a road that would eventually lead to the fire road. From that crossroads you could either go to the mountains the back way or head the other way for the reservation.

But as he reached the crossroads, from out of nowhere, something rammed him broadside. The last thing he heard was the din of twisting metal before he passed out.

The next day he woke up in the hospital with a serious brain concussion, bruises and a nasty gash near his eye. Frantic, he tried to reach Sadie, but the report from the Hensons came back that she wasn't at home.

When he awoke a second time, the nurse brought him Sadie's note and read it to him. The words ripped him to pieces.

JAROD LAY IN the clover remembering the pain until Volan nudged him. Feeling as if his heart weighed more than his body, he climbed on the stallion and rode home.

Avery confronted him in the tack room after he returned. Her brunette hair and bright smile reminded him of their father Colin's second wife, Hannah. She'd been a wonderful mother to Jarod, never pushing him. Avery was a little more aggressive in that department.

"When you didn't come in the ranch house with Connor, I knew you'd gone riding. Did it help?" Her hazel eyes studied him anxiously.

She could read most of his moods, but he didn't answer her this time. There was no help for the disease he'd contracted eight years ago.

"Grandfather was hoping to talk to you."

"I know. I'll go see him now."

"He's gone to bed, but don't worry, Connor and I told him all we could. Great Uncle Tyson came to the funeral with his family. It was so strange, all of us together on Corkin land after so many years of being warned off the property. I think it overwhelmed Sadie. She thanked us for coming, but clung to her little brother the whole time."

Jarod's thoughts were black. "Did Ned behave?"

Her mouth tightened. "Does he ever?"

"Tell me what he did."

"He asked a lot of questions in such bad taste it raised the hairs on the back of my neck."

"Like what?"

At his rapid-fire question, his sister looked startled. "I was standing by them when he asked if she and Zane had an interest in each other besides Ryan. He said he hoped not because he was planning to spend a lot of time with her now that she was back."

Jarod bit down so hard he almost broke a tooth.

"It was appalling, but no one else heard him. Sadie didn't answer him, but I was so angry I broke in on their conversation. That angered Ned and caught Uncle Grant's attention. He wasn't thrilled with his son's behavior, either, and got him out of there as fast as he could."

"Ned gave me an ultimatum the other night."

"What kind?"

"Not to show up at the funeral."

"That's no surprise. He was jealous of you from birth. It only grew worse when grandfather gave you more responsibilities for running the ranch. Ned couldn't handle it. But when you and Sadie became friends, that killed him."

"There's a sickness in him."

"I know. Sadie was never interested in any of the guys chasing after her, least of all Ned. He used to wait for her after school and follow her as far as Corkin property. Sadie never paid him one whit of attention because the only guy she could ever see was *you*."

Until Jarod had planned to make her his wife. Then she'd run like the prong-horned antelope, putting fifteen hundred miles between them. Had his accident been the excuse she'd been looking for not to marry him?

"After today she'll like him even less, but I guess it doesn't matter," Avery added.

He closed his eyes tightly. "Why do you say that?"

"The chances of her having to deal with him are pretty remote. She's got a home in California and a little brother to raise."

"With Zane's help?" Jarod didn't want to listen to another word.

"Forget what you're thinking. I asked her outright if she was involved with Zane. She said no and was shocked at the question. I think it actually hurt her."

Jarod's relief had him reeling.

"I have to tell you I'm envious of her. Ryan's such an adorable boy, I wish he were mine."

Those were strong words. Jarod heard wistfulness in her voice and eyed her with affection. "Your time will come, Avery."

Her eyes darted him a mischievous glance. "Are you trying to make me feel better, or did you have a vision about your only female sibling who's getting older?"

Her teasing never bothered him. He rubbed his lower lip absently. "I don't need a vision to know you're not destined to be alone. Ben's been crazy about you ever since he was hired."

Avery rolled her eyes. "That has to work both ways, big brother. If anyone ought to know about that, it's you. You're pushing thirty and until two months ago you had no prospects despite the fan club you ignore. Am I wrong or at long last has a woman finally gotten under your skin? Leslie's an extraordinary person, the kind I've been hoping you would meet."

"You and grandfather." But Jarod was too conflicted over Sadie to get into a discussion about anything. She'd just inherited Farfields, a place she'd loved heart and soul. Jarod couldn't imagine her leaving the land where she'd been born. But he'd been wrong about her before. Maybe she was involved with another man in California.

When are you going to learn, Bannock?

Chapter Three

It was Tuesday morning. Sadie had slept poorly and got up before Ryan, who was sleeping in the crib Millie had used for Liz. Zane had been installed in the guest bedroom and was still asleep. Though she'd come to the ranch to bury her father and take stock of her new situation, seeing Jarod after all these years had shaken her so badly, she was unnerved and restless. Through her friendship with Liz, she knew he hadn't married yet, though that made no sense when he could have any woman he wanted.

But recently Liz had dropped a little bomb that over the past few months he'd been seeing an archaeologist working in the area named Leslie Weston. Liz seemed to think it was more serious than his other relationships had been.

Her breath caught. *Had they made love? Were they planning to marry?* Sadie couldn't bear thinking about it.

From her bedroom window she watched Liz leave the Hensons' small house adjacent to the ranch house and head for her truck. No doubt she was on her way to work at the Rafferty vet clinic in White Lodge.

Pretty soon quiet-spoken Mac followed and started out for the barn to get going on his chores.

With a deep sigh, Sadie turned away and headed for the bathroom. Once she'd showered and washed her hair, she pulled on jeans and a cotton sweater. After blow-drying her hair and applying lipstick, she felt more prepared to face this first day of an altered life and turn the second stone.

To stay busy she fixed breakfast, woke and dressed Ryan for the day and then returned to the kitchen. She piled some cushions on one of the kitchen chairs for Ryan as Zane joined them to eat. Before the day was out, she'd take her dad's pickup and run into White Lodge for a high chair and a new crib.

Though she had everything she needed back in California, it would take time to ship her things here. While she was at it, she'd also buy some cowboy boots and start breaking them in.

Millie appeared at the back door. The housekeeper still had a trim figure and worked as hard as ever to keep the ranch house running smoothly. Her brown eyes widened in surprise when she walked into the kitchen and found the three of them assembled there. "Good morning, Millie. Come on in and eat breakfast with us." It was long past time someone waited on her for a change.

The older woman kissed Ryan's head before sitting next to him. "I think I'm in heaven."

"Good. You deserve to be waited on." Sadie brought a plate of bacon, eggs and hash browns to the table for her.

No sooner had Sadie started to drink her coffee

than they heard a knock on the front door. She jumped up from the table. "That'll be Mr. Varney. I'll show him into the living room. He's here to talk about the will."

The attorney from Billings had come to the graveside service and told her he'd be by on Tuesday morning.

"I'll take care of Ryan," Zane offered.

"Thank you." She got up and kissed her little brother's cheek. "I'll be back soon."

She hurried down the hall to the front room of the three-bedroom L-shaped ranch house. The place needed refurbishing. According to Mac, in the last few years her father had been operating Farfields in the red. He'd ended up selling most of the cattle. Toward the end he'd been too ill to take care of things and there'd been little money to pay Millie and Mac. The value of the ranch lay in the land itself.

Reed Varney had put on weight and his hair had thinned since the last time she'd seen him. He must be sixty by now and had handled her father's affairs for years. The man knew all the ugly Corkin secrets, including the particulars of the divorce, which was okay with Sadie since it was past history.

"Come in, Mr. Varney." She showed him into the living room. A couple of the funeral sprays filled the air with a fragrance that was almost cloying. Mac had taken some of the other arrangements to their cabin. "Would you care for some coffee?"

"No thanks." For some odd reason he wouldn't look her in the eye. She had the impression he was nervous.

"Then let's sit to talk." She chose one of the leather chairs opposite the couch where he'd taken a seat. As he opened his briefcase to pull out a thin file she asked, "How soon do you want to schedule the reading of the will?" For all their kindness, Mac and Millie should head the top of the list to receive the house they'd been living in all these years. She couldn't wait to tell them.

He rubbed his hands on top of his thighs, another gesture that indicated he felt uncomfortable. Sadie started to feel uneasy herself.

"Something's wrong. What is it?"

After clearing his throat he finally glanced at her. "The will is short and to the point. You can read it now. The particulars are all there." He handed her the file.

She blinked. Maybe her father had been in more financial trouble than she'd been led to believe. Taking a deep breath, she started to read. After getting past the legal jargon she came to her father's wishes.

Mac and Millie Henson betrayed my trust on my daughter's eighteenth birthday. Therefore they'll receive no inheritance, nor will my daughter, whom I've disowned.

Over the years several people have wanted to buy the ranch, but so far they haven't met the asking price. I have their offers on record. If no one else makes an offer within a month of my death, then the ranch and all its assets including my gun collection will be sold to the

*highest bidder through Parker Realty in Bill-
ings, Montana. My horse, Spook, has been sold.*

*No furnishings are to be touched. The new
buyer will either use or dispose of them. Under
no circumstances can the ranch be sold to a
Bannock.*

Sadie gasped and jumped up from the chair. Her
father had lived to drink, hunt and hate the Bannocks
with a passion. The meanest man alive didn't begin to
describe him. Forget the fact that he'd disowned her.
When she'd left for San Francisco, she never dreamed
he'd take out his fury on the Hensons like *this*.

"Does this mean he's thrown Mac and Millie out
with nothing?" Her eyes filled with tears. "After all
they've done for him over the years? The care they
gave him toward the last?"

Varney eyed her with grave concern before nodding. "However, Mr. Bree at the realty firm has asked
that the Hensons stay on to manage things until the
new buyer takes ownership. It's entirely possible Mac
Henson will be asked to continue on as foreman for
the new owner."

Daniel had died nine days ago. In less than a
month from now the eighty-five-acre ranch would
be sold? She couldn't take it in. Her father wanted
her and the Hensons off his land as fast as humanly
possible. When he'd told her to get out eight years
ago, he'd meant for it to be permanent. "What is the
sale price?"

"Seven hundred thousand. He was in a lot of debt."

Her mind was madly trying to take everything in.

"What about me, Mr. Varney? Am I supposed to clear out today?"

With a troubled sigh, the older man got to his feet. "Legally you have no right to be here, but morally this is your home and you can stay until the new owner takes up residence. As for your own personal possessions, you're free to take them with you. I'm sorry, Sadie. I wish it could be otherwise. To be honest, I dreaded coming here today. You don't deserve this."

Reeling with pain, she walked him to the door. "It's Mac and Millie I worry about. The ranch is their home, too. I can hardly bear it."

When Jarod hadn't showed up that night eight years ago, the Hensons were the ones who had tried to comfort her. She'd believed he had decided at the last minute that he couldn't go through with their marriage, and she would never have survived if they hadn't been there to help her get through that ghastly night.

Reed Varney shook his head. "When Daniel summoned me to the ranch, I begged him not to do this, but he was beyond reason."

She stared into space. "He's always been beyond reason." This proved more than ever why her mother had been forced to abandon Sadie.

If Eileen had stayed in the marriage, who knew what would have happened during one of his drunken rages when he'd threatened to kill his wife. Eileen's decision to let him keep Sadie had probably saved both their lives.

When Sadie had found out about Jarod's accident, her father had threatened to kill Jarod if she went to the hospital to be with him. He'd made her write a letter telling Jarod she never wanted to see him again and then he'd told her to get out of his house. Millie and Mac were afraid for her life and urged her to leave Montana and go to her mother in California, saving her once more.

"Thank you for coming," she said quietly to the lawyer.

"Of course. The number for Parker Realty is listed on the paper. They've already put an ad in the multiple listings section. Things should be moving quickly. I'll be in touch with you again soon."

The second he left, she grabbed the file and hurried to her bedroom to hide it in the dresser drawer. She never wanted the Hensons to know what he'd put in the will about them. They'd been wonderful surrogate parents to her. Somehow she had to protect them.

With that decision made, she grabbed her purse and left for the kitchen, determined to lie through her teeth if she had to. She found Millie at the sink and gave her a hug. "Hey! I made the mess and planned to clean it up."

"Nonsense. How did everything go?"

"Fine. Tomorrow I'll drive to Billings and meet with him in his office," she lied. "Where's Zane?"

"Outside with Ryan. If Tim Lawson was as terrific as Zane, then your mother was a very lucky woman."

"She was. So was I, to be raised by you and Mac. I love you and Liz dearly. You know that, don't you?"

"The feeling's mutual."

"You're my family now and that's the way it's going to stay." *No matter what she had to do.*

"Nothing would make us happier." They hugged again.

"I'm going to drive into White Lodge. Do you want me to do any shopping for you while I'm there?"

"We stocked up for the funeral so I think we're fine right now."

"Okay. See you later. Just so you know, tonight I'm going to visit Ralph Bannock. Zane will babysit Ryan." She hadn't asked him yet, but knew he'd do it.

Zane's wife had betrayed him with another man while he'd been in the navy. After he'd left the military, they'd divorced and, not long after, Zane had lost his elder brother, Tim. "Honey, I can do that."

"I know you can, Millie, but you spent enough time raising me. The last thing I want to do is take advantage of you. We'll be back shortly."

Sadie reached for the truck keys on the peg at the back door and hurried outside. She found Zane walking around with Ryan. He made the perfect father. His ex-wife had been the loser in that relationship. Sadie knew how much he'd wanted a family. It broke her heart.

She scooped her little brother from the ground before darting Zane a glance. "Will you drive me to town? We need to talk."

"Sure."

She handed him the keys to her father's Silverado and walked over to get in. They'd brought a car seat from California for Ryan and had already installed it in the backseat. Once he was strapped in securely, she climbed into the front with Zane and they took off.

Zane gave her a sideways glance. "I know that look on your face. You've had bad news."

"Much worse than anything I had imagined, but Mac and Millie don't know a thing yet. The fact is my father disowned me." She ended up telling him everything written in the will. "I've got three weeks from today to come up with a plan. I don't want the Hensons to find out about this."

"Of course not. That monster!" he muttered under his breath, but she heard him. "I'm sorry, Sadie." They followed the dirt road out to the highway.

"Don't be. With him, the shoe fits. The bottom line is, if I want to make my home on this ranch, I'll have to buy it from the Realtor in Billings. There was no mention in the will that I couldn't. I have some savings after working for your brother, but not nearly enough to make a dent. In the meantime I need to find a job in town and put Ryan in day care."

Zane grimaced. "I could give you some money."

"You're an angel, Zane, but you gave your ex-wife the house you both lived in, so you need to hold on to any money you've saved. I'll have to find another avenue to pay off the debt owing the bank so I can hold on to the ranch, but I've got to hurry."

"I've got an idea how you can do it." She jerked her head toward him, waiting for the miracle answer. "I could sell Tim's house in San Francisco."

Sadie made several sounds of protest. "After your divorce, mother willed it to you before she died because she assumed I'd inherit the ranch one day. She knew Tim would have wanted you to have it."

"You're forgetting she expected you to go on living there with Ryan."

"But it's not mine, and I don't want to live in San Francisco."

"Neither do I. I have no desire to be anywhere near my ex, so I've got another idea."

"What?"

"The house isn't completely paid off, but I could still get a substantial amount if I sell it. With that money, plus any you have, we could move here and become joint owners of the ranch."

Her heart gave a great clap. "You're not serious!"

"Yeah. Actually, I am. I spent a lot of years in the military and know I won't be happy unless I'm working outdoors in some capacity. So far I haven't found a job that appeals to me. I can help with the ranching for a while until I know what it is I want to do with the rest of my life."

"Zane, you're just saying that because you're at loose ends and are one of the great guys of this world."

"I'm saying it because I have no parents, no brother and I don't want to lose Ryan. I know you have nothing holding you in California. To be honest, I like the idea of being part owner with you. It'll be our investment for Ryan's future."

Her eyes smarted with unshed tears. "If you're really serious…"

"I'm dead serious. Take a look around. With these mountains, this is God's country all right. It's growing on me like crazy. I already like Mac and Millie. And the little guy in back seems perfectly content. Why don't you think about it?"

"I *am* thinking. So hard I'm ready to have a heart attack."

"Don't do that! If you wake up tomorrow and say it's a go, I'll fly back to San Francisco and get the house on the market. While I'm there, I'll put everything from the house and my apartment in storage for us. What do you say?"

She was so full of gratitude, she could hardly talk. "I say I don't need to wait until tomorrow to tell you yes, but I don't want ownership. The ranch should be put in your name for you and Ryan. I'll get a job and do housekeeping to earn my keep. In time we'll build up a new herd of cattle. Anything less and I won't agree."

He flashed her the kind of smile she hadn't seen since before Tim's death. Zane had dimples, too, an irresistible Lawson trait. "You sound just like your mother when she's made up her mind, but you need to think about this. There's a whole life you've left behind in San Francisco. Men you've dated. Friends."

"I know, and I've enjoyed all of it including my job at your brother's store. But with Mother gone, it hasn't been the same. Now that my father has died, I feel the only place I really belong is here."

After a period of quiet he said, "I can tell you this much. I feel this ranch growing on me."

Like Sadie, Zane needed to put the painful past behind him and get on with life.

"Tell you what, Zane. When I drive you to the airport tomorrow, I'll stop by Mr. Varney's office and let him know we have a plan for you to buy the ranch. He can inform the Realtor and we'll go from there."

"Sadie—" There was a solemn tone in his voice. "If things don't work out, we'll find another small

ranch for sale around here. Montana is in your blood.
We won't let your father win."

She had no words to express the depth of her love
for him. Instead, she leaned across the seat and kissed
his cheek.

On Tuesday night Jarod had just returned from the
upper pasture when he caught sight of Daniel Corkin's Silverado parked in front of the Bannock ranch
house. *Sadie was still here.* The blood pounded in his
ears as he let himself in the side door of the den on
the main floor. His grandfather's room was farther
down the hallway of the two-story house.

With Connor headed for another rodeo event in
Oklahoma, either Avery or their housekeeper, Jenny,
would have let her in. He planted himself in the doorway of the den. When Sadie left, she would have to
walk past him to reach the foyer. Since it had grown
dark, he didn't imagine he'd have to wait much longer. His grandfather tired easily these days.

As if he'd willed her to appear, he saw light and
movement at the end of the hall. She moved quietly
in his direction. When she was within a few feet he
said hello to her.

"Oh—"

"Forgive me if I startled you, Sadie. How's my
grandfather?"

She stepped back, hugging her arms to her waist.
He saw no sign of the vivacious Sadie Corkin of eight
years ago who'd caused every male heart in Carbon
County to race at the sight of her.

When he'd watched her galloping through the

meadow, blond hair flying behind her like a pennant in the sunshine, he'd hardly been able to breathe. The moment she'd seen him, she'd dismount and run into his arms, her hair smelling sweet from her peach-scented shampoo.

Without losing a heartbeat, he'd lay her down in the sweet white clover and they would kiss, clinging in a frenzy of need while they'd tried to become one. Just remembering those secret times made his limbs grow heavy with desire.

"He fell asleep while we were talking," she answered without looking at him directly. "I'm afraid I wore him out."

"That means you made him happy and left him in a peaceful state. When I had breakfast with him this morning, he was excited to think you'd be coming by. He was always partial to you and Liz." He almost said his grandfather had been waiting to welcome her into the Bannock family, but that would be dredging up the past.

"I care for him a lot." She shifted nervously. "I'm afraid I have to get back to Ryan now, so don't let me keep you. Good night." She darted away like a frightened doe spooked by a noise in the underbrush.

He'd promised himself to stay away from her, but the trail of her haunting fragrance drove him to follow her out the front door to the truck. By the time she'd climbed behind the wheel, he'd reached the passenger side. Not considering the wisdom of it, he got in and shut the door.

"What are you doing?" She sounded panicked.

Jarod forced his voice to remain calm. "Isn't it obvious? We have unfinished business, Sadie. While we're alone, now is as good a time as any to talk." He stretched his arm along the back of the seat, fighting the urge to plunge his hand into her silky hair the way he'd done so many times in the past. "To pretend we don't have a history serves no purpose. What I'm interested to know is how you can dismiss it so easily."

"I've dismissed nothing," she said, her voice shaking, "but sometimes it's better to leave certain things alone. In our case it's one stone that shouldn't be turned."

"I disagree. Let's start with that note you had delivered to me at the hospital. That was quite a turnaround from the night before when you'd promised to marry me. Or have you forgotten?"

"Of course not." She stirred restlessly. "I waited for you until dark, but you never came."

"Ned had been stalking me in town."

"Ned?"

He nodded. "I had to wait until I saw his Jeep disappear before I headed out to get you."

She struggled for breath. "I didn't know that. I was afraid to be out any longer in case my father realized I wasn't home or at Liz's, so I headed back. I thought you'd decided not to come, after all," she said in a barely audible voice.

"*Not come?* I was on my way to you when a truck blindsided me. Everything went black. A hiker found me and I didn't wake up until I was taken to the hospital in an ambulance. By then it was afternoon the next day. I couldn't reach you on the phone. Late that night one of the nurses brought me your note."

He felt her shudder.

"What happened, Sadie? For weeks I'd been asking you if you were sure about marrying me. You had every opportunity to turn me down before I went to the trouble of preparing for our wedding. Surely I deserve a better explanation for you not showing up than the pathetic one you sent me."

Her head was still lowered. "I—I'm afraid to tell you for fear you won't believe me," she stammered. "I've kept this a secret for so long, but now that my father is dead, you need to hear the truth."

He gritted his teeth. "Why didn't you tell me before?" he rasped. "It's been eight hellish years, Sadie."

"You think I don't know that?" She whipped her head around to face him. "I didn't hear about the accident until late the next day when Mac told me. The second I found out, I started out the door to go straight to the hospital. But that's when my father stopped me. He said if I went near you, he would kill you."

Jarod frowned. "Kill me? He'd been threatening to kill any Bannock that came near you on his property for years, always when he'd had too much to drink. Why did you suddenly believe him?"

"This time was different!"

He blinked. "Start at the beginning and don't leave anything out."

"After Mac told me about your accident, he gave me the keys to his truck so I could drive to the hospital. I left the house, but my father followed me out and forbade me to leave. I told him I was going to see you and he couldn't stop me. I was eighteen and he had no more right to tell me what to do. But before I could climb into the cab, he said something that made my blood run cold."

Jarod waited.

She stared at him in the semidarkness. "He warned me that if I ever went near you again, another accident would happen to you and you wouldn't survive it."

"What?"

Jarod's thoughts reeled.

"I was afraid you wouldn't believe me." She started to open the door to get out, but Jarod was faster and reached across to stop her.

He knew Daniel Corkin was demented when he got too drunk, but— "Are you saying he drove the truck that ran me down the night before?" Jarod caught her shoulder in his grasp, bringing their mouths within inches of each other.

"No." Sadie shook her head, unable to hold back the tears. "But my father had to be behind the accident. Otherwise why would he have said that? He probably paid someone to drive into you, and after all these years, that person is still out there."

Was it true?

He gripped her shoulder tighter. "I *knew* it wasn't a simple accident. When I felt that kind of force on a dirt road with no one else around, I thought it had to be a small plane making a forced landing that ran into me.

"It all happened too fast for me to see anything. The impact caused the truck to roll into the culvert and twisted the horse trailer onto its side. The police said it had to have been a truck, but after an exhaustive investigation, they couldn't find the person responsible."

Sadie moaned. "It was so horrific. I heard that Chief was injured, too."

"Yes, but he survived."

"Thank heaven. I don't know how, but someone knew we were planning to get married and word got back to my father. Maybe someone from the reservation did some talking in town. Oh, Jarod." She broke down, burying her face in her hands. "You could have been killed."

She was right about that.

"I can't bear to think about that night. There was evil in my father. I realized he *would* kill you another time given more provocation. At that point I did the only thing I could do and promised not to see you again. He made me write that note and then he told me to get out of the house and stay out. He obviously assumed I'd run to the Hensons."

Jarod heard her words, but it took time for him to absorb them.

"I was so terrified to learn you were in the hospital, and so terrified of him, I knew I had to get away and stay away. All these years I've wondered who could have done something so sinister to you. My father must have paid that man a lot of money he didn't have."

He sucked in a breath. "Whether your father was bluffing about the accident or not, his objective of separating us was accomplished. You were gone out of my life as if you'd never been there."

"Please listen to me, Jarod. In the note I wrote, those words were only meant to convince my father. How could you have believed them? I was going to be your wife!"

He stared her down, unable to fathom what had happened. Something didn't ring true, but he'd have to think long and hard about it first. He slowly released her arm.

"Just tell me one thing. Why did you go to your mother after she'd abandoned you for all those years? It made no sense. I couldn't come up with any conceivable explanation, so I finally had to conclude you couldn't bring yourself to marry me."

"Jarod," she pleaded, "I don't know how you could think that! When you didn't come and I still knew nothing about your accident, I thought you'd changed your mind about getting married, or maybe your uncle had urged you to put off the marriage for a while longer. I wanted to die when you didn't show up. Mac and Millie came in my room to try to calm me down. You have no idea what was going on inside me that night."

"That made two of us. I lay on that hospital bed incapacitated with no way to talk to you. My grandparents thought we were on the reservation enjoying our honeymoon."

"I didn't know that!" she half cried. "I was so upset Mac and Millie told me a secret they'd been keeping from me because my father had sworn them to secrecy. If they broke that oath, he would have thrown them off the property. Millie said the only reason they hadn't left him was because of me."

He shook his head in disbelief. "What secret?"

"They told me he'd threatened to kill my mother if she tried to take me away from him. Jarod, all those years I thought she didn't love me, but it was just the opposite. She always wanted me, grieved for me. She kept in touch with the Hensons every day to find out how I was. But they had to keep quiet because of my father."

"Is that the truth?"

"Yes, but I didn't know it until that moment."

Jarod rubbed the side of his jaw. "A mother's love," he murmured. "You wanted it more than you wanted me."

"No, Jarod. You have everything wrong."

"I don't think so," he argued. "When you heard about my accident, it was obvious you didn't want to be my wife or you would have found a way to get in touch with me at the hospital. You knew that when I got out, I'd come for you and we would have gotten away from your father. I wasn't afraid of him."

"But I *was!* He'd just admitted he would make sure you were dead if I so much as looked at you. I couldn't bear that, so I went to my mother. Don't forget he'd threatened her years earlier. My father was capable of anything! With a gun or a rifle in his hand, he was lethal. Since I'd turned eighteen, Mac and Millie urged me to get away from my father and go to her because he was out of control. Mac drove me to Billings."

Jarod felt as though a giant hand had just cut off his breath. "So you let Mac do that instead of driving you to the reservation where my uncle would have taken care of you until I got out of the hospital. You promised to love me forever."

He could barely make out her words she was sobbing so much. "You were my life, Jarod, but when I never heard from you after you recovered, I thought you didn't want me. I thought my life was over. Don't you understand? I was devastated to think you'd decided it wouldn't be wise to marry me because of my father. He hated you—hated all the Bannocks. You have to believe that the only reason I left was so my father wouldn't hurt you again."

A boulder had lodged in his throat. "How could you think that when I was prepared to be your husband and take care of you? I swore I would protect you. Do you honestly think I would have let him or anyone else hurt either one of us?"

"He managed it the first time."

Jarod's features hardened. "Why don't you tell me the real reason why you ran away from me? I'm warning you. I won't let you go until I get the truth out of you."

Tears rolled down her cheeks. "I *have* told you, but you're so stubborn you refuse to listen."

"You think I haven't listened? Did Ned get to you, after all?"

"No!" She sounded wild with anger. "I couldn't stand Ned. He revolted me."

"But he told you about my father, didn't he?"

She stared at him through the tears. "What are you talking about?"

"After all this time and all we've been through, are you still going to pretend you don't know the truth?"

"What truth?" she cried.

"My mother and father were never married."

Stillness fell around them.

"They weren't? I swear I've never heard any of this. Ned used to call you a bastard and a half-breed under his breath, but I knew he was insanely jealous of you. He had such a foul mouth, my friends and I always ran from him when he followed us around."

Sadie's earnestness shook him.

"Jarod Bannock, are you trying to tell me you think I heard about your parents and was ashamed to become your wife?"

Jarod struggled to hide the guilt rising up in him.

"You *do* think it! I can see it on your face. How dare you think that about me!"

"That's exactly how it was," he returned angrily. "You were playing a game with me—the half Indian. But you were a teenager then, living through a lot of pain and turned to me. I was three years older and should have known better than to believe you and I shared something rare."

"We did," she whispered, her voice throbbing. "Can't you understand that I was convinced my father would kill you?" Even in the semidarkness her face had lost color. "Listen to me, Jarod. I'm going to tell you something right now.

"Even if I knew about your parents, I was ready to live with you no matter what because I *loved* you. *I* was the one who begged you to take me away before I turned eighteen. Remember? I didn't care. I would have hidden out on the reservation with you. That's how deeply in love I was with you. So don't you dare credit feelings and motives to me that were never mine."

Gutted after what he'd heard, Jarod needed to get out of the truck. He started to open the door, but she grabbed his arm. "Oh, no, you don't! We're not through yet. I want to know why you never, ever told me the truth about your parents."

Jarod realized he couldn't avoid this conversation any longer. While he tried to find the words, she launched her own.

"It seems to me your cousin did a lot of damage I didn't know about, otherwise you wouldn't have held anything back from me. What did he tell you? That a white girl would never want you once she knew the truth? He got under your skin, didn't he? Well, we're alone now, so I want to hear the whole truth. You owe me that much before you walk away again."

He deserved that much and closed his eyes tightly before sitting back.

"Dad was twenty when he drove to the reservation to look at the horses. The Crow loved their animals and knew good horse flesh. My uncle Charlo showed him around. While they were talking, his younger sister Raven came riding up on a palomino. Dad told me she looked like a princess. He was so taken by her, he forgot about the horses. From then on he kept driving over there and finally told Charlo he wanted to marry her.

"My uncle told him she was destined to marry another man in the clan, but by that time Raven was in love with my father. At that point Charlo took him to meet their mother. Her word was law. She said her daughter was old enough to make up her own mind. They spent that night together on the reservation. It meant they were married. There was no ceremony. I was conceived that night."

"Oh, Jarod." She sniffled. "What a beautiful story. Did they live on the reservation?"

"On and off. Dad took her home to meet my grandparents. They loved my father and welcomed Raven. When she discovered she was pregnant, she spent more time with her family. I was born on the reservation. But Addie had prepared a nursery, so I lived in both places.

"That winter my mother caught pneumonia, and though my grandfather paid for the best health care, she died within six weeks of my birth and was buried on the reservation. My father was grief-stricken. It was hard to take me out to the reservation as often after that because of all the reminders.

"My Bannock grandparents helped raise me. Eventually Dad met Hannah at church and they married, then Connor and Avery were born. That's the whole story. Though secretly I knew Great Uncle Tyson's family didn't approve of what my father had done, they were never unkind to him or to me."

"Except for Ned," Sadie muttered. "He's as intolerant as my father. The fact that you're an exceptional man only makes your cousin angrier."

"There's more to it than that, Sadie. After my parents were killed in a freak lightning storm, Ned became more vocal about his hate for me and my background. He constantly tried to show me up. It grew uglier with time. But *you* were the crux of the problem. He wanted to go out with you himself, and I knew it.

"When I used to watch you compete at the rodeo, I knew Ned was in the crowd, wishing you'd go home with him after it was over. I loved knowing you and I had secret plans to meet later. I had too much pride knowing it was I you wanted."

She shifted in the seat. "I lived to be with you. That's why it kills me to think that Ned was able to undermine your faith in me once I left Montana. I had to write what I did in that note to sound believable to my father, but I can't believe you didn't read between the lines. I waited for weeks, months, years, hoping and praying I'd hear from you so I could tell you everything and we could make plans to meet."

"That works both ways, Sadie. I waited weeks for a phone call from you. Maybe now you can understand how devastated I was when you fled to your mother instead of marrying me.

"But after you'd gone to California and time passed, I realized you were right to escape me. Despite the Bannock name, I'll always be treated as a second-class citizen by certain people. If you had married me, you would have been forced to deal with the kind of prejudice Ned dishes out on a daily basis."

They'd reached an impasse. He opened the door. "Eight years have passed. You've suffered some great losses in your life and now have a child to raise. I only wish you the best, Sadie."

Her features hardened. She wiped the moisture off her face. "If you can accuse me of being afraid to be your wife after all we shared, then you never knew me. I gave you a lot more credit than that. Have you forgotten the evening we met in the canyon and I told you about a lesson we'd had on the Plains Indians and the great Sioux Chief Sitting Bull?"

"Vaguely." Jarod knew he'd always been so excited to be with her, he'd barely taken in everything she'd told him.

"That lesson changed my view of life, but it's obvious you need a reminder of how deeply it touched me. Did I tell you our teacher made us memorize part of Sitting Bull's speech before the Dawes Commission in 1877? I still know it by heart and got an A for it."

Jarod had had no idea, but he nodded.

"Sitting Bull said, and I quote, 'if the Great Spirit had desired me to be a white man, he would have made me so in the first place. He put in your heart certain wishes and plans, and in my heart he put other and different desires. It is not necessary for eagles to be crows.

"'I am here by the will of the Great Spirit, and by his will I am chief.

"'In my early days, I was eager to learn and to do things, and therefore I learned quickly.'

"'Each man is good in the sight of the Great Spirit. Now that we are poor, we are free. No white man controls our footsteps. If we must die, we die defending our rights.

"'What white man can say I ever stole his land or a penny of his money? Yet they say that I am a thief. What white woman, however lonely, was ever captive or insulted by me? Yet they say I am a bad Indian.

"'What white man has ever seen me drunk? Who has ever come to me hungry and left me unfed? Who has seen me beat my wives or abuse my children? What law have I broken?

"'Is it wrong for me to love my own? Is it wicked for me because my skin is red? Because I am Sioux? Because I was born where my father lived? Because I would die for my people and my country? God made me an Indian.'"

When she'd finished, Jarod sat there in absolute wonder, so humbled he couldn't speak.

"You don't know how many times I wanted to face my father and Ned and deliver that speech to them," Sadie told him. "I wanted to yell at them, 'God made you men white and Jarod's mother an Indian. So be thankful you were made at all and learn to live together!

"That speech made me love you all the more, Jarod. I can't believe you didn't know that. But as you said, it's probably that pride of yours. It's turned your heart to flint and stands in the way of reason.

"Do you know I've given you a second Crow name now that you've grown up? It's Born of Flint."

Born of Flint? That's what she thought of him? Everything was over.

"I wish you a safe journey back to California, Sadie."

Chapter Four

When Sadie walked through the back door of the ranch house Tuesday night, Millie was in the kitchen making coffee. She glanced at Sadie and said, "You look as bad as you did that night eight years ago. It can only mean one thing. Sit down and talk to me before you fall down, honey. Ryan's asleep and Zane's in his bedroom doing work on his laptop."

"Oh, Millie…" She ran into those arms that had always been outstretched to her. They hugged for a long time.

"You saw Jarod."

Sadie nodded and eased away. "I don't think it was by accident."

"No. He knew you were going to visit Ralph."

"He followed me to the truck. We talked about that ghastly night eight years ago. He said he couldn't come to the meadow until after dark because Ned had been stalking him in White Lodge. That's why he was so late."

"That doesn't surprise me one bit. Ned was always up to no good."

"But it was a revelation to me! When he thought it

was safe, he started for the mountains but got broadsided by a truck." She told Millie everything they'd talked about.

"Don't tell me you didn't believe him—" The tenderness in her brown eyes defeated Sadie.

"Of course I believed him," she half protested. "But back then I was dying inside. Now it is eight years too late. Millie—" She scrunched her fists in anger. "All these years I've wanted to hate him for not trying to get in touch with me."

Millie's voice was gentle. "You didn't reach out to him, either. It's a tragedy you both lost out on eight years of loving. Ah, honey…you were so young, struggling with too many abandonment issues. When he didn't come for you in California, the pain was too much for you."

"You should have heard him, Millie. He…he thought I left Montana because I didn't want to marry a part Indian. Did you know his parents got married on the reservation? But no one knew about it, certainly not Ned.

"I didn't realize Jarod suffered so much from Ned's taunting. He *had* to know none of that mattered to me. Can you imagine him believing I thought less of him because of his heritage?"

The housekeeper gave her a sad smile. "Yes. Jarod is a proud man like his uncle Charlo. But at twenty-one, everything was on the line for him. Don't forget your father's hatred of the Bannocks, let alone his hatred of anyone who wasn't of pure English stock.

"Wanting to marry you was a daring dream for any man, but as we both know, Jarod was always his own person. In his fearless way he loved you and reached out for you. But when you left Montana before he got out of the hospital, all those demons planted in his mind by your father and Ned caused his common sense to desert him for a while."

"I see that now," Sadie whispered, grief stricken. "But I was afraid my father would kill him."

"Don't you know about the great wounded warrior inside him? He needed you to believe in him, to believe he would protect you."

"You're right."

"Did you tell him tonight that you'd wanted to marry him more than anything in the world?"

Sadie wiped her eyes with the palms of her hands. "Yes, but he didn't listen. Do you know what he said? In that stoic way of his he wished me a safe journey back to California."

Millie studied her for a moment. "Perhaps he thinks you and Zane are romantically involved. Have you forgotten that fierce Apsáalooke pride so quickly? According to my daughter, Zane Lawson is the most attractive man she's seen around these parts in years."

"No, Millie. I cleared that up with Avery the other day when she asked about Zane. She's close to Jarod and would have told him." But Ned had been brazen enough to ask her about Zane.

Millie shrugged. "Maybe Jarod thinks you're involved with a man in San Francisco and are looking forward to getting back to him."

"It never happened."

"All I can say is, if you're going to be neighbors

with the Bannocks again, it wouldn't hurt to mend a fence that doesn't need to stay broken. Don't you agree? After all, Jarod's involved with another woman right now."

Pain pierced her. "I know. Apparently it's more serious than his other relationships."

"That doesn't surprise me. He's not a monk and he *is* getting to the age where a man wants to put down roots with a wife and children. Honey? Since you're not going back to California, perhaps you could tell him there is no other man in your life the next time you see him. If either one of you had done that eight years ago with a phone call or a letter, you might be the mother of one or two little Bannocks by now."

Except at that point in time, Millie hadn't known that Daniel was the person behind Jarod's accident, and still didn't. Sadie's father had talked to her outside where no one else could hear them. The horror of knowing her father would kill Jarod with little provocation was another secret she'd wanted to keep from the Hensons.

But the mention of one or two little Bannocks had Sadie swallowing hard. She'd entertained that vision too many times and suffered the heartache over and over again.

Sadie thanked Millie and said good-night. She tip-toed into the bedroom. Ryan was sound asleep, snuggled beside his blanket.

Good old Millie. Her sage advice nagged at Sadie as she got ready for bed. To mend that fence by telling Jarod there was no man in her life meant turning over the next stone. If she did tell him, she didn't know if she had enough courage to deal with the rejection of the grown man he'd become.

"Honey?" Millie peeked in her room. "I need to give you something. Now that you know the truth about that night, you should have this back." She handed Sadie the beaded bracelet Jarod had given her the night they'd made love and planned their future.

Sadie stared at the bracelet in disbelief. "I thought I'd lost it. You kept it?"

"Of course. I knew there had to be an explanation why he didn't meet you, but you were too wild with pain to hear me. When you took that bracelet off your wrist and tossed it across the room, I picked it up and put it away for safekeeping.

"Don't you know he would never have given you a gift like that if he hadn't loved you with all his soul? Jarod's a great man, Sadie. After you left, I cried bitter tears for both of you for years."

Sadie stared at the woman who'd been her mother through those difficult years. "What did I ever do to deserve you? I'll love you and Mac forever."

"Ditto. We couldn't have more children. You were a blessing in our lives, a sister for our Liz. We all needed each other."

Yes. Sadie wouldn't have made it without the Hensons.

She pressed the bracelet against her heart and fell asleep reliving that night in the mountains. *Jarod*...

So SHE *WAS* leaving the ranch. The Sadie he'd once known had gone for good.

Jarod stood outside the ranch house for a long

time. The sound of Sadie's truck engine echoed in the empty cavern of his heart, the one she'd likened to flint.

When he'd checked on his grandfather and found him asleep, he'd told Jenny he was going to drive out to the reservation to see Uncle Charlo and would be back by tomorrow afternoon. Again it meant putting Leslie off, but it couldn't be helped.

He'd met the good-looking, redheaded archaeologist from Colorado through Avery. The two women worked at the dig site near Absarokee, Montana, run through the University in Billings. They were unearthing evidence of Crow history. Leslie's looks and mind had attracted him enough to start dating her, but seeing Sadie again made it impossible for him to sort out his feelings.

The reservation crossed several county lines with ninety percent of the population being farthest away in Big Horn County at the Crow Agency. However his uncle resided in the small settlement on the Pryor area of the reservation in Carbon County, only an hour's drive from the ranch.

If Martha needed anything, she could call his uncle Grant. But if there was a real emergency, he could come right back.

AFTER SPENDING THE night on the reservation, Jarod drove straight to the ranch on Wednesday to look in on his grandfather. Since his hospital stay the month before, Ralph's condition could change on a dime because of the pneumonia plaguing him. Martha had just served him his lunch. She smiled at Jarod as he walked into the bedroom.

"I'll stay with him while he eats," he told her.

"He's in better spirits than I've seen him in a long time."

Jarod figured that might have had something to do with the visit from the gorgeous blonde on the neighboring ranch. Being with her last night had shaken him, though he wasn't sure in such a positive way.

You were my life, Jarod, but I thought you didn't want me. I thought my life was over. I was devastated to think you'd decided it wouldn't be wise to marry the daughter of Daniel Corkin. He hated you.

Even though he'd talked to his uncle, it had taken until early morning before the cloud over Jarod's mind had dispersed and he'd allowed himself to dig deeper for answers. Daniel wasn't the only person who'd hated Jarod enough to cause him injury. He could think of another man who matched that description.

A member of his own family.

Since Sadie's return to Montana, Ned had shot him glances that said he'd like to wipe Jarod off the face of the earth. Ned had always been up to trouble and had taken it upon himself to be chief watch dog of Jarod's activities. Was it possible he'd heard about Jarod's plans to marry Sadie?

Jarod couldn't imagine it, but if that was the case, then he understood the hate that could have driven Ned to prevent the ceremony from taking place. Couple that with his drinking and a scenario began to take form in Jarod's mind.

"I'm glad you're here, son," Ralph Bannock said. "We need to talk."

His grandfather's raspy voice jerked him from his black thoughts to the present. Since Jarod's father's death, his grandfather, whose thinning dark hair was streaked with silver, had started calling Jarod "son." Though he and Jarod were the same height, his grandfather had shrunk some. He was more fragile these days, and there were hollows in his cheeks.

He was propped against a pillow, sipping soup through a straw. Martha kept him shaved and smelling good. Today he had on the new pair of pajamas Connor had brought him.

Jarod spied a newly framed five-by-seven photograph placed on the bedside table. His breath caught when he realized it was a picture of his grandfather and Sadie taken when she couldn't have been more than six or seven. She was a little blond angel back then, sitting on the back of a pony.

His grandfather's eyes misted over when he saw where Jarod was looking. "Sadie gave me that last evening. I remember the day her mother brought her over to see the new pony. Addie took a picture of us and gave it to her. Sadie said that was one of the happiest memories of her life and wanted me to have it.... With that father of hers, she didn't have many good ones. There was always sweetness in that girl."

No one knew that better than Jarod. He'd never forgotten the day they'd rode into the rugged interior of the Pryors to find one of the wild horse herds. They'd come across a mare attending her foal, their shiny black coats standing out against the meadow of purple lupine. He and Sadie had watched for several hours. "I wish that little foal was mine. I never saw anything so beautiful in my life, Jarod."

The scene was almost as beautiful as Sadie herself. That was the day their souls joined.

Jarod knew in his gut Leslie Weston was becoming more serious about him, yet he kept holding back. It wasn't fair to her. She'd invited him to Colorado to meet her family, but he wasn't there yet.

When Sadie left again for California, maybe that would be the spell-breaker for him. So far no other woman had ever gotten past the entrance to that part of him where Sadie lived. She was his dream catcher, trapping the memories that would always haunt his nights.

Last night his uncle had listened to him before giving him a warning. "Consider the wolf that decides it is better to risk death for some chance of finding a mate and a territory than to live safely, but have no chance of reproduction. You don't know how many winters the Great Spirit will grant you, but they will be cold if you continue to torture yourself with insubstantial dreams that give no warmth."

Jarod knew his uncle was right. He could see a marriage working with Leslie. While he ranched, she'd be able to continue with her career. Together they'd raise a family. For a variety of reasons he felt she'd make a good wife. But would he make a good husband? The answer to that question was no. Not if he couldn't tear Sadie out of his heart.

"Son? Did you hear me?"

His head reared. "What was that, grandfather?"

"I said I need you to do me a favor."

"Anything." He sat in the chair next to the bed, emotionally shredded.

"It turns out Daniel is worse in death than he was in life."

Jarod sat forward. After what Sadie had told him about her father, he wasn't surprised. "What do you mean?" Sadie's father had cast a pall over their lives for too many years.

"He cut Sadie and the Hensons out of his will."

The news shocked Jarod. She'd said nothing of this last night. He shot to his feet. "But there's no one else to inherit!"

"That's right. On June third, the ranch is to be sold to the highest bidder. Parker Realty in Billings is handling it."

So soon? That was only two weeks away. Jarod's hands formed fists.

The lunatic was selling the place rather than give it to his own flesh and blood?

"I would buy it," his grandfather continued, "but Daniel thought of that, too. No Bannock will be able to touch it."

"But Sadie loves that ranch. It's her home. If nothing else, she'd want to keep it in her family."

"She told me she plans to buy it so she and the Hensons can live on the property until they die. It would be just like that lowlife Corkin to force her to come up with her own money to buy it back. You and I know her heart has always been here."

Jarod felt his heart skip a beat. Despite what everyone had been thinking, Sadie wasn't going back to California. Even when the circumstances pointed otherwise, deep down *Jarod had known.*

"Does she have the kind of money it will take?"

"She has savings, but Zane is flying back to California to sell the Lawson house. That money combined with hers ought to be enough to pay off the bank loan so they can hold on to it until they come up with more."

"'They'?" His nervous system received another shocking jolt. "What does Zane have to do with her ranch?"

"Everything! Being Ryan's uncle, he has decided to move here with her. Together they're going to do the ranching."

Jarod frowned. "Does he know anything about ranching?"

"She said he's a retired navy SEAL who just got divorced after finding out his wife was unfaithful. If he was courageous enough to defend our country and survive thirteen years in the military, it stands to reason he can learn. Mac will be there to help him."

His grandfather had an amazing way of humbling Jarod.

"One day she wants it to be Ryan's in honor of Eileen. Their mother put her heart and soul into that ranch before Daniel drove her away. What I want you to do is pay a visit to our attorney in Billings. Ned wants that ranch. He wants Sadie, too, but she was never his to have."

Their eyes locked. His grandfather's steel-gray ones stared at him. "If it wasn't for that accident, she would have been your wife!"

As if Jarod needed to be reminded.

"When Ned hears it's on the market, he'll try to fight the will on the grounds that a third-party designee won't stand up in court these days and anyone can buy it. I want you to get to Harlow before Ned does. Inform him of Sadie's desperate plight and make sure no one else gets their hands on her property. Block him with everything you've got." His gray eyebrows lifted. "I mean *everything*."

Jarod got the message. This was a mission he was going to relish. Ralph Bannock of the Hitting Rocks Ranch was a big name in the State of Montana and wielded a certain amount of power among the business community. For once Jarod planned to use that power for leverage.

"Don't worry about Tyson or your Uncle Grant," his grandfather continued, unaware of the tumult inside Jarod. "I'll take care of them. If they decide the blood between them and Ned is thicker than the blood between them and me, then there will be war. We'll have to get there before they do. Time is of the essence. I'll be damned if I'll let Daniel Corkin cheat Sadie out of her rightful inheritance. Addie wouldn't have stood for it."

Jarod remembered Ned's angry warning in the barn two nights ago about the war not being over. Little did his cousin know what he was in for. Though Ralph had always been Jarod's champion, until this moment he hadn't known how much he loved his grandfather. "I'll drive to Billings first thing in the morning."

"We'll keep this under wraps."

"I'm way ahead of you."

SINCE THURSDAY WAS Liz's day off from the clinic and she wanted to tend Ryan, Sadie had to wait till then to drive Zane to Billings to make his flight. Little Ryan cried when they walked out the back door. They both felt the wrench, but Sadie knew he'd be laughing in a few minutes.

After she dropped Zane off at the airport, Sadie met with Mr. Bree at Parker Realty and they talked business. He couldn't tell her about the other bids, but he did give her a price. If she could meet it, he'd be happy to sell the property to Zane.

She explained about the house in San Francisco, advising that Zane's agent would contact Mr. Bree with a notice of intent to use the money from the sale of the house to purchase the ranch. Everything depended on a quick sale. Sadie put down earnest money from her savings account. With that accomplished, she left his office and headed back to the ranch. She had a lot to discuss with Zane when he called her later.

Ryan was taking his afternoon nap when she returned. Now was a good time to get busy cleaning out her father's bedroom. So far she hadn't been able to bring herself to go in it. When she told Liz and Millie of her intentions, they wouldn't hear of it.

"Give it more time, honey," Millie urged her. "While Ryan's still asleep, why not put on those sassy new cowboy boots and take a ride on Sunflower?"

"She's a lot like Brandy once was," Liz commented. "Playful, with plenty of spirit. You'll love her. But Maisy's energetic, too. Go ahead and ride whichever one you want."

"Thank you." Sadie stared out the living room window facing the mountains. "I presume Dad sold my horse after I left."

"Along with half the cattle."

"Did he get rid of my saddle, too?"

"No. It's still waiting for you in the tack room." Millie got up from the couch and put an arm around her. "Don't dwell on the past. I happen to know a girl around here who never let a day go by without going for a ride."

Obviously, Millie knew she was on the verge of breaking down.

"Maybe for a half hour. If you're sure."

"What else have we got to do? Having a child in this house makes me feel useful again."

"It makes me want one of my own," Liz said on a mournful note.

So far every subject they'd touched on was painful one way or the other. "I'll get ready, but I won't take a long ride. If Ryan starts crying for me, call me on my cell."

Millie shook her head. "Whatever did we do before cell phones?"

If Sadie and Jarod could have called each other eight years ago…

But Sadie's father had forbidden her to have a phone. He didn't want guys calling her without him knowing about it. At Christmas, four months before she'd fled to California, Jarod had bought her one and paid for the service, but she'd been too afraid her father would find out. She'd made Jarod take it back.

If they'd been able to talk before his accident,

she would have known he hadn't deserted her. They would have communicated while he was in the hospital and their marriage would have taken place the second he got out....

You're a fool to dredge up so much pain, Sadie.

She put the phone she'd bought ages ago in her blouse pocket, then went in the bedroom to change into her cowboy boots. Just a short ride to the bluff overlooking the ranch and back.

After thanking Millie and Liz, she left the house through the back door and walked to the barn, lifting her face to the sun.

The smell of the barn flooded her with bittersweet memories. Horses had been her soul mates, just as Jarod had said. When her mom had left, this was the place where she'd come to cry her heart out and find solace. They's always listened and nudged her as if to say they understood.

Though the fights between her parents had stopped, for a long time the emptiness of no loving parent in the house had swallowed her alive. From her earliest memories, her father had been a gun-toting alcoholic. He'd always been gruff, though her mother had done her best to shield Sadie from him.

But somewhere along the way he'd turned hard and cold. After the divorce he'd just have to look at Sadie and she'd known he was seeing her mother. Sadie had learned to stay out of his way.

A neigh from the horse in the barn startled her, breaking her free of those memories. She discovered her cheeks were damp. After wiping the tears away, she walked over to Maisy's stall. The sorrel stared at her as if surprised to see a stranger.

Sadie moved on to Sunflower's stall. With a yellowish gray coat set off by a black mane and tail, the dun-colored mare was well named. She nickered a greeting.

Sadie rubbed her nose. "Well, aren't you the friendliest horse around here. Want to go for a ride? I know you're one of Liz's horses, but you won't care if I take you out for some exercise, right?" She marveled that her friend, who'd become a vet, was still Montana's champion barrel racer. But as she'd informed Sadie, this would be her last year of competition and she hoped to go to the Pro Rodeo Finals in Las Vegas in December.

The horse nickered again, bringing a smile to Sadie. She could saddle and bridle a horse in her sleep, and before long she had left the barn and was galloping away from the ranch. As the horse responded to her body language, the exhilaration she hadn't felt in years came rushing back. She'd done this before. She'd felt this way before.

Her inner compass told her where to go. She was on one of those rare highs and discovered herself racing toward the rocky formations in the distance where Jarod had first taken her to see the wild horses. Sadie knew he wouldn't be there. She didn't even know if the horses still ran there, but she was back now and this was one pilgrimmage she had to make.

In a few minutes she'd reached the place where her bond with Jarod had been forged. The deserted gulch held no evidence that anything had ever happened here, but cut Sadie open and you'd see his imprint on the organ pumping her life's blood.

Jarod. It was always you. It will always be you.

WHEN JAROD TOLD Harlow's secretary he needed to see his grandfather's attorney ASAP, he figured he might have to wait hours or come back the next day. But the two men were old friends. As soon as she buzzed her boss and told him who was out in reception, she smiled at Jarod.

"He says you can go right in."

"Thanks, Nancy." He walked across the foyer to the double doors and opened them.

Harlow started toward him. Though the older man was in his seventies and had a shock of white hair, he was a wiry, energetic individual. His shrewd blue eyes played over Jarod with genuine pleasure. "Come on in! It's always good to see you."

They shook hands before the lawyer took a seat behind his desk, motioning for Jarod to sit in one of the leather wing-backed chairs in front of it. "Has Ralph taken another turn for the worse?"

"His last bout of pneumonia left him weak, but he's still fighting."

"That's good to hear. And Tyson?"

"His macular degeneration along with ulcers has taken a real toll." The brothers were only two years apart. "I've come on my grandfather's behalf about something vital."

"Ralph appears to be depending on you more and more to run the Hitting Rocks Ranch. He couldn't choose a better man to be following in his footsteps."

Jarod's uncle Grant probably wouldn't like hearing that, but Jarod had always liked Harlow and felt the man's sincerity. "They're big ones."

Harlow chuckled. "Indeed they are." He pushed a stack of legal briefs to the side of his desk and leaned forward. "Tell me what's going on."

It didn't take Jarod long to explain the problem.

The older man touched his fingertips together. "What a tragedy, but there is a very simple way around the problem. If Ralph wants to make certain Sadie Corkin doesn't lose her ranch without her knowing he's behind it, I'll act as a straw buyer and purchase the property."

"It's going for $700,000."

He nodded. "When all the papers are filed and transactions made, Ralph can pay me and the land will be deeded over to Zane Lawson. He can work out the details with Ralph to get him paid back. No laws have been broken, therefore no grounds for a court case. That part of Daniel Corkin's will doesn't hold water. Anyone has the right to buy that ranch including a Bannock."

With those words Jarod felt his chest expand. Only a friendship as strong as the one his grandfather and Harlow had built over the years could have achieved this miracle. "How soon could you act on it?"

"Today if you want." He quirked one white eyebrow. "You're anticipating a bidding war?"

"According to Sadie, who confided in my grandfather, two other people made offers on the property before Daniel died. The place will be sold to one of them if no other offers come in before the deadline.

The ranch is already in the multiple listings online. I'm afraid once my cousin sees it, he'll outbid anyone else to make make sure he comes out on top."

"Which cousin is that?"

"Ned."

"Ah, yes. Grant's son, the one who's always been in trouble. Why would he want to buy that ranch?"

"Though close to a century has gone by without any evidence, Ned still believes there's oil on the land. He's determined to get his hands on it." *And on Sadie.*

"Do you know how many gamblers have squandered their lives going after that same pipe dream around these parts?"

"Ned has never been able to let it go," Jarod said.

"From what Ralph told me," Brigg mentioned, "that cousin of yours has some deep-seated problems. I recall hearing about the time when he and his friend were caught stealing some wild horses on federal land. It cost Grant plenty to keep that hushed up."

Jarod's brow furrowed in surprise. "I didn't know that. What happened?"

"Instead of ending up in jail, they were charged with drunk and disorderly conduct. It took influence with the judge and a lot of money to keep that under wraps. Ralph said Ned's father was continually bailing him out of some pretty nasty scrapes."

This was all news to Jarod. For Ned to have that kind of serious brush with the law underlined his cousin's dark side. Jarod had no idea his grandfather had confided in Harlow to this extent.

He winked at Jarod. "We'll get there before Ned

does. I'll phone Mr. Bree at Parker Realty after you leave and set things in motion."

"When my grandfather hears that news, it'll probably add several years to his life."

The lawyer smiled. "I owe him so many favors for sending business my way, I'm delighted to do this."

"We're indebted to you, Harlow. Sadie's been our neighbor since she was born. It's time she had some joy in her life." He stood to shake the lawyer's hand.

Harlow squinted at him. "I'll give you and Ralph a ring as soon as I've spoken with Mr. Bree."

"Good. I'll see myself out."

On the way to the underground car park, Jarod mulled over the new revelation about Ned. It triggered his memory to the time his cousin had accused him of stealing Chief. Though Jarod had gotten legal permission to keep the wild horse once he'd tamed him, Ned had been furious. Having always been in competition with Jarod, Ned might have decided to steal a wild horse to prove he could have one of his own, too.

Since Sadie had come back, his toxic behavior around Jarod had an edge of desperation that bordered on instability.

Ever since his accident, Jarod had wanted to know the identity of the person who'd intentionally tried to take him out. Sadie believed her father had been behind it. So much so that she'd left the state to protect Jarod. But if it had been Daniel, he would have arranged a series of accidents long before that night. Over the years Jarod had occasionally seen Sadie's father out hunting in the mountains. He could have picked Jarod off at any time.

He suspected that Daniel had used the accident as an excuse to frighten his daughter further, knowing how vulnerable she was at that point. The man had been born with few scruples, but he'd stopped short of murder, only threatened it.

When Jarod really thought about it, there was only one person he was aware of who truly hated him for personal reasons. That was his cousin...

The revelation coming from Harlow had made him see things in a different light. More and more he was convinced that his cousin was the guilty party and had gotten away with his crime for years now.

On the night in question, Ned must have arranged for a truck ahead of time, probably from one of the friends he hung around with when they went off to keg parties. After driving his Jeep around town to throw Jarod off the scent, he'd gotten that friend to drive him to the crossroads where he'd ambushed Jarod. Or maybe Ned had borrowed it and was alone when he drove into Jarod.

Needing evidence, Jarod decided to visit some auto paint and body shops while he was still in Billings.

Before Ned had returned the borrowed truck to the owner, he would have gone to a shop for repairs, but not in White Lodge, where the police had already done a search.

When he reached his truck, Jarod bought a hamburger at a drive-through before starting his investigation of the dozens of body and paint shops in Billings. The police had checked a few places here, but they could have missed some. Most places kept invoices, accounts payable/receivable ledgers and ex-

pense reports for a minimum of seven years, but gen-
erally longer. Sadie's birthday had been May tenth, a
Thursday. That narrowed the field as to time.

It was a long shot, but he might come across a business that had done some work for Ned. He would have
used an assumed name and paid cash.

One by one he interviewed the service managers,
hoping to come up with a lead. No one could give
him information on the spot. He left his cell phone
number for them to call him and also used his phone
to retrieve a photo of Ned from the ranching office
information for the managers to download.

Tomorrow morning he'd leave early for Bozeman
and go through the same process. It wouldn't take as
long to cover since it was a third the size of Billings,
a city with a population over 100,000.

On his way home, his cell phone rang. Hoping
it was one of the body shops, he clicked on without
looking at the Caller ID and said hello.

"Hi!"

His hand tightened on the wheel. It was Leslie. For
the life of him he couldn't muster any enthusiasm at
hearing her voice. The only emotion at the moment
was guilt that he couldn't give her what she wanted.
"Hi, yourself."

"Is this a bad time to call?"

"No. I've been going nonstop and am just leaving
Billings to drive back to the ranch. How was your
day? Any new finds?"

"A hide scraper made out of bottle glass."

Jarod nodded. "Sounds like traditional technology
meshed with a modern material."

"Exactly. I'd love you to work with me one of these days. Am I going to see you tonight?"

He'd already put her off once. "Let's do it. I'll meet you at the Moose Creek Barbecue in White Lodge at seven for dinner. You can tell me what else you've found."

"I can't wait to see you."

Jarod didn't feel the same way. "It'll be good to see you, too. I've had a ton of business to do for my grandfather and will enjoy the break."

"Jarod?" she asked tentatively. "Are you all right?"

He took a labored breath. "Why do you ask?"

"I don't know. You sound…detached."

"It's not intentional. I'm afraid it has been a long day. See you tonight."

After he ended the call, he realized he couldn't go on this way. Leslie needed reassurance, but Sadie's unexpected return to Montana had altered the path he'd been plodding since she'd left, throwing him into the greatest turmoil of his life.

What Daniel had told her that night had crystalized certain things for Jarod. If the statute of limitations hadn't run out and he could discover the proof, Ned would be facing felony assault charges for using a borrowed truck as a deadly weapon. Worse, because he'd left the scene of the crime without reporting it or getting help for Jarod, Ned would be looking at prison time.

If he didn't reopen the case, the most Jarod would do was go to Tyson and Grant with any evidence he found and let them deal with Ned in their own way.

His hand tightened around the phone, almost

crushing it. What if he did find enough evidence to have the case reopened?

If Jarod's uncle Charlo knew what was going through his nephew's mind right now, he would intimate that the reason Jarod hadn't received his vision yet was because his cry was selfish. Only those who were of exemplary character and well prepared received the truly great visions. With the taste for revenge this strong on Jarod's lips, he was far from that serene place his uncle talked about.

Chapter Five

Saturday morning Sadie got breakfast for her and Ryan and then they went outside to an overcast sky. The small garden plot on the south wall of the house where it received the most sun needed work. While she watched Ryan toddle around with some toys, Sadie prepared the soil, then laid out black plastic to warm it up, a trick she'd learned from Addie Bannock years earlier. In a week she'd plant seeds.

While her mouth salivated at the thought of enjoying sweet juicy melons all summer, her cell phone rang. She wished it were Jarod, yet she knew that was impossible. As Millie had said, Sadie needed to be the one to tell him there was no other man in her life. But that was complicated because he was seeing another woman.

Even if he wanted to call Sadie, which he didn't, he would have to use the landline because he didn't know her cell phone number. With a troubled sigh she pulled the cell from her pocket and checked the Caller ID. One glance and her spirits lifted.

"Zane! How are things going?"

"Couldn't be better. I've had all our mail forwarded to White Lodge. Right now I'm at the house sorting things. Tomorrow the moving van will come to put everything in storage. When they're through here, they'll load up the things from my apartment. How's Ryan?"

"Missing you. Just a minute. He'll want to talk to you." She walked over to her brother. "Ryan? It's your uncle Zane. Can you say hello?"

After Ryan greeted his uncle and babbled some other words not quite intelligible, she heard Zane chuckle and a conversation ensued with Ryan mentioning the juice he'd had for breakfast and one of the toy cars he held in his hand.

"You have to hang up now," she told the little boy. "Tell Uncle Zane bye-bye."

Ryan liked saying the words over and over, but finally Sadie put the phone back to her ear. "If I do the planting right, we'll have fresh honeydew all summer."

"How about some cantaloupe, too!"

"I'll plant some of those and maybe some green beans."

"Terrific. Have you heard from Mr. Bree yet?"

"No. I don't really expect to until you have a prospective buyer for Tim's house."

"Let's hope it's soon, but at least our Realtor has contacted him and knows we're serious. If all goes well here, I'll have the cleaners come and leave for Billings sometime Sunday in my Volvo. It can hold the main stuff you wanted me to bring along with my own."

"That's great. What about my Toyota?"

"The salesman at the dealership said he'd get a good price for it."

"I hope so. Dad's old truck is on its last legs. I need to buy a used one."

"Understood. Depending on how late I get away, it might be Monday night before I reach the ranch."

"We'll be waiting. Ryan will be thrilled. He keeps looking for you." Right now he was down on his haunches, pushing his little trucks and cars through the grass.

"I can't believe how much I've missed him."

Her throat swelled. "He's adorable."

"Amen."

"Is it going to be difficult to pull up stakes, Zane?"

"No. I'll always have my good memories, but my life isn't here anymore."

"I know what you mean. Much as I love San Francisco, my home is here."

After a silence, Zane told her, "Don't work too hard, Sadie."

"It's saving my life." Along with making a new home for Ryan, she needed to stay too busy to think. She'd tackled cleaning the house, including her father's bedroom. Now the outside needed attention. "Thank you for taking care of everything, Zane. I don't know what I'd do without you."

"We're family. Let's agree we both need each other. Because of you I can feel a whole new life opening up. When everything fell apart, I couldn't imagine putting one foot in front of the other."

She cleared her throat. "I've been there and done that."

"I know you have." He knew the secrets of her heart. "Talk to you soon."

"Drive safely, Zane." Her voice trembled. "If anything happened to you…"

"It won't."

As Sadie hung up, she felt a shadow fall over her. When she lifted her head she discovered Jarod standing there.

"Sorry," he said in his deep voice. "Once again I've startled you. Millie was out on the front porch washing windows and told me to walk around back."

After wishing he'd been the one who'd phoned her, she was so shocked to see him, she couldn't think clearly. Somehow on Jarod a denim shirt and jeans looked spectacular. "No problem. As you can see, I've been getting the ground ready to plant."

"Shades of my grandmother Addie."

She nodded. He remembered everything.

His enigmatic black eyes swept over her. "I drove over here to talk to you about the accident."

Jarod's reason for coming was as unexpected as his presence. Sadie struggled to keep the tremor out of her voice. "Since you didn't believe me about my father, I'm afraid any answers you need are buried with him."

He put his hands on his hips; pulling her attention to his hard-muscled physique. "I've given it a lot of thought and I don't believe your father was the culprit, Sadie. That's why I'm here."

Shock number two. "But he said—"

"What he did was use a scare tactic to frighten you away from me for good," Jarod cut in on her. "I'm convinced that when he heard I was in the hospital, he realized it was the perfect moment to play on your fears."

Sadie was afraid to believe it. "Then who could have done such an evil thing?" She removed her gardening gloves.

"I've been doing an investigation and hope to figure it out before long. I wanted you to know that no matter how much pain your father caused you, he wasn't responsible for trying to hurt me or he would have done it much earlier. Though he wished I hadn't been in your life, we both know he was a troubled man with a terrible drinking problem. But it didn't go as far as planning to kill me, so you can cross him off your list."

Her lungs had constricted, making it difficult to breathe. "But according to you, someone *did* want you dead."

His eyes narrowed on her features. "The police and I both felt that the accident had to have been premeditated. Someone went to elaborate lengths to set me up. It took someone whose dislike of me turned to hate. I'll give you one guess."

Suddenly she felt sick. *"Ned,"* she whispered.

"I'm afraid so."

"After you told me he'd been stalking you in town, I thought a lot about that myself. But for him to go after you like that…"

"It chills the blood to think he could have done it to his own family, but I can't rule him out as the prime suspect."

"I agree," she whispered. Being a year younger than Jarod, Ned had been a senior when she'd started high school. He'd always chased after her. The more she'd ignored him, the more he'd mocked her friendship with his "half-breed cousin."

"He never hid his dislike of you."

After his graduation Ned had hung out in White Lodge with his friends and followed her around whenever she went into town. His actions were repulsive to her.

"You're the one girl who never gave him the time of day, but he never stopped wanting you. As our love grew, so did his jealousy. It's my belief he'd been following me on those last few nights when we met in the mountains. But I didn't realize it until the night before you and I were going to leave for the reservation. I caught him spying on me as I rode to the barn."

Horrified, Sadie stared at him. "You think he was watching us wh-when—" She couldn't finish.

"That's exactly what I think. But he couldn't go to my grandfather claiming to have seen us when he had no reason to be watching us. That would have opened up a whole new set of problems for him."

"He was sick!"

Jarod nodded. "The next afternoon after I hitched the horse trailer to my truck, he saw me leave with Chief and knew I was getting ready to do something with you. So he set me up, but he needed an accomplice and couldn't use one of our trucks on the ranch."

"Who would help him do anything that hideous?"

"His best friend, Owen."

"Owen Pearson? Cindy's brother?" She was incredulous. "I know they used to drink and mess around like a lot of guys, but I can't imagine him doing anything like that."

"I found out from my grandfather that Ned and Owen committed a crime a few years ago but it was hushed up." Jarod told her what he'd learned from Harlow. "Ned could wheedle money from his father when he wanted. Don't forget he and Owen have been friends for years and got into so much trouble, Ralph claims it turned Grant prematurely gray."

"I didn't realize Ned gave your family that many worries. It's still hard for me to believe Owen would go that far."

"I've been doing my own investigation." Jarod reached in his back pocket and handed her a sheet of paper, which she opened. It was a photocopy of a receipt from a body shop in Bozeman. The repairs listed included grill and front fender work on a 2003 Ford F-150 pickup owned by Kevin Pearson of the Bar-S Ranch, brought in on May 10 and repairs completed May 16 of the year in question.

"Jarod—" She lifted her eyes to him. Streams of unspoken words passed between them.

"The manager of the shop didn't recognize Ned's picture. It's been too many years. But whoever took the truck in paid cash up front. I checked the police report on my truck, which was totaled. Once I contact the department that investigated my case and give them this receipt, then the case will be reopened to see if there's a match between the two vehicles."

"That means they'll be contacting the Pearsons about the truck." Sadie frowned. "What if it has been sold or traded in for another one by now?"

"The police will track it down. Owen will have to fess up to what happened to his father's truck. Unless, of course, it's a huge coincidence and his father's truck was damaged some other way. But if that was the case, why didn't he let the insurance pay for it?

"I'm afraid he has a lot of explaining to do. If he was helping Ned, then he'll have to make the decision if he wants to go to jail for him or not. But I'm not ready to act quite yet."

Sadie's eyes stung with salty tears. "I don't know why you have to wait. This couldn't be a coincidence. Ned could have killed you— All this time I thought it was my father." Her body grew tense. "Your cousin should go to prison for what he did. You were left to die—"

Her raised voice alarmed Ryan, who stood and came running to her with an anxious look on his precious face. She swept him up into her arms and buried her face in his neck.

"But I didn't," Jarod said in a quiet voice, tousling Ryan's hair. "I'm pretty sure he didn't intend to finish me off, just put me out of commission. As for his plan, it backfired because I was back on the ranch three days later and you'd fled to California out of his reach. Your departure put an end to any dreams Ned entertained about the two of you getting together."

"He was delusional."

"I agree. But now that you're back, he's going to make trouble again."

Her stomach muscles clenched. "What do you mean?"

"I know for a fact he hasn't given up on you. Avery

told me about the incident at the funeral when Ned approached you. Be careful around him."

That sounded ominous. "What aren't you telling me?"

"I suppose we'll all find out when this new investigation gets under way. I'll leave now so you can give your little brother the attention he's craving. He really looks like his uncle."

"It's the dimples. They run in the Lawson family. Mom fell in love with Tim's. It kills me Ryan has been deprived of both parents."

"He has a wonderful mother in you."

"Thank you. I'm planning to adopt him."

"Then he's a lucky little boy. Take care, Sadie, and remember what I said."

"Jarod? Wait—" she called to him, but he moved too fast on those long, powerful legs. She couldn't very well run after him with Ryan in her arms. Her brother needed lunch and a nap.

Sadie hurried inside, shaken by everything he'd told her and even more shaken by the things he'd only hinted at. Millie stood at the kitchen sink filling another bucket with hot water and vinegar. "Jarod was here a long time. Everything all right?"

"Yes and no." She didn't dare share the evidence Jarod had uncovered until he gave her permission. But one thing had become self-evident. Her longing to be with him was growing unbearable.

Millie started out the back door, then paused. Sadie thought she detected a faint smile on the older woman's lips. "After you've fed Ryan and put him down, come on outside where I'm working. There's something you ought to know."

With one of those cryptic comments Millie was famous for, Sadie hurried to feed Ryan and put him down with a bottle. The cute little guy had tired himself out playing and fell asleep fast.

She found Millie washing the windows at the rear of the house. "I'm back."

The housekeeper looked over her shoulder at Sadie. "When Jarod drove in, he was pulling a horse trailer. After he left, I saw him drive to the barn and pull around it. Kind of made me wonder what he was doing when the road back to his place goes in the other direction. If I were you, I'd walk down there and find out what's going on."

Sadie's heart raced till it hurt. Feeling seventeen again, she flew down the drive past her father's truck to the barn. But when she rounded the corner, Jarod's rig wasn't there and her heart plummeted to her feet.

After hearing her call to him, had he hoped she'd come after him? Until she had answers, she wouldn't be able to breathe. While she stood there in a quandary, she heard Liz's horses whinnying and wondered what was going on.

She opened the barn doors. "Hey, you guys. What's up?" She walked inside to check both stalls. All of a sudden she heard the neigh of another horse. It couldn't be Mac's. He was out working on his horse, Toby.

Sadie spun around. The light from outside illuminated the interior enough for her to see a gleaming black filly in the stall where she'd once kept Brandy.

Her body started to tremble as she moved closer to the three-year-old, which looked to be fourteen hands high.

This couldn't be the foal she'd seen in the purple lupine with Jarod when she was seventeen! That wasn't possible, but the filly had those special hooked ears and broad forehead that tapered to the muzzle, just the way Sadie remembered. On further examination she saw the straight head and wide-set eyes of Chief, the wild stallion Jarod had tamed.

"Oh, you gorgeous creature," she whispered shakily. Sadie didn't need to ask where this beauty had come from. "I'll be back, but first I need to know all about you before this goes any further. I promise I won't be long."

Sadie's feet seemed to have wings as she flew up the road to the house. "Millie?"

The housekeeper turned around. "I'm right here!"

"I've got to find Jarod. Do you mind watching Ryan until I get back?"

"Of course not, honey. What's going on?"

Sadie ran in the house to grab the keys off the peg. When she came out she said, "There's a new filly in the barn. I can't keep her. Jarod needs to come back and get it."

Before she reached the truck a voice of irony called out, "Good luck to that."

Five minutes later she drove through the gates of the Bannock Ranch. The spread resembled a small city. She took the road leading to the barn and corrals where Jarod would have parked the horse trailer. Intent on finding him, she wound around the sheds until she saw his rig in the distance. He still hadn't unhitched the trailer.

After pulling up next to it, she jumped down from the truck. As she reached the entrance, the man she'd come to see was just leaving the barn on his horse. Riding bareback, the magnificent sight of him ready to head out took her breath. His long black hair, fastened at the nape, gleamed despite the gathering storm clouds blotting out the sun.

They saw each other at the same time. He was caught off guard for once, and his eyes gleamed black fire as they roved over her, thrilling her to the core of her being. While she stood there out of breath, he brought his horse close before coming to a standstill.

She couldn't swallow. "I have to talk to you, Jarod."

How she envied him sitting there as still as a summer's day. "I'm going to ride to the upper pasture. Come with me."

Before she could respond, he reached down with that swift male grace only he possessed and lifted her so she was seated in front of him. He wrapped his left arm around her waist and tucked her up tight against him. The way his hand splayed over her midriff infused electricity in every cell of her body.

"Reminds me of old times," he murmured against her temple, "except this time I'll be able to see where we're going. Don't get me wrong. I like your new hairstyle, but now I don't have anything to tug."

That rare teasing side of Jarod had come out, the side she adored. Robbed of words, she was helpless to do anything but give in to the euphoria of being this close to him again. Though it had been eight years, their bodies knew each other and settled in as one entity.

Once he urged his horse into a gallop, the layers of pain peeled away, liberating her for a moment out of time. Heedless of the darkening clouds, they were like children who'd been let out of school and were eager to run until they dropped.

She quickly lost track of where they were going. This was like flying through heaven, achieving heights and distant stars unknown until now. Filled with delight, she heard laughter and realized it was her own. Through it all her body absorbed the fierce pounding of his heart against her back.

At one point it dawned on her he'd brought them to the pine-covered ridge that looked down on their favorite place. He reined his horse to a stop so they could enjoy the meadow with its vista of wildflowers in glorious bloom.

She gripped the hand pinning her against him. *"Jarod..."*

"I haven't heard you say my name like that except in my sleep. Did you ever dream of me?"

This was a time for honesty.

"Yes," she admitted quietly.

"Every night?"

Haunted by the agony she heard in his voice because it matched her own, she said, "Don't ask me that. It's all in the past. I came to find you because—"

"The filly is yours, Sadie." The authority in his voice signaled the end of the discussion. "Now that the war is over, consider it a peace offering."

She was still in shock over his incredible gift, but it was growing darker. "Jarod, we'd better go back before we get caught in the rain."

"It's too late. We'll stay in the shelter of these pines until it passes over. Volan needs a rest."

He slid off his horse in an instant and gripped her waist to help her down. After tying the reins to a tree branch, he walked her over to the fattest tree trunk and sat against it, pulling her onto his lap. By now the wind was gusting, bringing the smell of rain with it.

"This is only a small storm. We'll wait it out." He gathered her to him in a protective gesture. Cocooned in his warmth, she could stay like this forever. "If you're worried about getting wet, I promise I'll protect you."

She relaxed against him. "Tell me about the adorable filly."

"Chief was her sire."

"I *knew* it. She has the shape of his head and eyes."

"It took two tries with the black broodmare I acquired to produce her." She could tell by the softness in his voice that her observation had pleased him. "Her first offspring was a grullo I gave to Uncle Charlo's boy."

"You mean, Squealing Son Who Runs Fast?"

Jarod chuckled. "You remember."

"I remember everything," she confessed in a tremulous voice. "He must be fifteen by now."

"The perfect age to train his own stallion. But that was his childhood name. Now he's known as Runs Over Mountains."

"Sounds like he has some of the same genes that run through his noble cousin Sits in the Center."

He kissed the side of her brow, sending fingers of delight through her nervous system. "What happened to Born of Flint?"

Jarod had forgiven her. "That name belonged to my world when pain was my constant companion. But seriously, Jarod, no gift has ever thrilled me more. I love her already."

"Your filly has been registered as Black Velvet. Until now, she has lived at the reservation on my uncle's property. I've been getting her used to a saddle, but you'll need to break her in more before you take her riding."

Sadie gripped his hand harder. Velvet was the name she'd given the new foal they'd seen that wonderful day years ago. Now Sadie had her own filly, a horse who'd known nothing but Jarod's love. She had to clear her throat. "Velvet has been trained by the expert. Thank you doesn't begin to cover what I'm feeling, not when I've done nothing to deserve such a present."

"When my grandfather told me you were going to stay in Montana, I realized you would need a horse."

"Your uncle Charlo must be bursting with pride."

"What do you mean?"

"Do you remember the time you took me to meet him and his family? Before we left he took me aside and told me you possessed a very rare trait like your mother. It was the ability to hear the cries of the oppressed, the sick, the weak. He said that you weren't ashamed to help others.

"I didn't understand what he meant at the time, but I do now. After I visited Ralph last week he told you everything about my situation, didn't he?"

Before she heard his answer, the rain descended, first in individual drops, then it poured, yet they stayed dry. She nestled deeper in his arms, finding a comfort she'd never known in her life, except with him. Together they listened to the elements that had always made up their world.

His lips were buried in her hair. "You think I see you as a charity case?"

"I think that's the way you've always seen me. A cast-off waif you took pity on because it's in your nature. After eight years, you're still coming to my rescue, trying to right wrongs against me by giving me Velvet. I'll be indebted to you all my life for everything you've done for me in the past, but it's time you gave that side of your nature a rest in order to walk your true path."

He lifted his head in surprise. "My true path?"

"Mmm." The downpour was easing in intensity. She moved out of his arms and stood. "The one you used to talk about that will lead to your ultimate destiny."

After a long silence he asked, "What about yours?"

"Mine was revealed when my mother died and left Ryan to my care."

Before she gave in to her longing and begged him to kiss her, she needed answers about the woman who was in his life now. "Tell me about Leslie Weston."

Immediately he got to his feet. "Listening to so many wagging tongues tends to confuse the listener."

"If you're talking about the way you were confused with wagging tongues concerning me and Zane
at the funeral, you're right. But please don't be offended. I've heard she's a lovely woman who works
with Avery at the dig site. Your grandfather sounded
particularly taken with her, which means you're on
the right path."

"Grandfathers are prone to dream."

"Liz tells me that not only is Leslie a highly edu-
cated archaeologist studying the Crow culture, she's
also well-traveled and comes from a good family in
Colorado Springs. How important is she to you?"

"Why do you ask?" His tone grated.

Don't tiptoe around this, Sadie. "Because when
word gets out where Velvet came from, I don't want
her to misunderstand or be hurt."

After the telltale rise and fall of his chest, he said,
"The rain has stopped. We need to get back to the
ranch."

Instead of a protestation that the woman he'd been
involved with meant nothing to him, he was ready
to leave this sacred place. Sadie had her answer. She
just hadn't expected it to feel as if one of those wild
stallions they used to watch had just kicked her in the
chest, knocking the life out of her.

Schooling her features to show no emotion, she
turned to him. "This time I'll sit behind you. That
way I can tug on *your* hair for a change."

Her teasing produced no softening of his stone-
faced expression. As he walked over to Volan, she
followed him. "I liked the way you used to wear it, but
I'm glad you gave in to the right impulse to let it grow.

"I know you'll hate hearing this because you don't like compliments, but now that I'm grown up, I'm not afraid to say what I think. You're a very beautiful man, Sits in the Center. Leslie Weston would have figured that out the first time she laid eyes on you."

In seconds he'd vaulted onto Volan's back with practiced ease, then held out his hand for Sadie to climb on behind him. She settled herself and slid her arms around his waist. If she couldn't kiss the life out of him because he belonged to someone else, she could at least hold him in her arms for the ride home.

Judging from his reaction to her question about Leslie, this would be the only time she would ever be allowed to get this close to him again. As the rain that had cleared the air, this conversation had cleared away the last piece in the complicated mosaic of their lives. Their love story had come to its final, tragic close.

Chapter Six

Jarod's uncle Charlo knew of his nephew's struggle to let Leslie or any woman into his life while another woman lived in his heart. This Saturday afternoon Sadie's question ended the struggle. He knew what had to be done to end a situation that couldn't go on any longer.

As they rode back to Jarod's ranch in silence, his uncle's analogy about the wolf took on fresh meaning. It *would* be better to risk death for a chance to find a mate and a territory than to live through every winter in agony alone.

Weighed down by his thoughts, he was surprised to hear Sadie's sudden gasp as they approached the barn. He glanced over to see what had caused the reaction. If it wasn't Ned coming out of the barn on foot! Once again it was no accident he'd been hanging around. He must have seen Daniel Corkin's truck and put two and two together. Jarod thought his cousin looked a little green around the edges. Wasn't that jealousy's color?

Sadie's arms tightened around Jarod as he rode his horse straight to her truck. Aware of her fear, he threw his leg over Volan and pulled her off, then opened the driver's door. "In you go," he whispered, shutting it after her.

Their eyes met for a breathless moment before she started the engine and took off. He stood there watching until she'd driven out of sight.

Ned smirked at him. "Leslie's not going to like it when she finds out what you've been doing all afternoon."

Jarod turned to look at his cousin. "I'm afraid there's a lot more you're not going to like when your father hears you've been spending time in town minding other people's business rather than inspecting the machinery."

When Jarod had hired Ben as the new foreman, one of his jobs was to keep a close eye on Ned, who was lax in his responsibilities and played hooky when he thought he could get away with it. Ben reported Ned's activities to Jarod on a daily basis. Ned's assigned job was to keep all the ranch machinery in good condition and operational, but he often failed in that department, which added to Jarod's workload.

"What in the hell are you talking about?"

"The grain-cutting swathers and forage harvesters for one thing. They haven't been oiled or greased on time. That's your department. One of the grain trucks has a broken part that needs replacing. Have you taken a look at the Haybine mowers lately? If I were you, I'd get busy or it could all rebound on you."

Ned's cheeks turned a ruddy color, a sure sign of guilt. "What do you mean?"

"That's for *you* to figure out." From the corner of his eye, he glimpsed Rusty, the stable manager, and signaled to him. "We got caught in the storm, and now I'm in a hurry. Will you take care of Volan for me? He'll need a rubdown."

"Sure, Jarod."

Ignoring Ned, Jarod walked over to his rig to unhitch the trailer. The puddles from the cloudburst were still drifting away. Climbing into his truck, he drove out of the parking area without acknowledging his cousin and headed for White Lodge.

Leslie would be off work by now. He hoped to find her at her apartment. He knew she'd sensed something was wrong on their dinner date Wednesday. It was time they talked. She lived in an eight-plex near the center of town where they usually met before going out for the evening. He'd brought her out to the ranch one time to meet his grandfather, but it was easier for them to get together in White Lodge, the halfway point between her work and the ranch.

Both his grandfather and uncle approved of her. Charlo had been amenable to her interviewing him for a newsletter she contributed to about the Absarokee dig site. There was nothing not to like about Leslie. But she wasn't Sadie.

Pleased to see her Forerunner parked in her stall, he drove to the guest parking and got out of his truck. Taking the stairs two at a time, he reached her apartment and gave a knock she would recognize.

He didn't have to wait long for her to open the door. "Jarod—" She broke into a smile that lit up her brown eyes. "I didn't know you were coming tonight. Why didn't you say something at dinner the other night or phone me?"

"I'm sorry I didn't give you any warning, but this couldn't wait."

When he didn't reach to kiss her, her smile slowly disappeared. "Come in. Is this about your grandfather? Is he worse?"

He walked into her living room. "No. I'm happy to say he's doing better and off his oxygen for the time being."

"That's wonderful! Have you eaten yet? I just made homemade fajitas. Would you like one?"

"They smell good, but I'm not hungry. Go ahead and eat." He took a seat in one of her overstuffed chairs.

She frowned. "I don't think I can till you tell me what's wrong. You're not yourself. In fact, for the past two weeks you haven't been the Jarod I've known."

He shook his head. "I realize that."

Leslie perched on the arm of the sofa, studying him. "You wouldn't have come here out of the blue like this without a good reason. Have you decided you don't want to see me anymore?" He heard the pain in her voice.

Jarod met her searching gaze head-on. "I can't," he answered. She deserved the whole truth no matter how much it hurt. He was glad he hadn't been intimate with her yet.

Her features looked pinched. "Avery hinted that there was someone in your past. Are you saying you can't get over her?"

He got to his feet. "I thought I'd put her behind me, but her father died and now she's back in Montana for good. I was with her today."

She averted her eyes. "And the old chemistry is still working."

The blood hammered in his ears. "Yes. Don't get me wrong. We're not together. I don't know if we ever will be, but feeling as I do—"

"I get it," she broke in. "Do you mind my asking who she is?"

"Her name is Sadie Corkin. The Corkin ranch borders our property."

Leslie stood. "Childhood sweethearts?"

"Yes."

"That's an obstacle I'm not even going to attempt to hurdle. One of the many things I admire about you, Jarod, is your honesty, even when it's devastating."

"Leslie…I was trying to make it work with us."

She walked over to the door, her curly auburn hair swinging slightly. "I believe you and I give you full marks, but in the end, trying doesn't cut it. That explains why you weren't anxious to sleep with me, or to drive to Colorado with me."

"If she'd never come back, things might have been different."

"No." Leslie shook her head. "If she hadn't come back, our relationship would still have ended because it's evident you're a one-woman man. There aren't very many of those around." She clung to the open door. "I've loved every minute we've spent together."

"So have I."

"Because of who you are, I know you mean that."

"I do."

"But it's just not enough for me or you. Love means sharing a single soul inhabiting two bodies. That definition doesn't apply to you and me. I'm grateful you stopped by, Jarod, but now I need to be alone."

Jarod had no desire to make this any more painful. "Take care, Leslie." He kissed her forehead before leaving the apartment. He wished there was some way he could have spared her this hurt. No one deserved happiness more than she did.

On his drive back to the ranch, her parting comment played over in his mind. He and Sadie *had* shared one soul. That's why no other relationship had worked for him. But he still didn't know about the men she'd been involved with since she'd moved to California.

If there was someone important, she wasn't letting it get in the way of buying the ranch and living here. So many questions still remained unanswered where Sadie was concerned. But saying goodbye to Leslie had been the right thing to do.

When he entered the front door of the ranch house, the housekeeper came running. "I'm glad you're home. Your grandfather is in an agitated state."

He moaned. "I thought the doctor had taken him off the oxygen."

She shook her head. "It's not his health, Jarod. Tyson was here earlier and they quarreled." *Tyson?* "He's terribly upset about something and says he can't discuss it with anyone but you."

Jarod's gut told him this had to be about Ned, especially after their confrontation earlier. "Where's Avery?"

"She's not home yet."

"Thanks, Jenny." He hurried down the hall to

his grandfather's bedroom and found him sitting up at his desk near the window in his pajamas and robe. Though he was gratified to see Ralph was well enough to be out of bed, Jenny's mention of Tyson had filled him with concern.

"Grandfather?"

He looked around with a flushed face. "At last."

"What's happened?"

"What hasn't?" he said with uncharacteristic sharpness. "I'm sorry, son. I didn't mean to snap. I'm just glad you're home. Sit down. We have to talk."

Jarod pulled up a chair next to the desk. "I can see you've been going over the accounts."

Ralph's gray eyes flicked to his. "Tyson needed me to help him with the figures. He just left. I'm afraid we had it out. It's been coming on for a long time. After our father died, Addie warned me I should let my brother take his share of the ranch and make it his own place. But he begged me to go into business with him and I didn't have the heart to say no. For the most part we've gotten along. But with time, there've been issues over Ned. He doesn't have your instincts for ranching and never did.

"Your idea of developing two calving seasons a few years ago has brought in unprecedented profits. When Tyson and I went along with your plan, Ned fell apart and has been impossible ever since. Now that Ned has found out the Corkin property is up for sale, he's asked for a loan from Grant to buy it."

Jarod got up from the chair and started pacing. "Let me guess. Grant's money is stretched due to helping his other children, so he's come to Tyson for $700,000 for Ned to buy the place."

Ralph nodded. "Grant's always been afraid of Ned and doesn't know how to say no to him. It's Grant's opinion that if Ned made a break with the family business and had his own spread to manage, his son might turn into a real rancher."

"We know that's never going to happen."

His grandfather shook his head. "I advised Tyson it would be the wrong decision to give money to a grandson who could never make good on such an investment. But just as I feared, he got angry. My brother isn't well and not up for a fight with Grant. He told me he'd be back tomorrow for my consent. If I don't give it, he'll take the money out, anyway. Of course, it's his right as part owner."

They stared at each other before Jarod said, "What do you want to do? Tell Tyson you've already authorized Harlow to buy the ranch for Sadie and Zane?"

"Never. That has to remain a secret."

Jarod didn't need to think about it. "Then don't try to stop him, Grandfather. You love your brother too much, so make your peace with him and let him negotiate with Mr. Bree. When the time is almost up, Harlow will come in with a little higher offer and that will be it.

"In time Tyson and Grant will learn that Zane Lawson bought the ranch and no one will ever know the truth because the money came out of your savings account and mine. Tyson has no access to them."

His grandfather tilted his head back. "What do you mean *your* account?"

"I've been investing my money and plan to contribute. Sadie'd be my wife if things had been different."

"I know." Ralph's eyes dimmed. "When Addie and I heard about your accident, it was one of the worst moments of our lives. We could have lost you." His voice trembled.

Touched by those words, Jarod squeezed his shoulder. "Don't you know I'm tough like you? Now that you're feeling better, I have news. Let me show you what I found after doing some investigating about the accident on my own."

Jarod showed his grandfather the paper from the body shop in Bozeman incriminating Owen Pearson.

Tears rolled down Ralph's cheeks. "Oh, Jarod… All these years I've asked you to be the bigger man, which you always will be. To think Ned could have done such a thing. It explains why his behavior has grown worse over time. You have every right to go to the police with what you've found."

"That's true." For now he was holding off deciding what to do about it. "Did Sadie tell you she's going to adopt Ryan?"

"Yes, bless her heart." His grandfather reached for Jarod's hand. "Now tell me about that lovely woman you brought to the house a while back. When are you going to bring her again?"

"I'm afraid that's not going to happen, Grandfather."

"Why not?"

"I drove to White Lodge earlier this evening and told Leslie the truth. I can't be involved with her while I still have feelings for Sadie."

"You've done the right thing for Leslie and yourself," he murmured with what sounded like satisfaction. "A house divided against itself can't stand."

In spite of his turmoil, Jarod smiled. He bounced between two cultures. Both his mentors offered the same wisdom.

"So." His grandfather sat back in the chair looking relieved. "We'll keep all this to ourselves and wait a few more days before we tell Harlow to make the final move. When everything has been transacted, Harlow can contact Zane and they'll go from there."

Jarod's thoughts shot ahead. "It's good it will be in Zane's name." He gave his grandfather a hug. "I'll tell Martha to come in and help you get ready for bed."

Ralph tugged on his arm. "Do me a favor, son. Watch your back around Ned. I need you."

The feeling was mutual.

RYAN WAS ECSTATIC when Zane came into the kitchen on Tuesday morning. He'd arrived late Monday night. While the two of them walked down to the barn to visit the new filly Sadie had told him about, she had hurriedly put the things away that Zane had brought from California. Now Ryan had his toys and pictures, and his room resembled the nursery Eileen had made for him in San Francisco.

After lunch he went down for a nap with his favorite furry rabbit.

Zane was bringing in the last of his own items from the car when Sadie stepped out onto the front porch dressed in cowboy boots, jeans and a short-sleeved white blouse. She'd tied an old black paisley bandana around her neck for fun.

"You look cute in that."

"Thanks. When I saw it in the sack you brought in, it brought back memories. I thought, why not look the part."

"All you need is a cowboy hat."

She smiled. "I'm afraid my old one got lost years ago. While Ryan's asleep, I'll run into town and pick one up when I get the groceries."

"Take as long as you want. I plan to devote the rest of the day to him once he wakes up."

"He'll love that. We're so glad you're back safely."

"Me, too." His eyes glinted with curiosity. "That horse is a beauty. For Jarod to give you a present like that means he still cares for you a great deal."

She shook her head. "He feels sorry for me."

"Sadie—"

"It's true. He knew Dad sold my old horse. Before you say anything else, you need to know Jarod's involved with another woman and it's serious."

Zane frowned. "Did he tell you that?"

It was more a case of his not answering her question about Leslie Weston when they'd been out riding the other day. "I've heard it from his grandfather and from Liz, who's very close with Avery. Now, I'd better get going. See you later and we'll talk."

They only had two weeks left to work out an arrangement with Mr. Bree. So far she'd been living on some of her savings while they'd pooled their resources. With the days passing so quickly, Sadie's fear escalated that their best efforts might not be enough.

But she refused to think about that yet, or the possibility that Jarod might be getting married in the near future. Millie had sounded as though she thought it could happen.

After loading up on groceries in White Lodge, Sadie put the bags in the truck, then decided to buy herself a treat in the hope it would make her feel better. The Saddle Up Barn was just down the street. She'd drop by there for a cowboy hat.

It didn't take her long to find the one she wanted. Black, like her new filly, like…Jarod's eyes and hair. The band and sides of the brim were covered in a delicate gold floral pattern that picked up the gold-and-silver cowboy concho on the band. She was partial to the pinch-front, teardrop crown that gave it character.

After paying the bill, she walked out of the shop wearing the hat and was met by a barrage of wolf whistles from various guys passing by in their rigs. Their response reminded her of her barrel racing days in her teens. She'd almost forgotten what that experience was like.

Every time she and Liz performed at the county rodeo she'd watch for Jarod, hoping he'd be in the crowd with his family to cheer on Connor, who was a fabulous bulldogger. Being a contestant, she often carried the Montana State flag as they paraded around the arena for the opening ceremony. During those times when she was all decked out in her hat and fancy Western shirt with the fringe, she'd feel Jarod's piercing black eyes staring at her and almost faint with excitement.

The memories swamped her, causing her to forget she was headed for the post office. She needed to mail the thank-you notes she'd written to all the people who'd sent flowers for the funeral. While she was buying a book of stamps from the machine, she heard her name called out in a familiar voice and turned around.

"Avery!" Her heart raced to see Jarod's sister come up to her, a smile lighting her gray-green eyes. Avery and Jarod shared similar facial features that identified them as Bannocks.

"I've been following you since I saw you walking across the street. Do you know you caused about a dozen accidents out there?" Sadie laughed in embarrassment. "It's true. You used to knock them dead at the rodeo, but your impact is more lethal now."

"It's the new hat."

"That's bull and you know it. In high school the guys voted you Queen of Montana Days your senior year. To get that nomination, let alone win, you had to be able to stop traffic for *all* the right reasons."

"Stop—" She gave her friend a hug. Avery could make her blush.

"I'm glad I ran into you. Since Connor will be home, we're going to throw a surprise family birthday party on Monday the twenty-ninth, for Grandpa, who's going to be eighty-four. He's feeling so well we thought it would be fun to invite a few close friends. Our cousin Cassie will be coming from Great Falls, of course, and can't wait to see you. Naturally everyone on the Farfields Ranch is invited, including the Hensons, Ryan's uncle Zane and that cute little brother of yours."

Sadie could hardly breathe. It would mean facing Jarod, who would be there with Leslie Weston. Maybe they were celebrating more than a birthday. She felt ill at the possibility, but she'd have to go even if it killed her.

"Sadie, don't worry about Ned," Avery added. "Connor has orders to keep him away from you."

"Thanks." But Ned had been the furthest thing from her mind. "We'd love to come." Sadie marveled that she was even able to get the words out. "I'll tell Millie as soon as I get back to the ranch."

"Wonderful. It'll be very low key. Please, no gifts. I'm making his favorite homemade hand-cranked pineapple ice cream, Grandma Myra's recipe. When he sees what I'm doing, he'll want to help me."

"Don't let him do it, Avery!"

She chuckled. "Try telling him that. Come any time after six-thirty. Grandpa gets tired fast and goes to bed early."

"We'll be there. What can I bring?"

"Yourselves!"

Sadie gave her another hug. When Jarod had asked her to marry him, she'd been so thrilled that Avery was going to be her sister-in-law. Instead, Leslie Weston would be the luckiest woman on earth to become a part of that family.

"See you then, Avery." She watched her leave, then put the stamps on the envelopes and mailed them. With her heart dragging on the sidewalk, she headed back to the truck. How in the name of heaven would she get through the party when she knew Jarod would be there?

Maybe at the last minute she could claim Ryan was running a temperature. Zane could go without her. She'd send Ralph her apologies in a written note. Zane would deliver it with her gift and tell him she'd be over when Ryan was better. She and Ralph would celebrate with a card game.

On impulse she drove to Chapman's Drugstore and bought him two packs of playing cards and a card shuffler with new batteries. She also bought some wrapping paper and a silly birthday card Ralph would understand with his sense of humor. It said, "Grandfather still looks pretty good on his birthday. If it just hadn't been for_____." You could fill the line in with anything you wanted.

Without having to think about it Sadie wrote "the neighbors."

Chapter Seven

Avery had coordinated their grandfather's birthday party with Jarod and Connor's help. She'd hired caterers to do the cooking and serving out on the back patio. Jarod couldn't have been happier when he'd learned she'd included Sadie and the Hensons in the guest list.

Because of Ned, Jarod's afternoon ride with Sadie had ended abruptly, leaving things hanging. Since then he'd broken it off with Leslie, but due to the long hours of calving season, this would be Jarod's first opportunity to get Sadie alone and answer the question of Leslie's importance in his life.

The evening of the party, after a shower and shave, he put on a silky black sport shirt and gray trousers. This was a special occasion. Six weeks ago his grandfather had been in the hospital and Jarod had feared he wouldn't come out again. But he'd rallied and in some respects seemed better than he had been in several months. Jarod was convinced Sadie's presence on the Corkin ranch had had a lot to do with the change in him.

Ralph was furious over Daniel's shameless treatment of her. To help her keep the ranch in her family was a gesture that revealed the depth of his affection for her. Like Jarod, he was in this fight to win. The end of the month couldn't come soon enough for either of them. After Harlow bought the ranch, they could all breathe more easily again.

Once he was ready, he went downstairs. "You look distinguished in that new gray suit, Grandfather. It matches your eyes."

Ralph chuckled. "You think?"

"Connor has excellent taste."

"Come to think of it, you and I match," he said with a smile.

Just as he spoke, Connor walked into the bedroom wearing a tan suit. "Come on, you two. Everyone has started congregating out on the patio."

Jarod hoped that meant Sadie had arrived. He needed to tamp down the frantic pounding of his heart. He and his brother both linked arms with their grandfather and walked with him to the back of the house. Before they could see people, Jarod heard voices and smelled steaks cooking on the grill.

As they stepped out onto the patio, everyone clapped and sang "Happy Birthday." Jarod estimated the whole Bannock clan had showed up with at least twenty other family friends. His grandfather looked pleased with the turnout—sixty-odd people including grandchildren, young and old, sitting at the tables set up for the occasion.

Ralph thanked everyone for coming. "Go ahead and eat because that's what I intend to do. I'll bore you with a speech later!" His remarks drew laughter as Jarod and Connor helped him to his place at the head table.

"I'll get his food," Jarod said to his brother, who nodded.

He walked around the other side of the smorgasbord to fix his grandfather a plate. A quick glance at the assembled group revealed the Hensons had come, but to his disappointment no Corkins or Lawsons yet. His gaze traveled to Tyson and his wife's table, which included Grant and Pat. No sign of Ned, either.

Jarod needed to keep the line moving. His grandfather liked his steak medium-rare. After filling the plate, he carried it to the table and sat with him. Jarod wasn't hungry and told Connor to go ahead and get his food. His eyes went to Avery, looking particularly lovely in a deep red dress. She moved around, setting up a mike that could be passed around for people to make toasts.

In another five minutes Ned showed up. His father motioned him over to his table and the two men got into a lengthy discussion. Clearly, Grant wasn't happy about something, but that was nothing new.

As Jarod continued to look around, he saw Sadie and Zane slip in from the side of the house to sit with Mac and Millie. Zane held Ryan in his arms.

Sadie had dressed in a sophisticated orange, yellow and white print cocktail dress, an outfit she'd probably worn to dinner in San Francisco with some lucky man. The short sleeves and scooped neck exposed the tan she'd picked up since moving back to the ranch. Her windblown blond hair had the luster of a pearl. Jarod could find no words.

Before long one of the caterers wheeled out a cart carrying a chocolate birthday cake with lighted sparklers. The cake was in the shape of a giant cowboy boot with the word *Ralph* written in red frosting down the side. More of Avery's doing. Jarod gave his sister a silent nod of approval.

Their grandfather did the honors of cutting the cake. To facilitate matters, Connor and Jarod helped pass the dessert. When he neared Sadie's table and she looked up, it struck Jarod how the years had added a womanly beauty to her that he found irresistible. He couldn't take his eyes off her. "Enjoy your meal?"

"It was delicious," she said in a quiet voice, but a glance at her nearly full plate told him she hadn't been hungry, either. "I brought a present for Ralph. Where shall I put it?"

"I'll take it for you and give it to him."

"Thank you." She handed him a gift bag. The touch of her fingers sent a live current through his body. He walked to the head table and put the small bag in front of his grandfather. "It's a gift from Sadie," he whispered, then went back to handing out the cake.

A little while later Avery announced it was time for people to give toasts. Using the mike, everyone got in on the act, telling anecdotes about Jarod's grandfather that brought smiles and laughter. Finally it was Ralph's turn. With their help, he got to his feet.

"What a gratifying sight! If only Addie could be here with me. Thank you all for coming to help me celebrate. I don't know what I'd do without my three wonderful grandchildren who made this night possible. It's a very special night because one of our long-lost neighbors, Sadie Corkin, has come back to us after an eight-year absence, along with her new little brother, Ryan, and his uncle, Zane Lawson. I look forward to us being neighbors for years to come."

Only Jarod understood the meaning behind his grandfather's words and loved him for it. After Ralph showed Jarod the card she'd given him, emotion swamped him to realize what a burden her father's hatred had been to her.

"Thanks for this, Sadie." Ralph held up the card shuffler. "Sadie used to play canasta with me and Addie. I look forward to another game soon. I taught her how to play, you know." He winked. "Maybe this time I'll slaughter *you* instead of the other way around."

Amid the laughter and cheering, Jarod saw Sadie smile. A few minutes later she got up from the table with Ryan, who'd become restless. Anticipating her departure, he asked Connor to take care of their grandfather, then excused himself to walk through the house and catch up to her out front. No way was she going to get away from him tonight. He'd been living for it. Zane was right behind her.

"Leaving so soon?"

She looked shocked at Jarod's approach. "I'm sorry to just slip out like that, but it's past Ryan's bedtime and he was getting too noisy."

"Understood." He darted the little boy's uncle a glance. "There's no need for you to leave, too, Zane. Stay as long as you want. There's going to be dancing. I know three unattached females at the party who've been dying to get to know you. Since my duties are done for the evening, I'll drive Sadie and Ryan home in my truck."

Zane's brows lifted. "Would that be all right with you, Sadie?"

"What do *you* think? You've done so much baby-tending, it's time you had a night off. Jarod's right about the ladies. What's nice is, they're *all* beautiful."

With a chuckle, Zane kissed Ryan, and after a thank-you to Jarod, he headed around the ranch house to join the party.

SADIE WAS TREMBLING so hard, she was thankful she had Ryan to cuddle. For some reason Jarod had been alone tonight. She didn't know what that meant, but at the moment she didn't care because he wanted to take her home.

After she was settled, he reached around to fasten the two of them in with the seat belt. His nearness made her feverish. "I don't have a car seat for him, but I think we can manage to get you home without a problem."

"I'm not worried."

"Good." He shut her door and went around to the other side to climb in. "Your gift made Grandfather's night. Especially the card. He laughed till he cried."

"Cried would be the right word. My father pretty well ruined everyone's lives for years."

"Well, you're back where you belong and he couldn't be happier about it."

And you, Jarod? Are you happy about it, too?

Sadie wished she knew what was going on inside him. It wasn't long before they reached the ranch and she hurried inside with Ryan. Jarod followed. He'd never been allowed on Corkin property before, let alone to step across her threshhold. The moment was surreal for her.

"I'm trying to wean him off the bottle, but tonight he needs a little extra comfort after being around so many strange faces."

Jarod plucked him out of her arms. "Come on, Little Wants His Bottle." Sadie broke into laughter. "I'll change him while you get it."

There was no one in the world like Jarod. "I'm afraid he might not let you."

"We'll work it out, won't we," he said to Ryan. "I've changed my fair share of diapers at my uncle's house."

Delighted and intrigued to see him in this role, she left them alone long enough to half fill a bottle with milk. When she returned, she found Ryan ready for bed in a sleeper. There'd been no hystrionics. Jarod was holding him in his strong arms as they examined the animal mobile attached to the end of the crib. She paused in the doorway to listen.

"Dog," he told Ryan as he pointed.

"Dog," Ryan repeated. His blue eyes kept staring in fascination at Jarod.

"Now can you say horse?"

"Horse."

"That's right. One day you'll have a horse of your own."

Her eyes smarted. Jarod had always had a way with animals, but it was evident that the invisible power he possessed extended to little humans, too.

"I hate to break this up, but it's time to go night-night, sweetheart."

After she handed Ryan his bottle, Jarod lowered him into the crib. She tucked his rabbit next to him and Ryan started sucking on the nipple as he stared up at the two of them. Sadie went through her routine of singing his favorite songs to him. Pretty soon he'd finished most of the bottle and his eyes had fluttered closed.

They tiptoed out into the hall and went down to the living room. She turned to Jarod. "Thank you for helping me with Ryan. You were such a big distraction, he forgot to be upset."

A faint smile lingered at the corner of his compelling mouth. "I'm glad to know I'm useful for something."

She got this suffocating feeling in her chest. "I happen to know your grandfather couldn't get along without you."

They stood in the middle of the room. Jarod's eyes swept over her face and down her body, turning her limbs to water. "Do you realize this is the first time I've ever been inside your house, except at the funeral?"

"I was thinking the same thing, but I try not to let the ugliness of the past intrude. Ryan makes that a little easier."

"He's a sweet boy."

She could feel herself tearing up. "I just hope I'll be the mother he needs. It's a huge responsibility."

"You're a natural with him, Sadie."

"Thanks, but it's early days yet." Clearing her

throat she said, "Shouldn't you get back to the party before Ralph is missing you?"

"Connor's with him. I don't need to be anywhere else tonight. What I'd like to do is continue a certain conversation that came to an abrupt end when we discovered Ned waiting for us after the rainstorm. Mind if I stay awhile?"

Jarod...

Sadie was terrified she was going to hear news that would ruin the rest of her life.

"Of course not. Please, sit down."

After all the years her father had spouted his hatred for Jarod, it was nothing if not shocking to see him take a seat on the couch and make himself at home, arms spread across the top of the cushions. She sat rigidly on one of the chairs in front of the coffee table opposite him.

"When you asked me how important Leslie Weston was to me, I had my reasons for not answering you at the time."

Here it comes, Sadie. "I should never have asked you that question."

He leaned forward. "You were right to ask. Leslie wouldn't have understood about Velvet. How is your filly, by the way?"

"Wonderful." She stirred restlessly on the chair. "Jarod...you don't owe me any explanations."

"Then you're not interested to know why Leslie wasn't at tonight's party with me?"

Sadie lowered her head. "It's none of my business."

"Don't play games with me, Sadie. There's too

much history between us to behave like we're strangers."

"I agree," she confessed before eyeing him directly. "I thought she would be with you tonight. In fact, I was half expecting Ralph's birthday party would turn into an announcement of your engagement."

"You and a few other people, but it's never going to happen."

The finality of his words shocked her. "Why not?"

"We've stopped seeing each other."

Her heart ran away with her. "But I thought— I mean, I was led to believe your relationship was serious."

"I cared for her a great deal, but she wanted more from me than I could give her."

"You mean marriage."

"Yes. As long as we're being truthful, why don't you tell me how many men have proposed to you since you left Montana?"

There was no point in pretending there hadn't been men in her life after Jarod. "If any of them wanted to get married, I didn't give them a chance to get that close to me."

"Why not?"

She sucked in her breath. "Like you, I could tell they wanted a permanent relationship, but I wasn't ready to make a commitment."

For years she'd been in too much pain to even look at another man. When she finally did break down and start dating, no man came close to affecting her the way Jarod had done. He was an original. "How's that for honesty?"

"It's a start."

"Since we're going to be neighbors, I hope we can still be friends."

His black brows met in that fierce way they sometimes did. "That would be impossible."

His response was like a physical blow. "Why?"

"Because we've been lovers. There's no going back."

Heat suffused her cheeks. She shot to her feet. "That was a long time ago." She didn't want to talk about it.

"Too long. That's why we have to move forward. Marry me and it will be as if we were never apart."

"Jarod—" Maybe she'd just imagined he'd articulated her greatest wish. Sadie thought she might expire on the spot.

"A very wise person said it best when describing you and me. Love means sharing a single soul."

Tremors ran through her. "Sounds like your uncle talking."

"You're wrong. It was Leslie. After being with you the other day, I went to see her and broke it off. In her pain she admitted it was pointless to love someone who couldn't reciprocate that love. I wanted to make it work with her, but it never happened."

Sadie shook her head, so incredulous she couldn't take everything in. "You don't know what you're saying. Too much time has gone by. You can't still be in love with me." She'd hurt him too deeply. He wasn't the same with her. "We're different people now. I have a little boy to raise."

Jarod was on his feet. "Maybe we've both been in love with a memory, nothing more. But the strength of that memory has prevented us from getting past it. You're a liar if you deny you didn't want to make love the other day while we were out riding."

She'd wanted it so badly, he would never know what she'd gone through to control herself.

He moved to the front door and turned to her. "I'm asking you to marry me, Sadie. In church. In front of everyone. We need to do it soon while my grandfather is still alive and able to give you away. Once we're married, we'll have time to fall in love all over again. If we don't, then we'll just deal with it." He was silent a moment.

"Think about it," he said at last. "Ryan needs a father. I need a wife. I want children. When you're ready to give me your answer, you know where to find me. But keep one thing in mind. I won't ask a third time. This is it."

Jarod was out the door like an escaping gust of wind without giving her a chance to answer him. *Without touching her.*

She stood there long after she'd heard the sound of his truck fade. He'd asked her to marry him for a second time, but he'd meant what he said. If she wanted him, she would have to go after him.

What was it Millie had warned her about a few weeks ago? *Don't you know about the great wounded warrior inside him? He needed you to believe in him.*

Sadie *did* believe in him. She was wildly in love

with him. But it was clear he still wasn't sure about her. Not really. Otherwise he wouldn't have left so fast. He wouldn't have mentioned being married in church rather than on the reservation with his uncle Charlo doing the honors. He wasn't behaving like the Jarod she'd fallen in love with years ago.

It was up to her to prove her love for him. In the past they'd come together as equals. There'd been no need to chase because they'd been one. But that was back then. There was only one thing to do because she wanted the Jarod of eight years ago back again. The man who had no doubts about her, the man who'd ignored her father's threats and had come to steal her away to the reservation....

By the time Zane came home an hour later, she was out on the front porch waiting for him. "I'm glad you're back. Did you have a good time?"

"Yes. As a matter of fact I did." She heard a wealth of meaning behind his words that she intended to explore later. Right now she was in a hurry to find Jarod.

Zane studied her for a moment. "I'm surprised you're still up. What are you doing out here?"

"Waiting for you to get home. I need to go out again. Do you mind? Ryan's asleep."

"Of course I don't mind. But it's getting late. I'll worry about you being out alone."

"I'm just going to drive next door."

"Oh. Well, in that case…"

Zane didn't ask the obvious question. That was one of the reasons she loved him so much. "I'll only be as far away as my cell." She grabbed her purse.

With a subtle smile he handed her the keys. Sadie rushed past him to the truck.

When she arrived at the Bannocks and pulled up to the rustic ranch house, there were still half a dozen vehicles parked in front. Her heart raced to see Jarod's among them.

Making a quick decision, she walked around the side of the house, hoping to catch him helping with the cleanup. Instead, she ran into Connor, who was folding the round tables used for the dinner.

His eyes lit up in pleasure. "Hey! What are you doing back here?"

"I'm looking for Jarod."

"He's helping grandfather get to bed. I'll go tell him you're out here, but you're welcome to come inside."

"Thank you. I'll stay here."

He stacked the last table against the wall, then disappeared inside the house. She walked over to the swing and sat to wait. But it had grown cooler, so she got back up to move around.

"You wanted to see me?" Jarod's deep voice resonated inside her.

She swung around on her high heels. "I didn't hear you come out. Forgive me for intruding. Connor told me you were helping your grandfather, so if this isn't a good time, I'll come again."

He eyed her through shuttered lids. "If it was important enough for you to see me tonight, then let's not put it off." His terse comment alarmed her. "The temperature has dropped. Why don't we go back to your truck where you can be warm?"

Her truck wasn't the place she envisioned talking to him, but since he hadn't invited her in the house, it would have to do. She walked ahead of him, but was so nervous she stumbled several times on the rocky pathway. He was there to cup her elbow till they reached the Silverado.

Sadie climbed into the driver's seat. She had to hike up the dress she was wearing, and knew Jarod caught a glimpse of leg before he shut the door. She hoped he didn't think she was being provocative.

After he got in the other side, she said, "Where can we drive so there's no possibility of Ned watching our every move?"

"Is this going to take a while?" He sounded put out, but *was* he? Or could he be covering some hidden emotion? She had to find out.

Emboldened by her desperation to connect with the old Jarod, she turned to him. "Yes."

Something flickered in the recesses of his eyes. "How soon do you have to get back?"

"Zane's home for the night to take care of Ryan."

"Then we'll leave your truck here and take off in mine."

Sadie said a silent prayer of thanksgiving he was willing to listen to her. The next thing she knew he'd helped her down and walked her over to his truck. After opening the door, he gripped her waist without effort and lifted her into the passenger seat.

He drove them two miles up a badly rutted road that zigzagged behind the ranch house. It led to a shelter of pines where they could look down on the whole layout of the Hitting Rocks Ranch. Sadie had never been here before.

Jarod shut off the engine and shifted around, extending an arm along the back of the seats. She felt him tease her hair. "Old habits die hard. I have to reach farther to grab hold. Why did you cut your glorious hair?"

Sadie wasn't prepared for such a personal comment. "Off with the old seemed like a good idea after I got to California." She knew better than to ask him why he'd let his grow long. By doing so he'd made a statement that he was proud of his Crow heritage. It told Sadie's father and Ned Bannock to go to hell. She understood his feelings and loved him all the more for them, but she had to tread carefully right now.

He cocked his dark head. "All right. We're alone at last with no chance of being disturbed. Let's get this over with."

She'd been right. He didn't believe she believed in him anymore. "Why did you leave the house so fast? You didn't give me a chance to respond."

His searching gaze appraised her. "After the failure of our first attempt to become man and wife, I wanted to give you some breathing room before you made a decision about trying a second time. But it seems you didn't need it. Otherwise you wouldn't have come right over to the house again. I only need a one-word answer. Since I know what it is, I'll drive us back and send you home before it gets any later."

She moaned inwardly. "You're so sure of my answer?"

He grimaced. "The Sadie I once knew wouldn't have let me walk out of her house tonight."

Sadie took a deep breath. "The Jarod I once knew wouldn't have had to ask me to marry him a second time. He would have drawn me into his arms and told me we were going to get married as soon as it could be arranged."

His jaw hardened. "You spoke the truth earlier. Too much time has passed. We're different people now and can't go back."

"Isn't it sad that although our marriage didn't take place through no fault of our own, the fallout caused us to doubt each other. How does something like that happen?"

"We were young." His voice grated.

"That's not all of it, Jarod. Tell me something. What prompted you to ask me to marry you in a church in front of everyone?"

After a prolonged silence he said, "It's what every woman wants."

"That isn't what you planned for us the first time."

His body tensed. "I railroaded you into doing what I wanted. I thought I owned you. I believed you were mine. But I've since learned a man can no more own a person than he can the earth or the sky or the ocean."

Jarod's honesty touched her to the marrow. "How do you know it wasn't what I wanted, too? I would have given anything to have known your mother. You planned that wedding for us in her honor. It thrilled me. I've felt cheated ever since." Her heart was thudding out of control.

"You were too sweet and trusting, Sadie. I took advantage of you."

"Oh. So when you say we were too young, you really meant that *I* was too young to know my own mind."

"You weren't too young, but I know I influenced you."

"Don't you know you saved my life the day you found me sobbing on my horse? You helped me to know where to go with my sorrow. You comforted me. Every person could use that kind of influence. I was the lucky one to be able to turn to you.

"What saddens me is to realize that my being a Corkin caused you so much grief. To this day I wonder what I ever did for you to want me for your wife."

She had to wait a long time for the answer.

"Chief Plenty Coups taught that woman is your equal. She's a builder, a warrior, a farmer, a healer of the soul. All those qualities I found in you. That's what you were to me. I believed you loved me."

Jarod, Jarod. "Why past tense? I still do," she said. "That's never changed. It couldn't."

He'd turned his head to stare out the window. Sadie opened her purse and pulled out the bracelet he'd given her the night they'd made love.

"Jarod Bannock? Tonight you asked me to marry you. My answer is *yes,* but there's a condition. I want us to have the same ceremony you planned for us eight years ago."

Sadie got on her knees and moved across the seat to lean toward him, getting in his face so he had to look at her. She dangled the beaded bracelet in front of him. "I want Uncle Charlo to marry us on the reservation. I want your family to be there along with the Hensons. In my heart I know your mother and father will be watching and they'll approve because they know how much I've always loved you."

She'd finally caught his attention.

"Before you fasten it around my wrist for a second time to make this official, there's something vital you need to know."

"You're talking about Ryan," he said, reading her mind.

"Yes. He comes with me."

His chest rose and fell. "You're both flesh of your mother's flesh. Do you think I could possibly love him any less?"

"No," she whispered, brushing his mouth with her own. "You have an infinite capacity for loving. I adore you, Jarod."

Chapter Eight

Her words trickled through his mind and body like the wild, sweet Montana honey dripping from a honeycomb he'd discovered in a tree at the edge of the meadow years ago.

He studied the oval of her face, the passionate curve of her mouth so close to him he felt her breath on his lips. Moonlight illuminated the inside of the cab. Those solemn blue eyes were once again searching his. That was the way she used to look at him, as if he held all the answers to the universe.

"Aren't you going to put it on me?" He heard the slightest tinge of anxiety in her voice.

The bracelet.

She'd so mesmerized him, Jarod was slow to even breathe. He'd been convinced that when she'd fled to California, that token of his commitment had been lost or destroyed.

His fingers trembled as he caught the ends of the bracelet and fastened it around her wrist. The satisfying click echoed in his heart.

"Sadie—" Wrapping his arms around her, he lowered his mouth to hers the way he'd done eight years

ago; a kiss he'd relived in a thousand dreams. Yet this was no dream. His loving, precious Sadie was back in his arms, alive and welcoming.

For a while those desolate years they'd been apart seemed to fall away while their minds and bodies communicated their need for each other.

"Darling," she murmured over and over again, as if she, too, was overwhelmed by such emotion.

Sometime later he tasted salt on his lips. "Your eyes are wet," he whispered against her lids.

"So are yours. I can't believe we're together again. It's been such a long, long time." Her tear-filled voice reached his soul. They clung to each other, attempting to absorb the quiet sobs of happiness that shook them both. "I'm so thankful we've found each other again. Jarod— You don't know. You just don't know."

"But I do." Jarod kissed the contours of her moist cheeks, then her mouth, never satisfied. She looked and tasted beautiful almost beyond bearing. Their desire for each other had escalated to the point they couldn't do what they wanted in the confined space of the cab.

"I want you, Sadie. I love you. I'm going to drive us back to the ranch. You'll stay with me tonight."

She moaned her assent as he helped her to sit up. "This is going to be a fast trip, so hold on!" Within seconds he started the engine and put the truck in gear to head down the road.

Sadie flashed him one of her disarming smiles. "We don't need to be in a hurry. My father's no longer on the lookout. The situation has changed and we've got the rest of our lives to be together."

He grasped her hand and kissed it. "That's what I thought the night I was coming for you. Never again will I take another moment of loving you for granted."

"Neither will I." Her voice shook. "How soon do you think we can be married? I don't want to wait."

That sounded like the exciting Sadie he'd thought had disappeared forever. "I'll talk to Uncle Charlo in the morning." June third would make the perfect wedding day. By then the deed to the Corkin ranch would be in Zane's hands, but Jarod wouldn't settle on an actual date with his uncle until Zane owned it free and clear.

"The dreams I've dreamed, Sadie. My grandfather's health has to hold out long enough to see our first baby come into the world. I can hardly wait to feel movement inside you."

She nestled closer to him. "Millie told me that if you and I had communicated, we'd probably have one or two little Bannocks by now. It's all I've been able to think of for days now."

"When I saw you at the graveside service holding Ryan, I was imagining you with our child. It shocked me how strong my feelings ran. Watching you with Ryan, I knew you'd be the sweetest mother on earth. The sooner we give him a brother or sister, the better. Connor and Avery kept me from being an only child."

How he'd love it if he and Sadie were the ones to give his grandfather his first great-grandchild. Ralph would be overjoyed. Tyson already had three. Jarod's uncle Charlo would be overjoyed, too. He'd carried a heavy burden over the years watching after Raven's headstrong son.

She pressed against him to kiss his jaw. "What's putting that secretive smile on your face?"

He squeezed her hand harder. "In January my uncle told me it was time to go on my vision quest at the top of North Pryor Mountain. It had to be in an area with risks like falling and contact with animals. The more rugged and mysterious the better."

"The snow would have been too deep!"

"It nearly was, but he told me I'd be guided. He said I possessed the power to achieve my ultimate destiny by using the senses and powers already given to me. After four days of fasting, I came back down and told him my mind was still clouded."

"Four days?" she cried. "I could never have done that."

"To be honest, nothing was worse than the way I felt when you never got in touch with me." Sadie buried her face against his shoulder. "My uncle told me my quest wasn't in vain. With more time all would be made clear, but I had to develop patience because everything else in my life had come too easily."

She lifted her head. "Too easily? You lost your mother, then your father and stepmother!"

"But I was given an uncle, grandparents and siblings, a home, money, education, good health. Grades came without effort. I had everything I wanted. And when I decided I wanted Sadie Corkin, I went after her. By some miracle I was able to snatch her away from all the other guys who were hot for her."

"Jarod!"

"That's the word for it, and I was the worst. I came up with a secret plan to marry the one girl in the county who was off-limits to me. I would have succeeded, too. But fate stepped in and taught me life's most bitter lesson."

Jarod covered her hand with his own. "When Ben told me your father had died, all I could think about was you rather than your loss. Suddenly my uncle's comment about my quest not having been in vain came into my mind."

She kissed the side of his neck. "There wasn't a day in my life that I didn't yearn to come home and find out why you'd stopped loving me. We've had to endure so much needless pain."

"Not only us. Everyone who loved us was affected, Sadie."

"I know. I'm still having trouble believing we're back together."

They reached the ranch house in record time. He pulled around in front and parked. After shutting off the engine, he reached out to hold her in his arms.

"By morning you'll believe it. Tomorrow when I ask my uncle to help prepare for our wedding, I'll thank him for being a great and wise man who guided me through my trials on the way to finding my ultimate destiny. He'll give me one of those long sober looks, as if he can see into the future, but I know he'll be smiling inside."

"I know the one you mean. That's how he looked at me the night he praised you. He couldn't love you more if you were his own son."

"That's how I already feel about Ryan," he whispered into her hair. "But right now I want to concentrate on us. I desperately need to love you all night."

She looped her arms around his neck and clung to him. "I've been thinking about that and would rather we went back to my house. Yours is full of family and they don't know about us yet. It might be a shock when Connor and Avery see us walk out of your bedroom in the morning."

"A happy shock because I've been impossible to live with. They'll get down on their knees to you for coming back to me." He bit gently on her earlobe. "Zane could be a different story."

"You're wrong. We have no secrets. Follow me home. Our being together won't shock him since he knows how long I've been ready to walk through fire for you. His one reaction will be relief that we've been able to find each other again after our painful history."

"Then let's not waste another second." He got out of the cab and went around to help her down. Knowing she was all his to love had made him euphoric. Their mouths fused before he swung her around and carried her over to her truck. After putting her inside he shut the door. "I'll be right behind you."

A shadow crossed over her face. "Promise me." She couldn't prevent the tremor in her voice. "If anything happened to you now…" He knew she was thinking of Ned.

"I'll sit on your bumper."

Her expression brightened before she started the engine. He retraced the steps to his truck and they formed a caravan to the Corkin property. Connor knew Jarod was with Sadie. He'd phone if there was an emergency with their grandfather.

Jarod checked his watch. It was ten to one. For the first time in their lives they had nothing to worry about except to love and be loved. As he followed behind her, he anticipated their true wedding night. She'd always been fascinated with the bygone traditions of his mother's people. The vision of disappearing into their own tepee after the ceremony wouldn't leave him alone.

After Sadie had parked in front of her place, she jumped down from the truck and held out her hand to him. When he reached her, she ran toward the porch, pulling him as if she were in the race of her life. They both were.

But she had to get the house key from her purse. When he saw how she was trembling, he reached for it. "Let me." Within seconds he'd found it. After unlocking the door, he opened it and followed her into the living room.

"Sadie?" A light went on and they discovered Zane standing near the the window.

She came to a halt. "Zane. Is something wrong with Ryan?"

That was Jarod's first thought, as well.

"No, but I'm glad you're both here because we need to talk. Mr. Bree emailed me to let me know he has a client coming by tomorrow at 9:00 a.m. to look at the house and property." His gaze flicked to Jarod. "A little while after that your cousin Ned came by. When he found out Sadie wasn't home he left, but I was afraid he'd wait for her outside so I've been keeping watch. I didn't phone because I knew the two of you were together."

She frowned. "What did he want?"

His mouth thinned into a tight line. "*He's* the client planning to buy the ranch and do a walk-through with the Realtor in the morning."

"But he's a Bannock!"

"That part of your father's will won't hold up in court."

"So that *criminal* who came close to murdering Jarod is planning to buy this ranch out from under us?" Her outrage was as real as Jarod's. "Over my dead body! How dare he come by here this late to trample over our lives!"

"My thoughts exactly," Zane muttered. "He claimed he was hoping to talk to you at the party, but he saw you leave with Ryan so he thought he'd still find you up."

Sadie's proud chin lifted. Jarod knew that look. "What did you tell him?"

"That I was buying the ranch and had already put down earnest money. He gave me a superior smile and said that unless I was paying more than $700,000, I didn't have enough money to close the deal."

"Neither does he. I'm not sure he has a dime to his name."

Zane's brows lifted. "That may be true, but I thought I'd better tell you that tonight because June third is only four days away. I think we'd better start looking for another ranch around here within our price range."

The woman at Jarod's side had gone quiet. Much as he didn't want either Sadie or Zane to know what was going on behind the scenes, he needed to say enough to take the shattered looks off their faces. He put an arm around Sadie, pulling her close.

"He was bluffing, Zane. I do the ranching accounts. Sadie's right. Ned doesn't have any savings, and his father can't fund him any more loans. He certainly can't depend on his grandfather. Tyson has helped all his grandchildren to the point he doesn't have that kind of money, either. He's using scare tactics, but it won't work. Your bid is right in the ball park so don't give up."

"We won't!" Sadie declared. "I know it's Mr. Bree's job, but it infuriates me to think he has the right to come here with Ned, who would do anything to hurt me for loving Jarod."

After her revealing explosion, Zane eyed the two of them with interest. "Why do I get the feeling you've got something to tell me?"

Sadie extended her arm. "Jarod put this bracelet back on me tonight. It's the one from his mother's family he gave me eight years ago. We're going to get married right away."

A broad smile lit Zane's face. "That the best news I ever heard." He gave her a loving hug, then shook Jarod's hand. "When's the wedding?"

Jarod stared down at her. "As soon as it can be arranged."

"Good. It needs to happen fast. I have to tell you this girl has been dying for you."

"Zane—" Her blush warmed Jarod's heart. "You're the first person to know."

"When we've picked the date, we'll tell everyone.

We plan to keep it to family only. My uncle will be marrying us out on the reservation."

"That sounds like heaven," Zane said. "Little Ryan's going to have an amazing dad who'll open fascinating new worlds for him."

Jarod picked up a nuance in the other man's tone. In truth Zane had been the only father Ryan had known since he was born. Zane loved his nephew deeply, and was one of the most genuine, likable men Jarod had ever met. But their news had just changed his world again. "I hope one day to live up to the hero uncle Sadie raves about."

"That's nice to hear. Thanks, Jarod. Now that you're both home safely and have heard the bad news, I'll go to bed."

Sadie gave him another hug before he left the living room. When she turned to Jarod he planted his hands on her shoulders. "I'm going to leave."

"No—" She flung herself at him. It reminded him of the night before they were to be married. She'd clung to him then, too, not wanting to be parted from him. "We're not going to let Ned ruin this night for us."

"He doesn't have the power."

"Then is it because of Zane being here?"

"No, Sadie." He kissed away her tears. "But it *does* have to do with him."

She shook her blond head in confusion. "What's changed since we came in the house?"

"He just found out we're getting married right away. In his mind the plans you two had to ranch together have suddenly gone up in smoke. He sees his nephew slipping away from him and fears he might not be able to buy the ranch, after all. You told me he moved here with you to start a new life after his divorce, but tonight we dropped a bomb on him."

"I know," she whispered. "I had no idea he'd still be up and waiting for me to come home. When we told him our news, there was a look in his eyes that haunted me."

"I saw it, too. You need to go to him before he's in bed and reassure him that whatever plans we make, he's included in them in every way. He's going to be a part of our family now, the same way my uncle Charlo and his family are a part of us. But a talk like that could take the rest of the night. Before you know it, Ryan will be awake."

"You're right, but I can't stand to see you walk out the door."

"The last thing I want to do is leave, but you two need your privacy to talk. Before I go, give me your phone so we can program each other's cell numbers."

Once that was accomplished he pulled her into his arms again. "Call me after Ned and the Realtor leave. Knowing Zane is with you, I'm not worried. I'll pick you and Ryan up. We'll drive over to tell grandfather our news."

Sadie clasped her hands on his face. "You're the most wonderful, remarkable man I've ever known. I didn't think I could love you any more before we came in the house. Now I can't find the right words to tell you what you mean to me. This will have to do until tomorrow." She pressed her mouth to his.

Though he wanted to devour her, he couldn't do

that while Zane was in the other room. The man was in a state of hell Jarod wouldn't wish on the retired SEAL. He'd already lived through a war both at home and in Afghanistan, and Sadie was the one person who could make things right for him.

She had no idea she held the hearts of three men in her hands. As she'd told him earlier tonight, Ryan came with her.

"See you in the morning." He kissed her once more, knowing she was in safe hands with Zane until Jarod could take care of her himself.

On the drive home, he decided that tomorrow morning he'd leave early for Billings to do some business at the bank and talk to Harlow Brigg. Jarod wanted the attorney to make his offer to Mr. Bree before the end of the day and get the transaction finalized. Zane and Sadie deserved good news and they were going to get it.

When he got back to the ranch, he set his alarm for six. He wouldn't get the sleep he needed, but it didn't matter. Until this business was over, he didn't have a prayer of relaxing.

The next morning after he'd showered and dressed, he knocked on Connor's door. Their bedrooms were upstairs across the hall from each other. Avery's was at the other end.

"Come on in." To Jarod's relief his brother was up and seated on the side of the bed, putting on his cowboy boots. Connor looked up at him with concern. "Is grandfather all right?"

"As far as I know. This is about something else. I need to talk to my best friend. That's you."

Connor looked taken aback. "You're mine, too."

"I realize I haven't shared some of my personal thoughts with anyone over the years, not even you. It's the way I'm made. But like grandfather and Avery, I've always known you were there for me. You've never pried or overstepped. I could always count on you."

"Ditto. I wouldn't have made it through my divorce without you."

Jarod nodded. "We've been lucky to have each other. That's why I want to confide in you now."

Connor sat forward. "You sound so serious. What's bothering you, bro? After last night I figure this must have to do with Sadie." Connor eyed him with compassion. "Are the rumors true about her and Zane Lawson?"

Jarod caught a leg of the chair with his boot, pulled it forward and sat. "No. Last night I asked her to marry me for the second time and she said yes."

Connor jumped off the bed in shock. "Second time—"

"The first time was eight years ago. We'd planned for Uncle Charlo to marry us on the reservation. The ceremony was all arranged in secret so Daniel wouldn't get wind of it. Grandfather and I wanted to protect you and Avery. I was on my way to pick Sadie up with the horse trailer the night the accident happened."

For the next twenty minutes he filled his brother in on everything, including the tragic misunderstanding that had sent Sadie to her mom's in California.

"All these years Sadie thought her father was be-hind it, but that wasn't the case."

His brother shook his head in disbelief.

"The person who rammed me in the side of my truck had every intention of putting me out of com-mission. I didn't know until recently it was a deliber-ate act and I have what I call partial proof."

"What?"

Jarod reached into his pocket and then handed Connor the sheet of paper from the body shop in Bozeman. "Notice the date. The accident happened the night Sadie turned eighteen."

"Owen Pearson? But he's—"

"Ned's friend?" Jarod supplied.

Connor's expression turned dark. He walked around the room for a minute, rubbing the back of his neck. Then he turned to Jarod.

"I always thought there was something wrong about that day. When the hospital called, the whole family went en masse to visit you. Avery and I were terrified you might die. Both grandfather and your uncle Charlo must have aged ten years. But the only one who didn't show up was Ned.

"I remember Uncle Grant being particularly upset because Ned wasn't anywhere around. He tried to call him all day but Ned didn't answer his mobile phone. None of the hands knew his whereabouts and none of his friends had seen him, not even Owen. He didn't show up at the ranch until late the next night."

By now Jarod was on his feet. "Did the police question him?"

"I don't know, but I heard Uncle Grant say later that he'd had a date with one of the girls who worked at her mom's beauty salon in White Lodge. Rose, or Rosie? I can't remember. That's why he hadn't heard about the accident."

Jarod frowned. "I saw his Jeep in town that evening. It might be worth checking her out to see if she knows anything about that night."

"Do it, Jarod. Too many times I've wanted to strangle Ned with my bare hands for his treatment of you. If we could prove he or Owen was at the wheel of Owen's truck that night…"

"I plan to find out," Jarod's voice was harsh. "Did you know he's trying to buy the Corkin ranch?"

"Say that again?"

"Daniel didn't will it to Sadie. He put it up for sale. Ned's already found out about it."

"Our cousin?" Connor exploded with an angry laugh. "That's not only impossible, it's absurd!"

"He's going over there this morning with Bree from Parker Realty to make the inspection before he puts down the money."

"*What* money?"

"Tyson told Grandfather he's going to take out $700,000 for him. Uncle Grant believes if he has his own place, he'll become responsible and turn into a rancher."

Connor put up his hands. "Wait a minute here. You mean, Grandfather's okay with that?"

"No. He has his own plan working." Once again Connor was a captive audience while Jarod explained about Harlow's part in the private purchase. "We're making sure Zane ends up owning it. I'm going into Billings right now to see him."

Lines marred Connor's features. "Happy as I am to hear that, Ned's not going to take this lying down, especially when he finds out you and Sadie are getting married."

"That's why I've got to nail him for the accident. Once I know the whole truth, I'll confront him and put the fear in him about having to do some serious jail time. Thanks to your recall about the night I was in the hospital, I've got a valuable piece of information that could be the proof I need to implicate him." He hugged his brother. "I owe you."

THREE HOURS LATER he'd finished his business and finalized the details of the purchase with Harlow Brigg.

On his way back to the ranch, he phoned his uncle and broke the news. Charlo sounded elated, which didn't happen very often. They talked about possible dates for a ceremony and would make a final decision in the next few days.

When Jarod passed through White Lodge, he stopped at the Clip and Curl beauty salon. The sign said they welcomed walk-in traffic. He got out of his truck and entered the shop. The women stared at him as he approached the counter.

His gaze darted to the license on the wall. It belonged to a Sally Paxton. Her name meant nothing to him, but Jarod was determined to get answers. If this lead didn't reveal any new information, he planned to go to the Pearson ranch to confront Owen.

An older beautician washing a client's hair looked up. "Hi! I've never seen you in here before."

"I usually get my hair cut on the reservation. Does someone named Rose work here?"

"If you mean Rosie, that's my daughter over there."

A dark blond woman who looked to be Avery's age was sweeping the floor after the last client. She looked up at him. "You want to see me?"

"I was told you do a great job so I thought I'd come in."

"Who said that?"

"I heard someone telling the new vet over at Rafferty's."

"You mean Liz Henson?" He nodded. "That's nice to hear. We were part of a group of girls who hung out in high school, but she was usually barrel racing."

"I learned she's going to compete at the world championship in Las Vegas."

"Isn't that great? Be with you in a second. Go ahead and sit in the chair."

Jarod did her bidding. "I'm getting married soon and need the ends of my hair trimmed. Just an inch." This would be a new experience for him. Before he'd let his hair grow, he used to ask Pauline, Uncle Charlo's wife, to cut it.

She smiled. "Lucky woman." After fastening the cape around his neck, she undid the thong. "Do you know how many females would kill for gleaming black hair like this?"

"I hope not."

With a chuckle, Rosie washed and combed it before getting out the scissors. He noticed she wore a wedding ring. "You know I always admired Liz."

Glad he didn't have to get her back on the subject, he said, "Why do you say that?"

"She was serious about school and didn't drink like some of the girls."

"You're talking about the famous keg parties. Even though I graduated before your time, I heard they got pretty wild with Owen Pearson and Ned Bannock around."

"Ned was the ultimate party animal."

"Were you two an item?"

"That's a laugh. Do you remember a girl named Sadie Corkin? She barrel raced with Liz. All the guys were nuts about her."

His breath caught. "I remember hearing about her."

"Ned had it bad for her, but she couldn't stand him and every girl knew it. She moved right before graduation. It was weird her going away like that before she got her diploma."

You'll never know, Rosie.

After she'd tied his hair back again, he winked at her. "So you never dated him?"

"Are you kidding? Guys like that are toxic."

So that was another of Ned's lies. Jarod wondered why the police hadn't interrogated Rosie, but he was going to find out.

"You were wise to stay away."

She undid the cape. "My boyfriend made sure of it."

"Good for you." He pulled forty dollars out of his

wallet and put it on her table. "You did a great job. When I need another haircut, I'll be back."

"Congratulations on your upcoming wedding."

"Thank you, Rosie."

Chapter Nine

Sadie stood by to watch while Ned and Mr. Bree walked through the house inspecting everything. She could only imagine how much Jarod's cousin was enjoying this. The Corkin property had always been off-limits to the Bannocks. Now it was up for sale and Ned was sure he was going to become the new owner of Farfields.

But Jarod had assured her it wouldn't happen. Sadie believed him, which was the only reason she could stomach this vile intrusion into her life. She continued to watch in disgust as he handled her father's firearms. Before the funeral Mac had moved them from Daniel's bedroom to the hall closet, where they'd been locked up for safe keeping. Millie had insisted that with a child in the house, they would keep all the ammunition stored at their place.

"This is a fine collection." He flashed Sadie a strange smile. "Your father really knew his guns. I plan to buy a permanent display case for them."

There's something wrong in his head. That's what Jarod had told her years ago. Ned Bannock *was* mentally ill. A shudder racked her body.

"I believe we're finished here." Mr. Bree spoke up. Sadie immediately locked the closet. "Thank you for allowing us into your home, Ms. Corkin. We'll see ourselves out."

She nodded and followed them. Through the window she watched them drive away in a car with the Parker Realty logo on the side. Without wasting a second she rang Zane, who was on his way back from White Lodge with the Hensons and Ryan.

The Hensons were overjoyed to hear the news about Sadie and Jarod, but they still didn't know about her father's will and Sadie intended things to stay that way. Zane had taken Mac and Millie to breakfast with him and Ryan, not only to get them all away from the ranch while Ned was here, but to offer the Hensons a business proposition since he would be helping Sadie run the ranch.

Jarod had been so right about Zane. Last night she and Zane had talked for several hours until Sadie had convinced him nothing was going to change, only get better.

In a few minutes he came through the back door holding Ryan. Millie followed them inside. When Zane lowered him to the floor, Ryan grabbed him around the leg, wanting to be picked up again. "Hey, sport." Zane lifted him in the air with a happy laugh Sadie hadn't expected to hear again after he'd left her and Jarod last night.

Millie darted Sadie a secret smile. Nothing got past her.

As he poured some juice for Ryan, Millie pulled

Sadie into the front room. "When Zane told us the news, Mac and I were so happy, we almost burst!"

"You need to hear the whole story." After Sadie quickly filled her in she said, "I have to tell you, this bracelet worked its magic. Bless you for holding on to it all this time." She hugged Millie hard. "Without it, I don't know how long it would have taken me to break through that stoic barrier he sometimes erects."

"Maybe another ten minutes?" Millie quipped. "I can't wait to tell Liz. She left early to help with a foaling problem on the Drayson ranch."

"I'll phone her after I call Jarod."

"It's going to make her realize that if this can happen to her sister, it will happen to her, too, when the time is right."

"Of course it will. Oh, Millie. I can't believe this day has come. I never dreamed it would."

"Does Ralph know?"

She shook her head. "We're planning to tell him our news as soon as Jarod picks me up."

"Then don't waste another second. If you or Zane need me, just give me a call."

"You've already helped us so much."

"I wish you'd been there for breakfast when Zane asked Mac to teach him how to be a rancher. My husband could hardly talk he was so flattered."

"Zane's going to learn from the best."

"Honey—" She put a hand on her arm. "I'm sorry about your father, but I have to say how happy I am your mom ended up with Tim Lawson. I really like his brother."

"Me, too. Men like him and Jarod don't come along more than once in a century."

"You can say that again."

"And of course, I include Mac in that group."

Millie laughed, but Sadie could tell she was pleased.

While Ryan was still in the kitchen with Zane, Sadie walked in her bedroom to phone Jarod. He picked up on the first ring. "You must be psychic," he said. "I was just going to phone you. I'm one minute away from your door."

"I can't wait! I'll grab Ryan and meet you outside."

After renewing her lipstick and running a brush through her hair, she put on her cowboy hat. Once she'd stowed some diapers and small toys in her purse, she flew through the house to the kitchen. Millie must have gone home.

"Come on, cutie. I hate to tear you away from your uncle, but we're going with Jarod so you can get acquainted with your new grandfather-to-be."

Zane gave him a kiss. "See you later, sport."

Sadie rushed through the house and out the front door with Ryan. She was greeted with one of those ridiculous wolf whistles. Coming from Jarod, it was a total surprise. He was already out of the truck and had opened the rear door. 'You look good enough to eat."

"Jarod…" She moved closer, melting from the look he gave her. "Oh, you got him a car seat!"

"I picked it up in town on the way home." He took Ryan from her arms and strapped him in. "Hey, little guy. Remember me? We're going for a ride."

Ryan had fastened his attention on Jarod, but he didn't cry. Once they'd closed the door, Sadie and

Jarod reached for each other. Jarod pressed her against the side of the truck, causing her hat to fall off. She didn't care. Their emotions were spilling all over the place. It wasn't until Ryan started to get worked up over being ignored that Jarod lifted his hungry mouth from Sadie's, eliciting a protest from her. She was finding it impossible to let him go.

He looked different somehow. "Did you do something to your hair?"

"You noticed. There's a story behind it. I'll tell you about it later." He picked up her hat and helped her into the cab. After talking to Ryan and handing him a toy, Sadie pressed against Jarod for the short drive to the ranch.

"Tell me what went on with Ned."

A shudder ran through Sadie. "When he was handling one of the rifles, I was so sickened by him, I couldn't watch. He acted as if he already owned the place."

"It'll never happen."

"I believe you."

"Thank God." He put his arm around her and stopped long enough to give her a deep kiss before they ended up in front of the ranch house. Once inside, the housekeeper made a fuss over Ryan, who clung to Sadie.

"I'm sorry, Jenny. He's still getting used to people."

"That's natural."

"How's Grandfather?"

"Feeling so spry he gave Martha the day off. He's

out on the patio having lunch. I'll bring some for you, too."

"Thanks."

Jarod led Sadie down the hall and out the door to the covered patio where'd they celebrated his birthday. His grandfather's gray eyes brightened when he saw them. "Well, look at the three of you."

"Hi, Ralph. I can tell you're feeling much better." She kissed his cheek. "You saw Ryan before, but now he'd like to meet you."

"You're a good-looking little fella, aren't you?" He rubbed Ryan's head. "Just like your mom and sister. Sit down and join me."

Jarod helped her to get seated at the glass-topped table. She held Ryan on her lap while Jarod took his place next to her. Jenny brought out two more salads and rolls and glasses of iced tea.

"We're glad you're up because we have an announcement to make."

Ralph preempted him. "About time, too! When's the wedding?"

On cue, tears filled her eyes. "You know?"

"I knew the second I saw your faces just now. It's written all over you."

She reached out to squeeze his hand. "Does that mean you're happy about it?"

"Ah, honey, you know Addie and I were always crazy about you. So was my grandson. Otherwise he wouldn't have made preparations for your marriage the first time around."

Sadie lowered her head. "Jarod's accident changed our lives."

"Indeed it did, but that period is over."

They spent much of lunch talking about plans for the ceremony on the reservation. But after two hours Ryan got restless and it was time to take him home. Once Ralph was settled on the swing with his bifocals and the latest ranching magazine, Jarod picked up Ryan and they made their way back out to the truck.

He shot her an all-consuming glance. "I think it's time for everyone to have a good nap."

Her heart did somersaults as they pulled away from the ranch. But when his cell phone rang and he picked up to answer, her excitement was short-lived. A fierce expression crossed his face, the one that caused her legs to shake.

"What's wrong?" she asked as soon as he'd ended the call.

"It's nothing for you to worry about."

She sat straighter. "How would you like it if our positions were reversed and I said the same thing to you?"

He expelled a troubled sigh. "That was Ben. Fire has broken out in one of the sheds on the property. I've got to go, but I'll be back." As soon as they reached the Corkin ranch house, Sadie jumped out to get Ryan with Jarod's help. "We had a good time today, didn't we, little guy?" He lowered the toddler to the ground.

Sadie looked up at Jarod. "Please be careful."

"Always." He gave her a hard kiss before getting back in the truck. As he pulled away, she realized the Silverado was gone. Zane must have gone to town. This would have been the perfect opportunity for her and Jarod to enjoy alone time, but it would have to come later.

Much as she hated to see him go, there was something she needed to do. After she gave Ryan a bath she put him down for his nap, then got on the phone to speak to her heart doctor in California. His nurse said he wouldn't be able to return her call until after five California time. Sadie would have to wait.

Jarod wanted children. So did she. That was why this call was necessary because he didn't know about her arrhythmia.

Sadie was feeding Ryan dinner in his high chair when the phone rang at ten to six. She glanced at the Caller ID and picked up. "Dr. Feldman?"

"Is this Sadie Corkin?"

"Yes. Thank you for returning my call so fast."

"How are you?"

"Wonderful. I haven't had any problems since you put me on this last medication."

"That's excellent."

"The reason I'm calling is that since mother's passing, I've moved back to Montana and now I'm getting married to the man I told you about."

"What a lucky man. That's splendid news!"

"You can't imagine how happy I am, but he wants a baby soon. So do I. What do you think about my getting pregnant? After what happened to mother, I have to admit I'm frightened."

"It goes without saying you have to keep taking your medication and use a reliable form of birth control until you've seen a specialist. Let me assure you there's a whole new type of procedure for your kind of problem that's had a high success rate."

For the next few minutes he went on to describe the benefits and risks. "Where are you in Montana?"

"Near Billings."

"I'll look on my index. Let me give you the name of a specialist there, Dr. George Harvey, who performs procedures for your particular heart condition. I advise you to get an appointment right away. I'll send your medical records."

"Thank you so much, Dr. Feldman."

"You're welcome. I want to hear back and know what's going on with you."

"Of course." She hung up.

A whole new type of procedure?

How would Jarod feel if she had it done before they were married? But what if she went through with it and it didn't work? Haunted by all the what-ifs, she cleaned Ryan's face and hands before taking him outside for a walk.

She hadn't heard from Jarod yet and was starting to get worried. A few minutes later Zane pulled up in front of the ranch house. He got out of the truck and picked up Ryan, who was thrilled to see him.

Sadie smiled at him. "Where have you been?"

"Bozeman."

"How come?"

"I've been looking up job opportunities on the internet and came across an ad put out by the Bureau of Land Management. I decided to go in for an interview."

Sadie had thought he wanted to learn to be a rancher. Her surprise must have shown.

"Hey, don't worry. I'm not planning to go any-where. I can combine ranching with another job."

"You're going crazy around here already, aren't you?"

"No. I love it here, but I want to find something where I can use some of my skills, too."

"What kind of work was the BLM advertising for?"

"They need uniformed rangers to provide law en-forcement support. Because of my military training, I'm a natural for it. At the moment there's an open-ing in northeastern Montana. Naturally I don't want to go there. But I've learned there may be an opening soon with the national Community Safety Initiative for American Indians in this area so I can stay home on the ranch. On my days off I'll work with Mac."

"What would you do exactly?"

"Work on eradicating drugs, investigate crimi-nal trespassing and theft of government property in-cluding archaeological and paleontological resources. When I was talking to Jarod's sister last night, she told me there's a great need for that kind of protec-tion around the archaeological sites. She also told me about one of the rangers up in Glasgow who appre-hended a sniper after several people had been killed."

Yup. That sounded like it was right up Zane's alley. Sadie smiled inside. So that was what Zane meant when she'd asked him if he'd had a good time at the birthday party and he'd said yes. He'd been talking to Avery. Had she been the one to spark his interest in a BLM job?

In school Avery had been known as the Ice Queen. Like Jarod, she had a regal aura about her that in her case intimidated guys who'd wanted to ask her out. Not Zane. Sadie bet he'd danced with her as long as he'd felt like it.

"Sounds like an exciting prospect."

"Maybe. I've still got more research to do before I jump in." He flicked her a glance. "Is Jarod coming over?"

"Yes, but there's been a fire on Bannock property and he had to go. I still haven't heard from him. He's got to be all right, Zane."

"Nothing's going to happen to him. Have you fed Ryan?" She nodded. "Good. Why don't I put him to bed and give you a break?"

"Are you sure?"

"Positive."

"Then I'll let you, because I haven't visited Velvet all day." She hugged both of them. "My horse needs a daily walk around the corral and some loving."

His eyes danced. "Don't we all. You're lucky."

She grinned all the way to the barn. It appeared that finding a job that appealed to Zane had changed his whole outlook. After a career as a navy SEAL she'd feared he would never find anything as challenging. But this evening he looked and sounded happier than she'd ever known him to be.

Sadie was so glad for him and so in love with Jarod she thought her heart would burst. It must be a bad fire, otherwise he would never stay away from her this long and torture her. She prayed he wasn't in danger. *Please come home soon, darling.*

Chapter Ten

Jarod and Connor, along with Ben, their uncle Grant, two of their cousins plus other ranch workers, stood outside the smoldering heap that had been one of their hay storage sheds until a couple of hours ago. At one point Jarod had gotten out the backhoe to tear down part of the shed so the firefighters could finish extinguishing the flames.

The fire marshall walked over to them.

"It was a set fire."

"Damn," Grant muttered.

That wasn't a surprise to Jarod. There'd been no lightning, no faulty electrical wiring. Just pure arson. Luckily the shed had only been a third full and the fire hadn't spread to the other buildings. A fifty-thousand-dollar loss. Jarod couldn't help think of the senseless waste of man hours and valuable hay for the cattle. A new shed would have to be built.

"Have you got any enemies?"

Jarod could think of one and shared a silent message with Connor.

Their uncle shook his head, not saying a word, but he had to be worried his youngest son hadn't come running when the fire had broken out. Ned, who was supposed to be working in a nearby building, should have been one of the first to see the flames.

But his cousin wasn't anywhere around.

Jarod knew Ned wanted to buy Sadie's ranch, but if he'd found out someone had gotten in ahead of him with more money, he would have had plenty of time to light a fire in retaliation against his father and Tyson.

Connor and Jarod returned to the house, and Connor seemed to have read his brother's mind.

"We need to confront Uncle Grant and Tyson about the fact that Ned was nowhere around. Grandfather will hate it, but this can't wait."

"Agreed," Jarod replied grimly. "Particularly since I visited the beauty shop this morning and learned from Rosie she never dated Ned. He couldn't have been with her the night of my accident. Your tip gave me the proof I needed that his alibi was a lie."

"Do you suppose Ned found out he was outbid?"

"I do. Since our bid came in at $720,000, Bree probably phoned him to give him the bad news as soon as possible and Ned lost it."

"He's probably at the bar in town getting drunk."

"Maybe." But Jarod had a dark feeling and felt a cold sweat break out. "Let's talk to Uncle Grant right now. We'll go in my truck."

They headed for Tyson's ranch house half a mile away. Grant and his family were on the porch talking as Jarod and Connor got out of the truck and walked toward them.

"Have any of you seen Ned?" Jarod asked the question of all of them, but he was looking at his uncle.

"Not since breakfast."

"We're pretty sure Ned lit that fire," Connor said. "We also know that today he was outbid for the Corkin ranch. Someone else is buying it."

"Who?"

"Zane Lawson—he wants to be around to help raise Sadie's little brother."

"That's as it should be," Tyson murmured. He sounded a lot like Ralph just then.

Jarod nodded. "Ned's rage has been building for a long time, Uncle Grant. I have proof he had something to do with my accident eight years ago."

"What do you mean?"

He pulled the receipt from his wallet and handed it to his uncle. His cousins looked at the paper along with their father. "Notice the date. Call Owen's father and ask him about that Ford truck. The police would be interested to see the vehicle that almost got me killed.

"Ned used to follow me when I rode into the mountains to meet secretly with Sadie. His jealousy crossed the line. I never told you about those times. That was my mistake."

His uncle weaved silently in place.

"Today I learned that the excuse he made up about being with Rosie from the beauty shop in town that night was a lie. She never dated him. For some reason the police didn't follow up his story with her. You do realize that every time something bad happens, Ned isn't around and can't account for his whereabouts. His drinking problem is another indication that something's off. He needs psychiatric help and has for a long time. You know it, and we know it."

Grant looked shattered.

"You never had control over him. That part I've always been able to handle. But burning down the hay shed has endangered everyone, not to mention the financial loss. Tyson and Ralph are old and failing in health. I don't want them to be hurt by this."

Grant looked at his sons in alarm. "Boys? We've got to find him."

"We'll all help." Connor had fire in his eyes.

"Let's go." Jarod raced for his truck. When Connor joined him he said, "Before we look anywhere, I need to make sure Sadie is all right." His wheels spun as he took off for her ranch.

"If he has gone after her, at least Zane is there," Connor reasoned. "Ned would be no match for a former SEAL."

"You're right." Jarod broke the speed limit getting to Farfields. Relief swamped him when he saw the Silverado parked out front. "I'll be right back."

He jumped out of the truck and knocked on the front door. After a minute Zane answered. He smiled at Jarod. "You look and smell like you've been battling a forest fire, but Sadie will be so happy to see you, she won't care."

"I hope not. Is she inside?"

"No. She went down to the barn about an hour ago to exercise Velvet. You'll find her there or out in the corral. She's crazy about that horse."

"Thanks, Zane."

He ran back to the truck. "Connor? Come with me." His brother got out. "Where are we going?"

"To the barn. Zane said she's there, but it's getting late. I've got a feeling something's wrong."

They made their way on foot and checked the corral. No sign of her. Putting a finger to his lips, Jarod walked around to the front of the barn. The doors were closed. On a warm evening like this she would have kept them open. Jarod felt the cold prickle of sweat on the back of his neck as the dark feeling returned.

SADIE WAS READY to leave after walking Velvet back to her stall when she saw Ned standing there, a dangerous glint in his eyes. She'd seen it before and shuddered. There was no reason why he would be here except for a bad one. Aware she was alone, she felt a dual sensation of fear and nausea rise up in her.

"I don't know what you're doing here, but you're not wanted," she said, trying not to show how frightened she was. "Get away from the doors, Ned. I have to get back to Ryan."

Jarod's cousin had a strong physique like his father. She could try to push him away, but she couldn't stand the thought of touching him. He'd been drinking. She could smell it.

"No, you don't. Zane's there. We've got this whole barn to ourselves." His looks were attractive enough, but the way he leered at her made her cringe.

"Jarod will be here any minute."

"No, he won't." He gave her that insidious smile. "He's putting out a fire."

The mention of it alarmed her. "How do you know about that?"

"I'm a Bannock, remember? Anything that goes

on at the ranch I know about. What I'm here to find out is what you know about the buyer who outbid me for your father's ranch."

"What do you mean?"

"Bree called me this afternoon and told me he sold the ranch to someone else for $720,000. That kind of money doesn't grow on trees."

Her heart lurched. Zane's $700,000 bid had never stood a chance.

"I didn't learn the buyer's name, but the only person I know around here who can fork out that much cash is my half-breed cousin. He's a wealthy son of an injun, did you know that?"

"Don't you ever call Jarod that again." She almost spat out the words. "If he is wealthy, it's through hard work, something you don't know anything about."

Ned laughed. "O-oh. You're beautiful when you're angry, you know? But I'll do and say whatever the hell I feel like. Looks like he got what he wanted. There's oil under your land. He knows it, and he's been biding his time, waiting for you to fall into his hand like a ripe plum. Next thing we know he'll be drilling."

Sadie's body went rigid. There was no oil, but he wasn't listening. "What did he ever do to you?"

Ned cocked his head. "He got born."

"Jarod has as much right to life as you."

"Nature made a mistake."

Incredible. "Is that why you decided to drive Owen's truck into Jarod's eight years ago?"

His smirk faded. "What are you talking about?"

"You know exactly. I can see it on your face. You

followed him from White Lodge and picked your spot to ram him."

"Yeah. I did a pretty good job if I say so myself. He had it coming. But even if he could prove it, there's nothing he can do about it. The statute of limitations on that hit-and-run case ran out a long time ago."

She shook her head. "You could have killed your own flesh and blood."

"Nah. Don't you know an injun has nine lives like a cat?"

Ned had lost touch with reality.

"The body shop in Bozeman has proof Kevin Pearson's truck was taken in to be repaired the morning after the accident. Jarod showed me a copy of the receipt. You paid cash. With that evidence, I'll go to the police and reopen the case myself!"

His cruel smile sickened her. "Well, then, honey, before you do that, I might as well take what you've been giving to that no good bum."

He lunged for her and dragged her into one of the empty stalls, knocking her down.

Sadie screamed at the top of her lungs, upsetting the horses, who whinnied. He covered her mouth with a hand that smelled faintly of gasoline and climbed on top of her.

"You fight like a she-cat. What does that long-haired cousin have that I don't? Come on, baby." He'd straddled her. "It's time you showed me what you've got. You need to share. I've waited long enough. This is going to be fun."

With her wrists pinned above her head in one

hand, he ripped at the front of her blouse with the other, stifling her screams with his mouth.

Using every ounce of strength, she bit him as hard as was humanly possible. Warm salty blood filled her mouth.

"Ack! You little—" But she didn't hear another word because he was silenced by someone bigger and stronger who seemed to have come out of nowhere.

Ned spewed his venom, but it did no good. It was Jarod who had pulled him off her and now had him on the ground facedown in a hammerlock.

Connor was there, too. Together they tied his wrists and ankles with rope. The sheriff walked in on them as Jarod looked up at her. She'd never seen such fear in those black eyes. "Are you all right?"

"Yes." She tried to cover herself with the torn fabric of her shirt. "You got here just in time."

"Thank God." Jarod turned the sheriff. "We're glad you're here."

While Connor guarded Ned, the sheriff took her statement. Jarod led her outside before wrapping her in his arms. His body trembled like hers. "If anything had happened to you…" he murmured into her hair.

"He needs psychiatric help."

"That's what I told Uncle Grant earlier. We all knew who set fire to the hay shed. You're safe now and this whole ugly business is finally over. Come on. Let's get you home so you can shower and get cleaned up."

She buried her face against his chest as they made their way toward the house. "I was so terrified."

"So was I when I heard your scream, but he'd

rigged something against the doors from the inside so we had to climb in through the rear window to get to you."

"Oh, Jarod." Sadie broke down sobbing. "How did you know where to find him?"

"A strong hunch. He'd lost everything else. Knowing how his mind works, I suspected he'd come after you. Rest assured he'll never bother you or anyone else again."

An anxious Zane came hurrying down from the porch. "What's happened?" He sounded frantic.

"She's all right, Zane. Ned decided to pay her a visit in the barn, but Connor and I got there in time and now he's tied up. The sheriff's with them."

"Sadie—" The other man gave her forehead a kiss. "I'll go see what I can do to help."

While Zane took off at a run, Jarod entered the house and walked her through to her bedroom. "You've got blood all over you."

"I bit him so hard, I don't know if he has a bottom lip left."

He hugged her to his heart. "You're my warrior woman all right."

She let out a shaky laugh. "He'll need stitches."

"He'll need a lot more than that. My brave Sadie. You had to deal with him all those years."

"You've had to endure much worse, almost losing your life. He admitted to running into you with Owen's truck, but I don't think Owen was with him. He's insane."

"Shh. That's all behind us now." He stopped in front of the bathroom door. She felt his eyes rove over her, searching for marks and bruises. "What can I get for you?"

"Not a thing. My robe is on the door. I'll be out in a minute. Don't go anywhere!"

"As if I would. I'll be in the living room."

She clung to him until he walked away. After a shower and shampoo, followed by a vigorous brushing of teeth, she emerged from the bathroom feeling rejuvenated. No more Ned. That thought was enough to erase the horror of her experience.

Once she'd dressed in a clean pair of jeans and a cotton sweater, she entered the living room, where everyone had gathered, including the sheriff who needed to bag her clothes for the forensics lab. Jarod reached for her and put his arm around her shoulders.

Now that she was no longer terrified, she saw the soot on his arms and face. The shiny black hair she'd noticed earlier no longer gleamed due to the debris from the fire. Both he and Connor smelled of smoke.

The sheriff nodded to her. "Ms. Corkin? We're sorry to hear about the assault, but are thankful to learn you're all right. Mr. Bannock has been taken into custody and his family notified. If you don't mind my asking you some more questions, I'll leave as soon as we're through."

"That's fine." The next few minutes passed in a blur. After statements were taken, the sheriff left.

Sophie's gaze swept over the man she worshipped. "You and Connor fought a fire today and look absolutely exhausted. This is one time when I want you to go home. You need food and a shower in that order."

All three men chuckled.

Jarod's white smile shone through the grime left by the fire. "You mean you don't like me just the way I am?"

Her eyes smarted. "You know better than to ask me that question, but I'm thinking of your comfort. Please come right back. I'll be counting the seconds."

"Watch me." He gave her a hard kiss without touching her anywhere but on the mouth.

She walked them to the door. "Thank you," she whispered to Connor. "You and Jarod saved my life."

Connor kissed her cheek. "Any time, ma'am."

After they left, she closed the door and turned to Zane with such a heavy heart, she didn't know where to begin.

"There's something I have to tell you."

His mouth tightened. "Did Ned do something you didn't want Jarod to know about?"

"No. I told him everything. But while Ned had me cornered, he blurted that someone else's bid for the ranch came in higher than his." His ludicrous assumption that Jarod was the one who'd bought it revealed Ned's sickness.

Zane jumped to his feet. "Then that means we've lost the ranch."

"I'm afraid so. It's clear the bad news sent Ned's rage over the top, so he came after me." She could see the pain in Zane's eyes. "I know Jarod promised we'd get the ranch, but he's not in control of everything, so I have an idea. After we hear from Mr. Bree in the morning and know the fate of the Hensons, we'll go find us another place."

He shook his dark brown head. "You're getting

married. You and Ryan will be living with Jarod. *I'll* find me a piece of property."

"I want to help. Bring your laptop into the kitchen. Let's start looking."

"Not tonight."

"Yes, tonight! It's not time for bed. We have nothing else to do. I'm anxious to see what's for sale around here. Tomorrow we'll make appointments and go check the places out with Ryan. When Jarod comes back, we'll ask him if he knows of an opportunity for us."

She thought a moment. "Keep in mind it could be a month, maybe longer, before the owner wants to move in. That'll give us time to get resettled. If the Hensons no longer have a job, we'll take them with us."

He frowned. "What do you mean *us?* When Jarod gets back, you'll be making plans for your wedding."

"I'm not doing anything until I know there's a satisfactory solution for all of us."

AFTER A MEAL and a shower, Jarod took off for Sadie's ranch. With the threat of Ned gone for good, he had news for her and Zane they needed to hear. It couldn't wait until tomorrow.

Once he'd parked the truck, he hurried to the front porch and rapped on the door, thankful the last obstacle to their happiness had been removed and they could start planning their wedding.

The second Sadie opened the door, he pulled her into his arms. "I got here as fast as I could," he whispered against her mouth before devouring it. Her response was everything he could have asked for, but he sensed something was wrong. When he finally lifted his head, he saw a sadness in her eyes that had turned them a darker blue. He intended to remedy that situation right now.

"Where's Zane?"

"In the kitchen."

He brushed his mouth against hers once more. "Lead me to him. I've got news for both of you."

Her eyes misted over. "We already know what it is," she said in a quiet voice.

Surprised, Jarod shook his head. "You couldn't possibly know what I'm about to tell you."

"Ned told me while we were in the barn."

He frowned. "Told you what?"

"That Bree phoned him this afternoon and notified him an unknown buyer had purchased the ranch."

"So that *was* the final blow that sent my cousin on the rampage."

"I'm sure of it."

"Come on." He grasped her hand and walked her through to the kitchen. Zane looked up from the table where he'd set his laptop. Jarod saw the same sadness in his eyes. "Before another minute passes, I have an announcement to make."

Sadie clung to the back of one of the kitchen chairs. He could tell she was fighting not to break down. Jarod had seen that look too many times in their lives. He planned to wipe it away for good.

"The ranch and everything else on the property is yours, Zane."

Sadie looked as if she was going to faint. "Ned said you were the buyer, but I didn't believe him."

A dazed Zane got to his feet. "What's all this about?"

"We're not the buyers, and we aren't out any money. But Ralph and I didn't want Ned to get the ranch, so our attorney acted as the straw buyer to make certain you were able to purchase it before he did. Your offer was accepted, Zane."

"Jarod—" The emotion in that one word caught at his heart.

"Bree will be calling to set up a time for you to drive to Billings and sign everything. He'll give you the deed, and that will be it."

Zane cleared his throat. "I don't know what to say. 'Thank you' could never cover it." He walked over and gave him a long hug.

Jarod was moved by the other man's gratitude. "I'm the one who's in your debt. No amount of money could compensate for what you've done to help take care of Sadie and Ryan. We should have been married eight years ago, but that was not our path until now." He darted Sadie a speaking glance. "There's nothing else to prevent us from planning our future."

Zane's eyes had gone suspiciously bright. "I'm going to leave you two alone to get started on those plans."

"Did you hear all that?" Jarod whispered after Zane disappeared. Sadie was still clinging to the chair. He'd been waiting for her to run to him, but she hadn't moved. He reached for her. "What's wrong?"

Tears welled in her eyes. "How do you thank someone who's just given you the world? Tell me how you do that." Her voice shook. "I love you so desperately, Jarod, you just don't know. That's why

I'm so worried to tell you something that has to be said before we talk about the wedding."

"What's happened?" He sounded anxious.

She put her hands on his chest. "This is about the children you want to have with me."

He saw fear in her eyes. "Go on."

"There's no easy way to say this. I have a heart condition you need to know about."

His own heart almost failed him. "Since when?"

"At my last rodeo two weeks before graduation, I developed palpitations. My heartbeat accelerated abnormally during the barrel racing. Mac drove me to White Lodge to see the general practitioner at the hospital. He put me on birth control and a medication that really helped, but I had to stop the barrel racing. Then he advised me to see a cardiac specialist in Billings."

"*That* was the reason I couldn't find you after your performance that night?"

She nodded. Jarod was dumbfounded. "Since we were making plans to get married and I felt all right on the medicine, I decided not to tell you about it until after we were married. But three days later you had your accident."

"Sadie—" Fear caused him to break out in a cold sweat. He gripped her shoulders. "Your mother died of a bad heart having Ryan."

"That's true, but in her case there were extenuating circumstances."

He couldn't throw this off. "How serious is your condition?"

"Don't worry. It's not fatal. As you can see I'm

still alive and have been doing just fine on the medication."

"You haven't answered my question. What's wrong with you exactly?"

"Once I arrived in California and told Mother what had happened, she took me to see her heart specialist. I was diagnosed with paroxysmal supraventricular tachycardia."

"Explain that to me."

"It's called PSVT and occurs when any structure above the ventrical produces a regular, rapid electrical impulse resulting in a rapid heartbeat. The technique to fix it has been perfected and involves placing small probes in the heart that can destroy tissue and then are removed once the tissue is altered.

"The procedure is called catheter ablation. The doctor inserts a tube into a blood vessel and it's guided to your heart. A special machine sends energy through the tube. It finds and destroys small areas of heart tissue where abnormal heart rhythms may start. You have to go to the hospital to have it done."

"Did your mother undergo this procedure?"

"Yes, but it didn't work. Sadly, in her case, the arrhythmia brought on cardiac arrest, something very rare. Her older age and stress played a big factor in what happened to her. I'm thinking of having the procedure done before we're married. Otherwise I won't be getting pregnant because the medicine I take can cause a miscarriage. I'll have to stay on birth control and won't be able to give you a baby."

"I don't like it, Sadie. I don't want you to do anything that will put your life in more jeopardy than it already is."

"I'm not in jeopardy. Listen to me, Jarod. Today I talked to my heart doctor in California. He gave me the name of a specialist in Billings named Dr. Harvey who does this kind of procedure. I'm going to call tomorrow for an appointment. We'll go together. If I find out I'm a good candidate, I'd like to have it done right away."

He struggled for breath. "What if it isn't successful?"

"Then my other doctor told me they'd put in a pacemaker. But think how wonderful it would be if I could plan to get pregnant without the fear of something going wrong."

"I'd rather we adopted children."

"If it comes to that, then I'll get my tubes tied and we'll go in that direction. But more than anything in the world I want to try the procedure so I can have your baby and give it a good Crow name."

Jarod wrapped his arms all the way around her and buried his face in her hair. "More than anything in the world, the only thing I want is for you to be in my bed for the rest our lives. We have Ryan. Let's let that be enough for now. Later on we'll consider adoption."

"Will you at least be willing to go to the doctor with me?"

His eyes closed tightly. "You're asking too much. We almost lost each other before. I can't go through that again."

She eased herself away from him. "Do you really mean that?"

"I do. My mother died after she had me. Your mother died after Ryan was born. Now you're asking me to live through more torture while you undergo some procedure that could go wrong and you'd need a pacemaker to keep you alive?"

Her face was a study in pain, but he couldn't stop.

"What if that fails? Then it would mean another procedure and another until…" He shuddered. "I can't go along with it."

Sadie's complexion lost color. "What if I told you I've always wanted to have your baby and will do anything to make it possible?"

"Even chance death?"

"That won't happen! I want to do this for us. Remember what you told me a few nights ago? You said, *'The dreams I've dreamed, Sadie. My grandfather's health has to hold out long enough to see our first baby come into the world. I can hardly wait to feel movement inside you.'*"

He searched her eyes, gutted by this conversation. "I said that before I knew about your heart problem. Don't put me in this position, Sadie."

She looked at him with a pained expression. "I won't, because I can see your mind is made up." Her chin lifted in that unique way of hers. "You deserve to have your own baby. You'll make the most wonderful father on earth. So I'm going to do you a favor and release you from your commitment to me."

He stared at her, incredulous she would go this far.

"I shouldn't have accepted your proposal without telling you of my condition, but the night we got back together I wasn't thinking about babies. I was very selfish, only thinking about myself and my happiness. But let's be frank. There are many women out there like Leslie Weston who'd give anything to meet a man like you, and they don't have my heart ailment.

"I've always been a problem for you and it hasn't stopped. One day when you have a wife and several children of your own, you'll thank me. I love you, Jarod. I'll love you till my dying breath, but you shouldn't have to sacrifice every part of your life because of me. You did enough of that while my father was alive and it simply isn't fair to you. It's your turn to find happiness."

"You really want us to be over?"

"No. I want us to have our own baby, and the only way we can do that is for me to go to the doctor to see if he can do that procedure on me. If you're too afraid to even accompany me to the appointment to find out my options, then we shouldn't be together because I don't want to put you through that kind of agony. I'm a liability and have always been."

An overwhelming sadness filled her eyes, but Jarod knew she was determined.

"I—I think you should go," she said. "After fighting a fire and subduing Ned, you must be feeling worse than exhausted."

This just couldn't be happening, but it was....

With the blackness descending upon him, Jarod left the kitchen and headed for his truck.

"Sadie Corkin, you've just done the only terrible thing in your whole life."

Shocked at the tone of Zane's voice, she wheeled around white-faced.

"Because your voices carried, I didn't have to

eavesdrop. Don't let him go like this or you'll never get him back. You're the woman he's always wanted, but you just threw everything he ever did for you back in his face. Sadie… You don't tell a man it's either my way or nothing. Not a man like Jarod. You're talking about your lives here!

"The poor man hasn't had two seconds to digest all this new information. He's terrified you might die. Forget having a baby right now. Even if you didn't have a heart problem, how do you know you can get pregnant? And Jarod might not be able to give you children. You're only twenty-six. You've got years to worry about that. Jarod wants marriage. He wants to live with you. You've put having a baby before *him!*"

Sadie had never seen Zane so impassioned.

"If your positions were reversed," he went on, "and he'd given you an either/or proposition, I can guarantee you'd be in such horrendous pain I don't even want to think about it. Take my car. It's all gassed up. Go find him!"

Sadie half expected him to point a finger at her. "I don't want to see you walk in that door again without him. Remember, it's my house now. Your place is with your fiancé."

Zane was right. He was right about everything.

She dashed to the bedroom for her purse. He met her at the door with the keys. "Go get him, Sadie. All the man wants is to be loved."

"Thank you," she whispered against his cheek.

Sadie flew to the car with her purse and drove off.

Jarod usually went to the reservation when he was in pain. She knew that about him, but he'd only had a five-minute start. Just to make sure, she drove to the Bannock Ranch to check if he'd stopped there first.

Thank heaven she'd followed her instincts. There was his truck parked in front. She got out of the car and ran to the front door. Afraid to waken Ralph if he was already sleep, she knocked several times instead of using the bell. In a minute Avery opened the door.

"Sadie—"

"Hi," she said, out of breath. "Is Jarod here?"

"Yes. He passed me on the stairs a few minutes ago looking like death. You look the same way."

"I have to talk to him."

"Come on in and go up the stairs. His bedroom is at the end of the hall on the left. I'm glad you've come because you're the only one who can fix what's wrong with him."

Sadie rushed past her and raced up the steps straight into Connor, who steadied her with his hands. Her head flew back as she looked up at him. "I'm sorry, Connor. I didn't see you."

"Jarod had the same problem when he came up a few minutes ago." He grinned. "That's twice I've been run into tonight. Jarod's at the end of the hall on the left."

She nodded. "Avery told me."

"Then don't let me keep you. One piece of advice. Don't knock. Just walk in."

That wisdom from Jarod's brother told her everything. If she knocked and Jarod knew who it was, he'd tell her to go away and never come back.

Taking his advice, she hurried down the hall and started to reach for the handle when the door opened.

Jarod appeared, carrying a saddlebag and bedroll. If she hadn't caught up to him in time, he'd be off to the mountains and she would never have found him.

Without hesitation, she threw her arms around his neck and clung to him, forcing him to drop his things. "I'm sorry, darling." She covered his face with kisses. "Forgive me. The second the words came out of my mouth earlier, I wished I hadn't said them."

His body remained rigid. She knew she was in for the fight of her life.

"I want to live with you. You're all I want! We'll worry about children later. I wanted everything to be perfect for us, but as Zane let me know in no uncertain terms, nothing is perfect or set in this life. We need to seize our happiness while we can. There's no life without you. Please say you forgive me."

His grave countenance made him look older. "Only on one condition. That we leave for the reservation and ask Uncle Charlo to marry us tonight."

"Tonight? Isn't it too late?"

"No. I refuse to spend another night alone without you. It's your decision."

Sadie didn't have to think. "My place is with you."

Jarod's black gaze pierced through to her soul before he shut the door behind them. "Did you drive the truck over?"

"No. Zane's car."

"Give me his keys." She followed him to Connor's room. When he appeared with Avery, Jarod said, "We're getting married tonight." He handed him the keys. "Will you two see that Zane's car is returned to him? Tell him we'll be back tomorrow."

"Sure. Can you get a marriage license this late?"

"We'll take care of that later. We don't need one on the reservation."

"In that case, I claim my right to kiss the bride ahead of time." Connor pressed a warm kiss to her lips. "Take care of my big brother," he whispered. "He badly needs to be loved by a woman like you."

Sadie nodded and threw her arms around him. "I love you, Connor."

"Welcome to the family."

"Amen," Avery chimed in from behind them and reached for Sadie. "Grandfather and I have said every known prayer in the universe for this night to happen."

She laughed through the tears. "I love both of you, too, Avery."

They walked her and Jarod out to his truck.

As they drove away, Sadie waved until she couldn't see them any longer. After closing the window, she realized Jarod was on the phone talking to his uncle. Their conversation lasted a while before he rang off.

"I want you near me." He pulled her against him so possessively, it sent a tremor through her body that didn't stop, even after they reached the reservation.

Chapter Eleven

The Apsáalooke settlement of two thousand looked like a surreal painting in the moonlight. Most every home had a white tepee in its yard.

Though all the signs of modern civilization were there, in her mind's eye Sadie could see the proud, courageous warriors of years ago mounted on horseback in their search for buffalo. In a fanciful moment, she could imagine Jarod riding with them, his long black hair flying in the wind.

His mother came from this wonderful heritage. Tonight Sadie was going to experience a part of it. When they pulled up in front of his uncle's house, she was excited for what was about to happen.

Pauline Black Eagle was a lovely woman who came outside with her pretty eighteen-year-old daughter Mary Black Eagle and younger son George, otherwise known as Runs Over Mountains. They were all smiling as they greeted Sadie and Jarod.

His uncle stood on the porch steps in his plaid shirt, jeans and cowboy boots. *"Kahe,"* he called to them. Jarod responded and they spoke in Siouan, the language Sadie was determined to learn.

"My uncle just welcomed us. Let's go in."

They entered the house. Once inside the living room Charlo asked them to sit. Only in his fifties, the tribal elder had obtained a *Juris* doctorate from the University of Montana School of Law. He stood in front of them, an attractive male figure with black hair to his shoulders. His dark eyes fastened on Sadie.

"My nephew says he wishes to get married. Is that your wish?"

"Yes."

"I see you wear the bracelet of our clan."

She nodded. "Jarod gave it to me eight years ago."

His eyes glimmered with satisfaction. "I once told Sits in the Center that the wolf must decide it is better to risk death for some chance of finding a mate and a territory than to live safely alone. I am happy to see he took my advice…for a second time," he added, causing her to glance at Jarod, who stared at her with smoldering eyes.

"I'm sorry about the first time and all the preparations you made that had to be canceled," Sadie said.

"It was no trouble. We were sad that Jarod had to suffer from an accident. But tonight there is only happiness because the circle of your lives has brought you together again."

"I'm so happy I could burst."

The women smiled broadly.

"My nephew has told me of your great interest in our culture, so he wishes to recreate his father and mother's wedding night. Pauline has some things for you to wear. If you'll go with her and Mary, George and I will see to Jarod and meet you outside in back.

We've invited a few aunts and uncles to celebrate with you."

Jarod squeezed her hand hard before she followed the women through the house to one of the bedrooms. Sadie saw an outfit laid out on the bed.

"When my husband heard you were back from California, our clan made this deerskin dress and moccasins for you."

"But how did you know? I mean— Jarod and I hadn't been together for eight years."

"My husband sees many things."

Sadie shivered. She would always hold him in awe.

Pauline handed her the dress and Sadie looked at it with reverence. "The beading is exquisite. I'll always treasure it. Thank you from the bottom of my heart."

"You're welcome."

"You can change in my bathroom," Mary told her.

Sadie quickly removed her jeans and sweater, and emerged from the bathroom wearing the soft garment and moccasins. While she'd been changing, the other women had also donned deerskin dresses.

Pauline slipped the belt that matched the bracelet around Sadie's waist. *Bless you, Millie,* Sadie thought.

"You will please Jarod very much."

"I'll do everything I can to keep him happy."

"You already have or he wouldn't have asked you to marry him two times. Many of the women who are not married have given him a new name—*He Who Has No Eyes*. But they didn't know what my husband and I knew."

Sadie felt heat rush to her cheeks. Pauline was wonderful. She used her skills as a nurse at the tribal clinic.

Mary, who was attending college, handed Sadie the beaded earrings, which she put on. Though Sadie knew that with her blond hair she looked a fraud, it was exciting to play a role for a little while. The most important role of her life. *Jarod's bride.*

"Come with us."

She walked with them through the house and out the back door to the yard. A fire had been lit in the fire pit, casting shadows over the tall white tepee in the background. The magical setting sent goose bumps up and down Sadie's arms.

Several dozen extended family members stood in a semicircle. She marveled that Charlo could assemble so many of their loved ones this close to midnight. They nodded to Sadie, who stayed close to Pauline and Mary. Their presence showed how much they revered Jarod.

Another minute and Charlo came out the back door in deerskin pants and shirt, followed by George in a similar outfit. Jarod walked out last. To her surprise he was wearing modern-day jeans and cowboy boots. But he'd dressed in a black ribbon shirt with a V neck and long sleeves ending in cuffs the men wore for special occasions.

She knew black was the sacred color of the Apsáalooke. The ribbons reflected orange, green, blue and yellow, representing the elements. The intricate pattern would have been passed down through the generations and given to him by his uncle.

Jarod had never worn his hair in a braid before, at least not in front of her. She could hardly breathe, he looked so fiercely handsome. Suddenly his gaze fell on her. Time stood still as they communed in silence as she took in the gravity of this moment. A light breeze ruffled the tips of her hair. If there was any sound, it was the thud of her heart in the soft night air.

Charlo motioned for her and Jarod to come closer and face him. A hush fell as he began to speak.

"If Chief Plenty Coups were here, he would say the ground on which we stand is sacred ground. It is the dust and blood of our ancestors. Sadie… Tonight when you enter the tepee on this sacred ground, our First Maker reminds you to remember that a woman's highest calling is to lead a man's soul so as to unite him with his Source."

She wasn't sure how to respond but gave him a solemn nod.

"Jarod? Tonight when you enter the tepee on this sacred ground, our First Maker would have you remember that a man's highest calling is to protect a woman so she is free to walk the earth unharmed."

When he nodded, Sadie wanted to proclaim to everyone that he'd always protected her and had already saved her from Ned earlier in the day.

"The crow reveals the true path to life's mission. It merges both light and dark, inner and outer, and when in the darkness of emotional pain and turmoil, the crow will carry the lost soul into the light.

"Both of you have endured much sorrow over the years. Don't waste today letting too much of yesterday ruin your joy. Before you lie down together, give thanks for blessings already on their way and you will have peace."

What better advice could anyone give?

He lifted his hands. "Go now. May you live in eternal happiness."

They were married?

She asked the question with her eyes. Jarod's mouth broke into such a beautiful smile that her entire being was filled with indescribable love for him. He grasped her hand. Leading her around the fire to the tepee, he moved the buffalo covering aside so she could enter.

The tepee's cone shape was formed with dozens of poles and could hold five to six people. Blankets on top of buffalo skins had been placed on the floor. Nothing else was inside....

Jarod held both her hands. "My mother's culture didn't do marriage ceremonies, but I think my uncle did the perfect job of performing ours."

"So do I," she said softly. There was enough light from the fire outside to see each other. "Do you mind if we kneel right now and do what he said?"

He kissed both her hands before they got down on their knees, facing each other. "You say the prayer."

"Thank you. I want to."

Closing her eyes she said, "Dear God, my heart is full to overflowing for the many blessings Thou has given us. We will strive to live worthily of the blessings Thou has yet to bestow on us. I thank Thee for my husband, a great man and a great warrior. I thank Thee for Jarod's loving family both on the ranch and on the reservation. I thank Thee for my family, for the Hensons. Amen."

Jarod's eyes were fastened on her as she lifted her head. "Amen," he whispered in a husky voice. "You have no idea how beautiful you are to me, kneeling there in that dress to please me. Though I see a woman, I also see the sweet, vulnerable, lonely girl inside you who stole my heart years ago. I want to fill your loneliness, Sadie."

She cradled his face with her hands. "You already have. Uncle Charlo said not to dwell on the past. Tonight is the beginning of our future. There's something I want to do before we do anything else."

His breathing grew shallow. "What is it?"

"Take off your shirt first."

He looked surprised, but he did as she asked. Her breath caught to see his well-defined chest and shoulders emerge. "Now close your eyes."

As soon as they were closed, she moved around behind him and began unbraiding his fabulous hair. "I've been dying to do this since you came up to me at the funeral." She threaded her fingers through the glossy strands that fell loose and swung around his shoulders and face.

When she was finished she knelt in front of him. "You can open them now." Sadie almost fell back in amazement. "You're the most gorgeous man. I want an oil painting done of you exactly like this, sitting inside this tepee. After it's framed, I'll hang it in the most prominent place in our home with a small brass plate at the bottom that reads '*He Who Sits At My Side.*'"

Jarod's eyes glowed like black fire. He rose to his full height. She noticed the special belt he wore before he pulled her up and turned her around. Her body trembled as he undid the back of her dress, lowering it off her shoulders till it fell to her feet. His mouth found the side of her neck. "Come lie with me, my love."

A cry of longing escaped her lips as he laid her gently on top of the blankets. Looking down at her he said, "No painting of you could do you justice. I love you, Sadie. You're my heart's blood."

After plunging his fingers through her silky hair, he lowered his mouth to hers, giving her the husband's kiss she'd been waiting for since she'd fallen in love with him at fifteen.

Jarod— As their bodies melded, her heart and soul leaped to meet his.

MORNING HAD COME to the reservation. Jarod could see light through the tiny opening at the top of the tepee. He eased himself away from his precious wife, who still slept.

Jarod's hunger for her hadn't been appeased, no matter how many times they'd made love during the night. Now that he'd finally allowed her to sleep, he left her tangled in the blanket while he peered outside the entrance. The direction of the sun shining overhead told him it was at least two o'clock in the afternoon. That's why the interior was heating up.

He caught sight of their regular clothes along with a picnic basket of food Pauline had placed against the outside of the tepee. She'd taken care of everything to make their wedding night perfect.

After struggling eight years along a treacherous path, he'd obtained his heart's desire. Sadie was the most unselfish, giving woman he'd ever known.

Jarod breathed in the fresh air, aware that he felt

whole at last. The night had been so perfect, he never wanted it to end, but she would awaken soon and want to get back to Ryan. Recognizing his insatiable appetite for her, he decided he'd better get dressed or they'd be here for another twelve hours.

Once he'd pulled on his cowboy boots, he brought everything inside. He found his cell phone and watch among his clothes and checked for messages. Only one from Connor.

Grandfather is ecstatic and can't wait to welcome both of you home. Tyson and Ned's parents are inconsolable. The police need to know if you want to press charges. You have every right, bro.

"Darling?" He glanced over at his wife. The word still thrilled him. What a beautiful sight she made. Unable to resist, he leaned down to kiss her, which was a mistake. He wanted to climb under the covers with her and never come out.

"Why did you let me sleep?"

"Because you needed to after I wore you out." He put the basket in front of them. "Pauline fixed us a picnic."

"She's incredible."

"I agree."

"I saw you checking your messages just now. Anything from Zane about Ryan?"

"No. It was from Connor. Everything's fine. Let's enjoy our first meal together as man and wife."

They ate sandwiches and drank soda. "I'm so excited to be married to you, I can hardly take it in. Last night—"

"Was miraculous," he broke in. "No man ever had a lover like you."

Her blush delighted him. When he'd finished eating, he reached for his thong.

"Don't confine your hair. I love the way it flows."

"I'll wear it loose at night, but during the day it gets in the way."

She eyed him curiously. "Yesterday you were going to tell me why you changed your hair."

He swallowed the rest of his cola. "I paid a trip to the beauty salon in White Lodge to talk to a woman named Rosie."

In another minute she knew the whole story about Ned's fabrication.

"She washed and cut your hair!"

"What's wrong?"

"I want you to know that no other woman will ever be allowed to do that again."

Laughter poured out of Jarod. He pressed her back against the blankets, kissing her long and hard.

"I want your promise, Jarod."

"I swear I'll never go in there again."

"Rosie probably had a cow when she found out she was going to get her hands on the gorgeous Jarod Bannock."

"A cow?" he teased.

"You know what I mean. I bet she can't wait until you go back."

He couldn't stop laughing. "She's married."

"That doesn't matter. For years I've had to put up

with the way women look at you. It's been enough to give me a heart attack."

"Don't say that," he begged her, "not even in jest."

"Sorry. Happily, Pauline told me something about you that makes me feel a lot better."

"What's that?"

"The women on the reservation have been calling you He Who Has No Eyes."

More laughter caused him to bury his face in her throat. "That's because only one woman has ever held my heart."

"Have I told you I'm madly in love with you?"

"All night long," he murmured against her lips.

"Darling? What was Connor's message? I know it had to be something important or he wouldn't have sent it."

"Tell you what." He reached for her regular clothes and handed them to her. "After you get dressed, we'll freshen up in the house and then I'll tell you during the drive home. On the way we'll stop in White Lodge for our marriage license."

She smiled. "It's a little late for that, wouldn't you say?"

He didn't say anything, but fell back against the blankets to watch her.

"Close your eyes."

"That's one thing I can't do."

"The trouble with this tepee is that there's nothing to hide behind."

"My *Apsáalooke* ancestors knew what they were doing," he teased.

"Your *male* ancestors."

He loved it that she tried her hardest to pretend he wasn't there while she put on her clothes. Sadie never did seem to know how beautiful she was. Everything about her made her so desirable to him, and he was terrified of ever losing her. Their argument over her wanting that heart procedure still had a stranglehold on him.

Her blue eyes flashed. "I'm ready now, as if you didn't know."

"You did that far too fast for my liking. Next time things will be different."

"*How* different?"

"For one thing, we won't be in a hurry to go anywhere." His comment put color in her cheeks.

He gathered up their things and they left the tepee. No one was home when they went inside to use the bathroom. Jarod wrote a note and left it on the counter, thanking his aunt and uncle for everything.

We're now one soul in two bodies and have come into the light.

As they drove away from the reservation toward home, Sadie nestled up against him and pressed kisses to his jaw. "Tell me about Connor's message."

"Ned is in huge trouble. But I don't want to talk about him right now."

Sadie looped her arms around his neck. "You're such a noble man, Jarod Bannock." She started kissing him until he could hardly see to drive. "Sorry," she whispered when he had to slow down. "I'll behave myself until we get home."

"That's the next thing I want to talk to you about, *Mrs. Bannock*. I'm planning to build us our own home on the ranch, but until we've decided what kind we want and how big to make it, where is our home going to be for the next few months?"

"Would you mind terribly moving in with me? The nursery's already set up for Ryan, and it's only a few minutes away from your ranch and Ralph."

"Sadie, I'd live anywhere with you and can bring over some of my clothes. In fact, it's the Apsáalooke way for the husband to move in with the wife's family. But you'll need to feel Zane out."

"Honestly, I know he won't care. He's been looking for work."

"What about his plan to become a rancher?"

"With Mac's help, I think he wants to try to do both." For the rest of the drive home, she told him about Zane's interest in working for the BLM as a ranger.

When they arrived at the ranch, Jarod pulled up next to the Volvo. Sadie jumped out and they both hurried in the house.

"Zane?"

"In the kitchen, Sadie."

They found him alone. "Where's Ryan?"

He got up from the table where he'd been working on the laptop. "Millie and Liz wanted to watch him at their house. They're keeping him overnight so you can have some alone time."

"You're kidding—"

His eyes zeroed in on Jarod. "That's an amazing shirt you're wearing."

"It's a ribbon shirt with a design from his clan woven into the strips appliquéd to the fabric. Isn't it beautiful? Jarod wore it for the wedding ceremony."

"Nice." Zane's brows lifted. "What did *you* wear?"

"A beautiful, beaded deerskin dress. It's out in the truck. I'll show it to you."

"What are you doing home already? You're supposed to be on your honeymoon. I hoped you'd enjoy another night on the reservation at least!"

"We couldn't have done that to you. When I left here last night, I didn't even know if Jarod would forgive me. I caught him leaving the bedroom with his bedroll."

He grinned. "Yeah?" His gaze flicked to Jarod. "How long did it take you to decide to get married instead of high-tailing it to the mountains?"

"Not long," Jarod admitted.

"Well, now that you're here, I might as well tell you about the conversation I had with Connor and Avery last night when they brought back my car."

Jarod was all ears.

"They said they didn't know your plans yet, but figured if you two wanted to live here with Ryan for the next few weeks while you figure everything out, it could be like a honeymoon for you. Because of your grandfather, they know you wouldn't want to go away yet.

"In the meantime I'll temporarily move into your room, Jarod. It's only an idea, but let's be honest… You two need some space, and you won't get it at *your* ranch. We'll all split up the babysitting."

"It's a fabulous idea!" Sadie cried.

Jarod could see Connor coming up with that idea, but *his sister?* Avery was such a private person.

"My room's yours, Zane. I'm building Sadie and me a new house, so I don't plan to be in it any longer."

"In that case, why don't you two go see your grandfather? I understand he can't wait to congratulate you. When you come back, I'll drive over with a few of my things."

Sadie hugged Zane before they went back out to the truck.

"Before we leave, I want another one of these." Jarod gave her a kiss that she returned with such passion, he couldn't wait for night to come.

When he would have let her go, she clung to him. "I think I'm in shock. For almost thirty years this ranch was off-limits to you. Now we're going to live here and we're married, and Zane and Ryan are happy and it's all because of you and—" She couldn't finish what she was trying to say.

Jarod knew she was happy, but not completely. The next step on their path would be the decision about children. When he'd awakened this morning with her lying in his arms, he'd remembered something he'd been taught by his father about fear when they were trying to tame a horse out in the corral. It had been speaking to him all day.

Courage was not the absence of fear, but rather the judgment that something else was more important than fear. Sadie wanted his baby. He wanted to give her his baby. To do that, he had to overcome his fear.

Tonight they'd talk about his going to the doctor with her.

He drove them to the ranch. Ralph was waiting for them in the living room with Jarod's siblings. They'd thrown together a quick celebratory meal with champagne. For the next hour they sat around and talked about the ceremony and the outpouring of love from Charlo's family.

"Thank you for doing this for us. To be here with all of you in the home I've known all of my life, and to be with my wife, whom I've loved for so long, I—" Jarod couldn't go on. His heart was too full.

In his whole life he'd never known such a completeness of joy, but he couldn't forget Connor's text message. There was something important they needed to discuss.

"What's happened to Ned?"

Ralph cleared his throat. "He and Owen have both been taken into custody and will be arraigned before the judge. Naturally his parents are grieving. I told the police you were on your honeymoon. They want to speak to you when you get back and are waiting for you to press charges for the accident."

Jarod clasped Sadie around the shoulders before letting out a deep sigh. "Marrying Sadie has made me so happy, any feelings of revenge I've wrestled with have fled. In their place is a deep sadness."

Sadie nodded. "At this point that's how I feel about my father, too."

He stared at his family. "Ned has been sick for years, but I don't believe he's evil. Perhaps there's still time for him to heal if he gets the kind of intense therapy and counseling he needs. Tomorrow I'll have a talk with Grant. Even if it takes years, I'd rather see Ned go that route than face a felony charge. As for Owen, he was only doing what Ned wanted, but Owen wasn't the one who drove into me. I'd say he needs therapy, too."

"You're a fine man, Jarod," his grandfather told him, trying to hold back the tears. "You make us all proud."

"To finally have peace so we can get on with our lives means the world to us, doesn't it, sweetheart?"

Sadie kissed his cheek. "Jarod and I have loved each other for what has seemed like eternity. It's hard to believe we can actually plan for the future."

"We want a family, but first Sadie has to undergo an operation on her heart to fix the palpitations. I just found out it's the reason she stopped barrel racing."

Sadie's look of joy and gratitude made him realize it was the right decision.

"Once that's behind us, then we'll start to build our own home on the property. With Zane next door to help us raise Ryan, life couldn't get any better. Speaking of Zane, we need to get back to the ranch so he can start to move in here." Jarod got to his feet, pulling Sadie with him.

Sadie moved around the room to hug everyone. "We were given wonderful advice by Jarod's uncle. He said, 'Both of you have endured much sorrow over the years. Don't waste today letting too much of yesterday ruin your joy. Before you lie down together, give thanks for blessings already on their way and you will have peace.'

"Jarod and I are going to take his advice and re-member it. We love all of you."

Jarod's throat tightened.

He was going home with his angelic wife. Today was their first step to a shared destiny.

* * * * *

A sneaky peek at next month…

Cherish™

ROMANCE TO MELT THE HEART EVERY TIME

My wish list for next month's titles…

In stores from 18th April 2014:

❑ Expecting the Prince's Baby – Rebecca Winters

& The Millionaire's Homecoming – Cara Colter

❑ Falling for Fortune – Nancy Robards Thompson

& A Baby for the Doctor – Jacqueline Diamond

In stores from 2nd May 2014:

❑ Swept Away by the Tycoon – Barbara Wallace

& One Night in Texas – Linda Warren

❑ The Heir of the Castle – Scarlet Wilson

& The Prince's Cinderella Bride – Christine Rimmer

Available at WHSmith, Tesco, Asda, Eason, Amazon and Apple

Just can't wait?

Visit us Online

You can buy our books online a month before they hit the shops! **www.millsandboon.co.uk**

0414/23

Special Offers

Every month we put together collections and longer reads written by your favourite authors.

Here are some of next month's highlights— and don't miss our fabulous discount online!

On sale 18th April

On sale 2nd May

On sale 2nd May

Save 20%
on all Special Releases

When five o'clock hits, what happens after hours...?

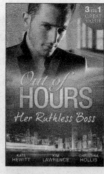

24 new stories from the leading lights of romantic fiction!

Featuring bestsellers Adele Parks, Katie Fforde, Carole Matthews and many more, *Truly, Madly, Deeply* **takes you on an exciting romantic adventure where love really is all you need.**

Now available at:

www.millsandboon.co.uk

Join the Mills & Boon Book Club

Want to read more **Cherish™** books?
We're offering you **2 more** absolutely **FREE!**

We'll also treat you to these fabulous extras:

- Exclusive offers and much more!
- FREE home delivery
- FREE books and gifts with our special rewards scheme

Get your free books now!

visit www.millsandboon.co.uk/bookclub
or call Customer Relations on 020 8288 2888